LIBRARY OF CONGRESS CATALOGING-IN-PUBLICATION DATA

Names: Uglow, Loyd, 1952– author.
Title: Slow train to Sonora / Loyd M. Uglow.
Description: First edition. | Waterville, Maine : Five Star Publishing, a part of Cengage Learning, Inc., [2017] | Series: The border army series | Description based on print version record and CIP data provided by publisher; resource not viewed.
Identifiers: LCCN 2017007831 (print) | LCCN 2017011338 (ebook) | ISBN 9781432834104 (ebook) | ISBN 143283410X (ebook) | ISBN 9781432836979 (ebook) | ISBN 1432836978 (ebook) | ISBN 9781432834135 (hardcover) | ISBN 1432834134 (hardcover)
Subjects: | GSAFD: Romantic suspense fiction. | Adventure fiction. | Western stories.
Classification: LCC PS3621.G56 (ebook) | LCC PS3621.G56 S58 2017 (print) | DDC 813/.6—dc23
LC record available at https://lccn.loc.gov/2017007831

First Edition. First Printing: August 2017
Find us on Facebook– https://www.facebook.com/FiveStarCengage
Visit our website– http://www.gale.cengage.com/fivestar/
Contact Five Star™ Publishing at FiveStar@cengage.com

Printed in the United States of America
1 2 3 4 5 6 7 21 20 19 18 17

THE BORDER ARMY SERIES

SLOW TRAIN TO SONORA

LOYD M. UGLOW

FIVE STAR

A part of Gale, a Cengage Company

GALE
A Cengage Company

Farmington Hills, Mich • San Francisco • New York • Waterville, Maine
Meriden, Conn • Mason, Ohio • Chicago

THE BORDER ARMY SERIES

SLOW TRAIN TO SONORA

LOYD M. UGLOW

FIVE STAR
A part of Gale, a Cengage Company

Farmington Hills, Mich • San Francisco • New York • Waterville, Maine
Meriden, Conn • Mason, Ohio • Chicago

LIBRARY OF CONGRESS CATALOGING-IN-PUBLICATION DATA

Names: Uglow, Loyd, 1952– author.
Title: Slow train to Sonora / Loyd M. Uglow.
Description: First edition. | Waterville, Maine : Five Star Publishing, a part of Cengage Learning, Inc., [2017] | Series: The border army series | Description based on print version record and CIP data provided by publisher; resource not viewed.
Identifiers: LCCN 2017007831 (print) | LCCN 2017011338 (ebook) | ISBN 9781432834104 (ebook) | ISBN 143283410X (ebook) | ISBN 9781432836979 (ebook) | ISBN 1432836978 (ebook) | ISBN 9781432834135 (hardcover) | ISBN 1432834134 (hardcover)
Subjects: | GSAFD: Romantic suspense fiction. | Adventure fiction. | Western stories.
Classification: LCC PS3621.G56 (ebook) | LCC PS3621.G56 S58 2017 (print) | DDC 813/.6—dc23
LC record available at https://lccn.loc.gov/2017007831

First Edition. First Printing: August 2017
Find us on Facebook– https://www.facebook.com/FiveStarCengage
Visit our website– http://www.gale.cengage.com/fivestar/
Contact Five Star™ Publishing at FiveStar@cengage.com

Printed in the United States of America
1 2 3 4 5 6 7 21 20 19 18 17

To my son, Joel, with blessings for your life's journey.

Prologue:
Spring 1911

"The wrath of a king is as messengers of death."

Proverbs 16:14

Rodolfo Escarra glanced across the opulent room at the massive grandfather clock. Five minutes to ten. The Old Man had said he'd come at ten, and punctuality was one of his virtues, even now. Ten it would certainly be.

Escarra shut his eyes. There was the hum of anxious conversation, that and the clink of ice in crystal glasses. Ice—a precious commodity in Veracruz in the month of May—but the Old Man had never let scarcity or cost stand in his way. He was, however, a man of relatively simple tastes. At least that had been Escarra's experience with him, confirmed by the tales and whispers of others through the years.

Uncertainty permeated the room. It was plain on the faces of the other men. This was, after all, the changing of the guard, and the first time in thirty years. But they were lesser men.

Several stood near Escarra—too near. Trujillo from Morelos was talking nervously to two others. Really the alcohol was talking. The smell was in the air—that, and a feeling. Why did other men partake of liquor? In that, he and the Old Man were alike. He smiled just a fraction. There was that story years ago about the fellow who'd sent the Old Man a bottle of mescal, knowing full well that he didn't drink. Had the fellow been allowed to live? It was impossible to remember. But, my, what he would've done to such a man—what he *had* done to more than one. Men learned not to joke at his expense. Yes, he was like the Old Man in that, too.

He walked over by a window, where the others weren't so close. A white-gloved steward appeared before him with a tray of drinks. The man kept his eyes down and seemed thankful to depart when Escarra shook his head.

The window was heavily curtained in lush velvet, drawn back to admit the morning sun across the waters of the Gulf. Escarra glanced at the street below. The crowds were there, jostling one another in the warm, humid morning. This was their last chance.

The door opened, and all heads turned in that direction. A man, one of the secretaries, peeked in for a moment. A collective sigh escaped from the gathered men, and the guarded conversation resumed as the door closed. The clock read just a fraction before ten now. The second hand ticked toward twelve. It passed the mark—one, two, three—and the door came open wide. The majestic white head was the first thing visible past the crowd of suits.

The Old Man still cut a fine figure, even in the dark gray suit and tie, flanked by men a head taller. If he'd had the familiar uniform, resplendent with half the chest in medals, he'd have seemed almost like a god. The moustache was part of it, thick, snow white, and sweeping down in graceful arcs past the upper lip. But the eyes were the key—stern and commanding, eyes that had never taken no for an answer. Escarra feared no man— but there had been a time . . .

That was all in the past now. The Old Man had been ruth-less—but Escarra had learned to be more so. Where the Old Man had been cruel, Escarra made himself demonic. The Old Man had used violence without hesitation, but Escarra trained himself to use it eagerly and in greater measure than his master. What had started so many years ago as an apprenticeship, and developed in his own eyes into a rivalry, had ultimately led to one result—at every turn he'd come to surpass his *Jefe* in the fine art of institutionalized terror.

The Old Man strode to the middle of the room and halted there, surveying his audience. They turned toward him like flowers to the sun. He didn't smile. He seldom had, through the long decades. Now every eye looked to him as master still—but of a kingdom shrunk to the limits of a single room.

The Old Man sought out his favorites, those who'd shown themselves faithful, even unto death—the deaths of others, of course, rebels, traitors, and the inconvenient. He said a word to a trusted lieutenant; spoke a blessing of thanks to a companion in arms; gave one a warning against too much mercy when judgment was within the grasp.

Others he passed by, those who had too great a love for accommodation or too little steel. Silence from him at this final occasion must've stung them like a brand. And ever he moved, to one and another, like a dark priest dispensing deadly benedictions. Escarra bided his time. The Old Man would seek him out if he deemed him worthy. If not—then to hell with the Old Man. One could be a pupil for only so long. Then, it would be time to take his rightful place as master and let the Old Man become simply an old man.

At length he appeared before Escarra, face to face.

"Escarra, my trusted friend. You will be strong." He squeezed Escarra's shoulder with a powerful hand. "The game is not played out yet."

Oh, but it was—for the Old Man. Escarra said, "Might I serve you where you're going?"

"A man without a country travels too light for many companions. Stay. Work. Wait."

Yes, yes. But not for the Old Man. His time was past.

The Old Man moved on, and when all in the room had been

greeted or shunned, he found a spot where, his back to the wall, he could address them all one last time.

"They won't push us from power so easily, eh?" This brought the shouts, the shaking heads, even from the more timid made bold by shared bravado.

From the window, Escarra looked down on the masses in the street, standing, waiting. They were there to cheer when the Old Man passed by. But was it for him or for his leaving?

"When I am gone," the Old Man told them, "keep faith in the *Acordada.*" He held out an open hand to one of his confidants, who gave him a sheet of paper. The Old Man glanced over it and then handed it on to a tall, heavy man, one of the circle close around him. "You will know what to do with these. They have been troublesome."

Escarra shifted his weight. They and many others.

The Old Man cleared his throat and looked across the group. "My time has come. I have given myself for Mexico, and no one can claim otherwise." He gave a dry, mirthless chuckle. "Madero has let the tiger loose. We will see if he can control it."

He glanced at the grandfather clock and started toward the door. The assembly parted before him. When he reached the doorway, there was no delay, no turning for a final look—he strode through, erect and deliberate.

And from his place by the window, Rodolfo Escarra saw the promise of a whole new world as Porfirio Diaz departed the room for exile.

CHAPTER 1

"Among all this people there were seven hundred chosen men left-handed; every one could sling stones at a hair breadth, and not miss." Judges 20:16

It came down to the last four rounds—two bullets for each man.

Lieutenant C. W. Langhorne wiped his thick moustache and relaxed in the prone position, waiting for his opponent, an infantry sergeant named Hambrick, to line up and take his shot. The man chambered his next-to-last round in the 1903 Springfield and settled into the firing position.

The sergeant's shooting had been nearly flawless all afternoon. The competition was grueling, one of the toughest Langhorne had ever participated in, his own cavalry team trading shot for shot with the infantry team that Hambrick anchored. Now, with the score tied, those last four shots would determine the outcome—win, lose, or draw.

Catherine had never cared for guns. Langhorne blinked quickly—there'd be time to think of her later.

He wiped sweat from his eyes and looked over at Hambrick, then downrange at the target, a thousand yards away toward the shore of Lake Erie. Maybe it was time to think of getting out of these competitions—after all, a man might start to lose his touch by the time he reached forty-one.

But not yet.

It was easy to figure what was going through Hambrick's mind—all the variables of wind, temperature, and humidity. Combined, they'd determine the unique point of aim at that one moment in time.

A man's voice, young and indistinct, drifted across from somewhere behind him, and Langhorne scowled and glanced back. A junior officer, it seemed, was guiding a young lady up into the gallery back of the firing line. It would've been nice with no spectators, only the marksmen themselves, but the annual competitions here at Camp Perry, Ohio, had become popular. Too popular. Apparently, some of the crowd didn't realize the intense concentration it took to hit a three-foot bull's eye at a thousand yards. Maybe they just didn't care.

Hambrick held rock steady and fired. The crack from his rifle wasn't particularly loud. Langhorne stared downrange, waiting for the result of the shot. There it was—a white disk lifted up from the men in the pits, a bull's eye. Five more points for the infantry.

Langhorne peered through his spotting telescope and began his own calculations. They'd become second nature over years of long-range shooting since he'd first put on the uniform in 1898. The red wind flags down near the targets showed a light breeze from right to left, matching the wind at his position. Heat waves shimmered under a late summer sun. And it was getting hotter. Not enough to call for lowering his barrel on this shot, though. Maybe on the final shot. His uniform was soaked with sweat from the humidity and the pressure. The dry desert heat of El Paso and Fort Bliss, home to him and the Fourth Cavalry, would feel so much better, but no sense wishing for what wouldn't come. At least the humidity had remained fairly constant throughout the day—no need to change elevation for that factor, either.

Langhorne chambered his round and threaded his left arm through the sling, drawing it tight. He laid his cheek along the stock and took a slow, deep breath, then held it. He brought the sights onto the target, held firm for the space of a couple seconds while his index finger took all the slack out of the trigger, then continued the pressure and fired.

The shot felt good—that usually meant a bull's eye. Moments later, the white disk confirmed it. Still a tie.

Now it was two bullets.

Langhorne relaxed a little as Hambrick prepared for his final shot. The wind seemed to be picking up, and the sergeant peered through his own telescope. Langhorne looked, too. The flags stood out a bit more at times but then collapsed now and then. Bad news—erratic wind was harder to figure into the calculation.

He glanced back at his second-in-command on the team, Sergeant Stone of the Sixth Cavalry. Stone had shot his last round a few minutes before and was watching the final duel. Stone, Hambrick, the men on all the teams—it was easy to feel at home among them. Marksmen were a special breed, serious, unflappable, competing against themselves more than against the other contestants, striving for consistent excellence, match after match, shot after shot.

Crack!

Hambrick's shot came sooner than expected, and Langhorne looked toward the target—another bull's eye. The pressure settled on him now like a sack of oats across his shoulders.

A tie was the best his team could get now. That wouldn't sit well with Lieutenant-Colonel Stemmons, the regiment's acting commanding officer. The colonel was a fierce competitor and an excellent athlete, having captained more than one athletic team as a cadet at West Point and competed in the 1900 Olympic Games in Paris—he'd recounted the whole story to

Langhorne whenever he could force an opportunity. Although Langhorne's rifle team represented the army's entire cavalry arm, Stemmons had appointed himself something of an unofficial team sponsor and was quick to direct and criticize whenever he was present at practice or match. If he'd be unpleasant about a tie, there'd be the devil to pay if they actually lost the match.

Stemmons would be back there now, pacing like an angry tiger just behind the firing line. Langhorne didn't look around—no, block out everything but the shot.

That shifting of the wind was troubling, and it seemed even more erratic now, just thirty seconds since Hambrick's last shot. There was no way to foretell the sudden gusts and calms, so Langhorne settled on the general wind direction and speed. He made the barest adjustment on the wind gauge.

He loaded his last round, took one final look at conditions, then settled into firing position to wait for the breeze to steady again. He fought down the impulse to hurry, to get it over with. He waited, his hands grasping the weapon like a vise. The breeze seemed to steady from the right and hold for several seconds. He brought the sights onto the bull's eye and began the steady squeeze that would bring the trigger back to the tripping point. Now was the time.

"Here, let me take a look at it, my dear." The words floated across from the gallery a split second before Langhorne fired, and he tightened ever so slightly at the instant of firing. He didn't flinch—it was much less than that. But it was movement nevertheless, maybe imperceptible to anyone watching, but movement.

Langhorne stood up, gathered his gear, and walked quietly over to Sergeant Stone. The sergeant peered downrange for the result of the shot, but Langhorne didn't need to look—it would be no bull's eye. A moment later, Stone confirmed it.

"Close four." He frowned, looked Langhorne in the eye, and spoke softly. "Sorry, sir. I knew that jackass talking would throw you off. Couldn't tell it by looking at you, but I knew."

Langhorne had recognized the voice—the same young officer who'd spoken out earlier in the gallery. He was coming down from his seat now with the rest of the spectators, and chatting with an elegant young lady on his arm.

Hambrick and his infantry team approached Stone and Langhorne, and there was handshaking and sincere congratulations all around. It was tough to lose, tougher that it was his shot that lost it for his team, but he was still proud of them—and proud of the infantry team as well.

The officer in charge of that team, Captain Moore, nodded toward the milling spectators.

"That's the one, Langhorne, that blond lieutenant over there with the girl." He looked grim. "I tell you, there's no excuse for what that fellow did. I'm gonna go over and chew on him for a while. We'll see what his girl thinks of him then."

"Sir, I'd rather—"

Moore was already moving, though, so Langhorne set down his gear and walked reluctantly along.

Moore slipped through the crowd on the trail of the blond lieutenant. As he and Langhorne came within fifteen feet, Moore called out.

"Lieutenant, stand fast there!"

The young officer, a cavalryman, halted and turned around, looking surprised and amused. "Are you addressing me, sir?" he asked, still holding the young lady lightly by the elbow. Langhorne heard Deep South in the fellow's accent.

"I most certainly am," Moore answered. Moore was tall, as tall as Langhorne, and he had three or four inches on the young man, but the fellow didn't appear intimidated.

"Well, what may I do for you then, Captain?" His voice was

pleasant enough, no edge of irritation or insolence that Langhorne could tell.

"You've already done too much," Moore said. "Do you have any idea what your speaking out at a crucial point in this match has done? Don't you realize you ruined Lieutenant Langhorne's last shot?"

"Why, no, sir." He chuckled. "How could I have ruined the fellow's shot? I was only in the gallery, keeping the lovely Miss Higginbotham here company."

The lovely Miss Higginbotham smiled at the compliment, and Langhorne looked at her for a moment. Lovely, all right. Hair a little lighter than Catherine's.

Moore's frown deepened. "Understand this, Lieutenant. A few whispered words, a cough, tapping the foot—anything loud enough to be heard down on the firing line is enough to mess up a man's shot. If you're going to watch a match, you ought to have the decency and decorum to keep silence during the shooting." He cocked his head and stared hard at the young man. "Do I make myself clear?"

Miss Higginbotham looked aghast at the dressing down, but her escort didn't appear fazed in the slightest.

Langhorne fidgeted for a moment. Why had he come along with Moore? The match was over, lost fair and square, and the poor girl had no part in the trouble.

"Not entirely clear, sir," the young lieutenant replied amiably. "I fail to see how my efforts to render assistance to this young lady when a gnat flew into one of her lovely green eyes should have any material effect on some chap's rifle shot. What was his name, Langrich?"

Langhorne frowned at that. "That's me—and it's Langhorne." Self-centered kid.

The lieutenant looked from Langhorne to Moore. "But, gentlemen, how can you tell me that a few whispered words can

16

have such a deleterious effect when men on the field of battle have to use those same weapons amidst a horrifyin' din? 'Cannon to right of them, Cannon to left of them, Cannon in front of them, Volleyed and thundered.' Et cetera, et cetera. That's Tennyson, of course."

Langhorne shook his head. The fellow had overstepped his bounds now.

Sure enough, Moore leaned forward like a bulldog.

"Mister, I don't tolerate insubordination in any form." He glanced quickly at the girl and back. "And being in the company of a young lady doesn't give you a free pass."

"But, sir," the lieutenant replied, a pleasant, guileless expression on his face, "can you not agree with me that weighin' a bull's eye in one hand and Miss Higginbotham's eye in the other, that to a gentleman certainly, hers is by far the more important consideration?"

That was it for Langhorne. Woman present or not, the silver-tongued Southerner was about to get a dressing down that he wouldn't forget. At that moment, however, the unmistakable command voice of Lieutenant Colonel Stemmons carried across the grounds.

"Langhorne! Over here, now!"

Langhorne looked at Stemmons then back at Moore. "Sorry, Captain. Thanks for tryin'." As he started across the lawn to what was bound to be a dressing down of his own, the young lieutenant's voice followed him.

"Say, old man, I'm sorry it threw you off, but it's not as if it were anything serious. There'll be plenty of other shooting matches."

Langhorne wasn't so sure there'd be any more for him. Stemmons stood with feet wide apart, his hands on his hips. The colonel's jaw was set, and he looked as if smoke might stream from his nostrils at any moment. While Langhorne was still a few yards away, however, another officer of Stemmons's rank stepped up to the latter, a wicked grin on his face.

"Jack, I believe you owe me something."

Stemmons turned to face the man, but his fierce expression changed not at all. "I'll settle with you in a minute, Powell."

Lieutenant Colonel Powell grunted. "Not too keen to pay your rightful debts, are you?"

Stemmons didn't reply but just stood there, glaring.

"Our bet was for a hundred dollars, Jack," Powell continued, speaking loudly enough for everyone within thirty feet to hear . . . and still grinning. Langhorne stayed back, watching. The baiting wouldn't make his own talk with Stemmons any easier, but there was a certain satisfaction in it, nevertheless.

"I know what the damn bet was for," Stemmons answered. "Not that I think it was a perfectly fair match. I could cry foul on our man Langhorne's last shot. I'm sure you saw how some moron in the stands threw off his concentration."

Powell shook his head slowly and held out his hand. "A hundred dollars, Jack."

Stemmons pulled out his wallet and leafed through the bills in it. He picked several out and practically tossed them at the other man.

Powell counted them and looked back up. The grin was still there. "Well, Jack, I don't know whether they teach you to count in the cavalry or not, but three twenties don't add up to a hundred dollars." He held out his hand again. "Come on, pay up. You make me wait much longer and I'll hit retirement."

"I don't normally carry that kind of money. You'll have to take my receipt for the rest." Stemmons pulled out a note pad and pencil and began scribbling. He held out the paper to Powell a little more politely than he'd handed him the money.

Langhorne kept his eyes averted from the scene, but it was plain the confrontation had caught the attention of the officers and civilians nearby. That wasn't good.

Powell made a show of holding up the receipt and studying it. Finally, he turned back to Stemmons.

"You won't try to leave town without paying the rest, will you, Jack?"

"Go to hell," Stemmons muttered.

"It's just that I remember that time down in Maryland at the horse race." Powell shrugged innocently.

"Go to hell."

"With a hundred dollars, I could go in style." Powell started chuckling, gave a brief nod, and drifted away toward a man and woman across the lawn and began a conversation with them.

Langhorne stepped up immediately and saluted. Stemmons glared at him.

"Well?" It was loud enough for anyone interested to hear.

"My responsibility for the match, sir. I should've made that shot."

"You're damn right, you should have." He stared for several seconds, as if he were expecting excuses, but Langhorne didn't offer any. You didn't blame the bad luck, or take credit for the good. Stemmons finally continued. "My grandmother could've made that last shot."

"I should've made the shot, sir."

"But you didn't." Stemmons seemed to think for a moment. "Which brings us to why. Maybe you can't shoot worth a damn. That's the simplest explanation, isn't it?" He moved his face closer to Langhorne's and stared hard. "If so, then what the hell are you doing as leader of the cavalry rifle team?"

Stemmons obviously didn't expect an answer to that one, so Langhorne waited for the colonel to continue.

"You're a senior lieutenant, acting commander of B Troop for what—the past six months since Halvorson left? Then you pull a stunt like this, blow an important competition and make us look like a bunch of old ladies, and you expect to get the troop permanently—and promotion to captain to boot, I'd wager?" He snorted. "Not very likely, mister." His eyes narrowed. "That brings us to the other possibility. You muffed the shot on purpose. You threw the match."

What? If that didn't beat everything!

"I just missed the shot, sir," Langhorne said, with a little more than normal emphasis.

"It could be for money," Stemmons said, his voice taking on a note of disgust. "Maybe some other considerations. Who knows?"

Langhorne's face got warm, but he kept his voice steady. "I don't throw matches, Colonel."

Stemmons kept going as if Langhorne hadn't even spoken. "Anyway, we'll sort this mess out. An investigation sounds like the correct approach to me, and then a board of inquiry. Incompetence or misconduct—I don't see any other possibilities in your case." Stemmons leaned in close again. "No one makes a fool out of me, Langhorne. You'll be lucky to command the Bachelor Officers' Quarters at Bliss after this. That's all."

Langhorne saluted as Stemmons turned on his heel, and the colonel stalked away without bothering to return the salute.

Langhorne took a deep breath. How did you put all this in order? As acting commanding officer of the regiment—the permanent CO, Colonel Vandreelan, being on temporary duty at the Army War College in Washington—Stemmons certainly had the power to launch an investigation and convene a board of inquiry. Langhorne frowned. Yes, he'd be exonerated. Vandreelan would probably chew out Stemmons when he heard about it, too. But the damage would be done. Stemmons would likely issue Langhorne a letter of reprimand regardless of exoneration, and that letter could stay in his service record from then on, shooting holes in every opportunity for promotion. More than that, Stemmons might even have him transferred out of the Fourth, the closest thing he'd found to a home and family since Catherine—and Amy. He tightened up for a moment, like he usually did.

Langhorne wiped his hand over his moustache. A lot had happened in the last ten minutes. He felt a tap on his back and turned around quickly, face to face with Lieutenant Colonel Powell.

"It's Langhorne, isn't it?" The colonel looked serious now. "You're a damn fine hand with that Springfield, son."

Langhorne almost smiled at the last word. Forty-one was old for a first lieutenant, but then he'd gotten a late start—the war with Spain had been irresistible.

"Thank you, sir."

"I heard Stemmons read you the riot act." He grinned again. "Hell, anybody who *didn't* hear it would have to be deaf. Did he really say he'd convene a board of inquiry about this thing?"

"That's what he said, sir."

"Hm. That's taking the competition a little too seriously if you ask me. But Jack Stemmons was always like that. He and I were at the Point together, you know. He was a hot shot among a hundred other hot shots there. I like winning as well as the next man, but he made it a religion. And he's never changed since."

"I suppose not, sir." Langhorne was treading carefully now. Superiors were off limits to criticism or complaint. It was best to avoid even getting close.

"Well, anyway, Langhorne, that was some of the best shooting I've seen in a long time."

"Your infantry team won the match, Colonel."

Powell nodded. "They were on top of it, too. No doubt about that. But you expect that from the infantry." He grinned again and Langhorne smiled at the joke. Then Powell looked serious again. "But what Stemmons said—did some noise from the gallery mess up your last shot?"

"Distractions come with the match, sir. We all have to put up with 'em."

Powell eyed him. "You look like you might've had to put up with them when it really counted. You've been under fire before." It was more statement than question.

"Yes, sir, a few times." Powell didn't reply, but his look told Langhorne to go on. "Cuba. The Philippines. Peking."

Powell's face lit up. "Peking!" He laughed. "Now there's a hell of a campaign, one I always wished I'd made." Suddenly, he checked his watch. "I've got to catch a train back to Washington."

"Yes, sir, and I've got to catch one back to the border—tonight."

Powell hesitated a moment then cocked his head. "You don't know any company grade officers down there who can speak Spanish, now do you, Langhorne? I mean fluent."

"No one but me, sir."

There was a spark of something in the colonel's eyes. "You don't say." He put his hand on Langhorne's shoulder and maneuvered him away from the knots of men and women still talking.

Langhorne watched him closely. It had been an unusual question. Powell lowered his voice.

"I need a man, a j.o.—first lieutenant, captain, it doesn't matter—who speaks Spanish and who knows how to handle himself. I need him right away. Thought I had one back in Washington, but I got a wire an hour ago. Seems he's come down with typhoid. If that's not the luck o' the Irish for you."

"With respect, sir, I doubt if Colonel Stemmons would consider cutting me loose for whatever this is when he's ready to start that investigation."

Powell smiled. "That's where clout comes in, Lieutenant. I'm at the War Department General Staff."

Langhorne raised his eyebrows.

The colonel continued. "If I cut the orders, you're in, regardless of what old Jack wants."

It sounded tempting—but so did a lot of "opportunities" in the army.

"Can I ask what it's about, sir?"

"That'll be brought out in six days—if you decide to volunteer."

Langhorne didn't say anything. But there were definite possibilities.

"Think about it, Langhorne. You'll be out from under Stemmons's thumb for three or four weeks. More or less independent duty—working with my aide, in fact. I'll even stroll over to the War College and get Ben Vandreelan's endorsement on your orders. That ought to make you feel better, and it'll sure as hell nix any wrench Stemmons might try to throw into the works." He frowned and cocked his head. "You're on good terms with Vandreelan, aren't you?"

That settled it and Langhorne grinned. "The best, sir."

"And by the time you get back to your duty station after this is over, Ben'll be back from the War College and in command of the Fourth again. So is it yes or no, Langhorne?"

"You must sell iceboxes to Eskimos, Colonel."

Powell laughed. "I'll have advance orders wired to your command tomorrow, so we get the jump on Jack Stemmons. There's not much love lost between us, you know. I just wish I could see the old s.o.b.'s face when he reads your orders."

Langhorne frowned for a moment. He *would* see Stemmons's face, and his reaction—it wouldn't be pleasant. But even Stemmons wouldn't try to buck orders from the General Staff.

23

Langhorne looked Powell in the eye. "I want to thank you, sir."

"Don't mention it. You're helping me out as much as I am you. My old Aunt Mabel would call you an answer to prayer. If I prayed, I'd probably say that, too."

"I *do* pray, sir," Langhorne said. He smiled. Things were looking up, more than at any time that day. "That won't knock me out of the running, will it?"

Powell chuckled. "Why should it? Where you're going, you'll need all the help you can get."

CHAPTER 2

"And Moses sent them to spy out the land of Canaan,
and said unto them, Get you up this way southward, and
go up into the mountain." Numbers 13:17

Langhorne skirted the parade ground at Fort Bliss and turned
in at the post headquarters building. He'd been conducting
mounted drill with his troop when the messenger found him
and told him to report to Lieutenant-Colonel Powell in room
four. The advance orders Powell had wired to the regiment five
days before were safely in Langhorne's pocket.

He entered the building and walked past the maze of cabinets
and electric fans, sweating clerks and desk sergeants. He nodded at an acquaintance here and there—thank God he wasn't
bound to a desk, at least not yet. Outside room four, he checked
his wristwatch, then knocked and entered. Powell was alone in
the office, seated behind a scarred wooden desk at the far end
of the room and seeming to relax in the warm air stirred by
another of the fans as it swept in a lazy arc from side to side.

Langhorne stopped in front of the desk and saluted. Powell
returned it and held out a set of papers.

"Your original orders," he said. Langhorne took them and
scanned the first page. Powell grinned. "I hope the advance
copy I wired was enough to keep Stemmons occupied."

"Yes, sir." *Occupied* didn't quite do justice to the colonel's reaction—a fuming, cursing, ranting scene, with more than one trash can kicked into walls and furniture. Langhorne had kept his temper; what else could he do? It was a little easier to keep cool because as much as Stemmons might huff and puff, he definitely wasn't going to blow this particular house down—not when the orders came from the War Department General Staff.

And so the confrontation had ended, with Stemmons practically throwing the advance orders at Langhorne and ordering him out, a vague and ill-defined threat left drifting in the atmosphere about what would happen when Langhorne returned from his detached service.

Langhorne looked over the orders carefully now. They mentioned few specifics; just like the advance copy, they simply instructed him to report for unspecified temporary duty under the War Department representative—obviously Powell—at Fort Bliss.

Powell chuckled. "You look a bit puzzled, Mister Langhorne."

"I was expecting some details, sir. Where I'm goin' and what I'll be doin'."

"Of course you were. But that's something we thought best not to commit to writing." He motioned to one of four straight wooden chairs facing the desk. "Make yourself comfortable, and I'll give you those details while we wait for the other gentlemen."

Langhorne sat. It would be good to hear what the colonel had in store for him. And who were those "other gentlemen?"

Powell poured himself a glass of water from a pitcher on his desk and took a sip, then looked at Langhorne.

"Stationed here on the border, you probably keep a closer eye than most on what's happening across the river. With Diaz out after the treaty in May, and Madero a sure-thing for president, it might seem like things are cooling off in Mexico. But Secretary Stimson isn't convinced, and I can say candidly that I'm not either. Some of the same men who helped Madero take Juarez last spring don't seem too happy with him now. And, frankly, a lot of people, President Taft and the secretary included, see trouble in Mexico in the short term or later."

So it was Mexico—no real surprise. But the other questions remained.

Powell said, "You know, American companies have tens of millions of dollars invested in Mexico. Mostly in mining operations, oil, and other natural resources, but also railroads. Plenty of smaller businesses, too. Mexico is a rich country."

"Yes, sir."

"But they don't have the means to develop it themselves, so they've looked to our businessmen to do it for them until they get the capability."

Langhorne nodded. There were the stories of his engineer friends Kaminsky and Worth, who'd been involved in Mexican copper and silver mines in Chihuahua and Sonora. Their tales painted a picture of untold but untapped wealth, of armies of *campesinos* who'd break their backs digging in exchange for a couple of pesos a day—and apparently that was good money by the standards of other industries in Mexico—and of an endless cycle of mule trains loaded down with high-grade metal.

Powell took another sip of water. "So what happens if the whole show in Mexico goes to hell in a hand basket? What if his friends turn on Madero and his government—if he ever gets around to forming one?"

"I suppose Mexico won't be such a pleasant place to do business anymore," Langhorne replied. Was American capital going to be the key point in this discussion? A lot of Mexicans were likely to die, many might lose the little they had, but that seemed to pale—in the eyes of the government at least—in comparison to the loss of American dollars.

Powell frowned at him. "You don't have to agree with the

administration, Lieutenant, but don't let your disapproval show too much. Remember, we're supposed to leave politics to the politicians."

Langhorne took a deep, slow breath. "I'm a soldier, sir. I'll follow orders."

"Good." Powell smiled and started to continue, but there was a sharp knock on the door. It opened and two infantry officers entered, exchanging salutes with the colonel. Powell made a quick introduction of Captain Mattox and Captain Alderman and offered them two of the remaining chairs.

"I was just bringing Lieutenant Langhorne up to date on the situation in Mexico," Powell told them. He turned back to Langhorne. "The captains are assigned to the general staff with me. They'll be part of this mission, but not working directly with you. I'm expecting another officer momentarily—my aide. He'll be with you on at least part of the mission."

Powell walked over to an easel to one side of his desk and flipped a map over so it could be seen by the others.

"Mexico."

Lines connected various points in the country in a rough pattern, with a number of large areas completely devoid of any of the lines.

"You may recognize the country's rail network," Powell said. He tapped at El Paso and Juarez. "From here we've got the Mexican National Railroad running all the way to Mexico City." Then his finger followed a parallel route from Juarez to the south, a little farther west than the first. "And this is the Mexican Northwest. It runs along the eastern base of the Sierra Madre Occidental before turning east to join up with the Mexican National again at Chihuahua City. From there, the line runs south, branching out here and there to connect with most of the important cities in the central part of the country. Those lines between El Paso and Mexico City are the most important part of the country's railroad system."

Then his hand shifted to the west, to the southern border of Arizona. "Here at Nogales the Southern Pacific of Mexico runs south through the state of Sonora, then Sinaloa, hitting all the important towns, and all the way into the little territory of Tepic, where the line ends. There are plans to extend it farther south, and there's a branch line under construction to connect it with the Mexican National network to the east, but it'll be years before it's completed."

Langhorne stared at the map. It took railroads to keep large military forces supplied and in the field nowadays. But whose military forces?

"So what we intend to do," Powell continued, looking now at the two captains, "is send you, Mattox and Alderman, south from here on the Mexican National and the Mexican Northwest. You'll meet up at Chihuahua City and travel on into central Mexico, stopping at the important cities along the way—Durango, Monterrey, San Luis Potosi, Torreon, Mexico City, and others. I expect you to use your own initiative as far as the route goes, although I'll provide a list of American consular officials and businessmen to contact along the way."

Then he turned to Langhorne. "And while they're going through the central part of the country, you and my aide will be doing the same along the West Coast in Sonora and Sinaloa." Powell pulled several manila folders and a cardboard box out of one of the desk drawers and set them on the desktop. He handed a folder each to the two captains and to Langhorne.

Langhorne opened his folder and glanced over the top sheet of paper, which was a list of the American consuls and businessmen in Hermosillo and Guaymas and other towns along his route in the west.

"As you can see," Powell began, "you have quite a few people to contact. Basically what the secretary wants you to do is talk with each of these individuals, get their feelings on the political situation in their area and the country as a whole. Find out if they think peace and order are likely there or if they see the whole thing disintegrating." Powell leaned forward. "I want to know—Secretary Stimson wants to know—firsthand from people we can trust—you—if things are likely to develop that'll require military intervention. Obviously, that'll be a last resort if it does happen, and we'll follow the strictures of international law, but it's a definite contingency."

Powell looked from Langhorne to the two captains, but when they said nothing, he continued.

"There's a second part to your mission. In the event we have to intervene, we'll need the best intelligence we can get about the country—especially the rail transportation network. You'll gather information on carrying capacity, condition of the tracks, bridges, repair facilities, rolling stock, fuel, and water—anything that can give us an idea of how many troops we can transport or supply in different parts of the country, the northern states in particular."

Langhorne nodded. Now the job was clear—and interesting. He'd been into Mexico briefly on a number of occasions, but this trip would be more extensive. What would things be like in the interior? One news report would have the country sinking into civil war; another painted it as a paradise under the enlightened leadership of Madero.

Powell said, "You'll find two different letters of introduction for you in those folders. Pull them out and I'll explain what they're for."

Langhorne found the first one, prominently marked as *Confidential* and addressed generally to American consuls and other government officials. It identified him as being on official business for the War Department and required that any U.S. official give him complete cooperation.

"You're to present the 'confidential' letter as your credentials whenever you make contact with any official of the United States government—State Department, consular officials, or whatever," Powell said. "When they see that, they'll work with you. You'll need to interview the U.S. officials in the cities in your area. Get a fair appraisal of the situation, the way they see it. Find out if they think there'll be peace or more fighting. Ask them how the typical Mexican in their area likes Americans. Ask if they think there's much danger to American lives and property. There may be different opinions on these things, but if we talk to a lot of our people down there, we hope to find a rough consensus."

Langhorne raised a finger. "How should we get this information back to you, sir?"

"Well, not by mail or wire—that'd be too dangerous. Of course if you get into trouble, send us a wire, but for the actual information you're gathering, it'll have to wait until you're back on American soil. Until then, keep it in here"—he pointed to his head—"and in some brief notes if you want, as long as you make them vague and abbreviated enough that no one else could make sense of 'em. If you can put them into some code that only you can decipher, so much the better."

Mattox and Alderman exchanged grins, and Powell stared hard at all three officers.

"I want you to understand very clearly that you're gathering intelligence in a foreign country. In other words, you'll be engaged in espionage. It's a serious affair, and you could be in real trouble if Mexican authorities take you into custody— especially if they find any information on you about the rail system. To make matters worse, we don't know who's in charge in the areas where you'll travel. It may be officials appointed by Madero, holdovers from the Diaz government, revolutionary juntas, or maybe just men who were bandits last year and now they're considered military commanders."

He nodded toward their folders. "To make your situation a little safer, we've given you a second letter of introduction."

Langhorne pulled out the other letter, and the two infantry officers did likewise. He started to read it over but stopped abruptly when he noticed the name listed.

"Pardon me, Colonel, but I've got the wrong letter. This is for somebody named Christopher Lockhart."

Powell shook his head. "It's no mistake, Lieutenant. We want the world to think that your name is Chris Lockhart and, if you'll read a little further, that you're a newspaper correspondent for the *Washington Weekly*. Mattox and Alderman have similar letters. These should relieve you from suspicion—to a certain extent, at least."

Langhorne read through his letter. It introduced him "to whom it may concern" and asked that they render him all aid possible and appropriate in gathering and reporting the news related to the situation in Mexico. It was simple, straightforward, and a lie.

"With respect, Colonel, I won't go along with this."

The words appeared to take Powell by surprise, and for a few moments he said nothing. Finally he frowned, and there was a hard edge to his voice when he spoke.

"What the hell are you talking about, Langhorne?"

"I stopped telling lies a long time ago, sir."

"This is in the service of your country."

"A lie's a lie, sir."

Powell cocked his head, a sarcastic smile on his face. "What if a lady asks you how her new hat looks when it looks like hell? You're gonna say it looks 'very becoming, my dear,' or some such crap as that."

"No, I'm not, sir." Langhorne held Powell's eyes. "If I don't think it looks good, maybe I can find something to compliment about it. Maybe I'll like the color, or the stitching . . . or the feathers, and tell her so. But I won't lie about it."

Powell looked for a moment like he was about to rant like Stemmons, but then he let out a long sigh instead. He turned on Mattox and Alderman. "And what about you two—any objections to using your aliases?"

Neither man objected, and Powell told them they could leave for a few minutes. As soon as they'd shut the door, he turned back to Langhorne.

"And what do you propose to say when somebody asks you what you're doing in Mexico?"

"I'll tell 'em I'm there on business. This is government business, after all."

"And what happens if they ask you who you work for?"

"I just won't say. I can tell 'em I'm interested in Mexican railroads. That's the truth."

Powell scowled. "And if they demand to know?"

"I'll take my chances, sir. Believe me, I'm not trying to be a guardhouse lawyer, but I won't lie."

"Langhorne, telling the truth is a part of the code of conduct expected of officers. I follow it, too. But this situation is special. You're not bound by it here."

"That's not the only code I follow, Colonel."

Powell frowned. "What?"

"I told you at Camp Perry—I'm a praying man, sir. A Christian man. For me, anyway, that means I don't lie."

Powell just shook his head. "I never figured you for a religious fanatic."

"I'm sorry, sir, but if this mission requires me to lie—I suppose you'll have to find another volunteer." Langhorne pictured the consequences. Stemmons would push ahead with his board of inquiry or whatever else he had in mind to make life miserable, to ruin him.

Powell stared at him for a long moment. "I don't have time to find someone else. All right. You may not be willing to lie, but you'd sure as hell better keep quiet then if somebody asks who you work for. Is that clear?"

So he was still going! The tension went out of his neck and shoulders, and he smiled just a little.

"Yes, sir."

"You're a hard-headed son of a gun, Langhorne. I'll have another letter typed with your real name on it." There was a knock on the door, and Powell said, "Enter."

A young first lieutenant stepped in. He had blond hair and what a woman might call boyish good looks. The fellow looked familiar, but . . .

"This is my aide, Calvin Jester," Powell said. Jester seemed a little puzzled himself—probably couldn't recall where they'd met, either.

"You and Jester'll be working together in Mexico," Powell said. Langhorne stood up and extended his hand. The moment they shook, there it was—the confrontation at the Camp Perry competition. It seemed to dawn on Jester at the same instant.

Powell glanced from one to the other, frowning. "You know each other?"

Jester grinned. "We haven't had the benefit of a formal introduction, but we have, uh, passed the time of day, you might say."

"Time of day, huh? What happened? Did you two get into it?"

Jester gave a disarming smile. "Why, Colonel, you know I'm a peaceful man. I wouldn't think of comin' to blows with another gentleman."

"There was a girl involved somewhere in this, wasn't there?" Powell looked to Langhorne.

Langhorne stared hard at Jester. "I'd say it was a question of professional courtesy, one officer to another, sir."

Realization appeared on the colonel's face. "Jester's the one who spoiled your shot?"

Langhorne didn't speak, but Jester did. "Why, Colonel, I've already apologized quite profusely to the lieutenant."

"You can tone down the North Carolina drawl, Jester, and your overabundant charm," Powell said.

"It's South Carolina, sir," Jester said. "And to answer an earlier question of yours, the young lady was only involved incidentally."

"There's always a girl, isn't there?"

"I certainly hope so," Jester replied, with a rueful smile. "I admit I have a character flaw—much like the great figures in literature, in fact. With the ancient Greeks, it was *hubris*. With me, it happens to be a weakness for the fair sex."

"Is that so?" Powell said. "I've got one officer who's short on character, and one"—he turned toward Langhorne—"who's got too much of it. Jester, you know that Langhorne, here, refuses to go in under an assumed name? What do you think about that?"

"Maybe he didn't fancy the name you wanted him to assume, sir."

"He simply refuses to lie," Powell said.

"Was there any mention of a cherry tree in the conversation, Colonel?"

Powell ignored the remark. "Lieutenant Langhorne has very strong religious convictions, Jester. Perhaps he can help you curb some of your baser instincts."

"I truly would not wish that task on any man, Colonel," Jester said.

"And I checked the lists. Lieutenant Langhorne is up for captain. Obviously he's senior to you—by several years, in fact, so he's in charge. I might add that he's seen action in multiple campaigns during his career so far."

Langhorne watched Jester. There wasn't much hope for that promotion as long as Colonel Stemmons had any input to the board, but it was good to get the clarification on seniority. A little of Jester's wit would go a long way.

Jester smiled. "Quite an impressive record, I'm sure."

"Let me put it more directly," Powell said. "You're going into Mexico with a religious zealot who can put a bullet through your heart at a thousand yards. You might want to tread lightly."

Powell wasn't smiling, but the humor just showed in his eyes.

"I shall endeavor to creep about on tiptoes, if necessary, sir," Jester said.

"You do that. Now both of you have everything you should need in your folders. There's a letter of credit, so you can draw expense money through the consuls at any city you visit. You'll get an initial draw of fifty dollars apiece from the paymaster this afternoon. You can wire for more along the way, if the letters of credit won't work."

Jester smiled. "Now that does provide solace, Colonel. We Jesters are accustomed to a certain modicum of comfort."

"We'll get receipts, sir," Langhorne said. Now it was his turn to smile. "And I'm sure we'll be able to keep expenses down. A two-dollar hotel sleeps as good as a five."

"Good, good," Powell replied. "A couple more things." He pulled two leather belts out of the box on his desk and handed one to each man. "Notice the flap on the inside of your belt. There's a hidden pocket under the flap for your money and the 'confidential' letter to the consuls."

"What about weapons, sir?" Langhorne asked.

"Take your own side arms. Just keep them out of sight." Powell opened a desk drawer and pulled out a newspaper clipping. He handed it to Langhorne. "That's Augustin Medina."

Langhorne studied the grainy photograph of a heavyset man

with a moustache and Vandyke beard. Jester craned his neck to look at the picture.

"Señor Medina has extensive property in the state of Sonora," Powell said. "His hacienda is a few miles northeast of a little town called Agua Blanca on the west slope of the Sierra Madre. You'll cross at Nogales on the Southern Pacific of Mexico, pass through Hermosillo and Guaymas, then get off at the town of Corral. The main line continues south, but you'll change trains and take the branch line that runs northeast up toward the Sierra. Detrain at Agua Blanca, and Señor Medina should have someone waiting to take you to his ranch."

Langhorne quickly scanned the article that went along with the photo. "Who's Medina?"

"A Mexican businessman. Co-owner of a copper mine with an American company. Owns ten thousand acres of ranch and timber land and a lot of cattle. We want you to talk with him, get as much information as you can from him about conditions in that part of Sonora. See what he thinks is going to happen now that Diaz is out of the picture."

"Does he know why we're coming?" Langhorne asked.

"Yes. He's supported Diaz in the past but wanted better education and working conditions in Mexico. He's what they term a *cientifico,* kind of what we'd call a Progressive here, something like Teddy Roosevelt."

Langhorne asked, "Why's he willing to work with the United States? He realizes we're thinking about possible intervention in the future?"

"He realizes it. He thinks it may be the best thing for Mexico in the long run—if there's the threat of anarchy. He's a businessman, after all, and stability is one of the most important considerations in his mind, for his own interests but also for the country. And the fact that his first wife was American may have influenced his ideas."

"So we'll visit with him and then go on to see the consuls and American businessmen in the cities along the route?" Langhorne asked.

"That's right. One of you can backtrack up the rail line to Hermosillo and Guaymas, then go by sea, if it seems feasible, south to Mazatlan and the other ports. Then inland to Guadalajara—again, that's only if it's practical. It's doubtful we'd go that far south even in a major intervention."

"And the other one of us takes the train south from Corral?" Langhorne asked.

"Right. Possibly, you'll be able to meet up in the south and ride back together. If you need to telegraph me, make sure not to say anything suspicious. Use my name, care of the *Washington Weekly*." Powell gathered his papers together. "You gentlemen had better pack your gear. You'll be on the ten-oh-five west for Nogales tonight." He stood up, and Langhorne and Jester rose.

Langhorne looked over at Jester—hopefully the kid could cut it.

"I'll take the railroad south after we leave Medina, and you can ride the ship, if it's all the same to you."

Jester looked pleased. "Definitely. The salt air might do me good. So we might say it's one if by rail and two if by sea. Think of what Mr. Longfellow could have done with that."

CHAPTER 3

"And not many days after the younger son gathered all
together, and took his journey into a far country."
Luke 15:13

Calvin Jester slept through most of the train ride from El Paso
to Nogales, Arizona, waking just when it pulled in, with the
release of a great hiss of steam, sometime around daybreak.
Damn but the conductor must've tried to be as loud as he
could, walking down the aisle and calling out their arrival.

"End of the line, folks. Everybody'll have to get off."

Jester frowned and stretched and looked around the car.
There were only a handful of people by now—someone had
said Nogales was on a spur off the main Southern Pacific line.
A lone woman near the back of the car wore a trim grey suit
and big hat—maybe thirty, nice looking but not overly pretty,
and in need of a little more rouge. Married, by the look of
her—too bad.

"Jester!" Langhorne's voice sounded like he was on the
parade ground with his troop. He looked grim; but then he
always seemed to look that way.

Jester leaned closer and spoke in a low voice. "Remember,
my name is supposed to be Jackson. Charles Jackson."

"Save that for Mexico. Let's find some breakfast before we
head south." He led the way down the aisle, standing aside for

39

the lady and tipping his pearl-grey Stetson hat as she passed. Jester gave her an elaborate bow and something of a flourish. That seemed to please her. She smiled, didn't she? Then she was past and stepping down out of the car, and he and Langhorne followed her out.

Nogales, Arizona, and its Mexican twin sat in a desert basin surrounded by mountains every bit as parched. Was there a more desolate looking place anywhere? Certainly a far cry from Charleston, worse even than El Paso. Well, at least things couldn't get any worse than this, where they were going.

The few low buildings got fewer and shabbier out from the station. The station itself was right at the border. That was a surprise. The track just continued south without interruption past a smaller station on the Mexican side, and then on to a waterless infinity.

The actual border ran down the middle of an empty corridor maybe fifty yards across, stretching out of sight to east and west. An American sentry stood out there, and at least he looked soldier enough to handle the little Mexican guard a few yards south, a seven-foot border obelisk between the two like a miniature Washington Monument. How nice it would be to be back in the capital now to look on the real thing instead of in this hell hole.

He and Langhorne deposited their trunks with a porter and walked across a street to a little café where they had ham and eggs and some of the worst coffee ever. Langhorne, strange specimen that he was, seemed to relish the stuff, black and steaming hot. Jester doctored his with plenty of sugar and a good dose of cream, which curdled when he poured it in.

Langhorne gave him a sly grin. "You'll like it better on the other side. Mexicans have a special way with coffee."

"You mean this is coffee?"

"It'll wake you up."

They hired a couple of Mexican *cargadores* to haul their trunks across the line to the Mexican station, and Langhorne bought their tickets south. The fellow actually did have his uses, bantering back and forth with the clerk in rapid-fire Spanish. How did anyone converse in it? The proper Castilian version had been difficult enough in Spain.

Jester said, "You know, I spent six months in Madrid a dozen years ago when my father was a diplomat there. The language didn't stick, though."

"You don't say. I got us passage through to Hermosillo." Langhorne handed him a crude ticket. "We'll have to pick up one for the next leg there. It's not like the States, where you can book a trip from New York clear to the West Coast."

Jester raised his eyebrows. It was more words than Langhorne had spoken to him since Fort Bliss. "When do we leave?"

Langhorne gave a dry chuckle. "Supposed to be about nine, but maybe, maybe not. Down here, things happen when they happen, which is hardly ever on time. Just relax."

Jester forced a smile. "Now that is one thing I do know how to do, sir."

Then without warning Langhorne strolled out into the cleared area along the boundary and headed right toward the Mexican sentry. What in the devil was Langhorne doing, trying to start a war?

The young sentry watched Langhorne nervously and shifted his rifle in his hands.

Jester turned for a moment and gauged the distance back to the American station—just in case.

Langhorne called a greeting to the sentry, then the words, *"Quien vive?"*

"Viva Madero!"

Langhorne just nodded and turned back toward the Mexican station. Jester fell in beside him and leaned close.

"What was that all about?"

"Easiest way to find out which faction's in charge here. They use it as a challenge and countersign these days in the field." Langhorne sat on a bench, and Jester dropped down beside him. "Things may change as we get farther in. I don't think Madero has the whole country in hand, at least not yet."

Jester swallowed and stared down the long, straight tracks south into nothingness. Ten minutes in Mexico, and already it seemed to shut out everything familiar. Langhorne leaned back and tilted his hat down over his eyes. Relax, he'd said. Maybe in three or four days—but by then it would be time to split up.

The train started for Hermosillo two and a half hours late, but no one seemed to notice or care except for one loud, redheaded American who'd driven the ticket clerk to distraction with his complaints.

Jester stuck his head out the window as they pulled out. The border obelisk was there, a hundred yards back—might as well have been a hundred miles. It would be so easy to jump out of that train and trot back down the tracks to the good old U.S.A. So easy. But that was just a thought. The obelisk got smaller and smaller until it finally disappeared in the distance.

Oh, well. He glanced around their coach. It really wasn't too bad, comparable to an American passenger coach, but of course dirtier and in need of a fresh coat of paint. There were a few other Americans, along with several Mexicans, decently dressed and polite, in the same car with him and Langhorne.

The train had hardly picked up momentum out of Nogales when it started to slow down. The puffing of the engine diminished with their speed, and before two minutes were out, they were settling to a stop at a tiny station identified by a crude sign as Eucina. Several Mexicans—individuals, pairs, and one family of six—boarded, all but one man heading into the third-class cars immediately behind theirs. The new arrivals

42

were definitely poorer looking than the original passengers.

One haggard, shawl-covered woman waited on the platform while a man, probably her husband, boarded the train. She had the look of a spooked horse, and Jester locked eyes with her for an instant. What could she be afraid of?

The pattern of short runs repeated itself many times as they lurched south, stopping at places with names like Cibuta, Cumeral, and San Ignacio. Far more boarded than got off, and the great majority were ragged and hungry looking, as bad as sharecroppers in the Carolina Low Country. Soon the third-class coaches were overflowing, and numbers of the latest arrivals perched on the outside staging platforms between cars.

Many of the poorer looking passengers, especially the entire families, brought their dinners onboard. Soup, beans, tortillas, even an occasional boiled chicken—feet and all—were produced, usually by the mother or wife, and consumed right where they sat.

Jester nudged Langhorne and nodded back toward the platform between their car and the next one, where a man and woman and two ragged children were munching on tortillas.

Langhorne looked up from the Bible he'd been reading. "Yeah, they're the smart ones. We came unprepared."

The crowding only got worse. Another couple of hours, and many of the newcomers were being seated in his and Langhorne's carriage. Jester wiped sweat from his face with his handkerchief, but it didn't help much, especially since some of the damned windows were stuck in the closed position. And with every new stop, there were more warm bodies to pack into the car. Langhorne looked miserable, too, often running his finger around the inside of his stiff white collar.

Jester's shirt was plastered to his skin now, and he leaned forward and flexed his back to break the clinging fabric free.

"I never thought I'd long for a good khaki uniform to wear."

Langhorne nodded. "Yeah, and to be on a horse instead of in this sardine can."

Jester shut his eyes and took a deep breath of the warm, pungent air. The Medina ranch was in the Sierra Madre, and mountains were usually cool.

Sometime in the afternoon, the train reached the town of Noria, a bit larger but no more modern than the other hamlets they'd passed through. Jester remained seated as the train crept to a stop, and waited for the inevitable influx of new passengers into the crowded coach. Stretching his legs out on the station platform would've been akin to heaven, but somebody would probably get his seat. Having to stand the rest of the way to Hermosillo while Langhorne looked on in derision wasn't a pleasant prospect, no matter how stiff his legs were.

Just then there was a shouted command outside and a flurry of activity much more energetic than anything up to this point today. Outside Jester's window a man in a white military uniform hurried past, followed by two others in civilian clothes and big sombreros but carrying rifles, and they came up the steps onto the train. A moment later they were in the doorway at the front of the coach, and Jester's stomach tightened. The man in the white uniform stood there, looking up and down the rows of passengers crammed together in the sweltering car.

Suddenly, a man seated right behind Langhorne bolted into the aisle and scrambled toward the back. The three soldiers shouted, and they pushed as quickly as they could after him through the crowded aisle. The fugitive elbowed past several passengers and literally climbed over one old man too slow to get out of his way. Jester and everyone else in the car stared in shock.

The fleeing man reached the back of the coach a good twenty feet ahead of his pursuers, and looked to be home free, but another rifle-wielding soldier appeared at that door at the same moment, blocking the man's escape. In obvious panic, the man reversed his course, pushing back up the aisle right into the arms of the officer and the other two soldiers. The fugitive thrashed and twisted, scratching the face of one of the soldiers badly, but they pinioned his arms and dragged him on toward the front door of the coach.

As they came abreast of Langhorne and Jester, the prisoner made a wild grab at Langhorne's lapel.

"Please, Señor, help me!" the man cried, tears streaming down his face. One of the soldiers wrenched the man's hand loose, and they hustled him the rest of the way up the aisle and out of the car. They hauled him a few yards away on the platform and then stopped. The officer gave a quick order, and two of the soldiers held the man there, one by each arm. The third soldier followed the officer as he re-boarded the train and started into their car again, pushing roughly back down the aisle. The officer's eyes seemed to Jester to be on him and Langhorne, and sure enough, the man stopped when he reached them.

Jester's stomach did a somersault, and the officer pulled out a big revolver. He said something to them in Spanish, which sounded like a question. Jester glanced at Langhorne, who hesitated a few moments, then spoke.

"We're Americans."

The officer said something else.

Langhorne turned his palms upward. "If you're asking whether we know that fellow, we don't. Never saw him before."

Out on the platform the prisoner raised his voice, sobbing as he cried out to the two soldiers holding him. He had to be pleading for his life.

The officer glared at the prisoner through the window momentarily then turned back to Langhorne and said something else, definitely threatening by the tone of his voice.

"We don't know him," Langhorne said.

The officer seemed about to speak again, but at that moment the prisoner outside jerked free of his two captors and bolted down the platform toward the rear of the train. The two guards were after him in an instant, and the officer and soldier inside rushed up the aisle, out the door, and off the train, joining the pursuit. The poor fellow didn't make it more than twenty yards before the soldiers overtook him and wrestled him to the ground.

All eyes in the train car were riveted to the spectacle outside. Just as the five men started forward again on the platform, the prisoner held firmly by a soldier on each side, the train jerked and the engine began a slow, pronounced puffing.

The train started creeping forward now, but the four soldiers and their prisoner were almost even with Jester's car. He held his breath—were they going to come back aboard?

They made no move to do so. Instead, they reached the end of the platform and stepped off, angling toward a small adobe structure fifty yards away. As the train slowly pulled abreast of the building, the men stopped there. The prisoner was struggling mightily by now, and one of the soldiers stepped into the building, returning a moment later with a wooden chair. They forced the man to sit on it, one soldier pulled off the prisoner's suspenders, and another one quickly tied him to the chair with them. Two soldiers shoved the man and chair against the wall of the building, and then all three soldiers formed a line facing him a few yards away.

Jester stared. It wasn't going to happen. It couldn't! The officer gave a command, the three soldiers brought their rifles up to their shoulders, the prisoner uttered a final pitiful plea, the officer gave a second command, a sharp volley burst from the rifles, and the prisoner was dashed back against the wall by the impact. He teetered there on two of the chair legs for several long seconds. Then he fell forward onto the dirt, still tied to the chair by his own suspenders. The train gradually gathered speed and left the bloody scene behind in less than another minute.

Jester looked at Langhorne beside him but couldn't speak. His heart pounded as if he'd just run a hundred yards. All through the coach, excited and horrified chatter seemed to erupt at once. Langhorne had a grim expression on his face, and finally he spoke.

"Makes you realize they play for keeps down here. Poor fellow." His eyes softened for a moment. "Could I have done somethin'?"

Jester just shook his head. He cast one last wary glance back out along the tracks, then finally found his voice. "How come you didn't answer that officer in Spanish?" He managed a nervous grin. "Cat get your tongue?"

"More like our throats. I just thought it might be best to be the dumb American. Kind of a hard call to make."

Jester let out a long, exhausted sigh and closed his eyes.

When Hermosillo finally came, they got off, bought a cool melon drink, then another, from one of the many ragged vendors at the station, and stretched their legs for half an hour before climbing onto another train for the trip on to Guaymas. Progress was just as slow, but the distance was much shorter. It was wonderful to finally reach the city and check into the Hotel Hidalgo for the night.

When they finished dinner a little before sunset, they left the hotel dining room and went for their rooms around the open interior veranda. Jester had to jiggle his key just right to get his door to open.

"I don't think I've ever wanted to see anything more than I want to see my bed right now," he said while Langhorne stood a few feet away.

"I wouldn't stroll around barefoot in there after the lights are out. No telling what kind of varmints you might run into on the floor."

Jester was in kind of a relaxed haze, and he smiled. "I shall be sure and wear my shoes then, should nature call me."

"Shake 'em out first."

Inside his spacious room, Jester stripped to his undershirt and drawers and lay back on the brass bed. He shut his eyes, but the scene of the execution came back suddenly, just as vivid as it had been in real life, and he sat up. He had one book of his two-volume Shakespeare, and, exhausted as he was, he read a couple of sonnets, then marked his spot with a sheet of hotel stationery. Right after sundown he spread the big louvered shutters that opened onto a cool courtyard along the back side of their rooms. A breeze drifted in immediately. If it weren't for the execution—and that was a very big *if*—there could be worse duty than taking a slow train to Sonora. With his hands clasped behind his head on the pillow, his eyes flitted aimlessly around the room, and in the waning light they settled on something scurrying along at the base of one wall.

He finally drifted off to sleep much later than he'd hoped, visions of multi-legged critters dancing in his head.

"I must say, this makes amends for any unease I felt during last night's slumber," Jester said as he dug into breakfast the next morning at a leisurely nine o'clock. Langhorne just grunted in reply and continued scribbling away in a notebook.

They sat in rattan chairs at a table along a shady veranda facing a side street. The meal was exceptional, including glasses of orange juice chilled in a bowl of ice, hot coffee—Langhorne had been right about the excellent quality of the Mexican version—fried eggs, beans, bread, and cheese, all for a couple of pesos each. Langhorne had awakened him at seven, already shaved, dressed, and looking like he'd been up for hours, but after finding that the train wasn't likely to leave until past ten, he allowed Jester to stay abed for another two hours.

Jester savored the meal and watched the local folk going about their daily migrations. A surprising number were children, and, rather than going to school, most seemed to be working, hawking merchandise or refreshments mostly. Then, of course, there were the women. They drew his eyes like magnets despite his valiant efforts to the contrary—not the matrons, but the younger women who passed under his vantage point. What a pleasant prospect indeed. Some were dark skinned, others as fair as many back in Washington or South Carolina, but almost uniformly their hair was very dark. He focused on the hair, and particularly of those who didn't cover theirs with a *rebozo*. It was smooth, lustrous. Yes, duty in Mexico might not be so onerous after all.

He gave Langhorne a quick glance to see if he was similarly engaged. He wasn't—hardly surprising, although it would've been gratifying to see the fellow distracted like mere mortal men by the Sirens of Guaymas. Instead, he kept at his writing.

"Your muse has inspired you to jot down a few lines of verse, I suppose," Jester said with a straight face.

Langhorne looked over, then quickly back down at his notebook. "Yeah, I was composing the *Mexican Odyssey*, but I can't figure out how to say 'golden boy who thinks he's on a holiday' in Greek."

Jester raised his eyebrows. Perhaps the man had a fairly active wit after all—and at least a rudimentary acquaintance with the Classics.

Langhorne continued in a low voice. "Trying to jot down a few notes of what we've seen so far. Without making it sound too official. Just an interested traveler's observations." He checked his wristwatch and snapped the notebook shut. "We'd better be up and about and get to the station."

The train east from Guaymas today seemed to cover ground a great deal more quickly than yesterday's had. Langhorne said they had eighty miles to the town of Corral, where they'd change, and the first half of that stretch only had four stops. After the midway point, though, the stations became as frequent as they'd been yesterday, so they didn't pull into Corral until mid-afternoon. After an hour's wait, their new train northeast on the little spur line got underway.

Jester watched the Rio Yaqui flow past beside the tracks until he thought he'd die of boredom, with stops at one tiny station after another until they finally came to a halt at Agua Blanca. The place was hardly a town, more an overgrown village whose one link to the outside world appeared to be the rail spur. It was warm when they stepped off the train about five o'clock, but the mountains to east and west now seemed nearer and considerably taller than they had earlier, and the higher elevation might bring a cooler evening.

The train pulled out immediately after depositing them and their trunks, along with one other passenger, on the platform.

"You said it only had two more stops?" Jester asked.

"Yeah. Then it ends at the mountains."

The near empty dirt streets of Agua Blanca were a far cry from the bustling scenes at Hermosillo and Guaymas. Jester looked over at Langhorne.

"They're supposed to send someone for us from Señor Medina?"

Langhorne nodded. "Supposed to. The hacienda is a ways farther on."

Jester noticed two men on horseback, well armed and wearing tailored, pearl-grey pants and shirts and beautifully trimmed grey sombreros, riding down the street toward the station.

"Do you think those gentlemen might be the ones?"

"Let's hope not. They're *rurales.* Kinda like a Mexican version of Texas Rangers. If they were lookin' for us, it might be the end of our business down here."

Jester watched them until they'd passed the station.

Langhorne pointed to a wagon and team standing across the street fifty yards away. A pair of saddled horses were tied to the gate of the wagon, and one man sat on the seat holding the harness reins.

"That's the kind of outfit I'd expect Medina would send. He knows we'll have baggage." He walked away toward the wagon, down off the platform and onto the street, and Jester followed.

As they approached, two vaqueros came out of a little shop, grain sacks on their shoulders, and headed for the wagon. They reached it first and tossed the bags into the back, then turned to face the Americans. The taller and older of the two waited until Langhorne was within a few yards, then spoke.

"Are you want to go to the hacienda of the Señor Medina?"

"*Sí,*" Langhorne answered. Then he continued in quick Spanish—Jester gave up trying to follow it after the second word—and the vaquero broke into a grin. He replied and motioned for Langhorne and Jester to climb up into the wagon bed and then sent the other vaquero back over to the station.

"He's getting someone to bring our trunks," Langhorne said.

The ride to the Medina ranch took three uncomfortable hours. The trail followed a small, winding river farther into the hills until they became true mountains. Then the wagon and the two outriders struck out across meadows and slopes, climbing through stretches of pine forest alternating with grassland and scattered scrub oaks.

The country was beautiful but lonely, and Jester tried to

draw Langhorne into conversation along the way, but the latter seemed content to enjoy the ride in silence, making no more than a comment here and there on the fine suitability of the land for grazing cattle.

The sun had been down for an increasingly chilly hour and a half, and the land in complete darkness for an hour, by the time the wagon finally pulled through an ancient stone gateway and into a huge courtyard. A row of blazing torches in sconces along the wall of the largest building augmented the vivid starlight to illuminate the courtyard. It looked to Jester to be over a hundred feet wide and not quite as deep. Lights twinkled in the windows of the large building, beckoning him in after the long, bone-jarring ride. The wagon pulled up in front of that structure. It had to be the main residence of the hacienda.

Langhorne stood and stretched, then vaulted over the side of the wagon, and Jester followed him. Immediately, a tall, heavy man in a dark suit appeared in the doorway of the house and strode out toward them. As he came closer, Jester could see a welcoming smile on his face. The man looked about fifty.

"I am Don Augustin Medina," the man said, extending a hand to Langhorne and bowing his head for an instant. "My home is your home. I am at your orders."

He shook hands with Jester as well, and Langhorne made the introductions to Medina. Medina said something in Spanish to his men, and then he led Langhorne and Jester into the house. A short, older man in a tight, black jacket met them.

"This is Carlito, my trusted friend and servant," Medina said. "He will show you to your rooms and see that your luggage is brought to you. We will have *cena* in half an hour. Carlito will call you." With that, Medina bowed and left them in Carlito's care.

As they followed the man down the corridor and turned left into another, Jester realized how hungry he was. Years ago in

Spain, *cena* had been a full evening meal, eaten late about nine or ten. Would it be similar here?

Carlito opened Langhorne's door first and ushered him in. After a few words, he came out and motioned for Jester to follow him farther down the hall. Jester glanced back and gave Langhorne a quick nod.

Forty minutes later a light knock sounded on Jester's door. It was Carlito, who escorted him down to Langhorne's room and then led both men past the corridor from the front door and into the next doorway to the right.

They were the first to arrive in the room. It was large, like the dining room at Jester's family's rice plantation back home in the Low Country. This room, though, was more sparsely furnished. The table was grand, indeed, and set for six. The only other things besides the table and chairs were a large, ornate mirror on one wall and an elaborate buffet holding dishes and cutlery. Jester's eyes were drawn to a double set of French doors on the outside wall. Torchlight from the courtyard played on the glass, giving a cozy feel to the room. It was good to be in out of the chill night air.

In a few moments Señor Medina joined them, smiling and asking if they'd found their rooms comfortable and their luggage undamaged. He spoke excellent English and seemed genuinely hospitable. Carlito drifted over by the buffet and stood attentively.

Quiet female voices down the corridor caught Jester's attention amid the conversation with Medina, and he and Langhorne both turned toward the door. An elegant woman, probably in her late thirties, was the first to step through the doorway. She wore a long dress of black velvet. Her hair was black and was gathered on her head just like the ladies did back home, and her skin was alabaster, quite a striking and attractive contrast. She smiled warmly when she saw him and Langhorne.

"Gentlemen," Medina said, holding out his hand toward the woman, "may I present my lovely wife, Guadalupe Maria Velasquez de Medina." He introduced the Americans.

Langhorne smiled and gave a brief bow.

"*Con mucho gusto,* Señora."

Jester felt a touch of envy for the man's linguistic ability, but then simply said, "Señora," bowing deeply with a flourish of his hand in the most courtly traditions of his state. It seemed to have the desired effect, causing the lady to give a tiny, apparently appreciative, gasp. As he came up from the bow, he glanced quickly toward Langhorne, but the man didn't seem to have noticed Jester's coup.

Señora Medina beamed. "It is such a pleasure to welcome you to our home. We seldom have visitors, and especially not ones so gallant as you gentlemen." Her English was more heavily accented than her husband's—delightful.

The lady moved to a chair at the table, revealing behind her a woman of nineteen or twenty in a long, dark blue dress. The girl smiled graciously as she stepped forward, and Jester was suddenly very glad that his country had called him to this duty.

"And this," Medina said, "is the most precious of my blessings—my only child, Fabiana."

The girl held out her hand, and all Langhorne did was shake it briefly and smile.

Jester stared at him for a moment—was the man so caught up with duty or religion that this beauty didn't stir him? When she then offered Jester her hand, he bent down and brushed it with his lips with all the elegance his upbringing in Charleston society could bring to bear.

"Enchanted, Señorita," he said, holding her eyes in a long gaze.

"Señor, we are delighted." Her voice was pure American.

Hadn't Powell said Medina's first wife was from the United States?

Fabiana was an inch or two taller than Guadalupe Medina, and her hair was a rich, dark brown. Like her mother, or stepmother, she wore it gathered on top of her head, but several ringlets fell tantalizingly down to her shoulders. Her eyes held something he couldn't identify with certainty—mischief, humor? Possibly a glimpse of fire? It was his duty as a gentleman to uncover the mystery.

Medina's voice cut into Jester's musings and brought his attention to another individual who had apparently been waiting in the background while the ladies took center stage. The man nodded briefly to Langhorne and Jester as Medina introduced them.

"My brother-in-law, Esteban Velasquez." Medina's smile had disappeared, and Velasquez wore an aloof expression. He seemed to look beyond Jester and Langhorne rather than directly at them. The man looked about thirty-five.

With the introductions completed, Medina took his place at the head of the table, and Carlito unobtrusively directed Langhorne and Jester to their chairs. Jester found himself seated next to Medina, with Velasquez to his left and the delectable Fabiana directly across the table. Langhorne sat to her right and Señora Medina to his right at the other end.

Jester glanced across at Fabiana in her chair, and he blanched for an instant—there was the scene, clear as it had been on the train, of the poor fellow tied to that chair, terrified, and shot dead a moment later. Then it was over. Jester forced a smile back onto his face.

Carlito moved quietly behind their chairs, pouring wine for everyone first and then ladling soup into each person's bowl from a pot on a serving cart. Medina tasted his wine and nodded to the servant. Jester wasn't sure of Mexican table etiquette, but when he saw his host begin, he knew it was all right to start eating. The soup was smooth and creamy, with a mild vegetable taste, but he could not determine the main ingredient. Fabiana must have noticed his uncertainty, for she caught his eye.

"*Calabaza,*" she said, watching him closely. After a few seconds, she said, "Squash."

Jester smiled back at her. It might be worthwhile to learn enough Spanish to carry on a conversation.

"Delicious."

Medina looked from him to Langhorne. "We are eating a heavier meal tonight than we normally do because we knew you would be very hungry after the long ride out from the station."

Between spoonfuls, Langhorne said, "We appreciate your consideration, Don Augustin. Breakfast was early."

From her place at the end of the table, Guadalupe Medina spoke. "Surely you did not come all the way from the border today."

"No, ma'am. We stayed in Guaymas last night."

"Ah, of course." She smiled.

Jester said, "It was a comfortable night, once the sun went down."

"Yes," she said. "The sea breezes help."

Medina held his spoon in midair for a moment as he spoke. "You'll find that here the problem is not keeping cool enough at night, but warm enough."

"It'll be a welcome change," Jester replied. "Washington is swelterin' this time of year, and then El Paso was like an oven."

"Oh, do you work for the American government, then?" Guadalupe asked.

Jester caught the quick frown in Langhorne's eyes. He'd said too much, hadn't he? He searched for a quick response that would steer the conversation away, but Medina came to his rescue.

"No, my dear. Mr. Jester is in private business." He turned to Jester. "What business was it, Señor?"

Jester smiled to cover his nervousness. "The newspaper business. I'm a correspondent with the, uh, *Washington Weekly.*"

Guadalupe smiled. "How interesting." She turned to Langhorne. "And you, Señor?"

"I'm studying the Mexican rail system."

"I am surprised that you can learn anything from our railroads," she replied. "When I have traveled in the United States, your trains are much nicer." She smiled. "And they run when the schedule says they will."

Jester focused on Langhorne—would he be able to continue the conversation without resorting to fabrication? The thought of the sober fellow sweating out the lady's interrogation was amusing.

Langhorne smiled. "I'm sure I'll be able to learn a lot that'll be of value to us."

The answer was good, and Jester was mildly disappointed. But things might not always be so easy.

Medina looked somewhat ill at ease and spoke quickly. "Are you gentlemen familiar with the cattle industry?"

Jester raised his eyebrows—the old boy had changed subjects smoothly enough. "Not at all, I'm afraid. Any animal bigger than a hound is beyond my familiarity—horses excepted, of course." He smiled as he finished, and Fabiana grinned at his confession. He held her eyes for a long moment.

"And you, Señor Langhorne?" Medina asked.

"I grew up around cattle. Worked 'em till I was about thirty." A cloud seemed to pass across his face as he said the words, but it was gone again in an instant.

Carlito was clearing away the soup bowls. The cart had been replenished with several large covered serving bowls, and the man began to serve each person from a big platter with slices of roast beef, starting with Guadalupe.

As soon as Langhorne had been served, Medina spoke to him again. "I will show you our cattle operation, or part of it. Possibly tomorrow."

Velasquez spoke for the first time, looking across at Langhorne. "We have many more animals than you have on ranches in the United States."

"How many head?" Langhorne asked Medina.

"About six thousand," he replied. "But I know some of your ranches in Texas rival many in Mexico." That last statement sounded almost apologetic to Jester, and Medina cast a sharp glance at his brother-in-law.

Velasquez looked from Langhorne to Jester. "Our hacienda has four thousand hectares of grazing and timberland." It sounded like a challenge.

"My brother-in-law lives in town," Medina explained. "He *visits* on our hacienda occasionally. Someday I think he hopes to have a ranch of his own."

Guadalupe and Fabiana both stared at Medina now, and Guadalupe looked uneasy.

Carlito served everyone from a bowl of boiled potatoes, and for a few moments the conversation ebbed. Jester felt the tension ease.

Guadalupe seemed to force a smile. "Señor Langhorne, may I ask how you like our country so far?"

Langhorne answered with a smile, in perfectly flowing Spanish.

It was a nice touch, Jester had to admit—but he still couldn't understand more than a few words, something about the people being wonderful.

Langhorne's reply drew smiles from all three Medinas and even from Carlito, but nothing more than a grunt from Velasquez.

"That is very kind of you, Señor," Guadalupe said. "We are a proud people." She paused and glanced at her brother. "But cruel to one another in many ways." A troubled expression came onto her face. "You know that many in our nation are very poor, but I don't know if you are aware that numbers of those are treated shamefully by the wealthy and powerful."

Velasquez held up his fork as if to emphasize his words. "Now that will not continue after Francisco Madero assumes the presidency. He will put an end to such injustice"—he cast a hard glance at Augustin Medina—"*and* confiscate the lands of those oppressors and distribute it to the *deserving*."

Jester stifled a grin. The man must've believed himself to be at the head of that list. Perhaps an innocent question might cool the atmosphere again.

"But I thought Señor Madero already was the president."

"He is—by the will of the people," Velasquez proclaimed.

"But he has not yet assumed the office officially," Medina said. "That will not come until November."

Jester said, "That's still two months away. What happens until then?"

"That is, as you say, anybody's guess," Medina replied. Carlito held a platter of rice before his master, but Medina continued speaking. "Some areas are following orders from Madero and his lieutenants, but others still remain under the same officials from the Diaz administration. There has been no transfer of power yet in many localities and even some entire regions. That worries me." He finally helped himself to the rice, but his eyes remained on his guests.

Guadalupe said, "My fondest hope is that the poor will no longer be at the mercy of the powerful once Señor Madero has finally taken office."

Langhorne cocked his head and asked, "How will he help them, Señora? The peons have to work for somebody. I understand most of 'em don't own land of their own to farm."

"Land reform," Velasquez said quickly. "Madero will take the land from those who don't deserve—"

"Nonsense!" Medina said. "Who is to decide the deserving and the undeserving? Don Francisco Madero is a great *hacendado* himself. Any distribution of land from the great estates must be done gradually and with fairness, or the country will slip into anarchy."

Jester glanced at Velasquez. The man was fuming.

Medina continued. "I trust Madero to desire land reform. The country needs it desperately. But whether he will have the strength of will to bring it about successfully, that I do not know."

"I *do* know!" Velasquez said. "He will do it. That or the people will rise as one man." He slapped the table. "And justice will be done."

Guadalupe said, "I fear that politics will not help the poor of Mexico unless true sympathy for them grows in the hearts of those who control the new government."

"Bear with me as an outsider," Jester began, "but I agree with the lady. Power corrupts, as we say, and who knows if the new leaders won't grow to be just as disagreeable as the old?"

"That is my fear," Guadalupe said. Her eyes seemed to take on a great sorrow. "Today, this very night, men and women— even children—are being tricked into slavery, taken to what they think are good jobs in the Yucatan and the Valle Nacional in Oaxaca, and instead finding themselves working for no pay, living in places not fit for even the pigs." She looked at each one of the men in turn. "They have no chance. They are worked until they collapse and die. And then more innocents are shipped in to take their place. *That* is the great evil, the poison that is polluting our country. I only hope that I can have a part in bringing an end to it forever."

Jester let out a long, quiet sigh. Further talk of politics seemed pointless now in light of the lady's fervent declaration, but he wanted her to clarify something. Hopefully his question wouldn't offend Medina.

"What you're speaking of, Señora, is the peons working for the landowners?"

She shook her head. "No, Señor. That is bad enough, the debt that the peons have to the *hacendados*. They can never pay it." She looked at her husband for a moment and smiled. "My husband, of course, pays his workers a decent wage and treats them fairly. No, what I am speaking of is worse, and so few even seem to know that it exists. It breaks my heart."

Jester's mouth went dry. There was his own family's history, their plantation and . . . everything. Whatever he could say of comfort to the lady might well smack of hypocrisy, in his own mind at least.

Langhorne was the one to speak. "None of those people are lost to God."

Guadalupe smiled sadly. "No, I suppose they are not. But how I wish I could help them."

Medina said, "Let us talk no more tonight of sadness. This is a practice that took ages to develop, and it will take a long time for it to be eradicated." He smiled and raised his wine glass. "To our guests," he said. "May their visit be one of peace and benefit to them, to us, and to our precious nation."

They all raised their glasses, and then they drank. All except Langhorne. Jester frowned at him and saw that Medina had noticed Langhorne abstain. Medina seemed about to say something, but Langhorne spoke first.

"I mean no offense whatever to your hospitality, Don Augustin. I never drink alcohol." He paused. "For religious reasons."

Medina broke into a smile. "And I take no offense, Señor. I am a believer in freedom of conscience for every man." He motioned for Carlito to bring a bottle of wine to him. When he received it, he held it up for Langhorne and Jester to see.

"This hacienda has produced its own vintage for centuries. The soil, the slopes, the climate all seem to come together in a perfect harmony to make the most exquisite grapes in the north of Mexico."

"I'd count it as a personal favor, Don Augustin," Langhorne said, "if you'd allow me to see your vineyard. I may not drink, sir, but I have a great love for land that produces good crops." He smiled. "Where I grew up in West Texas, it's dry and only fit for grazing."

"It would be my pleasure to show you. Perhaps tomorrow, and we can see my cattle as well—some of them."

"I'd like that, sir," Langhorne said.

The rest of the meal was spent in lighter conversation, and by the time they'd all finished the dessert of green melon and golden peaches, Jester was satisfied and pleasantly warm from several glasses of the very excellent Medina vintage.

The men all rose as the ladies began to excuse themselves.

"Thank you for a delicious meal, Señora Medina," Langhorne told her.

Jester said, "For a wonderful dinner and for your charming company," bowing to both Guadalupe and Fabiana. His eyes lingered on the girl, and she returned his gaze more boldly than he'd expected.

Velasquez was looking at the girl, too. "Fabiana, allow me to escort you to your room," he said with a slight bow of his own.

"Thank you, no, *Tio* Esteban." The refusal seemed to catch Velasquez by surprise, and after a few seconds he frowned and looked away.

The ladies said their gracious goodnights and slipped out of the room, and Medina turned to Langhorne and Jester.

"If you would join me, I would like to discuss some things

with you in my office." He gestured toward the hallway door. They filed out and turned down the hall, leaving Velasquez uninvited and, to Jester's eye, silently offended. With Medina leading, they walked down to a small room with a huge polished wooden desk and three comfortable armchairs. A kerosene lamp was lit on the desk, as were a number of candles in sconces on the walls and in a brass candelabra on a small table.

Jester inhaled deeply. The aroma of tobacco permeated the room, a pleasant smell even though he smoked nothing other than an occasional good cigar.

Carlito had entered behind them and stood by the desk now as Medina indicated two of the armchairs, then dropped into the one behind the desk. He opened a humidor and held it out to the two Americans, who declined, then picked out a cigar for himself. He took a whiff, looked satisfied, and cut the tip off with a small penknife.

"*Aguardiente,*" he said to Carlito. The servant fetched a squat brown bottle and three small snifters from the side table, while Medina scratched a match into life on the sole of his boot and lighted his cigar. He seemed to suddenly remember something and looked over at Langhorne and smiled. "Forgive me, Señor Langhorne. Could I have Carlito bring you something else instead? Coffee perhaps?"

"Please."

Once they all had their drinks and Carlito had shut the door as he left, Medina spoke.

"My apologies for this small room. It serves as the office for the business affairs of the hacienda." He looked around. "And it gives me a place of retreat and solitude when the female voices grow too insistent." He grinned for a few moments then his face grew serious. "My friends, let us now discuss the real reason for your visit."

Langhorne glanced at Jester, then turned back to Medina.

"Don Augustin, I understand that you're concerned about the stability of your country."

"Yes, very much so. President Diaz, for all his faults, has given us a long period of stability, law, and order. It has allowed business to grow and the country, in general, to become more prosperous. You heard my wife's concern over the injustices done to the poor—and I share that concern, believe me. But change can be either beneficial, or it can be harmful. I see the need for change, for more freedom for the poor, for their fair treatment. But it has to be accomplished in an orderly, lawful manner. Otherwise, it could bring great destruction to our country." He leaned back in his chair and puffed on his cigar, his eyes on Langhorne.

"In your business interests," Langhorne said, "I believe you have some joint ventures with American partners. A mining company, I think?"

"Yes. The Cerro Mojado Copper Mining Company in the northern part of this state. I like the way my American partners do business. That kind of efficiency is what Mexican businesses need. And they make a practice of treating their workers well." He leaned forward. "Do you know we pay our workers more than twice the usual rate in the other industries in this country?"

"I wasn't aware of that, sir," Langhorne said, "but then, I'm not a businessman." He took a sip of coffee. "Can you tell us how the workers feel? Are they satisfied? Do you think there'll be trouble with them now that the Revolution is a fact?"

Medina seemed to consider the question for a moment, and he shook his head. "I don't foresee labor trouble, no large strikes or violence like Cananea, if"—and he emphasized the word strongly—"the new government acts strongly to maintain law and order. If not, however, if Madero gives in to the more radi- cal voices among his supporters, then I fear there will be much bloodshed. And not just at the mines, but in every industry and business."

Jester just watched and listened, but Langhorne didn't seem to need any help. So why not sit back and enjoy his brandy? It was a rich amber color, and a bit more fiery than what he was used to drinking back home. But this was Mexico.

Langhorne asked, "Would you be in favor of U.S. intervention if Madero doesn't act strongly and things seem to be getting out of control?"

"Such intervention, as I understand it, would have the primary motive of protecting *American* business interests in Mexico, rather than Mexican interests—is that correct?" Medina was staring at Langhorne.

"That would be the reason behind any intervention of ours, from what our superiors have told us," Langhorne replied, glancing briefly at Jester.

Medina looked down at the desk momentarily, then back up. "I suppose I understand that. A nation must look to its own interests."

"I think what we're looking for," Langhorne said, "is circumstances where U.S. interests and Mexican interests would run parallel. Do you believe that under certain conditions, intervention would benefit both countries? And would the Mexican people, at least here in the north, support our intervention?"

Medina took a long draw on his cigar, held the smoke for possibly fifteen seconds, and finally blew it out toward the ceiling. He smiled and nodded his head. "Yes, I believe it would be supported, at least by the majority, if the alternative was chaos and anarchy."

Langhorne smiled. "That's what we wanted to know, sir." He took a long drink from his coffee cup. "Would the Mexican business leaders come out openly for it and help win the support of the rest of the people, do you think?"

"I think they would, the great majority. You must understand, Señor Langhorne, that we are not just businessmen, but patriots as well. We want what is best for Mexico—and for the Mexican people. That is where many of us have parted ways with Porfirio Diaz. He seemed to care for the country—but not the people, if you can grasp my meaning. And that is why I have my hopes in Madero, where I think the two interests coincide."

Jester barely nodded. The man's reasoning seemed sound. He and Langhorne exchanged glances. They'd heard what they needed.

Langhorne drained his cup. "I appreciate your talking so plainly with us, Don Augustin."

"The pleasure has been mine," Medina said, smiling. He got to his feet, and Jester and Langhorne followed suit. Medina opened the door for them and ushered them into the hall, where Carlito stood waiting. "Carlito will provide anything you need tonight. Rise when you wish in the morning. I hope to show you our ranch tomorrow."

The long day's travel and the excellent brandy joined forces now to call Jester to his bed—but not without anticipation of tomorrow.

CHAPTER 4

"I made me great works; I builded me houses; I planted me vineyards." Ecclesiastes 2:4

The sounds of morning had been floating through Jester's mind for half an hour before he finally stirred under the warm bed-covers. Soft light filtered in through the curtained windows. He opened his eyes and blinked to clear them. Last night's wine and brandy had left the hint of a dull ache in the top of his head.

He groped on the bedside table for his wristwatch and held it up. Ugh—not quite six o'clock. Langhorne had probably already dressed, taken a five-mile ride, and read half the New Testament. Jester grinned. Did the man ever . . . No.

He washed up and shaved, then dressed in a rough khaki shirt and heavy trousers. Just as he was pulling on his suspenders, a quiet knock sounded at the door. Carlito wished him a good morning and said there was hot coffee and *pan dulce* in the dining room.

"Is Señor Langhorne up?" Jester asked.

"Yes, Señor. He is awake for maybe two hours."

Jester stifled a smile. Sure enough. The fellow was an open book—and not a very long one, at that.

When Jester entered the dining room, Langhorne was by the buffet, his hand around a cup of steaming coffee.

"Don't you ever drink anything else?" Jester asked, still suppressing the smile.

"Water, when it's pure. Milk and buttermilk, when they're cold."

Jester walked over to the silver coffee pot on the dining table and poured himself a cup. "You, sir, seem to be a man without vices."

"We all have vices, Mr. Jester. The ones I've already got are trouble enough without taking on any new ones."

Jester studied him for a moment. Vices—like what, snoring? He glanced over the platter of breads and rolls sitting beside the coffee pot. "So this is *pan dulce.*"

"It's sweet and it's bread—just not too sweet. Some good peaches there." Langhorne nodded toward a bowl of the fruit down the table.

Jester picked a roll and put it on a saucer, then scooped up a hunk of butter with a knife and spread it on the roll.

"If you don't mind eating and talking at the same time," Langhorne said, "why don't you come to my room, and we'll figure when we need to leave here and get on with our business. Can't very well wander around outside before the family's up."

Jester didn't reply. The hacienda had charm—as did its female occupants. The idea of leaving held no appeal. But he followed Langhorne out into the hall with his coffee and roll. They started to the left toward their rooms, but the sound of an old woman singing nearby caught Jester's ear.

"Wait just a moment, if you please," he said, turning back down the corridor toward the sound. Langhorne followed, and, at the next door, they stopped and looked in. Jester frowned—wasn't this the same old woman he'd glimpsed last evening just before dinner? She knelt now over a stone trough, working what looked like a stone rolling pin back and forth. She sang a simple verse over and over as she worked. Jester glanced at Langhorne, who motioned for him to come back down the hallway toward their rooms.

"She's grindin' corn," Langhorne said, "or more like hominy. For tortillas. I would've expected the flour kind here in Sonora—they seem partial to 'em. But maybe that's just up north by the border."

"Looks like hard work."

"You see 'em at it for hours on end sometimes." Langhorne reached his door and led Jester in. "Here in Mexico, it's just like they say, 'Woman's work is never done.'"

Jester pushed the door shut. Langhorne sat on the bed and motioned him to the room's only chair.

Jester looked out through the open curtains. A high stone wall about fifty feet back of the house enclosed an area dotted here and there with low trees and vines. A semi-circular fountain stood on the midpoint of that wall. A few stone benches and wooden chairs were set comfortably among the flora. The early morning sun just peeked over that stone wall, dappling the ground with gold.

"Pleasant prospect," Jester remarked.

"Don't get too comfortable. We'll need to move on tomorrow or the next day." Langhorne was studying a small map.

"Oh, let's not be hasty, old man."

Langhorne looked up quickly, frowning.

Jester gave an innocent smile and waved one hand. "Just a friendly expression, I assure you, sir. It in no way was a reflection on your age."

Langhorne shook his head and looked back down at the map. "We have a lot of ground to cover once we leave here, and there's no reason to drag our feet. We said you'd be taking Hermosillo and Guaymas, then goin' south by boat. I'll have to take the main rail line south from Corral."

"That is my recollection as well," Jester drawled. "But I fail to see the necessity for haste." He grinned just a little. "Especially after making the acquaintance of the charming Miss Fabiana last evening. I feel it would do a disservice to our government were I to leave without learning all I can of her. As a representative of the feelings of the Mexican people as a whole, of course."

"Oh, of course," Langhorne said wearily. He looked hard at Jester again. "Lieutenant, has it occurred to you that we're here to do a job, that you're getting paid for this, and that you're under orders?"

"Certainly, sir." Jester dropped his smile. Finding the limits of Langhorne's tolerance might take a delicate touch from here.

"And that our superiors need the information we get as soon as possible, so they can make the best preparations in case we have to act?"

"Now that you put it that way, sir, I fully understand. Therefore, I'm prepared to sacrifice one of the days I had hoped to spend here." The grin crept back onto his face. "And be satisfied with remaining at the hacienda for just the next five days instead of six."

Langhorne let out a long, slow breath. "I'll give us two days, no more."

"But that—"

"Is an order, Lieutenant Jester." Langhorne looked him square in the eye.

"Precisely my point, *Lieutenant* Langhorne," Jester said pleasantly. "My bar is just as silver as yours, sir."

"But you haven't worn it as long. We've been through this already, if you recall. Colonel Powell laid things out pretty clear—I'm senior. I'm in command. Two days."

Jester shrugged. "Oh, well. I did try. Two days will have to satisfy me. Perhaps we can stop back by on the way home—so I can renew old acquaintances."

"Better not plan on forming any close *friendships* with the ladies of this house, Mr. Jester. Men down here don't look kindly on guests taking liberties with their wives and daughters."

"I assure you, sir, that I had no intention of taking liberties with any married woman. And as for the daughters." He smiled slyly at Langhorne. "Well, healthy young ladies have certain physical and emotional needs, just like healthy young men. Why, it's only natural. You wouldn't want me to act contrary to nature, now would you? I mean, it might actually lead to physical illness to stifle those needs too strictly."

"Enough!" Langhorne slapped his hand down on his leg with a snap like a rifle shot.

Jester felt his smile evaporate. So Langhorne could really get angry—or was it just dramatics, what they called "command voice"? No sense in pushing things.

The two sat in uneasy silence for a few seconds. Jester glanced around the room, and finally focused on two books on the bedside table.

"You're a reading man." It seemed a safe way to renew the conversation. "Anything interesting?"

Langhorne picked up the larger volume, leather bound and obviously well used, and he handed it across to Jester. "The Bible. Ever heard of it?"

Jester smiled nervously. "One of the great literary works of the world." He opened it and leafed through a few pages.

"It's a lot more than just a good story," Langhorne said. There was another, briefer period of silence. Finally, Langhorne took a long drink from his coffee cup and smiled. "We'd better finish our *desayuno* and get ready for Señor Medina in case he wants to show us around the ranch."

Jester relaxed and passed the Bible back, then took a big bite of his roll. A little hesitantly, he pointed toward the smaller book on Langhorne's table. "What's that one?"

Langhorne tossed it to him.

Jester read aloud from the title page. "*An Apache Campaign in the Sierra Madre* by John G. Bourke." So this was Langhorne's idea of pleasure reading.

"They chased a band through this region in the eighties," Langhorne said.

Jester grinned. "You're not plannin' to fight any Indians, now are you, Lieutenant Langhorne?"

"The Apaches are on our side now." Langhorne said it with a straight face. "Or hadn't you heard?"

"I think I picked it up somewhere. I'm glad we share a common interest."

"Reading?"

"Well, it's certainly not Apaches. My family insisted I receive a literary education, and, I have to admit, I'm quite glad for it now. It gives me great pleasure."

Langhorne seemed about to speak when there was a light knock on the door. He answered it, and Carlito told them Señor Medina planned to go riding and wondered if they'd like to join him. Jester downed the rest of his coffee, and they followed the man down the corridor and through an outside door on the end of the house.

"Did you have something to eat and drink?" Medina asked when they joined him on the covered gallery that stretched the length of that side of the house. Langhorne assured him that they had.

Jester looked right and left along the gallery. It was about eight feet wide, with round stone columns every ten or twelve feet, connected by Romanesque arches like those in some of the churches he'd seen in Spain. Large terracotta tiles paved the floor. A couple of wooden benches along the wall offered shady spots to sit and look out across the open courtyard toward the stables and the other buildings. The houses back in Charleston had big verandas like this, but they were wood rather than stone and tile. This gallery must enclose the house on three sides. The fourth side probably butted up against the tall stone outside wall around the entire enclosure.

"I thought we would take a ride this morning while it is still cool," Medina said, "and let you see some of the hacienda's lands."

Langhorne nodded and smiled. "That would be a pleasure, Don Augustin."

"Indeed it would, sir," Jester said.

"Good, good," Medina said, nodding his head. "My daughter will join us, if that meets your approval."

Jester caught Langhorne's eye and smiled. Langhorne responded with a quick, warning stare. Jester kept smiling.

Medina led them across the courtyard toward the stables. When they reached it, he gave orders to the men there, and four horses were quickly saddled and led out.

Just then, Jester noticed the girl, coming out of the same door they'd just used and striding confidently toward them. She was a picture, dressed in matching maroon trousers and jacket over a white shirt. That was a surprise—apparently skirts and side saddles weren't mandatory for women in Mexico after all. The girl's dark brown hair was down, hanging thick and lustrous several inches below her shoulders and gathered by a gleaming silver clasp.

She cast him just one glance, but seemed to look him up and down in that instant. It was hard to tell whether there was a smile in her eyes, but they seemed to hold some sort of mischief. She stood on tiptoes to kiss her father's cheek, and he gave her a warm embrace with one big arm around her shoulders.

"Gentlemen," Medina said, ushering them to the waiting horses. He mounted a powerful black stallion, just the sort of animal Jester expected the man would ride. Fabiana's horse was a tall thoroughbred gelding, and Langhorne had a big bay mare. Jester took the reins from one of Medina's men and climbed up on a palomino gelding.

Medina turned the head of his stallion and led off at a trot toward the front gate of the walled compound. Jester looked up at the gatehouse that flanked the opening as he rode past. It was like going forth from a castle in the Middle Ages. The thick stone walls and firing loopholes made it clear the gatehouse was built for more than decoration.

They turned north out the gate and rode for a long meadow beneath a pine-covered slope that angled to the northeast. The air was chilly and patches of ground fog still clung to the meadow as the early sunlight spread over a widening area. Jester inhaled deeply of the scent of pines. What a delightful change from the dry desert air of the preceding days.

Medina led them up into a cluster of hills interspersed here and there with more lush meadows in which scores of cattle grazed. A few mounted men stood lazy watch over the herds and doffed their sombreros as the party skirted the animals.

They rode for almost half an hour in that direction, Medina pointing out pastures used at various times of year, perennial springs, and other points of interest to a cattleman's eye, while Fabiana occasionally called their attention to the more picturesque elements—the striking peaks of the Sierra, long meadows of lush grass, and rugged rock outcroppings or cliffs. At several points, Langhorne and Medina were so locked in cattle talk that they scarcely seemed aware of Jester and Fabiana's presence.

The girl apparently noticed it, too, and after a while she and Jester were casting sly grins at each other whenever the other two would go off on another exchange of ideas. Jester kept his eyes on Fabiana—admiring her was a much more rewarding use of his time.

Finally, they pulled up at the edge of a rocky canyon, possibly a quarter mile across. On the bottom at the far side, rusty, abandoned equipment stood next to a huge heap of slag. An ugly gash pierced the side of the canyon, just above the slag.

Medina pointed across. "An old mine from when I was just a boy. Not very productive. They had a big cave-in and never reopened it."

Fabiana looked at Jester and Langhorne. "Many of the miners died."

One of the higher, pine-clad peaks of the Sierra, miles in the distance, formed a backdrop to the ruined mine. Jester studied the contrast of pristine mountain and decaying mine.

They turned southeast and rode past more herds and meadows. At one point on the edge of a flat stretch of short grass, Jester looked over at Fabiana, and the glint of a challenge came into her eyes. She was off with a bound, and Jester followed a half second later, galloping toward a lone pine tree standing a hundred feet tall. It wasn't much of a contest, with Fabiana's gelding much more horse than Jester's mount, but he laughed just as heartily as she did when he reached the pine three lengths behind her.

"Getting slow in your old age?" the girl asked. Jester watched her for a moment, her face flushed from the race and her chest rising and falling with each breath.

"Apparently so," he agreed. He started to add "but not at everything," then thought better of it. Medina and Langhorne rode up to join them, and Jester reluctantly turned his eyes away from Fabiana. Four was definitely a crowd today.

Medina studied her and Jester for a few moments, then led them all west. After another ten minutes, the walls of the hacienda compound came into view a quarter mile off to the left. They paralleled the north wall then angled left toward the meadow they'd passed at the beginning. Medina pulled up and pointed at a group of pens and a large, low barn two hundred yards west from the gate. He looked over at Langhorne.

"The pens will hold three hundred head. Let me show you." With that, he spurred into a trot across the grassland, Langhorne falling in beside him, and Jester and the girl coming along behind. Fabiana looked bored with the prospect, and she allowed her horse to fall further behind her father and Langhorne. Jester kept pace with her.

When they'd dropped back twenty-five yards, she pointed off at an angle, and Jester noticed a little shack at the edge of a copse of stunted oaks a few hundred yards away. The shack almost blended into the backdrop of trees. The girl gave no explanation, but turned in that direction, with Jester in step beside her. Finally he could make out a man sitting out front, under an overhanging *ramada* of branches.

He was an ancient fellow, with a face like well-tanned leather, grizzled gray hair, and a bushy moustache of the same color. They pulled up before the house, and the old man gave a gap-toothed smile. He struggled to rise, but he finally managed it, pulling his straw sombrero off and holding it with both hands across his stomach.

"Patrona," he said, bowing stiffly, then expressing a long greeting in Spanish that Jester couldn't quite understand.

She smiled and said, *"Buenos dias, Viejo,"* as she and Jester dismounted and dropped their reins.

Jester muttered a *Buenos dias* as well, then turned toward her and leaned close. "What did Viejo say?"

"It's an old style of greeting that means 'May God give you a good day and health.' Sometimes they add more to it. He's about the only one here who ever uses it anymore. Oh, and Viejo isn't his name—it just means 'Old Man.' " She looked at Jester with that glint in her eyes. "Let's go inside. You'll find his house interesting."

Jester's eyes narrowed. There was something she wasn't telling him. But what could he do but follow her into the shack after the old man?

The inside was dim, with a low ceiling full of dust and cobwebs. A small table and two chairs stood on one side of the single room, and along the other side was a rough, shallow shelf running almost the entire length of that wall, waist high. Boxes large and small, glass jars with rusty lids, and various other containers covered most of the shelf. A thick coating of dust was evident on them, as well.

"He's a collector," Fabiana said.

Jester decided not to ask the obvious question, but just followed her as she strolled casually around the room, exchanging pleasantries in rapid Spanish with the fellow. Jester's eyes became more accustomed to the dim interior.

Apparently in response to something Fabiana said, the old man picked up a jar and unscrewed the lid. He held it out for Jester and the girl, and they both peered inside at a mass of dried leaves.

"Those are a remedy for chills and fever," she said. She pointed to another jar, and the man dutifully opened it and presented it for their inspection. It was filled with large flat seeds. She turned to Jester and smiled. "For cuts and wounds."

She pointed next to a bundle of dried yellow stems hanging from the ceiling. After a quick exchange with the old man, she looked at Jester and held his eyes. There was something impudent in her gaze, as if she were making fun of him and enjoying it secretly. He didn't mind at all.

"And those," she said, ". . . who knows if it's true, but Viejo says those are for the young man who wants all the girls to follow him like mares after their stallion."

She was trying to embarrass him—that was plain—to make him blush at the suggestion. But he'd been playing games with girls more sophisticated than she was for too long to oblige her. He stared back without blinking.

"Never found the need."

She was the one that turned red, and after a few awkward seconds, she walked on and pointed to a shriveled object hanging from the ceiling. Jester started—a dried rat. He looked around more closely now and noticed several other desiccated creatures—rats, toads, and lizards—hanging by strings.

"Good for almost anything," Fabiana said, "when you make it into broth. Or so Viejo tells me." She seemed to be watching for a reaction.

Jester smiled. It would be good to make up for embarrassing her.

"I think I'd rather just remain ill."

She smiled in return and looked back along the shelf. A curious wooden box with a few small holes bored in the side caught her attention, and she reached out toward it.

In an instant, the old man uttered a cry of alarm, and his hand shot out and grasped her wrist before she could touch the box. Her eyes blazed for a moment, but the old fellow had a look of real concern on his face, and her expression softened. He released her wrist immediately and slowly pulled the box toward him. He motioned for Jester and the girl to come close and look down at it. *"Cuidado,"* he said, and he carefully took hold of the lid and slid it an inch to the side.

A little sunlight was coming in through the door now, and the old man angled the box so that the light fell inside it. Jester pulled back by reflex—a big straw-colored scorpion stood poised inside. The man shut the box again after a few seconds.

Jester took a deep breath. It would be nice to bid the old man adieu. The girl made no move to leave, though. Instead, she pointed toward another box, a smaller one painted dark red. This one had smaller holes. The hairs on the back of Jester's neck stood up.

The old man held the little box before their faces and slid the lid back, just as he'd done before. Jester couldn't see anything in this one at first, but then he spotted it in the darkest corner—a slim red scorpion, much smaller than the other one. The old man closed the top again quickly and shook his head at both of them.

"*Muy malo,*" he said. He launched into a further explanation—nothing Jester could follow. When it was over, he looked at Fabiana for translation.

She seemed a little spooked. "He says the little one is much more poisonous than the big one. It can kill or paralyze a person."

The old man hobbled across to a big wooden box on the floor and beckoned Jester and the girl over. On closer inspection, Jester saw that it was an old Sears and Roebuck shipping crate. Viejo tapped on the lid, and an indistinct rustling sound came in answer from inside. Cautiously, he raised one edge of the heavy lid a few inches and motioned for them to take a look.

Jester touched Fabiana's arm lightly and drew her with him up to the crate. They peeked in tentatively and both stepped back quickly.

"Not my first choice for a pet," Jester said, glancing sideways at the girl.

She gave a momentary grimace. "Nor mine. I think he milks them for the venom."

Jester forced a smile. "And I think it's time we rejoined your father."

"Yes, let's do that," she replied, smiling brightly. With thanks and an *adios,* she left the old man, and Jester was right behind her. The bright chilly morning felt good out in the sunshine again. The smell of roasting beef was in the air, drifting on the breeze from the hacienda.

Langhorne and Medina were riding toward them, and Jester and Fabiana mounted their horses and fell in alongside the two, and they all headed for the gate of the hacienda.

"Strange old fellow," Jester said to her. Medina apparently heard, for he called over his shoulder in reply.

"A bit eccentric but harmless. We furnish him with a goat and some corn on occasion. In turn, he helps us when my family or my workers are sick."

Jester turned to Fabiana. "You trust his remedies?"

"We have no physician." She shrugged. "And we always seem to get better. Of course, there was the vaquero who was gored by a steer. He died." She shrugged again and smiled. "But I like the Old One."

CHAPTER 5

"And behold another beast, a second, like to a bear, and it raised up itself on one side, and it had three ribs in the mouth of it between the teeth of it: and they said thus unto it, Arise, devour much flesh." Daniel 7:5

They all had *almuerzo,* the late, big breakfast, at nine forty-five by Jester's watch. Fabiana was there, along with Señor and Señora Medina and her brother, Esteban Velasquez, all seated around the dining table with Jester and Langhorne. Huge silver platters, one with fried eggs resting on tortillas and garnished with a red sauce, and the other with thin grilled beefsteaks and onions, sat on the ancient table where the diners could help themselves. On each end of the table was a plate with a huge stack of hot corn tortillas. Finally, there were bowls of peaches and grapes. Carlito kept each person's cup replenished with hot coffee.

Jester was suddenly ravenous, and he focused his attention on the food more than the conversation. He ended up eating three of the eggs and one of the larger steaks, along with several tortillas and a ripe, sweet peach, but that didn't stop him from glancing across the table at Fabiana occasionally, and she always seemed to be eyeing him, with a little subdued smile playing on her lips. Whatever could the dear girl have on her mind?

Velasquez, to Jester's left, didn't say two words during the entire meal but seemed intent on putting away as much food as humanly possible. He looked up at the others only rarely, and then with a dark expression on his face.

Guadalupe Medina was again, like the night before, the essence of grace and hospitality. She wanted to know if Langhorne and Jester had been comfortable in their rooms and if they'd enjoyed their morning ride.

When Jester drained his final cup of coffee, Fabiana leaned in close to her father and had a brief whispered exchange with him. He finally smiled indulgently and nodded his head.

He looked at Jester and said, "Señor, I have requested my daughter to show you the portion of the hacienda within the outer walls—if you would find that agreeable."

Jester smiled. "I assure you, sir, that I could find nothing more agreeable." Velasquez sniffed loudly.

"Good, then," Medina said. He pushed his chair back and stood up, along with the others. Langhorne came around the table, and the two walked out the door together.

Fabiana beckoned Jester to follow her outside through the open French doors, in the direction of the gatehouse. He nodded and smiled at Señora Medina as he left, and noticed Velasquez snatch a peach and stomp out after them. The man certainly couldn't be planning to tag along uninvited. No—Velasquez stopped on the gallery and stood frowning while they walked away.

"Let me ask you, Miss Medina," Jester said, "about the term *hacienda*. I'm not quite sure whether it means the main house here or this entire walled-in area with all its buildings."

"It means both," she replied. They passed the big round fountain in the middle of the courtyard between the house and the gate. "We also call the ranch itself the hacienda."

He smiled at her. "Three meanings, then. You make everything clear to me."

Just before they reached the gate, she had him turn around and face the main house. "This open area," she said, indicating the huge courtyard, "we call the main *patio*. The gate here is called the *zaguan*."

He looked back at the gatehouse for a moment. "And what do you call the gatehouse here?"

She looked serious. "We usually call it the gatehouse." Then she laughed.

The laugh did it—she had to be the most beautiful girl he'd ever seen, or darn close. It wasn't safe to look at a girl for that long, but mighty hard to stop. She turned away then and continued the tour.

"Over there," she said, pointing to the line of buildings to her left, "we have the wine room against the outer wall, then the stables, which you saw earlier. Then on the right are quarters for some of our workers."

"Your father's vaqueros live there?"

"No. They live in a bunkhouse outside the walls, or if they're married, in little shacks of their own out there." Next, she pointed right, where a long arcade extended along the outer wall from the gate to the wall of another building. "This covered area is the *portales,* and at the end of it is the chapel."

Jester chuckled. "You even have your own church. I *am* impressed, Señorita."

"You can call me Fabiana."

"And you can call me Calvin."

"But you are so much older," she said seriously. "It would be improper. I think I must call you Señor Jester."

She was toying with him now. He didn't mind it a bit.

She searched his eyes, still looking serious.

"Or maybe I should call you Viejo."

"I think that name is already taken," he replied, looking back into her eyes.

She was on the verge of a grin—that was obvious. Perhaps if he smiled, then she wouldn't be able to keep from it any longer. So he smiled, and that did the trick. She tried to cover it up by looking away and starting across the patio. He hurried to keep pace beside her, and she took his arm as they walked. What a pleasant way to spend the morning.

Jester happened to glance to his right as they came abreast of the main house, and there was Velasquez leaning against one of the pillars and glaring. It was a bit more comfortable when they were past the front of the house and blocked from the man's view.

"Your, uh, *uncle* appeared none too happy."

She frowned and shivered. "He makes my skin crawl." She pulled him out of sight behind the workers' quarters and stopped to look up at him. "You know he's not my blood relation, just my stepmother's brother?"

"I had gathered that."

She sighed. "I probably shouldn't tell you this, and you must promise not to tell my father or my stepmother." She reached out and fingered one of the buttons on his shirt and smiled just for a moment, then let go of it.

He raised a hand. "Cross my heart."

"Esteban thinks he will marry me and take all of this someday."

Jester frowned. "Your father certainly wouldn't allow it." That much was obvious from last night at dinner.

"You're right, thank goodness. But if anything should ever happen to Papa—then, who knows?"

"You don't think your stepmother would go along with that."

She stared off for a moment. "I don't think so—but I don't know if she would be strong enough to resist him. In Mexico, a man has great power over his family."

"Quite a distasteful prospect." A picture of Esteban with his

84

greedy hands . . . No.

She looked at him fiercely. "And it's not you he's wanting to marry. It would be unendurable."

He started to take her hand but maybe that would've been too forward. He cocked his head and looked down at her instead. "Don't you worry." His voice was almost a whisper. "I'm certain nothing will happen to your father."

She gave him a little smile and murmured, "Thank you."

She seemed more relaxed now and showed him the orchard of peach and apple trees behind the workers' quarters, and the vegetable garden back of the stables. They strolled past an open room that backed against the stables and smelled of a strong mixture of wood smoke and rancid meat. Cowhides were curing on frames inside under the watchful eyes of a dark, shriveled old man whom Fabiana identified as a Tarahumara Indian.

They came back around toward the main house now, and she pointed out the family's private patio behind it. Jester looked closely. That must've been what he'd glimpsed through Langhorne's window. It was lush with vines and shade trees, a cool oasis in the growing heat of midday.

"Now all that's left is the chapel," she announced, heading for the front gate again. Velasquez was gone from his vantage point by the house, and Jester smiled. Hopefully, the fellow wasn't lurking somewhere, watching them now.

After they walked through the *zaguan* and outside the wall, Fabiana stopped and faced back around toward the gate. She pointed across the top of the opening, where large, archaic letters were carved into the stone lintel beneath a medieval crest:

Sol contra Gabaon ne movearis et luna contra vallem Ahialon.

"Latin," Jester observed. "Mine's a little rusty, but it says something about the sun and moon not moving."

A voice spoke from behind them, making them both jump. It was Langhorne.

"Sun, stand thou still upon Gibeon; and thou, Moon, in the valley of Aijalon."

Jester turned and raised an eyebrow. "Why, what a pleasant surprise to find you here, of all people. And I had no idea you were a Latin scholar, on top of all your other accomplishments."

Langhorne grinned and tipped his hat to the girl. "I'm not. I just memorized the verse a long time back. It's from the book of Joshua."

"Chapter ten, verse twelve, I think," Fabiana said. She laughed. "I'm afraid it's the only Bible verse I ever learned."

Jester turned to her. "The man's a veritable walking Bible. You can't imagine how handy that comes in, in his line of work."

Langhorne looked a little embarrassed for once. "Well, if y'all will excuse me, I'm going back inside after my look at the chapel. Señor Medina had to sign some letters, so I took a few minutes to come out and see it. Oh, and Jester, you might have Miss Medina tell you about the other name for the hacienda." He headed in through the *zaguan* and was gone.

Jester looked at her. "What was he talking about?"

"Let's walk on to the chapel, and I'll tell you." She started toward the southwest corner, where a long stone structure jutted out fifty or sixty feet forward from the wall. "The name of our hacienda is *El Valle de Ajalón.* You can understand that it follows from the inscription."

"Certainly," Jester replied. "A beautiful name."

"The other name that Señor Langhorne spoke about is hardly ever used. It is *Hacienda de la Luna de los Apaches.*"

"I think even I can translate that one," Jester said. "Hacienda of the Apache moon." He raised his eyebrows and smiled. "Rather spooky."

"Yes. The story goes that this area was plagued for centuries by Apache raiders coming down from the north. They seemed to come when the moon was full, especially in the autumn."

She stopped as they reached what had to be the door of the chapel.

"Why don't you finish the story before we go in," Jester said.

"Sometime in the eighteenth century, our ancestor the Marques de Medina, a great and valiant warrior for the King of Spain"—she stopped for a moment and smiled—"took the field against the Apache with a force of soldiers. He marched for many hours."

Jester took on an expression of mock solemnity. "How noble."

She matched his expression. "Oh, yes. Anyway, he caught the Apache band by surprise, right on this very land where the hacienda stands today, and in a battle that lasted all night under the full moon, he utterly destroyed them. It is said that he prayed for God to cause the moon to stand still high in the night sky to give his army light to kill every last one of the Indians."

"You have interesting relatives."

She smiled now. "Yes, and successful ones. For his victory, the Marques received a grant of thousands of acres here where the battle was fought, and it, of course, became the *Hacienda El Valle de Ajalón* to commemorate the victory."

"Quite fascinating," Jester said. He held out his hand toward the door. "Shall we go in?"

They entered the chapel, cool and dim. Two rows of benches flanked a central aisle running from the back, where he and Fabiana stood now, to the altar at the front. Tiny square windows stood high on the side walls. They had stained glass scenes, but they were so small that it was difficult for him to make out the pictures. The place had a dusty, unused look. Jester noticed a number of boxes stacked by the entry along the back wall.

"Doesn't get much business these days, looks like."

"No. It hasn't been used as a church many times since I've been alive. Occasionally a priest would come and say Mass for the people on the hacienda, but the last time must've been five or six years ago. My stepmother would like to see it cleaned and put back into use, but it's been impossible to find a priest to come and serve. I care little for such things, and Papa doesn't have time to spare for them."

"Langhorne must have been disappointed when he saw the place."

Fabiana seemed to study him. "You don't like him much, do you?"

The question caught him by surprise, and Jester waited a few moments before answering. "He's a hard man to like, but"—he shrugged—"a hard man to dislike, as well. I hadn't really thought about it before you asked, but I suppose it's because he's so earnest about everything. Being around him makes me feel rather guilty. For I don't know what."

She did not reply but appeared to consider what he'd said.

Half an hour later, Jester was sitting with Langhorne on the front gallery of the main house, relaxing in the shade with a cool glass of fruit juice.

Jester stretched and looked around him. Across the sunny main patio, a couple of horses in the stables tossed their heads as a worker brought them fresh hay.

"I don't know about you," Jester said, "but I wouldn't mind retiring to a spot like this."

There was a twinkle in Langhorne's eye. "Not plannin' to marry into the family, now are you?"

Jester chuckled. "I could do worse."

Just then, Guadalupe Medina stepped out the front door and stopped, glancing around the patio. They stood up, and she smiled at them.

"Please," she said, "take your seats. I was just looking for my husband."

They assured her that they hadn't seen him, and she thanked them and disappeared back inside the house again.

When he was sure she was out of earshot, Jester turned toward Langhorne and smiled expansively. "Guadalupe Maria Velasquez de Medina." He said the name slowly, deliberately, lingering over it. "They do know how to name their women, don't they? It's like a song."

"I'll grant you that. But remember, it's *Señora* Guadalupe Maria Velasquez de Medina."

Jester shook his head, smiling. "She's a lovely woman, I admit, but I have no designs on her, I assure you. The Jester men respect the marriage bond." He looked at Langhorne, but who could tell if the fellow believed him or not?

"And you'd best be careful with the daughter. Remember you're a guest under her father's roof."

Jester shot him an annoyed glance. "Yes, Mother."

Heavy footsteps came toward them from around the corner, and in a moment Medina came into view. He spotted them, smiled, and hurried forward.

"My friends, I was hoping to find you still out here. My wife said she had seen you. Do you have enough to drink? I will call Carlito if you need something."

They both thanked him and shook their heads. Medina sat down in a rattan chair next to Langhorne and stretched out his long legs, crossing the ankles. He wore a beautiful pair of intricately tooled brown leather boots. He looked past Langhorne at Jester.

"My daughter said she told you the story of our hacienda, how it got its name."

"Yes, Don Augustin, she did." Jester smiled. "It was quite colorful."

"But it is more or less the truth," Medina said. "Of course those old tales have fantastic things added to them—the moon standing still and all that—but in its essentials, the story tells what actually happened. The battle is duly recorded in the annals of the Viceroyalty of New Spain."

"The Apaches must've given a lot of trouble to the people in this part of Mexico back in those days," Jester said.

Medina leaned toward Jester. "I tell you, Señor, there are people alive on this ranch who have faced the wrath of the Apache—in Agua Blanca, here at the hacienda, throughout the Sierra Madre. The old man whose house you visited this morning—as a child he saw his mother and father cut down by a raiding party not a hundred meters from that very house. I myself remember hearing of the raids when I was a young man."

The statement caught Jester a little by surprise, and he looked at Langhorne.

"You saw my book," Langhorne told him. "That campaign was only about twenty-five years ago."

"I guess I didn't give it much thought," Jester said. "Indian trouble has always seemed far removed from the here and now."

Medina pointed across the patio toward the chapel. "Did you notice how tiny the windows were? And have you wondered why we have such a high, thick wall around the house and buildings?"

"I noticed the windows." Jester raised his eyebrows. "So it's all for the Apaches."

"The whole place is designed for defense," Langhorne said. "The gatehouse, too."

Medina smiled. "Aren't you glad we don't have to worry about them anymore? Yes, we live in a much safer world now."

That was when they first heard the yelling far out in the grassland to the north.

For a moment Jester just sat there, listening. Then Langhorne jumped to his feet, and Jester and Medina sprang up an instant later. They all raced for the *zaguan.*

When they burst out of the front gate, a wagon was a hundred and fifty yards away and coming fast. The driver slapped his team with the reins, wildly urging them on at a lumbering gallop while two mounted vaqueros kept pace beside the wagon. One person was on his knees in the back, holding on to the sideboard and bending over a shapeless bundle on the wagon bed.

Jester jumped to one side and Langhorne and Medina to the other as the wagon careened through the gate. The driver stood up and heaved on the reins, leaning back hard to stop the rushing horses. One vaquero leaned from his saddle and grabbed the headstall of one of the team and helped bring the wagon to a halt in a swirl of dust, just in front of the stables.

Jester, Langhorne, and Medina ran to the wagon. It was no bundle on the wagon bed but a man, a badly injured one. Jester stared at him. If the frenzy of the driver and vaqueros was any indication, he might yet be alive.

Medina spoke rapidly, and the vaqueros and driver, along with Langhorne, gently hefted the injured man off the wagon bed and onto the ground.

Langhorne stepped back and leaned toward Jester. "We'd better keep out of the way unless you have some medical training I don't know about. Medina and his men probably know what to do."

The man wasn't conscious, but his chest rose and fell, the breathing labored and erratic. Jester watched them cut off the man's bloody shirt and peel it back, tugging it away from dark patches of dried blood that stuck to the fabric. His right arm flopped over onto the dirt in the process, and Jester swallowed quickly. The four fingers and half of his palm were gone, leaving nothing but the thumb and the heel of his hand. His shredded right trouser leg seeped blood.

The scene drew workers and vaqueros from every building inside the walls, and in less than a minute Señora Medina and Fabiana hurried out of the main house toward the crowd. Guadalupe knelt beside her husband and began speaking rapidly, but apparently not to him. She had to be praying.

Jester looked over at Fabiana. She'd stopped well back of the injured man. Jester worked his way past several onlookers and over to her. Maybe he could comfort her. She turned toward him, looking pale and anxious. He slipped a hand under her elbow to steady her.

"Thank you," she said.

"I thought you might need a little support."

"I've never been good with sick people."

A loud cry from the injured man made them both jump and then focus on him again. Medina and the other men all began talking loudly at once, sounding nearly in panic. The victim's back arched, and several powerful spasms shook him. Then he slumped loose and silent back on the ground. Medina shook him several times but got no response, then looked around gravely at the others. Guadalupe and several other women, as well a couple of the men, crossed themselves, and two women began to wail.

Jester looked at the girl and spoke as gently as he could. "I'm afraid he's gone. Did you know him well?" It was more to distract her from the tragedy than to learn the answer.

She frowned. "He's been a vaquero here for two or three years. I never knew his name."

Medina got four of his men to carry the dead man to the chapel. Medina remained there beside the wagon and questioned one of the vaqueros. The cowboy pointed vaguely north and jabbered away, with many gestures. Jester tried not to stare, but the man seemed almost ready to break into tears. Finally, Medina patted the vaquero gently on the shoulder and allowed him to follow the body toward the chapel.

"Elonzo!" Medina called out, looking back and forth across the crowd. Moments later, an older, tough looking fellow wearing boots and spurs appeared before him. Medina spoke rapidly to the man, who nodded quickly, then turned toward the stables and shouted something to several of the vaqueros standing nearby. Medina started toward the main house and motioned for Langhorne and Jester to walk with him.

"The dead man was called Hector Sanchez," Medina said. "One of my men and the women will care for the body. They know the method of preparation."

Jester raised his eyebrows.

Medina must have taken it as surprise. "Death has visited the hacienda before." They reached the door on the end of the house and stopped under the gallery roof. "I've ordered a man to ride to Agua Blanca for the priest. We are going out to find the animal and kill him. Please take your ease while we are gone."

"I'd like to join you if you could use an extra man," Langhorne said.

"You are welcome to accompany us," Medina replied. "But it could be dangerous."

"I know."

"I'll come along, too, if you don't mind," Jester said.

Medina nodded. "Of course. I will get my coat and join you in the office." As he walked off down the corridor, Jester turned to Langhorne.

"Now exactly what kind of animal are we going after?"

"I thought you heard. *Oso pardo.*"

"Oh, a brown bear," Jester said. That was better. It didn't sound too fearsome.

Langhorne looked hard at him. "What we'd call a grizzly."

The excitement in the courtyard seemed even greater now than when the injured man had been brought in, as Don Augustin Medina's hunting party made ready to go forth against the brown bear. The same wagon stood ready, with a fresh team of horses hitched up and two hounds and a bulldog in the bed, watched over by a man who sat beside them.

"I think they want the hounds fresh when we get to the spot where they last saw the bear," Langhorne told Jester as they crossed the patio toward the wagon and five waiting saddle horses. Fabiana was there, standing beside her stepmother, and Jester caught the girl's eye for a moment and gave her a nervous smile. She didn't return it but looked apprehensive.

Don Augustin had furnished them with arms, .30-30 Winchesters from a well-stocked gun cabinet hidden behind a panel of false books in the office. He himself carried a beautifully polished Mauser 7-millimeter bolt action that drew an admiring word from Langhorne. Jester had slipped his personal side arm, a Colt .38-caliber service revolver, into his jacket pocket, and he saw Langhorne had his older Colt .45-caliber service revolver in a holster at his waist.

Guadalupe put her arms around her husband and held him in a long embrace, one from which he finally had to pull away with a smile and an admonition not to worry about him. Fabiana came to him then, and he grasped her by the shoulders and gave her a quick kiss on the cheek.

Langhorne mounted his horse, the same mare he'd ridden that morning, and Jester climbed up onto his palomino. Two vaqueros, young but experienced looking, sat tall on their mounts, big felt sombreros enhancing their height. Their horses danced excitedly, and the men made little effort to keep them still.

Finally, Medina mounted his black stallion. Elonzo climbed

up onto the wagon seat and shook the reins to start the team forward. Guadalupe and Fabiana, along with several other women and a number of men, followed them out through the *zaguan* and stood watching and waving as the hunting party turned north and kicked into a fast trot.

Jester cast one long glance over his shoulder as they were about to cross a low ridge that would cut off the view to the hacienda. The folks were still waving although too far away by now to distinguish individuals clearly. Nevertheless, it looked like Fabiana standing off from the others, her hand waving over her head. It had to be for her father.

They rode, mostly at a trot, for half an hour along fairly easy paths and gentle grades that the wagon could negotiate. Finally, the terrain grew too rugged for the wagon to continue at anything faster than a slow walk, and they all pulled up. Elonzo climbed down from the wagon seat and lowered the tailgate while the man in back untied the dogs from the sideboard and jumped down. They leaped to the ground after him, and he had all he could manage to restrain them from dashing off immediately and dragging him along behind.

"Elonzo will stay here with the wagon," Medina said. "The spot where poor Hector was attacked is this way"—he pointed up a little valley clad in scattered pines—"by a small stock pen."

He turned his stallion in that direction and led out, slowly enough that the man with the dogs could keep up. Three hundred yards up the valley, they came to the stock pen. A short distance away the ground was trampled and churned up in an area twenty feet square, and a big steer lay there, twisted and partially devoured. Blood and more trampling were evident thirty or forty feet from that, and the men stopped there, looking down at the spot.

"This has to be where they found Hector," Medina said. "He must have come upon the bear after it killed that steer. He had no chance to get away from it." He shook his head sadly then looked around at them. "Unleash the dogs."

And the race began. The hounds circled for just a few seconds before baying loudly and taking up the chase at a run, northwest along the slope of the little valley. The horsemen followed at a lope, the short-legged bulldog struggling to keep up.

Jester rode beside Langhorne, back a few yards from Medina and his two vaqueros.

Langhorne leaned toward him. "I wish we had a little heavier firepower," he said. "Grizzlies are big animals."

Jester didn't answer, but Langhorne probably knew what he was talking about. The thrill of the chase began to work now as they threaded between the pines, crossing over ridges and down the slopes on the other side. His horse slipped and lost his footing here and there but was on the way again after a few seconds, and the others were having it the same. Once a low branch almost knocked him out of the saddle—he managed to duck at the last minute but still received a stout blow on the back from it. In the excitement he barely took notice.

He called across to Langhorne, "Sounds like they've really got him on the run."

Langhorne barely looked over. "I'm not so sure."

Along the way, they passed broken branches, trampled vegetation, and scars gouged in the soft earth. The baying of the two hounds was their beacon, but it was difficult to tell how far ahead they were.

After probably two miles of the pursuit, the pitch of the dogs' voices seemed to change. In another half minute it was definite. The long baying cries transformed into a ferocious, continuous blend of barking and fierce growling, punctuated once or twice by a deep bellowing roar that sent a cold shiver up Jester's spine. Being able to see what was happening up there would've made things easier.

Suddenly, one of the hounds shrieked loudly, and there was silence.

A few hundred yards later, a thicket of hardwood saplings looked as if a storm had just blown through. Movement off to his left caught Jester's eye, and he reached toward his rifle in the scabbard under his right leg, but then he saw that it was just one of the hounds, tail tucked and slinking back and around toward him and the other riders. Langhorne did pull his rifle, so Jester retrieved his as well. Medina and his men had theirs out and ready, too. They all slowed to a walk and fanned out a few yards apart.

Not far into the thicket they came across the other hound. Its back had been broken, and its body was laid open from chest to tail like a gutted fish. The bulldog went forward and sniffed nervously around the dead hound and the ground nearby. Finally, the other hound came back up, too, its earlier bravado evaporated.

The dogs didn't seem to be much good from that point, so Medina decided they'd push on ahead without waiting for the animals to lead the way. The bear's trail wasn't difficult to see, especially where the brush was thick. They followed it down a fairly steep slope that got rockier as they neared the stream at the bottom. On up the other side they rode, still at a walk. Finally, they came out at the top of that slope into a huge meadow possibly half a mile across, dotted with bunches of saplings and bushes and just a few clearings of lush green grass.

"Looks like a forest fire might've gone through a few years back," Langhorne said.

Medina stopped and spoke quickly in Spanish to his vaqueros, then turned to Langhorne and Jester. "I think we need to spread out. We have no idea where he is in this meadow, and I fear we will miss him if we stay together."

Jester said nothing. Staying bunched up seemed like a better idea, but it would be awkward to display too much caution in the presence of the others.

Medina took the center, with his two men fanning out to his left a hundred fifty yards apart, and Jester, then Langhorne, flanking him on the right at similar intervals. They started through the meadow still at a walk, and, before long, Medina and his men were both hidden from view. Langhorne was still visible for another minute, his rifle resting across the pommel of his saddle. Finally, he, too, was out of sight, and Jester opened his eyes a little wider. A brown monster seemed likely around every bush.

The meadow broadened out as he moved forward, but the patches of saplings and brush grew thicker. Was he even still walking a straight line or, instead, veering right or left toward one of his companions? After maybe fifteen minutes passed, it was like being the last man in the world. Could his friends and the bear have all abandoned the area?

Half a minute later, as he walked his horse out past a stand of bushy saplings, there was movement off to his left, and he whirled to face it. Medina looked his way at the same moment. They recognized each other, and Jester let out a deep sigh. Medina looked relieved and rode over. He dismounted and took off his hat for a moment, wiping sweat from his forehead. Jester sat there in his saddle. A cool drink of water would taste mighty good.

He was looking over to see if Medina had a canteen when a flash of tawny brown charged them from the brush to the left. With the most unearthly, paralyzing roar, the creature was upon them, laying Medina low with one mighty swipe of its right paw.

Medina's horse bolted away, and Jester's mount reared high in panic, catching him unready and dumping him from the saddle hard onto his back. He tried to breathe but couldn't. The grizzly took down the terrified horse with one blow, shred-

bared, and poised one of his massive arms for the killing blow. Jester stared up at the creature and heard another shot from right behind. He saw the color brown descending on him, and then everything went black.

CHAPTER 6

"And there followed him a great company of people, and
of women, which also bewailed and lamented him."
Luke 23:27

Mourning descended on the Hacienda del Valle de Ajalón that
evening and carried on the next day. Don Augustin Medina, the
Patron, was dead, torn and broken like a discarded doll. He now
lay beside his man, Hector Sanchez, in the chapel, with flowers
surrounding them and candles burning on all four sides. The
women had done their best to cleanse the bodies and make
them presentable—if that was the right word—for the rituals of
wake and burial, but the grizzly's handiwork was impossible to
undo or disguise.

Langhorne sat on a bench just behind Guadalupe Medina
and her brother. A few other mourners were scattered on the
benches there in the chapel. The señora wore black from head
to foot, and it made stark contrast to her white skin, seeming
paler yet because of the ordeal she'd gone through. She was
weeping. Velasquez was dressed in a black suit and tie, and he
looked decidedly nervous, his head turning first one way, then
another, and Langhorne could see his hands fidgeting with the
hem of his coat. The man had made no attempt to comfort his
sister during the half hour they'd sat there.

Langhorne thought for a moment about Jester. The fellow

was lying in his room now in the main house, attended off and on by Sofia, an old woman servant of the Medinas. It was tricky getting Jester back to the wagon from the site of the bear attack, but Langhorne had finally rigged a travois out of long pine poles, with the help of the two vaqueros, and they dragged him to the wagon on that. The jarring wagon bed turned out to be much rougher on Jester than the travois, so after fifty yards, Langhorne transferred him back to the travois for the trip to the hacienda. The wagon had sufficed for Señor Medina's body.

Guadalupe shook her head suddenly and stood up, with one hand holding onto the bench for support. Langhorne rose with her and steadied her with a hand on her elbow. Velasquez stood a moment later and took hold of the same arm, challenging Langhorne with a cold stare. Langhorne released her but didn't move away. She looked at him with troubled eyes.

"Please, Señor Langhorne. I must know what happened . . . how it happened, to my husband."

"You'd better sit back down, Ma'am," he said. They all sat, with Guadalupe keeping her eyes on Langhorne while Velasquez sat staring straight ahead.

It was a gruesome story, and Langhorne considered how to tell it as gently as possible. The last thing the poor lady needed was more grief—but the story couldn't be completely sanitized.

"Well, you know we rode out to the spot where the other man had been attacked, and that's where we set the hounds loose. It took us quite a while to catch up to the bear." He stopped and looked closely at her. She wouldn't care about the details of the chase, just the crucial points.

"Anyway, we figured we were getting close, and then the dogs caught up to him." No need to mention the killing of the one hound. "They couldn't take him down, of course, and he got away from 'em. We decided to spread out to find him. It was a big, open meadow we were in but with lots of saplings and undergrowth, so you couldn't see more than a few yards. There was maybe a hundred-fifty yards between us, which I guess was a mistake, but we didn't want him giving us the slip, and we had a wide area to cover."

Langhorne stopped again. Maybe it would be best to stop. But she looked into his eyes.

"And then?"

"Calvin Jester and your husband came together in the middle of that meadow and found the bear. I guess really he found them. It seems he took 'em by surprise. They only got off one shot between 'em." Langhorne looked down for a moment, then back up at her. This part would be the most delicate. "Don Augustin . . . um . . . died instantly, from what I could make out." At least he hoped that had been the case.

Guadalupe was hanging on, but it was plainly agony for her. She spoke in almost a whisper.

"And Señor Jester? He was able to kill the bear then?"

"Well, he and I both shot the thing. The bear almost killed him in the process, though." He saw the scene again, as he had a hundred times since the long ride back to the hacienda the previous evening—him rushing to the sound of the fight; Jester feebly trying to fend off the grizzly after taking terrible punishment; Medina sprawled on the ground, literally torn limb from limb. Langhorne shot out his entire magazine into the animal at a range so close he could almost touch it, all while trying to drag Jester out of harm's way. Then came the doomsday sound of his hammer clicking down on the empty chamber—Catherine and Amy seemed mighty close at that moment, and the thought had actually calmed him. Then Jester's rifle was there on the ground, and he grabbed it up, managing to put one more round—the killing round it turned out—into the bear's head. The giant animal had been ready to finish Jester, and it came close to doing that as it fell on him, eight or nine hundred pounds of dead weight. They'd dragged it off Jester with ropes and horses.

Guadalupe leaned toward him, and there was pain in her eyes. "Did my husband . . . say anything? No, he couldn't have. You said he died instantly."

Langhorne slowly shook his head. "I'm sorry, Señora."

"I want to thank you," she said. "You and Señor Jester, for going with my husband and helping him."

"I wish I could've done more. A lot more."

"Please excuse me now," she said. He nodded and she stood and walked over to two other women sitting on a bench on the other side of the aisle. He knew one of them to be Hector Sanchez's widow.

Langhorne watched Guadalupe Medina for a moment. Dignity. Selflessness. Taking the time to thank him when he'd been able to do nothing more beneficial than bring back her husband's body. Now putting aside her own grief to comfort the other widow. A remarkable woman.

He slipped out of the chapel and walked back through the *zaguan* toward the main house. He'd seen Jester an hour before, but he wanted to check on him again. As he crossed the patio and stepped under the gallery and out of the sun, he thought for a moment of Fabiana Medina. How was she holding up to this ordeal? She seemed devoted to her father and had to be suffering over his loss, but he'd seen very little of her since the tragedy.

He walked in through the side door of the house and down the transverse corridor to Jester's room. He hesitated for a few moments, then knocked twice, very lightly, and opened the door a few inches. Jester was alone, apparently asleep, so Langhorne went in and sat down in the room's lone chair, facing the bed.

Langhorne's eyes wandered across the little table beside the

105

bed. A blue bottle of liquid and a smaller bottle of pills sat on it, both left by a slight Mexican doctor with a bald head and round eyeglasses, the local physician in Agua Blanca. A trusted vaquero had ridden hard from the hacienda last evening to fetch the doctor for Jester, and the pair had finally reached the ranch about midnight.

The doctor was more competent than Langhorne had expected, given the remoteness of the region. The man cleaned and dressed the wounds on Jester's body where the claws had caught him, bound his chest tightly to secure the cracked ribs, and popped the dislocated arm back into place, securing it in a sling to prevent further injury. He diagnosed a severe concussion, which Langhorne figured had come either from Jester's being thrown from his horse or from the dying bear falling on top of him. The doctor ordered complete bed rest to help recovery from the concussion—a recovery that the doctor warned wasn't a certainty.

Jester hadn't regained full consciousness since the attack although he opened his eyes occasionally for a few seconds and twice had tried to speak. The words came out garbled and unintelligible to Langhorne and the others, but it still seemed to be a positive sign.

Now Langhorne sat there watching Jester's chest rise and fall in slow rhythm. The young fellow could be hard to take—self-centered, disrespectful, showing more regard for enjoyment than duty. But now he was in bad shape. It was anybody's guess whether he'd pull out of it, or when. Langhorne shook his head slowly. Instead of his troop of cavalry back at Bliss, this was his command now, one irresponsible, badly injured lieutenant—who'd had the guts to stand up to a grizzly bear. Sometimes command felt like being a father.

The doctor hadn't been able to stay, and Langhorne took responsibility for cleaning Jester's wounds and changing the bandages. He'd learned how to apply a tolerable battle dressing in Cuba and later in the Philippines. He was training old Sofia to take up the task, though, along with her cooking and cleaning duties. In a day or two, she'd have to take over because Langhorne had a train to catch.

There was a tap on the door, and he stood up and opened it. Fabiana's pretty brown eyes were red and a little swollen from crying. He held the door open for her and ushered her to the chair.

Langhorne smiled sadly at her. "How are you getting along, Miss Medina?"

She didn't return the smile but glanced down at her hands, then back up. "It's difficult." She swallowed and shook her head. "Papa was the most important person in the world to me. I don't know what I'm supposed to do without him."

Langhorne shifted his weight from one foot to the other. What could he say that would be any help to the girl? The best thing he could think of was, "I hope you and your stepmother can support each other, help each other get through this."

Fabiana cocked her head slightly. "She didn't know him like I did. She didn't love him like I did. There was no one like Papa."

Her words about Guadalupe didn't sit well, but it was a family matter—certainly not any of his business. Instead, he pointed over at Jester, asleep and breathing evenly.

"I think he'll recover in a few days."

Just the hint of a sad smile touched her lips. "He *must* recover."

Surprising fervency, but he just smiled and chuckled. "He'll do it. He's strong. Hardheaded. Not many men can have a bear fall on 'em—" He stopped abruptly—it was a stupid thing to say. Fortunately, another knock came on the door, and they both turned to look.

Old Sofia entered timidly, bowing to the girl and then to

Langhorne, and asked in Spanish if it was time to clean the señor's wounds. Langhorne said yes. She'd brought a bottle of wine and a stack of clean white bandages, which she set beside the medicine bottles. She waited for Langhorne to carefully remove one of the old bandages covering Jester's slashed arm. Then she held out the wine bottle toward him. He didn't take it, though—she was going to do the cleaning herself, to give her practice. The wine would be a good antiseptic, too, and it was plentiful here at the hacienda. Sofia applied a fresh bandage, then tentatively started in on the next wound, on Jester's stomach. When she finished all the dressings, Langhorne nodded and smiled at her.

"*Bueno.*"

The old lady smiled shyly at the praise and then began to wipe Jester's face with a clean bandage that she moistened in a bowl of water. She continued the sponge bath, wiping one of his arms next, stopping to dip the bandage in the bowl and wring it out. She carefully offered it to Fabiana, asking if she wanted to help minister to the señor.

The girl shook her head rapidly, looking very uncomfortable, and turned and hurried out of the room. Surprising. Langhorne looked at Sofia and shrugged, smiling, and she smiled back, then continued with her cleaning.

Langhorne stretched his legs later by strolling around the hacienda compound, looking in on the various workers. One of the men was a skilled carpenter, and he'd put his talent to use building two stout coffins out of pine. He carved a cross into a circular slab of pine and screwed it down tight onto the lid of Señor Medina's casket, and then, at Guadalupe's request, affixed a similar emblem to Hector Sanchez's coffin as well. The coffins were finished that afternoon, and it was decided to bury the men then, even though that was more quickly than was customary. The warm daytime weather made further delay unwise.

Langhorne leaned against the wall outside the carpenter's shop and listened while the fellow sanded out the last rough spots. He'd only known Augustin Medina for a day, but it was almost as if he'd lost an old friend. Medina was a kind and gracious host—he probably treated most everyone that way, a good epitaph for any man.

The priest came out from Agua Blanca. That was probably more for Guadalupe's comfort—and Hector Sanchez's family—than for any wishes Don Augustin might have had. Padre Espinoza didn't seem to have much interest in the families or the departed themselves. In fact, he dealt with everyone from Guadalupe to the poorest servant at the hacienda as if they were objects rather than human beings, and he went through the rituals of funeral and burial with no more feeling than Langhorne had seen from some clerks conducting an inventory.

After a perfunctory service in the chapel, which was crowded with almost every soul at the hacienda and most of the vaqueros from the outlying stations of the ranch, the procession was formed and started off in a slow march out the big doorway and to the south. The little *campo santo* stood on a slight rise two hundred yards from the hacienda wall. Workers had labored for hours to dig the graves deep enough in the stony ground.

The pallbearers set the coffins down beside the open graves, and the lids were removed again while Padre Espinoza went through the motions of his office. Langhorne noticed a few articles of clothing and small objects in both coffins, familiar items that the dead men had used frequently. When all was finished, the family members tossed a handful of earth into the coffins—not onto the closed coffins after they were lowered into the graves, as the custom was back in the United States. Then the lids were secured, the bodies committed to the ground, and the souls to the Lord. The entire ceremony had been punctuated by a great deal of weeping and wailing, especially by the Sanchez family, and Langhorne stood back at a respectful distance as the mourners began the lonely journey back toward the hacienda gate.

Langhorne alternated the rest of that day and evening between sitting in Jester's room and reading out on the gallery. The entire hacienda was uncomfortably silent as if people were afraid to speak. Fabiana sat by herself in the private patio behind the main house or remained out of sight altogether, and Guadalupe kept to her room during the remainder of that day and night. Velasquez, however, didn't appear to be very broken up about his brother-in-law's death. Langhorne watched him pace deliberately around the compound, stopping to gaze at the individual buildings and look over the horses in the stables. He had the look of a man appraising merchandise.

Once, when Langhorne happened out on the back gallery, Fabiana was sitting near the fountain on the east wall. She probably didn't need to be disturbed, so he just stood there to stretch his legs for a minute before returning to his bench around the corner. At that point, Velasquez appeared from the back door of the house and went straight to the girl. He stood over her, and they had some brief conversation—Langhorne was too far away to hear what was said. She rose to her feet as if to walk toward the house, but Velasquez blocked her path with an arm against the shade tree beside the fountain. He took a step closer to her.

That was enough. Langhorne moved nearer and coughed loudly, and they both turned to look. Langhorne held the man's eyes in a hard stare, and after a few moments, Velasquez turned on his heel and stomped off around the house toward the *zaguan*. Langhorne nodded to Fabiana, then returned to his bench.

Dinner was laid out well after sunset, but Langhorne found Velasquez was the only other person in the dining room, and they ate in virtual solitude. There was no point in trying to engage the man in conversation. Velasquez gave his full attention to three helpings of the *guiso de puerco* and tortillas that Carlito had laid out on the table, washed down by an entire bottle of the hacienda's vintage.

Langhorne retired late after spending an hour at Jester's bedside. He slept sporadically, like he did in the field with his troop, waking every couple of hours to check on the sentries and the horses—only in this case it was Jester. Early in the night Langhorne heard snatches of weeping every time he woke up—it must've been Guadalupe or Fabiana. But after midnight everything was silent. Around five in the morning, Langhorne figured his sleeping was over for that night, and he shaved and dressed.

The others didn't stir until around eight, although Carlito rose and made coffee in the kitchen at first light. Langhorne took a cup back to his room—it tasted wonderful and helped revive his body after the interrupted sleep of the night. About nine-thirty he left his reading and peeked into the dining room to see if anyone was about. Velasquez was getting up from the table, leaving a plate with the remains of steak and eggs. Did the fellow do anything but eat? He gave Langhorne a black look as he brushed past him and out the door. Langhorne settled down to a similar breakfast brought by Carlito, and spent the next half hour alone in the dining room.

Finally, he heard movement in the hallway and looked at the door. Maybe one of the ladies or at least someone besides Velasquez was coming. No one appeared, however, and he started to step out onto the gallery but then heard voices coming from somewhere down the hall. It was a man and a woman, and they didn't sound happy. Something to do with Jester? Langhorne hurried to find out.

The voices were coming from the office, though, and one of them was Guadalupe's, speaking rapidly in Spanish. The door was open, and he stopped in the hallway before he reached it.

"Tell me what you were doing in here," she demanded.

The masculine reply was too low to be intelligible. It could be Carlito. Better just to go on about his own business. Just as he was passing, however, the man raised his voice—Velasquez.

"Remember who I am, sister."

"It is you who does not know," she said. There was still heat in her voice. She glanced over her shoulder as Langhorne tried to pass, and motioned for him to stay. Then she turned back to her brother. "This is the hacienda's business office, and I am the *patrona* here. You have no reason to be here, especially not looking through our ledger."

Velasquez glared at Langhorne a few seconds, then faced Guadalupe again. "He is the one who has no business here. He is nothing but a guest, a hanger-on."

"But he is *my* guest, and this is *my* hacienda, *my* house, brother!"

Velasquez spoke again, but his voice no longer sounded angry. "I am the rightful man of the family now, Guadalupita. A family must have a man over it. You know that."

"I stopped being Guadalupita when I married," she said. "Now I am Guadalupe Maria Velasquez de Medina, mistress of this hacienda." Her voice broke a little when she continued. "The man of this family is dead. And you have not replaced him. You never will."

Velasquez shot another withering look at Langhorne. "We will speak of this later—when we have no interlopers standing where they do not belong." He very deliberately opened Don Augustin's humidor and took two of his cigars.

Langhorne watched Velasquez. He could force him to give

back the cigars, but how would that turn out? Guadalupe was probably glad for his presence, but she might not like him strong-arming her brother.

Velasquez again brushed past Langhorne, taking no care and begging no pardon. When he was gone, down the corridor, Guadalupe looked distraught and embarrassed.

"I am sorry, Señor Langhorne," she said, shifting to English now. "I do not wish to involve you in our family troubles, but"—she shook her head as if in frustration—"my brother thinks he can overwhelm me now that . . . Augustin is . . . gone."

"I never did like bullies."

"I wish I could say he is not, but . . ."

"The only way is to stand up to 'em." He grinned. "You were doing a pretty fair job of it."

She smiled sadly. "I fear that I will be doing it much more from now on. Esteban is not a man who gives up easily."

"I'll be glad to give you any help I can." How much benefit it would be to her and how much she'd be willing to accept—those were the questions. It was a little like walking through a dark and unfamiliar room, not knowing if there'd be an obstacle at the next step.

"You are kind," she said. "I believe you to be a man I can trust." She glanced away for a moment, toward the other side of the small office, and then looked back at him. "It would be more proper for us to talk outside, I think, on the gallery."

He stood aside to let her come out the door and then followed her down the corridor and to the front door. She led him along the gallery and took a chair by a flowering vine. He sat on a bench a few feet away.

She said, "My brother has always been a man of appetites, without satisfaction. He has wanted money, power—but they have always eluded him, it seems."

"How long has he lived here with your family?"

"Oh, he does not live with us. That seems to be what he has in mind now, but he has a house in Agua Blanca."

"Does he have a business there?"

"He is an attorney—of sorts."

Langhorne didn't answer. He'd known one or two of that kind of lawyer.

Guadalupe continued. "He has very few clients. In fact, he frequently borrows money from me and my husband."

Her voice had a catch on the last word, and tears welled up in her eyes.

He gave her a moment to recover her composure. "If you don't feel well enough to talk now, Señora Medina, we can continue later."

"No, I am all right," she said finally. "I feel that I need to talk, to keep my mind occupied. I am not good at sitting in my room and weeping for hours on end—although I did much of that yesterday."

Langhorne smiled. She could continue at her own pace.

"As I was saying," she began, "Esteban does not have the income to support himself in the style which he believes is his right. His habits also demand money. He inherited the majority of our father's estate, but that did not last many months."

"I can pretty well imagine. Like they say, you can choose your friends but not your relatives." Maybe it had been the wrong thing to say. However, she didn't seem to take offense.

"He is my brother, and that counts for something. But he seems to be interested in nothing but himself and his own plans. Of course, those plans include my stepdaughter."

Langhorne leaned forward, frowning. "What?"

Guadalupe looked down and sighed deeply. "Yes. Esteban has mentioned to me that he would like to make Fabiana his wife. Since there is no blood relation, it would not be illegal, but it would severely violate the rules of propriety. Of course I never let Augustin know of it. He might have killed Esteban. He certainly would have banned him from the hacienda."

"And what about Fabiana? Does she have any interest in him?" If she did, it would be a surprise. The only person the girl seemed to be interested in was Calvin Jester—although the pain of her father's death might have snuffed out that interest, too.

"From what she tells me," Guadalupe said, "she cannot stand the thought of such a marriage."

"Then it sounds like your brother doesn't stand much of a chance of marrying her."

"Until two days ago I would have thought as much." She shrugged. "But now . . ."

"How much power does a man in his position have in this kind of situation?" he asked.

She shrugged again and gave a sad smile. "Who knows? A man in Mexico has more power over his family than one in the United States, I think. And since Esteban is an attorney, he has the advantage over me in knowing the law."

"Have you considered hiring a lawyer yourself?"

She looked puzzled. "No. I had never given it a thought. It has always seemed to me that attorneys were for dealing with strangers, not your own family."

"I understand. But if your brother's trying to take advantage of you and Fabiana, it might be the only way to guard your own interests."

"Yes, I see," Guadalupe said. "Thank you." She looked down at her clasped hands for several moments, and her face seemed to betray turmoil inside. She lifted her head suddenly. "I apologize for being so occupied with my thoughts. I cannot seem to keep my mind on anything but Augustin for very long. It must be hard for you to understand."

"Not hard at all." Langhorne glanced down. "I've gone through something similar."

She looked at him with more interest. "Oh? Would you tell me?"

Langhorne swallowed hard, twice. It still wasn't easy to talk about. "I, uh, lost my wife and little girl. It was back in ninety-nine."

Guadalupe's face looked as sad as Langhorne felt. "I am very sorry. An accident?"

"Epidemic. I don't know if you recall it. Maybe it didn't hit Mexico. Influenza, they said." The words came slowly, and with them the ache deep in his chest. It wouldn't make him cry.

"I think I remember the epidemic," she said, leaning toward him a bit. Neither of them spoke for maybe fifteen seconds. Finally she continued. "You have helped me—just knowing someone else shares a like sorrow."

He nodded his head. "Misery loves company." She seemed puzzled, so he added, "It's an old saying," and that made her smile.

"What were their names?"

"My wife was Catherine. And our little girl was Amy." As he said his daughter's name, something grabbed his throat—the same as always.

"I know you loved them very much," she said.

"Still do. And I'll see them again, one of these days." That hope, that portion of his faith, was maybe the most precious of all.

"Yes." She seemed to really mean it. "I love my husband, too."

Fabiana's words came back to him, what she'd said in Jester's room about her stepmother.

"How's your daughter taking all this?" he asked.

"She is sad, of course, and angry, I think."

"At anyone in particular?"

"Possibly at everyone." She lowered her voice. "Fabiana is a proud girl, and one who has been indulged in many ways." Her eyes shone as she continued. "How her father loved her, doting on her. And she worshipped him in her way, more by following his example than anything else. Perhaps his good qualities have not yet had time to develop in her to their full extent."

"I suppose she's at an age where we couldn't expect her to be perfect yet"—he grinned—"like we are, huh?"

She smiled in return, a joyful smile.

He stared at her for a long moment. She really was a beautiful woman—but she was also just two days a widow. And there was duty to think about.

"Her father had such high hopes for Fabiana," she said. "And I do, too, of course."

"Certainly. She's a fine young lady."

"I know she thinks highly of your friend, Señor Jester."

"Yes, he seems to be a favorite with the ladies." He grinned again. "I guess it's that blond hair of his. That and his Southern drawl."

"You seem to have a certain *drawl,* yourself." She had a little trouble with the word.

"Texas accent. It's a bit different from his."

"Oh, Texas." She smiled. "I am not certain whether we should be enemies or friends."

"Yeah. Texas and Mexico—they're kinda like the married couple who can't get along *with* each other, but can't get along *without* each other, either."

She laughed. Then her expression became serious again. "Do you think your friend will recover?"

"I believe so. I hope so. The main thing, I guess, is that he wakes up before much longer. Even after that, it'll be a while before he's able to get around. I'm sorry to have to burden you with having him here for so long."

"It is our pleasure. As I told you, we have so few guests here that it is a blessing when they do come. I only wish I had a servant to watch over him constantly. It is very difficult to get servants out here on the edge of the wilderness. I am afraid that Sofia has too many other duties to give him the attention he needs."

"She's learning to change his bandages, and she keeps him comfortable," Langhorne said. "Would it be all right with you if I move on and take care of my business once Jester wakes up? I think he'll be out o' the woods then." He smiled. "Out of danger, I mean. I hate to leave him for you to care for, but my business is urgent."

"We will be happy to keep him as long as necessary—and as long as he wishes after that."

That was kind of her. But with Velasquez around, it would be easier to leave the two women if Jester was at least conscious again and able to lend them some support.

CHAPTER 7

"For the good man is not at home, he is gone a long
journey: He hath taken a bag of money with him, and will
come home at the day appointed." Proverbs 7:19-20

Jester regained consciousness just after sunrise the next day.
Langhorne was in the room, sitting by the window looking out
at the morning. Jester stirred and mumbled something, just as
he'd done several times before. Langhorne figured he'd lapse
back into silent sleep. This time, however, he let out a long sigh
and opened his eyes wide, looking around the room. He shut
his eyes tightly and opened them again, focusing blearily on
Langhorne.

"What a sight to wake up to," he said, his voice sleepy.

Langhorne looked hard at him. "You must be Rip van
Winkle." Then he had to grin. "Glad to have you back in the
land of the living. Coffee?" He held up his own.

Jester smiled weakly. "Not out of that particular cup, sir. But
I would be very obliged if you could get me some."

Langhorne was already on his feet and heading for the dining
room. He brought back a fresh cup and a buttered sweet roll,
and Sofia followed him into the room and shut the door behind
them.

Jester looked surprised at the old woman's presence.

"I forgot," Langhorne said. "You haven't made Sofia's

acquaintance." He chuckled. "But she knows you pretty well by now."

Jester's raised his eyebrows. "I hope I shouldn't be too mortified by what you and your minions have subjected me to."

"Nothing a newborn baby doesn't have to go through."

Jester raised his bedclothes and glanced underneath. "Well, I am thankful at least that you don't have me in diapers."

Langhorne translated Jester's words for Sofia, who laughed quietly as she stepped up to the bed and turned the sheet and blanket back to Jester's waist. She started right in on the bandages.

"Hey. Might I not have that coffee first?" Jester protested.

"Babies don't get to eat till the woman says so," Langhorne said.

"They do if they cry loud enough."

Langhorne grinned. The poor fellow deserved to eat if he wanted to. Langhorne told Sofia, and she smiled and bowed, backing out the door. Jester took the steaming coffee and sipped it gingerly. He kept at it until half the cup was gone.

"I didn't realize how thirsty I was."

"A couple o' days without anything but a sip or two o' water at a time—give you more and you might've choked."

Jester rubbed a hand over his face. "I see that Sofia didn't get a chance at using a razor."

"She's not your full-time valet. You're just an extra duty for her, kinda like scrubbing a floor."

"You make me sound rather important." Jester finished the rest of the coffee and held his cup out for Langhorne, who set the roll on the table and started for the door.

He almost collided with Fabiana as he went out. She recovered quickly and slipped past Langhorne with a polite smile. He left the door slightly ajar.

Langhorne took his time. In Jester's condition, no one should object to the girl being in the room with him for a few minutes. He poured himself a fresh cup of coffee in the dining room and stepped out onto the gallery. The morning air was crisp, with a feel of autumn in it. He took in a deep breath. It would be nice to stay on at the hacienda a little longer. That wouldn't do, though, not with Jester on the mend and Powell and the generals hungry for information. He took a drink, then went back into the dining room and poured another cup of coffee for Jester.

When he walked back into Jester's room, Fabiana was holding half the roll in her hands, and Jester was munching away. They both looked up suddenly. He swallowed and she pulled off another piece and fed it to him. He looked extremely satisfied with the treatment, especially so, it seemed, since Langhorne was witness to it.

"I brought you more coffee."

"I think I'll finish this roll first," Jester said. He smiled up at Fabiana. "It's a slow process—as weak as I am." The drawl was very distinct.

"Then I'd better call Sofia back in to help," Langhorne said, keeping a straight face.

"Oh, no, please." Jester looked more serious. "Don't trouble the dear old girl. I believe I'm feeling stronger already." He began to eat more quickly as the girl dutifully fed bites of pastry into his mouth.

Langhorne was glad when the doctor made another trip out from Agua Blanca to check Jester that day and was pleased with his progress. Nevertheless, the man cautioned that the patient should take the recovery slowly and not exert himself. He might lapse into a fever on and off as he recovered, and if so, he should stay in bed. Above everything else, he was to avoid any further injury to his head. The wounds, too, were healing, but they had to be kept clean and swabbed regularly with wine or another antiseptic to avoid infection.

Langhorne had been watching Jester closely. For all his banter, the fellow tired very easily. It was obvious he was a long way from getting back on his feet again. And Fabiana, despite her fascination with Jester, didn't seem to take naturally to the role of nurse. Feeding the playful patient was one thing, but when it came to dressing his wounds or sitting with him when he lapsed into an exhausted sleep, the girl drew back, leaving things to Sofia.

When the doctor started back to town, Langhorne had his trunk packed and hitched a ride on the hacienda's wagon. He left Guadalupe Medina and Jester a rough itinerary but no timetable firmer than the promise to return to the hacienda once he'd done what he needed to do. The trip to town was a slow one, giving him plenty of time to wonder whether he was doing the right thing, leaving Jester still laid up.

Langhorne managed to catch a train that afternoon in Agua Blanca bound for Corral. He made connections there back to Guaymas and Hermosillo, where he planned to contact the U.S. consul and spend the night. Then he'd retrace his route back through Guaymas and Corral and on to points south in Sinaloa. It was a cumbersome passage, but there was no way to avoid all the backtracking since Jester wasn't along to cover his half of the cities.

Langhorne spent that first night in a modest hotel in Hermosillo. After breakfast, he located the American consul, a man named Jackson, and spent an hour and a half with him. The consul recommended he also speak with two other American businessmen living in the city. All three expressed good opinions of the Diaz regime, primarily for the stability and order that it had maintained there. Jackson in particular had grave misgivings about Francisco Madero and the likelihood that he'd be able to provide a government as beneficial for business as Diaz had. As for U.S. intervention and how it would be received by the Mexican people, the men all believed it would have to come sooner or later, and they were decidedly optimistic about the reaction of the Mexican population, especially those of "the better sort," in Jackson's words.

When Langhorne went on to Guaymas that afternoon, he found a poorer looking population and an uneasy, dissatisfied mood on the streets and in the marketplaces. The acting U.S. consular official there, a factory owner named Williamson, told him that some of the old Diaz officials were still in control of the local government apparatus and that they were spending their time collecting all of the bribes they could in anticipation of losing their jobs during the changeover to a Madero government. Most people were merely holding on, hoping the new government would restore services to a satisfactory level and bring an end to the widespread corruption.

He had a meeting with several other Americans late in the day, and all but one expected U.S. intervention within six months to three years. The lone dissenter, a young physician, thought the Madero government would do fine without the need for American "adventurism" as he called it, and warned that if such intervention did come, it would be greeted by the Mexican nation rising in arms to oppose the U.S. forces.

After finding a room at the Hotel San Lorenzo near the railroad station, Langhorne decided to walk around the area, observing the rail facilities for his report. He noted track conditions, sidings, and a repair facility for locomotives and freight cars, but he was unable to get a look inside it. Finally, he caught a mule-drawn streetcar for five centavos that took him down to the harbor. A single railroad track ran from the dockyards back to the station. He was careful to note all the information in an abbreviated form—no one was likely to be able to decipher it.

After having dinner in a restaurant near his hotel, Langhorne decided on another walk before returning to his room. The evening was pleasant, and walking felt good after all the time on trains in the past two days. The streets were dirtier than they'd been in Hermosillo, though, and the people lacked the carefree air of those in that city. Once he saw two policemen beating a poorly dressed Indian and dragging him away between them. Langhorne stopped a short man in a dingy white shirt and tie, and asked him quietly what was going on. There was fear in the man's eyes, and he hurried off after explaining that the victim was a Yaqui Indian.

That explained a lot. The Yaquis had been the special targets of Diaz's wrath for years—the newspapers in El Paso had been full of it. Apparently the government wanted their land, but the tribe had proven to be difficult adversaries for the Mexican army to beat. The rest of Langhorne's walk was uneventful, and he returned to the hotel to finish his notes before turning in for the night.

The next day was a long one, with him on the train most of the day. The tedious trip gave him plenty of time to think about Catherine, and Jester. He crossed the boundary between Sonora and Sinaloa in the early afternoon and didn't arrive in Culiacan until a little after sunset. The streets around the station had a few people but appeared dark and forbidding, so he hired a coach to take him and his trunk to the Hotel Canales, where he slept like a dead man.

After taking a streetcar across town the next morning, Langhorne found the American consulate. It was in a solid looking stone building in the main business district among banks, offices, and small shops. In the light of morning, the city seemed much less sinister than it had the previous evening, and Langhorne nodded to several of the people he passed as he crossed a crowded street and entered the consulate.

Ushered into the office of Consul Robert Hurley by a clerk, Langhorne removed his hat, introduced himself, and waited for the clerk to step back outside, then quietly pushed the door shut. He pulled his secret letter of introduction out of the pouch in his belt and handed it across to Hurley.

"Hm," was all the consul said at first as he read the letter. There was silence for a minute or two except for the sound of the electric fan blowing back and forth from the top of a filing cabinet. Finally, he looked up and passed the letter back. "I'd heard something about this, but, frankly, I didn't know whether they'd ever send anyone down here. It's a long way from the border."

"I've been in Sonora for about a week," Langhorne said. "Had to leave my other man, injured, at the Medina hacienda up in the Sierra."

Hurley shook his head. "Don't know the place. But I haven't had occasion to be in that part of the state very often." He was a tall man with sandy hair, probably somewhere in his late thirties.

"What I'd like to talk about is how you think things'll work out with the new government," Langhorne said. "The War Department wants to know whether Americans down here feel we'll have to send troops in to protect them and their business interests."

"Yes, I gathered that from the letter."

"I also want to find out as much as I can about the condition of the Mexican rail system in these states. If we have to move troops and supplies, we'll need to have a good idea of the capacity of their railroads."

"Understood," Hurley walked over to a table where a tray held a pitcher and some glasses. "Water?"

Langhorne said, "Please," and the consul poured two glasses

and brought them back to his desk.

Hurley settled back in his chair. "Well, let me see. First of all, I think Mexico—at least this area—is in for a slow, painful, and probably dangerous transition from the Old Guard to the New Guard. Sure, the Old Man is out."

"Diaz."

"Yeah. But that doesn't mean all the officials, police, troops— everybody with a stake in the old government—are going to just give up the reins and retire to the sidelines. Madero and his people are going to have to take power forcefully if they want to get it at all. The Diaz bunch has been in for decades, and they're not going quietly."

Langhorne took a drink. "You think it'll come to civil war?"

Hurley blew out a long, slow breath. "Maybe. Maybe not. If Madero comes on strong, if he makes everyone know who's in charge and he gets his people all over the country to do the same at every level, then things will probably be okay. Mexicans like a man who means business." He frowned and shook his head slowly.

"Sounds like you don't think Madero does."

Hurley shrugged. "He's an honest man, by all accounts. But I have my doubts that he's, I suppose, ruthless enough to get the job done. The Diaz organization has deep roots, here and all over the country. Maybe least of all in the north, up along the border in Chihuahua and Sonora. But down here and further south, they're still plenty strong. It reminds me of a snake—you can cut the head off, but the body still whips around for a long time afterwards. Here in Culiacan, for instance, I still haven't seen a strong body of Maderistas come to take over, and Diaz abdicated months ago."

Langhorne sipped at his water, more out of habit than thirst. Things needed sorting out. "From what you say, there might as well not have been a revolution, at least here."

Hurley seemed to consider the statement. "That's about the size of it."

"And the people? What do they think . . . the average man?"

"They're scared stiff. Diaz and his people had them buffaloed and still do. There's still a battalion of three or four hundred soldiers under their old Porfirista officers out in the *cuartel* at the edge of town. *Rurales* are still under arms, enforcing the law in the countryside—but not taking orders from Madero, at least not yet. And the police organization . . ."

"What about it?"

"Strong as ever. Maybe not quite as open. But the real police power never has been what you see on the streets. It's tied in with the whole system of wealth and influence down here. I don't know whether that'll ever be rooted out."

"Sounds like trouble," Langhorne said. "Does Madero have any organized support around here?"

"Oh, there's plenty of support for him," Hurley said. "But what he needs are troops here. Or at least he needs to shoot those Porfiristas out at the *cuartel* and put his own officers over that battalion. Now if you're talking political support, that's a little better, I suppose. It's not just the poor who like Madero; I'd say half or more of the middle class do, too. Businessmen, professional people, the intellectuals such as they are."

"But they don't have guns."

"That's it, in a nutshell." Hurley's eyes brightened, and he cocked his head to one side. "Would you like to take a walk, Langhorne?"

"Wouldn't mind stretching my legs." Get out onto the streets and see things firsthand—that would be fine. He stood up and waited while Hurley pulled on a coat and grabbed a straw hat. As they went out past the clerk, the consul told him they probably wouldn't be back until after lunch.

They walked past the cathedral, glistening white in the morning sunshine, with two tall, thin towers in front and a broad dome farther back. It flanked the plaza, cool and inviting with its trees and walks and benches—like the patios and galleries of the *Hacienda Ajalón*. Would Jester be well enough to go outside yet?

Hurley led him across the street and on for several blocks until they reached a big iron bridge spanning the sluggish river. "That's the Rio Tamazula."

"Pretty impressive bridge."

"Yes, they can be proud of it. Named after Father Hidalgo, the one who helped them break away from Spain. Thing's only a few years old. Still under construction when I came down here."

Langhorne looked across the river. That side was mostly brush country—no houses at all. The town spread out in the other directions, though, low and white, with occasional palms against the blue sky. A few mountains showed in the distance, but the air was heavy, not crisp like at the hacienda.

Hurley led him back up the street in the direction from which they'd come. They passed through the long, shady *portales* across from the cathedral and plaza, and the brief coolness was delightful until they came out into the sunshine again. The consul continued across the main part of town, pointing out the Apolo Theatre and the governor's palace. Along one side street a few blocks from the cathedral, Langhorne noticed several businesses with men and women standing around the front doors. Others were crowded inside the buildings, waiting in lines before big desks. The sign in front of one advertised it as the Delgado Contract Labor Company.

Hurley shook his head, frowning. "They're kind of like employment agencies back in the States. Kind of."

The people along their route went about their business with an easy, unhurried pace. Langhorne was used to it by now from

128

the past few days. Even so, something seemed different, something hard to pin down. Was it their eyes—a wariness that strained even their smiles and laughter? Maybe it was just his imagination.

He and the consul stopped in front of a modest building a little before noon, and Hurley pointed at the lettering above the doorway—*La Voz de Culiacan.*

"*The Voice of Culiacan,*" Langhorne said. "A newspaper?"

"Yes. And there's someone inside I'd like you to meet."

They went in and Langhorne found himself in a large, hot room crowded with tables, trays of metal type, frames, stack upon stack of blank newsprint, and bottles of ink. A big, complex apparatus—apparently a printing press—took up much of the back wall.

A slender young man in white shirt and black trousers and a black apron was working at one large table, laying type into small frames. He looked over at them, and Langhorne nodded at him, then turned to the consul.

"The editor?"

Hurley shook his head. "No, his helper—Jorge Rodriguez is his name, I think." Hurley led the way to a small office at the back. A well-groomed, intelligent looking man of about thirty-five sat behind a battered old desk, banging out a page on a Remington typewriter. He looked up at them with a harried expression.

"Mr. Langhorne," Hurley said, "I'd like you to meet Señor Diego Sandoval, editor of *La Voz.*"

Sandoval stood up and gave Langhorne a brief bow before extending his hand. "I am pleased to meet you, sir." He shook hands with Langhorne and then with the consul.

Hurley said, "Langhorne is down here investigating the business climate, and he's interested in learning how the common people of Culiacan are getting along and whether they're happy and productive workers."

Sandoval raised one eyebrow. "I see. And are you hoping to find employees for a new business venture, Señor, ones that you can pay as little as possible?"

"Not at all, Señor Sandoval," Langhorne said. "I'm just gathering information. I'm no businessman."

Sandoval seemed puzzled for a moment and looked at Hurley. The consul nodded.

"Langhorne's telling you the truth, Diego. And I'm sure he'd like to find out the truth from you—on the Diaz organization, the wealthy class here in Sinaloa, and what that all means for the Mexican working man."

The frown left Sandoval's face, but there was no smile. He seemed to be sizing up Langhorne.

Hurley said, "If you don't have plans for *comida,* I wonder if you'd join us."

Sandoval nodded toward the unfinished page in his typewriter and said, "I regret that I cannot. This story must be ready this afternoon. And I have to write the editorial, as well. We will not be finished here until well after sundown."

Langhorne glanced at Hurley, then turned back to Sandoval. "Then would you join me—or us if the consul can make it—for *cena* tonight? I want to hear what you can tell me about conditions in this part of the country. I'd consider it a personal favor, Señor Sandoval."

The editor hesitated a few moments, then gave a brief smile and nodded his head. "I would be delighted. Will you meet me at the Metropolitan Restaurant about eight o'clock?"

"I'll look forward to it," Langhorne said.

El Restaurante Metropolitan was the nicest dining establishment in Culiacan, with tuxedoed waiters, linen tablecloths, and fine tableware. When Langhorne and Hurley walked in at eight, a waiter led them to a table in the middle of the restaurant. Langhorne frowned—a less prominent location would've been preferable, considering the conversation he expected to have with Sandoval, but the tables near the back were all taken. Hurley ordered a bottle of wine but had to start on it alone when he found that Langhorne was a teetotaler. By the time Sandoval showed up at eight forty-five, they'd discussed everything from local boxing and bullfighting to Mexican marriage customs.

Hurley leaned toward Langhorne with a wry grin as the editor walked over. "Punctuality isn't a virtue down here." Langhorne smiled, then turned to face Sandoval as the waiter seated him at their table and poured wine into his glass. The men exchanged greetings and then ordered, and the waiter left them.

"Thank you for joining us," Langhorne said.

"It is my pleasure."

Hurley held up his wineglass. "Gentlemen, to a productive discussion." Sandoval raised his glass, and Langhorne lifted his coffee cup. The consul glanced at Sandoval and smiled. "Mr. Langhorne doesn't indulge in alcohol. I heard somewhere that you're not supposed to trust a man who doesn't drink."

Sandoval said, "I believe that there are more reliable indications of a man's character."

Langhorne liked the editor.

To Sandoval, Hurley said, "We had quite a walk around town today. I believe Mr. Langhorne saw everything of importance in the city."

"But did he see the people?"

"They're the most important of all," Langhorne said.

"Precisely," Sandoval said, nodding.

"We saw plenty of 'em," Langhorne continued. "Mostly everyday folks, not many that looked wealthy."

Sandoval took a sip of wine. "Good. You must understand the people in order to understand conditions here in Culiacan and in all of Sinaloa." He shrugged. "For that matter, in all of Mexico."

"I think you know what I'm interested in learning about, Señor Sandoval," Langhorne said. "Why don't you tell me how things stand."

"I would be delighted."

Their waiter appeared with French bread and butter and ladled savory onion soup into a bowl for each man. When he had gone, Sandoval continued.

"As you probably know, our country has suffered under the heel of Porfirio Diaz for thirty years. Two years ago, with a new presidential election scheduled for 1910, many of us across the nation felt conditions were right to take a stand against reelection of the Old Man for yet another term. Anti-reelection clubs formed in many cities, including Culiacan. I joined the local club, in fact. We had high hopes that change—a change for the better—was coming. At the last minute, Diaz decided to run again, and that, of course, led to his overthrow by the people. You hear Madero's name, but it was the people themselves who rose up and forced the tyrant to abdicate. Madero has been merely a symbol, a representative of the people as a whole."

Langhorne listened quietly and ate the excellent soup and bread. The editor was quite a talker.

"So now, where do we find ourselves?" Sandoval continued. "I believe the word in English is *interregnum*. Diaz is gone and Madero is yet to assume office. And all of Mexico is waiting to see if things will be different when he does, if the old system will crumble and a new day will dawn. Perhaps it will, but until then the old evil continues unchecked, at least here and through most of the south. Those with wealth and power, the main *hacendados,* are as strong as ever. The federal army may have been defeated in the north, in Ciudad Juarez and along the border, but here it has not been disbanded, nor has it begun taking orders from Francisco Madero."

The waiter next cleared away their soup bowls and brought their entrees and vegetables and a *sopa seca* of fried rice. He set a grilled Delmonico steak with onions and peppers before Langhorne, a similar steak before Hurley, and half a roast chicken before Sandoval. After bringing fresh coffee for Langhorne and more wine for the other two men, the waiter departed, and they were able to resume their conversation.

"Tell me, Señor Sandoval," Langhorne said between bites, "what it's like to be an average man here in Culiacan. I'm pretty familiar with conditions in the countryside, on the ranches and haciendas, but not in the larger towns and cities."

"Here in Culiacan, the people work at good jobs or poor jobs, whatever they can find," Sandoval said. "That's not so different from any other place, I suppose. But what is different—intolerable, in fact—is the corruption and the hold that the powerful have on everyone else. The police, the military, the government officials all work with one objective and one only—to maintain their power and the wealth and power of those above them. They have no reservations about cheating, swindling, imprisoning, or even murdering anyone if it will enrich them or keep their control over the people."

Langhorne glanced at Sandoval's hand—it was gripping the edge of the table, his knuckles white. The man had kept his voice under control, but his eyes were on fire.

Hurley said, "I took Langhorne down the street where Delgado's and the other labor companies are."

Sandoval looked at Langhorne. "You saw them, then." He frowned and shook his head slowly.

"They cheat the people they find jobs for?" Langhorne asked.

The editor chuckled bitterly. "If only that was all they did."

"What do you mean?"

Sandoval leaned closer. "Those labor agents are the first step in a system of slavery that rivals the one that existed in your country."

Langhorne frowned. Guadalupe Medina had described something like that. This was a subject beyond his specific orders from the War Department. But it did have a bearing on the political climate in the country, that and the feeling of the Mexican people. More than that, though, it was—if true—a terrible injustice.

"I want to know about it."

Sandoval said, "I will do better than that."

CHAPTER 8

"The people of the land have used oppression, and
exercised robbery, and have vexed the poor and needy:
yea, they have oppressed the stranger wrongfully."
Ezekiel 22:29

By nine in the morning, Langhorne had dressed and breakfasted
and was walking out the front door of his hotel. It wasn't hard
to find the way back to the newspaper office.

Diego Sandoval rummaged through a cabinet in a back
corner of the big press room, sifting through old editions of *La
Voz*. He nodded to Langhorne when he noticed him but kept at
his task until finally pulling one particular paper out with a look
of satisfaction. He stood up and spread the paper open on a
work table, motioning Langhorne over.

"You see." He pointed at an article on the front page. "Read
that, if you will."

Langhorne noticed the date of the newspaper—eighteen
months before. He had no trouble with the Spanish. The article
was entitled, in translation, "The New Slavery, the Old
Serfdom." It was an exposé of a corrupt contract labor system
that took advantage of Yaqui Indians and poor laborers in Sonora and Sinaloa and trapped them into perpetual servitude for
wealthy *hacendados* and government officials in Yucatan and
other southern Mexican states. The style was pure muckraker—

that was familiar enough from the American press. This one had Diego Sandoval's byline.

"Not a pretty picture," Langhorne said.

"The reality is even worse." Sandoval took the paper back from Langhorne, folded it, and replaced it in the cabinet. "Now you have an idea about the evil system. But you will see a little of it in a few minutes. Shall we go?"

Even if they'd shuffled along at an old man's pace, they would've reached the street of the labor contractors in just a few minutes, so small a city was Culiacan. Sandoval put a restraining hand on Langhorne's arm.

"Let us observe for a while from here." He motioned toward a stone bench under an awning, half a block from the nearest labor company.

From their seats, Langhorne had a clear view of the half dozen such establishments on that block. In front of each one, there was a small line of poorly dressed men and two or three women, just as on the day before. The front doors were open, and the line of people extended inside. Others stood in ones and twos across the street from the companies. Shy? Afraid?

Nothing unusual happened during the ten minutes or so that they watched. The people in line moved slowly inside, with a few more walking up and joining the end of each queue.

Sandoval leaned a little closer and spoke in a low voice. "The labor agents work in league with wealthy men in the south, as I wrote in the article you read. This is the first step in the whole wicked process. The agents put handbills around the town and sometimes run advertisements in the newspapers. *La Voz*, needless to say, refuses to run them, but other papers have no such scruples." His voice was taking on the same bitter tone he'd used the day before.

"Your article said they lured people in," Langhorne said.

"Yes. The handbills promise steady work at reasonable wages, a situation very attractive to many in this country. They have to be willing to live in the states of the south, but they are promised opportunities to return to their homes and families two or three times a year, paid by their employer. Of course, it's all nothing but lies."

"What do the laws say about all this?" Langhorne asked.

"This is very much against the law and the national constitution," Sandoval whispered. "But that matters little when the officials charged with enforcing those laws are involved in breaking them."

Langhorne glanced again at the folks in line. It might not be true—but something told him it had to be.

"Makes you want to go in there and clean house."

"That, my friend, would be a very dangerous thing to attempt. There is an alliance between the labor agents, the local criminal element, the government authorities including the police, and many of the wealthy families in this area and around the nation. It stretches from here down into the states in the south and through every level of government. How naïve it was of us to think that by getting rid of the one man, Porfirio Diaz, we would free the country from corruption and injustice. This alliance remains, like a huge web of evil, ensnaring men and women by the thousands."

Sandoval pointed at a man coming out of one of the agencies, the Ortega Company. Unlike the other companies on the block, the line going into this one had dwindled to three.

"He is one of the agents," Sandoval said, "and he has come out to recruit more from among the timid ones on this side of the street."

Sure enough, the man crossed the street and began talking to several of those loitering on that side. He seemed to settle on one woman, a Mestiza with a black and green *rebozo*, to make his sales pitch. With animated gestures and a broad smile, he carried on a lengthy conversation with the woman—really, the agent seemed to be doing most of the talking.

"He is telling her all of the wonderful things that will come if she pays his fee and allows him to place her in a job in the south," Sandoval said, his voice heavy with irony.

Langhorne kept watching. "Do they work 'em in the fields?"

"The fields, the cane mills, wherever they need labor. The people sign the contract and pay the commission, and then the agents ship them south like cattle or make them walk the hundreds of miles to the plantations and farms. Once they get there, the poor people never see freedom again. Of course, the pay never comes either. They simply work until they die. There are always new bodies to replace them, and they come very cheap."

"How cheap?"

Sandoval grimaced. "Fifty pesos. Who would have thought a human life would have so little value?"

"Some of them must try to escape—don't they?"

"It is difficult with a chain around your ankle. And they are locked into filthy sleeping quarters at night. Besides, with the little food they are given, most of them barely have the strength to work, much less to run away."

Langhorne shook his head. "It's hard to imagine. They make the women work in the fields, too?"

"The ugly ones," Sandoval replied. "If they are pretty, the master often takes them into his house to cook and clean . . . and for other 'work' not so pleasant—married or single, it makes no difference."

Langhorne stared off at nothing in particular for a moment now. It wasn't so hard to believe, this slave labor system—there were always people ready to take advantage of the weak—but that didn't make it right.

He looked back at the labor agent and the woman again. The

man reached out and took hold of her elbow, trying to draw her along with him. She hesitated at first, but after maybe half a minute, she picked up a small suitcase and let him lead her across the street and in through the agency's front door.

He turned to Sandoval. "What happens now with her?"

"The agent will take his 'commission' and have her sign a contract. He keeps the fifty pesos that she pays him, and then he receives the same amount for her from whoever buys her at the other end, so you see the agents make a double profit. They probably won't send her away until tomorrow, along with a number of others. Tonight she will sleep comfortably with the other recruits in the back of the building. They make things seem safe and normal until they get them on the train or walking south. Then, it is too late."

Langhorne kept watching the building and the other labor agencies long after the woman had disappeared inside. He found himself grinding his teeth.

Sandoval looked over at him. "Now you know how I have felt for years, watching this happen day after day, with no power to interfere."

"You're sure the police won't do anything?"

Sandoval chuckled bitterly. "They are part of it, as I said. They make a show of 'investigating' reports, but nothing ever comes from it. If we push too hard, they retaliate against us."

Langhorne frowned. It felt like butting his head against a wall, trying to come up with something, anything, that would actually do some good. Finally, he stood up, shaking his head.

"Why don't we just call it quits."

Sandoval got to his feet. "Yes. There is little more we can see. Now at least you have witnessed the situation for yourself."

Langhorne was about to start back toward the newspaper office, but the woman appeared again, walking out the door of the Ortega agency. The same agent hurried after her, and she stopped and turned. They spoke for a few moments, and she nodded her head obediently, then continued up the sidewalk, away from Langhorne and Sandoval.

"You think she's backed out?" Langhorne asked.

Sandoval shook his head. "No. She would not do that when he already has her fifty pesos."

"I'd walk away and let him keep the money if I was her."

"My friend, fifty pesos is a great sum to a girl like that. She probably had to save for more than a year to get it."

Langhorne nodded his head in her direction. "I'm gonna see where she goes." He started off, and the editor followed a moment later.

The woman was in no hurry but walked steadily for a couple of blocks until she came to a tiny storefront selling tacos, sweets, and soup. Langhorne angled across the street toward the place, Sandoval still beside him.

"What do you plan to do?" Sandoval whispered.

"Tell her what she's getting herself into."

"I do not think she will listen."

They stopped a few feet behind her as she stood at the counter, buying a bowl of pork and hominy soup. When she turned around with her food, Langhorne stepped closer and spoke in Spanish, as gently as he could.

"Señorita, may I talk to you?" He pointed to one of the little tables on the sidewalk. "Would you sit down with us?"

She looked frightened, and younger than he'd thought, really just a girl of eighteen or twenty—about what Amy would've been now. Her eyes darted back and forth between him and Sandoval, and then up and down the street. A number of other people, men and women, were nearby, and she seemed to lose a little of her fear.

"Please," Langhorne said. "I'm not going to hurt you. I just want to talk."

Silently, she stepped over to the table and sat down. Langhorne and Sandoval joined her. Her eyes were still wide as she looked from one to the other.

Langhorne smiled to reassure her. "Please, go ahead and eat. We mean you no harm."

She made no attempt to eat but dropped her gaze to the tabletop.

Langhorne kept his voice gentle. "Do you realize that the men at the Ortega agency are going to cheat you? They've taken your money, and they'll send you to a terrible place in the south where you'll have to work like a slave for no pay."

She swallowed and looked at him. "No. The man said I will have a good job and be paid three pesos a week. They will give me food every day and a clean bed to sleep in."

Langhorne shook his head. "He didn't tell you the truth. He's an evil man, Señorita." If he could bring out the whole story now, as Sandoval had told him, and convince her of the danger . . . But that would be too much.

Sandoval introduced himself and told her that he was the editor of *La Voz*. By the look on her face, that knowledge seemed to bolster their credibility. Then he introduced Langhorne.

"American?" she asked.

"Yes," Langhorne said.

She spoke in English next, with a strong accent. "I worked for American man. A businessman. For one year. Here in Culiacan. I cook, I clean, I nurse his sick wife."

Langhorne looked closely at her now. She was a short girl, moderately dark skinned. Her lips were full, her nose broad, and she had large, trusting brown eyes. Kind of pretty after a sort—then there was Sandoval's comment on the fate of pretty women in the labor system.

He leaned toward her. "You can't go with those men at the agency, Señorita. I don't want them to hurt you."

She stared at him for ten or fifteen seconds, indecision in her eyes. Then, abruptly, she stood up and started quickly away, back in the direction of the labor agencies.

Langhorne hurried to follow, with Sandoval right behind.

"What are you going to do?" Sandoval asked him, as they weaved between other pedestrians on the sidewalk.

"Depends on what they do, I guess." The girl was only a few yards ahead of them. At least she hadn't started running.

They covered the blocks back to the agency in a very few minutes. Langhorne hurried ahead now and caught up with the girl just before she reached the door. He put a hand lightly on her shoulder and said, "Please!"

She stiffened for an instant, but at least she stopped. She didn't turn, though, so he stepped around in front of her. He shook his head slowly.

"Don't go in there. Don't."

The confusion was plain on her face, and tears welled up in her eyes.

The labor agent who'd been with her earlier chose that moment to rush out the door. He was lanky, with matted hair and a dirty brown shirt, and Langhorne could smell him. The agent grabbed the girl by the arm and started pulling her inside.

Langhorne felt his own fists clinch.

"No!"

The man ignored him and took a step toward the open door, the girl's arm still in his grasp.

"I said no!" Langhorne told him in Spanish.

Surprise showed for an instant on the man's face, but then he scowled and leaned in toward Langhorne.

"If you know what's good for you, you'll mind your own business!" He held Langhorne's eyes in a stare and started backing in through the open door, pulling the girl along with him. "Come on!"

142

She began to sob now and struggle.

"I don't want to go with you. Let me go."

"You'll lose your contract and your fifty pesos if you don't go! Do you want to be fined and go to jail?"

Langhorne clamped down on the man's wrist with his left hand and jerked the girl's arm from his grasp.

Fury flamed in the man's eyes.

"She's mine!"

Langhorne broke his nose.

Sandoval stepped forward and put his arm around the girl's shoulders.

Langhorne said, "Take her across the street until I settle this."

"Watch out," Sandoval said. "There will be more of them inside."

Curious onlookers were gathering on both sides of the street, but they all gave Langhorne a wide berth.

He walked over to where the man sat in the doorway with his legs apart. One hand covered his mouth and the broken nose, and blood was streaming between his fingers. Langhorne stood over him and glared down. Now fear joined the pain already in the man's eyes.

"You have the fifty pesos she gave you," Langhorne said in Spanish, loudly enough for the crowd to hear. He pulled out his wallet and counted out some bills. "And here are the fifty pesos you'd get when you sold her to the men from the south." He tossed the money at the man. "She owes you nothing. Don't ever bother her again."

Langhorne turned and strode deliberately across to Sandoval and the girl—no hurrying or looking back. This battle was won, and now was the time for a disciplined withdrawal before the enemy could mount a counterattack.

When the three of them were more than a block away, loud, angry voices started up back toward the agency, but Langhorne still didn't look back. Sandoval cast one quick glance over his shoulder and grinned.

"They seem to be arguing. It must be the other ones from inside." He shook his head. "You, Señor, have a great deal of nerve."

"What else was I supposed to do? I wasn't about to let 'em take her, I promise you that."

Sandoval laughed. "No, no. I applaud you. We honor such courage in this country. What we will do now, I do not know, but your courage is beyond question."

"I don't know, either, but I'm glad I did what I did." He looked down at the girl, walking between them. "It changes things when they're not just a face in the crowd anymore."

"Indeed, it does," the editor said, still smiling.

Langhorne kept his expression blank, but that didn't keep him from thinking. Maybe it was all over—but then again, maybe it wasn't. Do what was right and let God take care of the consequences—good teaching from his mother, but sometimes easier said than done.

They reached the newspaper office and ducked inside after checking to see that they weren't being followed. Sandoval called to his assistant, Jorge, to get the girl some coffee to steady her nerves and had her sit down.

The young man smiled when he brought her the coffee, and then stood there a little longer before starting back to his work. He cast a glance over his shoulder at her as he walked away.

She thanked them humbly and told them her name was Luna Garcia and that she was from Culiacan. She had no living relatives there, her widowed mother having died the previous year. That was when she'd found the job working for Mr. Dawes, the American businessman. Unfortunately, he'd returned to the

United States a month ago, and she'd had no success finding work since then until finally going to the labor agency as a last resort. She finished her story and looked at both of them with her sad brown eyes.

"I have no one, no family to protect me. What can I do?"

Langhorne raised his eyebrows at Sandoval and shrugged. "What do you think? We can't turn her out on the street."

Sandoval frowned and looked down at the table. "I have no place for her at my home." He glanced around the printing room. "She cannot stay here."

"Poor girl hasn't eaten for a while, either. She left her soup on the table." He cocked his head as he looked at her. "I can get you a room at the Hotel Canales where I'm staying."

She recoiled at the words, fear and mistrust on her face.

Langhorne felt the color rise in his own face, and he smiled at her. "It'll be a room of your own, and I'll stay clear. I promise."

"I am chaste!"

"And you'll stay that way, Luna."

She didn't say anything more, but it was obvious she was still uneasy.

Langhorne turned to Sandoval. "And what happens to her tomorrow?"

"She cannot stay in Culiacan."

She spoke slowly, sadly. "I can go back to the man at the agency. My suitcase is still there. It is everything I have. I will ask him to let me work. I will beg him. It is the only thing I can do."

Her hands were clasped tightly in front of her on the table, and Langhorne placed one of his big hands over both of hers. She looked over at him, and he smiled at her.

"Don't worry, little girl. Nobody's gonna hurt you while I'm around." An idea came into his mind, and he turned to

Sandoval. "I stayed several days at a hacienda up in Sonora, right along the western edge of the Sierra. They're good people. My associate is still up there, recovering from a bear attack, of all things." Associate? Maybe *friend* would've been a better word—but maybe not.

Sandoval peered at him. "Well?"

"Anyway, the lady of the house, Señora Medina, seems to be a kindred spirit with you."

"I don't understand that term."

"She thinks like you. She has the same ideas on this labor agency business. Says it's the worst thing in the whole country now, worse even than what the peons on the ranches have to put up with."

Sandoval slowly nodded his head. "Go on."

"I think she'd be glad to try to find the girl a job, maybe in the town near their hacienda. The lady wants to help people who've suffered at the hands of these labor agents. It's worth a try anyway. Is the telegraph office at the railroad station?"

"Yes, it is. Be careful, though. Your telegram may find its way into the hands of the authorities."

"I will. Now let's go have a good *comida,* then get Luna a room. After that, I'll send the telegram. Probably won't be much chance for an answer before tomorrow."

Langhorne's telegram couldn't provide the details he would've liked. A letter would have been preferable for the lengthy explanation he wanted to present, but that would've taken far too long. He put it in English—the operators could send it that way but might be less likely to understand it all.

To Señora Guadalupe Medina, Hacienda El Valle de Ajalón, Agua Blanca, Sonora
Have redeemed young woman Luna Garcia from labor agents

Culiacan (stop) Urgent she finds job out of area (stop) Can
you help find her one (stop) Great danger for her here (stop)
Signed: Langhorne

He started to leave the name of his hotel with the operator, so the man could send him Guadalupe's reply when it came, but Sandoval's warning came to mind. No, better to just check back at the telegraph office for any answer.

When Langhorne got back to the hotel, Sandoval was waiting with Luna at a table out on the patio. She seemed a little overwhelmed, but she gave him a shy smile when he sat down. A tall fruit drink sat in front of her, courtesy of Sandoval, no doubt.

"How do you like your room, Luna?" Langhorne asked.

Her smile broadened, and it seemed to light up the entire patio.

"Very nice, Señor. Thank you very much. It is like the house of Señor Dawes. Very nice." Suddenly she looked worried. She dug in a pocket and pulled out a small coin purse. "But I do not know how I will pay for the room." She showed them the coins in the purse. "I have only two pesos left."

Langhorne and Sandoval laughed.

"Señor Sandoval and I will pay for what you need till we can find you a safe place to live," Langhorne said. The girl looked relieved but still a bit apprehensive. Who could blame her?

For some reason, Fabiana Medina came to his mind, so self-assured in comparison with Luna. But that wasn't totally accurate. Around Jester, she seemed bold and more mature than her age one moment, but then she'd shrink from getting her hands dirty the next. Maybe the boldness was just an act. The Medina girl might be just as frightened by the world as Luna seemed to be.

They were certainly different in their appearance. Fabiana was more slender, with finer features and lighter skin and hair.

Still, Luna had a kind, vulnerable look. She needed protection from the world's wickedness. Her large brown eyes were like those of a child. Would Amy's eyes have looked . . . ?

Langhorne glanced again at Luna. The sooner she was in a place of safety far from Culiacan, the better.

CHAPTER 9

"And Joseph's master took him, and put him into the
prison, a place where the king's prisoners were bound."
Genesis 39:20

On the afternoon that Langhorne left the hacienda, Fabiana
was talking with Calvin Jester in his room when she saw the
fever return to his eyes, just as the doctor had predicted. It
continued, on and off, into the morning of the fourth day. Old
Sofia ministered to his needs as if he were a sick child, bringing
him food and drink during the periods when the fever abated,
and bathing his brow with a cool, wet cloth when it burned the
hottest. Fabiana came and went, checking on his condition
several times each day. Twice she did the feeding instead of the
old woman, spooning soup into Jester's mouth or playfully passing him grapes and bites of melon when he was cool and awake.
He was fun to be with on those occasions, smiling and bantering with her, obviously enjoying the special treatment.

During the times when he was feverish, drifting in and out of
a troubled sleep, Fabiana kept her distance. If she happened
into his room at such a time, she'd quickly withdraw. By the
second day of the fever, the situation was growing tiresome,
almost intolerable. He needed to be well where they could enjoy
each other's company and their flirtations, she fancied.

His blond hair was particularly fascinating. She'd only been close to two people—both women—with that color hair before. It made him look like a Greek god. And his face, his smile—the corners of her mouth turned up just a bit whenever she thought of them. He had to be the most handsome man—even more than her poor father.

On that fourth morning, Fabiana came to his room just after finishing her *almuerzo* of enchiladas and fried eggs. Sofia was there, straightening the things on the table, and she bowed quickly and slipped out, leaving the door halfway open. Fabiana reached for the knob, then took her hand away.

Jester lay on his back, breathing deeply, obviously sleeping well. She brushed his forehead with her fingertips, and his skin was cool. His hair was fairly short but curly, and on impulse she toyed with one lock at his temple.

He went suddenly rigid, stretching his entire body, and she jerked her hand away, her heart beating fast. He closed his eyes tightly then opened them and looked around the room, apparently unaware of her caress. His eyes showed recognition, and he grinned sleepily and bowed his head to her.

"At your feet, Señorita," he murmured.

She blushed and smiled. His words had taken her by complete surprise. "I beg your pardon," she said finally.

Jester sat up in bed, pushing his pillow up against the iron headboard to support his back. "At your feet," he said, more clearly this time. He was smiling and observing her closely. "Sofia told me that's what your young men say to young ladies when they want to show them special regard."

"Well, I don't, uh . . . Why would you ask her something like that?"

"Oh, just idle curiosity."

She finally smiled again. "Thank you." He certainly knew how to pay a compliment—Esteban and his calculating flattery were completely outclassed.

"Miss Fabiana," he said, "I truly feel that a little sunshine would do wonders for my constitution after being cooped up so long in this room." He looked around. "It is, I grant you, a lovely room, but I need to feel the sun on my face."

"I think we can manage that," she said. He reached out toward her, but she retreated out of range. "I'll get Sofia, and she can help you out onto the patio." She hurried through the doorway and down the corridor toward the kitchen, laughing silently—oh, the look on his face.

Jester leaned heavily on the old woman while they made their way out to the shady patio behind the main house. He hobbled along in his pajamas and robe, casting a pitiful look of mock forlornness over his shoulder at Fabiana, who followed a few paces behind.

He was such an actor—but quite a nice looking one. There was that young man she'd seen in a stage play once when she and her mother—her real mother—had visited family in Ohio during the last year of her mother's life. They'd gone backstage after the final curtain, a privilege of wealth and social status, and met the cast. The young actor looked nothing like Jester, having a thick head of long, black hair and a fine Roman nose, but there was resemblance in their manner, the same humorous jauntiness.

Sofia helped him settle onto a wooden bench in the sunshine, and Fabiana sat across from him in a reclined chair and sent Sofia inside to fetch orange juice for them. Jester shut his eyes and turned his face toward the sun. He smiled, his face bathed in the golden light, and Fabiana smiled, too. The sunlight must've felt wonderful on his skin after the days inside.

They talked of unimportant things and sipped orange juice. Jester's face was pale, most likely his natural coloring, reinforced by the long stay indoors. After a few minutes, though, that coloring seemed to have deepened a bit into an appealing ruddiness.

Now Fabiana noticed someone standing on the gallery near the corner of the house. Her stepmother was bending over a big potted shrub. Fabiana watched her out of the corner of her eye for several minutes while exchanging small talk with Jester. Guadalupe didn't seem to be cutting flowers or watering—they had a hired man to take care of the plants. She had to be spying—as if they'd do anything improper out here. Guadalupe was very conscious of propriety, too conscious of it. The woman should mind her own business, and propriety be damned.

"I'm going in for a moment," Fabiana said, and she started toward the spot where her stepmother was piddling with the plants. Fabiana passed as close to Guadalupe as she could, almost brushing her. Good! There was the look of embarrassment on her stepmother's face—it served her right.

Fabiana strode on around the gallery and into the house through the north door by Jester's room. She hurried on down the corridor but with no particular destination in mind—just walking out her anger.

She looked in at the kitchen door. Sofia was busy peeling and cutting vegetables, and a younger woman was cleaning the pots and pans. The old woman looked up and smiled hesitantly, and Fabiana stepped in and looked around. It was a foreign place. She'd never spent much time there.

An ironing board stood in one corner of the room, and Fabiana walked past it, noting the black flatiron cooling on a shelf nearby. A stack of folded clothing lay next to the iron. The shirt on top looked like one of Jester's.

"Are these Señor Jester's clothes?" she asked the old woman in Spanish.

"Yes, *Patrona*. I washed them this morning and ironed them just now. I tried to fold them just the way he likes."

"He's particular about that, is he?"

"Yes, *Patrona*. I will take them to his room now."

"No, I'll do it," Fabiana said. The old woman smiled and nodded, and Fabiana took up the stack of shirts, trousers, and underclothes and carried them out. She paused for a moment at the corridor that led to the open back door—Jester was still on the bench—then continued on down the other corridor to his room.

It seemed strange being in the room without him. The bedclothes were rumpled where he'd gotten up, and the pillow was still propped against the headboard. His masculine scent permeated the room—that wasn't altogether pleasant. But after all, he'd been sick.

Fabiana set the clothing down on the bureau. She pulled the drawers open one by one. The first two held underclothes, socks, and shirts, and she placed the freshly laundered ones in them.

The third drawer held the trousers. Fabiana moved Jester's belts and suspenders, which were atop the trousers, to the top of the bureau, so she could lay the newly washed pairs in. When she was putting the belts back on top of the folded pants, her finger touched something rough on the inside of one of the belts, and she glanced down at it. What was a zipper doing on a belt? But her father had had a belt with a zipper, too—she remembered now—a money belt.

She stared at the belt for maybe fifteen seconds, and she slowly smiled. She laid the belt out flat on the bureau top. Was he carrying a great deal of money? Not that she'd ever take it, but it was Calvin Jester's. Anything associated with him was interesting.

She glanced at the open door. Her heart began to beat faster, and she walked over and quietly pushed it shut.

Back at the bureau, she held the belt down flat and slowly worked the zipper open. It was stiff, and it took an effort to move it the ten or twelve inches of its length. With her thumbs, she pulled open the stiff leather to see if anything was in the hidden pocket. There was some paper money, and she smiled mischievously—secrecy made things exciting. She carefully worked the money out of the tight leather. Less than thirty dollars—a little disappointing. Perhaps Calvin Jester wasn't quite so mysterious after all.

She smiled again. What if she wrote a mysterious note, unsigned and in a disguised hand, and placed it among the bills for him to find later? That would be fun, making him wonder who'd found his secret bankroll. But then she frowned—he hadn't spent any money since coming to the hacienda, and he wasn't likely to until after he left. The joke wouldn't be funny if he wasn't around for her to see the puzzlement on his face.

She refolded the bills and started to stuff them back into the pocket. But there was something else in the pocket—a paper. It was wedged in tightly and folded and refolded several times, and she started working it out slowly, taking care lest she tear it. Just then, footsteps sounded in the hallway, and she practically jumped. She froze for a few seconds, staring at the door and not daring to breathe. But the steps went past and faded down the corridor.

Fabiana paused for a moment to let her heart return to normal. She pulled the curtain aside slightly and glanced out the window. Her stepmother was nowhere in sight—that was worrying—but Jester was still where she'd left him, on the bench. He seemed to be dozing.

Carefully, she went back to her task, and in less than half a minute she had the paper out. She opened it to look. Learning a secret about this dashing blond stranger would be exciting.

It was a bigger secret than she'd imagined.

Loud knocking on his door at seven that morning caught Langhorne in trousers, shoes, and undershirt, shaving in front of a wall mirror. He quickly wiped his face with a towel and put on a white shirt before going to the door.

Two grim looking men in ill-fitting coats stood there. One was tall and powerfully built, with a face that looked like it had seen its share of violence. The other was of medium height and wiry. His features were sharp, and he had a sparse moustache that needed trimming.

The smaller man flashed a kind of badge, said his name was Vega, and asked if he was speaking to Señor "Langornay."

"I'm Langhorne."

"You will come with us." They positioned themselves on each side of Langhorne.

He glanced right and left. Fighting wouldn't be smart. No sense in giving them any excuse to exercise the *ley fuga* and shoot him for trying to escape.

They let him take his letter of introduction—the unclassified one—and his wallet, but nothing else. The secret letter was still hidden in his belt.

They marched him through the hotel lobby, drawing a few darkly curious glances from patrons and staff. A carriage was waiting out front, and the policemen were careful to place Langhorne between them on the bench seat back of the driver. It took only a few minutes through Culiacan's lightly traveled streets to arrive at the *Carcel Municipal,* or city jail.

It was a modern looking stone and stucco building, layered like a wedding cake, and with graceful arched doorways like the ones at the *Teatro Apolo* that Consul Hurley had shown him. Langhorne had bailed plenty of drunken soldiers out of jails, but this one had a funny feel about it. Was he even under arrest, or was he just here for questioning?

Vega furnished the answer as soon as they went through the door. He took Langhorne by the arm and walked him into a room with peeling plaster and three spindly chairs.

"Sit down. You are under arrest, and I'm going to ask you

some questions."

Langhorne kept a poker face, but his pulse was pounding. This had to be for punching the labor agent.

"What am I charged with?"

"Attempting to buy a young woman for immoral purposes."

Langhorne stared at the man and then almost laughed.

"What am I supposed to have done?"

Vega leaned close, glaring down at Langhorne. "Be silent! Empty your pockets."

Langhorne handed his wallet, a few coins, and a handkerchief over to the policeman, along with his letter of introduction. Vega put everything but the wallet down on an empty chair.

"Do you deny that you took a young Mexican woman named, uh, Luna Garcia to the hotel where you are staying?"

"No, but—"

"Did you pay fifty pesos to an employee of the Ortega Labor Company for the girl?"

Langhorne frowned. "I paid him to get her free of those men. Not for any other reason."

"Did you take her to the Hotel Canales and keep her overnight?"

"We got her a room of her own."

"We?"

Too late to call it back now. "Señor Diego Sandoval and I."

Recognition showed in Vega's eyes, that and an odd glint that Langhorne didn't like.

"Ah, the newspaper man. So the girl stayed last night at the hotel?"

"She didn't have any other place to go, and I wouldn't let her go back to the Ortega people."

"Why not? How do you know this girl?"

This was frustrating—but there was no reason to let Vega see it. "I don't know her, except since yesterday when the man at the labor agency tried to force her to go with him. I didn't like it, so I stepped in."

"Do you usually assault honest businessmen when you 'step in'?" Vega looked through the wallet as he talked, pulling out the paper money.

"Honest businessmen? He was trying to swindle the poor girl and trick her into slavery."

"Slavery is illegal in Mexico. It does not exist." Vega folded the money and put it into his shirt pocket then tossed the wallet onto the chair with Langhorne's other things. He looked down at Langhorne. "Who are you, Señor?"

"C. W. Langhorne. You have my letter of introduction right there."

"Yes." Vega glanced over the letter again. "This is from a man named Powell at the newspaper the *Washington Weekly*. It says you work for him."

"That's right."

"And what are you doing for him here in Culiacan?"

Langhorne took a deep breath. He could say he was a correspondent—but he just couldn't swallow that. "I'm here to study Mexican railroads," he said finally. The next question might not offer such an easy answer.

Vega frowned and stared at Langhorne for several moments. Then he started to laugh. "An American wants to study *our* railroads? You are more stupid than I thought."

He took Langhorne by the arm and led him toward the door. He stopped there without opening it. In a conspiratorial tone, he said, "You are in very serious trouble. Mexican law holds the virtue of its women in high regard and severely punishes those who commit such outrages."

CHAPTER 10

"Then let them which be in Judaea flee into the
mountains." Matthew 24:16

Spending a day and night in the *carcel* wasn't as bad as Langhorne had expected. There had been no beatings, no intimidating gangs of toughs, not even an attempt by Vega and his cohorts to extort more money. In fact, surprisingly few inmates of any kind were there, and they looked more like hospital patients than criminals. The lack of any food—now that was the worst thing. Like he'd heard somewhere before, Mexican jails made the families and friends responsible for providing food for inmates.

Finally, a couple hours after sunrise, Langhorne got the attention of the jailer, a fat and sweaty man of about fifty, and promised him five pesos if he'd get a message to Hurley about his predicament.

When the consul arrived an hour later, the first thing Langhorne did was get Hurley to pay the jailer. Then the man let the consul into the big cell that Langhorne shared with two emaciated inmates. Hurley wore a wry grin.

"Buying a young woman for lustful purposes?"

Langhorne didn't smile. "*Immoral* purposes. Of all the ridiculous, trumped up—"

Hurley stopped him with a wave of his hand. "Langhorne,

this is Mexico. They do things differently down here." He started to laugh.

"All right, have your fun," Langhorne said sharply. "But when am I gonna get out?"

"Exercise some patience. I'm having to, as they say, 'clear up a little misunderstanding' with the authorities. Talked things over with an officer named Vega. It seems he's taken a liking to you, wants to give you a break."

"What he wants is to break the bank."

"Anyway, this Vega is willing to drop the charges against you if you just pay the fine and the damages."

"He's already cleaned out my wallet. That was twenty-three pesos."

There was a noise from the other side of the cell, and Langhorne turned, along with Hurley. One of the other inmates had sat up and was watching.

Hurley looked back to Langhorne. "You keep close track."

"It's Uncle Sam's money. I'm responsible for it."

The consul nodded. "Commendable. Vega asked for a hundred pesos, all together." Langhorne whistled and Hurley continued. "That's for the fine and for the labor agent's 'pain and suffering.' I think that's the legal term for getting your nose flattened." He smiled for an instant. "I'm not a violent man, but I would've paid to see that, you know. Those labor companies are a scourge."

Langhorne shook his head, frowning. "A hundred pesos."

"Oh, I talked him down to sixty—forty for the fine and twenty for the nose. I've had lots of practice with people like Vega since I've been in Mexico. Express regret, offer to make some arrangement, then threaten to call in the Marines when the price is too high. That's the way this kind of negotiation usually goes."

Langhorne finally grinned. "Marines, huh? What about the cavalry?"

"Figuratively speaking. We can bring some diplomatic pressure to bear, and they usually listen to reason. You've heard that expression, 'the carrot and the stick.' "

"I've also heard of the 'Big Stick.' "

"Wrong president."

"Anyway." Langhorne held out his hand and shook Hurley's. "Thanks for stepping in."

"Don't mention it. This may be the only U.S. 'intervention' you'll have any part of. By the way, did they get any information out of you?"

Langhorne shook his head. "I was sweating for a little while there during the questioning, but then Vega just stopped and had 'em lock me up."

"You wouldn't have lied if they'd asked point blank?"

"Glad I didn't have to find out. Now how about getting me out?"

Hurley called the jailer, who let him out but locked the cell door back in Langhorne's face. The consul disappeared into another room for a few minutes, then came back in and spoke to the jailer again. This time he opened the cell. Langhorne said *adios* to the two wretches in the cell, handing them the coins Vega hadn't looted, and walked out, following Hurley through the outer room and on toward the street door. Vega was sitting behind a desk, making a show of ignoring the Americans, and Langhorne gave him a hard look as he passed.

"Let's get you some breakfast," the consul said as they stepped into the morning sunlight.

That sounded good, and they headed to the hotel, where Langhorne drank what seemed like half a gallon of hot coffee and ate three eggs, fried patties of mashed beans sprinkled with cheese, and several slices of good buttered toast. He pushed away from the table and stretched. Things were definitely looking better.

Hurley peered at him across a coffee cup. "Now what about this girl?"

"Your friend Sandoval and I got her a room here night before last." He frowned suddenly. Was she even still there? It'd been twenty-four hours since the policemen had spirited him away. "I have to check on her." He started to rise, but the consul motioned for him to sit back down.

"Relax. I ran into Sandoval this morning, and he assured me she was still here in her room. Apparently, he'd just looked in on her."

Langhorne let out a deep breath. "It's almost funny, these crooked police and crooked labor agents. Seems like they've got all the people scared stiff, but they strike me as nothing but a bunch of con men."

The consul's expression became grave. "Now that's where you need to watch out, Langhorne. I know this seems like petty corruption, the kind of thing we read about in New York or Chicago. And some of the people come across like comic opera, or those motion picture shows with the silly looking villains."

Langhorne nodded and Hurley continued.

"Only it's not comedy, and these men aren't so stupid. They can be very dangerous, believe me. You can't just look on the surface. It's kind of like mice in a barn. You may see one here and there, but there's a whole lot more that never show their faces. And they're the ones you really have to watch out for. Remember what Diego Sandoval said the other night at dinner." Hurley seemed to think of something, and pulled out a telegram. "He wanted me to give you this."

Langhorne smiled. It had to be the answer. His eyes scanned the paper.

"Señora Medina—at the ranch where we were staying. She says she'll take the girl in, give her a job there at the hacienda, working in the house." That was perfect. Luna would be out of

161

the reach of the labor agents and the entire system, and Guadalupe could watch over her. He smiled and looked across at Hurley. "She says we can send the girl on right away. Can you help me get her on the right train? She'll need a little money and the price of the ticket."

"Sorry, but my job is helping Americans, not Mexicans. Sure, I'll get you the money you need, but I can't interfere in purely Mexican affairs. They'd kick me out fast."

"Sandoval, then."

"He's your best bet. And what about you? When are you moving on to your next stop?"

"Tomorrow, I suppose." There hadn't been much time to think about it since the trouble with the labor agent, but the mission wouldn't wait.

Hurley pushed his chair back and stood up. "Now I've got to get back to the consulate. Stop by on the way to Sandoval's, and I'll have your money waiting. I'd like to get a look at this girl who's caused you so much trouble. I hope she's worth it."

Langhorne stood up, too. Anybody in her fix would be worth it.

Langhorne checked Luna Garcia out of her hotel room as casually as possible, but two or three of the hotel staff still watched them slyly as he and the girl walked across the lobby and out the door. It felt better when they came out onto the sidewalk and started across town, and better still just to have a safe place to send her.

Langhorne didn't tell her about Guadalupe Medina yet, but just said he'd found someplace safe. He bought her a quick breakfast at a stand on the way, and the girl ate it gratefully as they walked. He kept a wary eye in all directions, just as wary as if he'd been on mounted patrol along the border, but no one on the busy streets seemed to pay them any special notice. They reached the office of *La Voz* just before eleven and slipped inside.

Sandoval approached them with concern on his face. "I am relieved that you are out of jail. I did not know if you would get off so easily."

"Just took a little money," Langhorne said. He smiled and held up the telegram. "I've found a safe place for Miss Garcia." He looked at Luna. "A woman I know up in Sonora, with a big hacienda in the Sierra, has offered to take you in and give you a job."

Luna's face lit up at the news—and again she seemed to brighten the whole room.

"This señora wants me to come and work for her?" Luna asked, as if she couldn't really believe the news. "She will let me stay at her hacienda?"

Langhorne nodded. "That's right. She's very glad to have you come there and stay. You'll be safe from the labor agents and have plenty to eat and a decent place to live."

Tears came to the girl's eyes, and she took Langhorne's hand in both of her own and bowed her head, thanking him, God, and the Virgin Mary over and over.

A few moments of that were enough to make him squirm, and he gently pulled his hand away and made her look up at him.

"Now we've got to get you on the train up to Sonora." He turned to Sandoval. "You think she'll be okay traveling alone?"

The editor frowned. "I cannot guarantee it. Perhaps I could send Jorge with her as far as the last stop. He would see that she found the kind lady, and then he could return."

"Sounds better that way." He glanced quickly across the room toward Jorge and spoke in a lower voice. "He's a reliable fellow, is he?"

"Completely," Sandoval replied. "Not a physically powerful man, as you see, but I would trust him with my life." He looked at Luna. "Or hers. He wants to destroy the system of slave labor as much as I do."

"I suppose we'd better ask him if he's willing to go with her."

Sandoval's eyes twinkled. "He'll be willing. Did you see the way he looked at her yesterday when we brought her in? He was like a puppy."

"Yeah, I noticed," Langhorne said, grinning for a moment. The girl smiled shyly and looked down. "I guess that settles it."

Sandoval called Jorge over and explained the situation to him. The young man didn't smile, but the excitement was obvious in his eyes.

"I have much typesetting to do," Jorge said to Sandoval. "I should not go." There was no conviction in his voice.

"Sometimes there are more important tasks than setting type," Sandoval said. "I need you to go." He glanced quickly at Langhorne, then back at Jorge. "Even though I know you would rather stay and work."

The young man looked down, then over at Luna, who was paying no attention to the conversation, then back at Sandoval. "Well, if you insist, Señor Sandoval, I will go."

Sandoval clapped him lightly on the shoulder. "Thank you, Jorge. I take it as a personal favor."

It took almost another hour for Jorge to pack an overnight bag in the room where he lived behind the newspaper office and for them all to help Luna buy a few things she needed for the trip to replace what she'd lost in her suitcase. Then the four of them rode a mule-drawn streetcar to the station, arriving in time for Luna and Jorge to make the last train north for that day.

The girl seemed nervous as she waited with them on the platform, and Langhorne kept checking his watch; it was almost like sending his own daughter out into the unknown, with the next friend a long day's rail trip away. He gave her shoulder a reassuring squeeze, and she looked up at him like a little girl.

Langhorne forced a smile. "Luna, there's a man named Calvin Jester up at that hacienda. He's not a bad fellow—but don't believe everything he says."

She threw her arms around him for a moment, and he breathed a prayer that she'd reach the hacienda safely. The next moment, Jorge took her by the hand and led her onto the train. A couple of minutes later, the steam whistle blew, and the locomotive began the slow chugging that started the train north. As it pulled sluggishly out of the station, Langhorne turned to Sandoval.

"Everything ought to be okay now." Even as he said it, he looked all around the station.

Sandoval suggested that they enjoy a hearty *comida* at a decent restaurant that he knew a few blocks from the office of *La Voz,* and Langhorne was quick to agree. There was nothing more to do for Luna now, and relaxing over a good meal sounded great. They walked toward the restaurant along streets that were nearly deserted, most of the townspeople apparently enjoying their midafternoon mealtime as well. As they passed by one café, Langhorne glanced in and found himself locking eyes with Vega. The policeman looked as startled as Langhorne felt, but they both looked away, and Vega made no move to get up from his table.

At the restaurant that Sandoval had chosen, they had meatball soup, roast beef, potatoes, and French pastry for dessert. All told, they spent an unhurried hour and a half eating, and Langhorne felt comfortably satisfied when they finally rose to leave.

Most people were still off the streets, and it was nice not to face crowds of other pedestrians. Sandoval was good company, a man who spoke his mind honestly and straight out.

While they were still a couple of blocks away from the newspaper office, the editor looked over at Langhorne and gave a rare smile.

"Who is this man that you warned Señorita Garcia about?"

Langhorne grinned—the young blond lieutenant and his smooth Carolina drawl. "Probably not someone you'd like. He has trouble being serious about anything."

Sandoval seemed to ponder that for a few moments, and his smile faded. "I see. Yes, I have little time for silliness. I have seen too much of the world's cruelty for that."

They turned down a side street a block from the office.

"Plenty of that," Langhorne said, "but sometimes a smile can make things easier to get through. Like the Bible says, 'A merry heart works good like a medicine.' "

"Perhaps. But I know nothing of Bibles."

Langhorne looked over at him. What a shame.

Rushing footsteps came from behind, and he glanced back for an instant—two men were running at them. Sandoval cried a warning, and Langhorne looked forward again just in time to see a third man catch Sandoval square on the ear with a walking stick, knocking him to the pavement.

Langhorne only had time to shove that man away, then turned to face the other two. One went for Sandoval, landing a vicious kick full into the editor's side as he got to his hands and knees. The other man came straight at Langhorne with a club, swinging high for the head. Langhorne jerked backwards but not enough, the club numbing his jaw with a glancing blow.

He ignored the pain and punched straight into the club man's teeth. The blow stunned the man long enough for Langhorne to wrench the club away, then bring it down with all his strength. The collarbone shattered like a dry branch, and the man dropped, screaming.

The other two were all over Sandoval, one kicking and stomping while the second rained blows on the editor's head and shoulders with the walking stick. But now they faced about at Langhorne. For a moment he and the two eyed one another for an opening. Then Langhorne swung the club high—when in doubt, attack!

The man danced out of reach, and the other pulled a knife, a short, ugly wedge of steel. They came at Langhorne in tandem, stick to the right and knife to the left. Langhorne drifted left, trying to put the knife man between him and the one with the stick.

What a sad place to die this would be.

A narrow alley was a few yards behind him, and he backed into it—now they could only come at him from one direction.

Someone out on the sidewalk started to groan—probably Sandoval.

The knife man said, "I'll hold this one. You get Sandoval." Immediately the man with the stick turned away.

It was now or never to save Sandoval. Langhorne yelled at the knife man, like a recruit learning the bayonet, and brought the club overhead and down. The man slipped back out of the way, and Langhorne pressed forward, the club out front to keep the knife at bay. He was out on the sidewalk again. The second man stood over Sandoval, the walking stick raised high.

"No!" Langhorne cried.

The walking stick came down, there was a thud, and then a grunt from Sandoval.

The knife man flashed his weapon at Langhorne, laying open his left arm. Langhorne gritted his teeth and swung the club down hard on the man's wrist. The knife clattered to the sidewalk, and the man shuffled backward in agony, supporting the broken wrist with his good hand. Langhorne shoved him down to get to Sandoval's attacker. The editor was face down, fifteen feet away, groaning and trying to lift his head.

Langhorne was off balance, stumbling forward. The man

with the stick was so far away. The walking stick rose, slowly it seemed. Then it crashed down again.

Sandoval was still.

A wave of strength and sorrow erupted in Langhorne, shutting out everything but the determination to kill. The assassin had time enough to turn, but that was all. Langhorne dropped the club and grabbed the man by shirt collar and belt in one swift motion, his momentum carrying them both toward a brick wall facing the street. Langhorne swung the man headfirst into the wall with all his strength. There was a sickening crack, and the man seemed to melt onto the ground.

Langhorne heard a low, fierce growl come from his own mouth, and he turned to find the other two attackers. One was already gone, and the knife man was staggering away, still cradling his ruined wrist.

Nausea rolled over Langhorne, but he forced himself to kneel beside Sandoval. He could still be breathing—but he wouldn't be. Sandoval was gone.

A terrible fatigue hit Langhorne as all the furious energy drained from his body, and he knelt there gasping for air.

Hurley took Langhorne to a doctor to tend to his injuries, a Mexican physician that the consul used himself. The man worked quickly and competently, and the two were out and walking to the consulate in less than an hour.

The consul shook his head, looking down at his feet. "It's hard to believe Diego Sandoval's dead. Such a tragedy. I didn't agree with all his positions, but he was a fine man."

"An honest one," Langhorne said. His left forearm burned where the knife had laid the flesh open. Twenty-one stitches and a thorough cleansing with iodine didn't help matters. His jaw hurt, too, although the physician said there was no break. But what was all that compared to Sandoval?

Hurley watched him as they walked. "Could you use a drink? You still look a little shaky."

"No drink. Coffee, maybe."

"You and your coffee. You drink more of the stuff than any mortal I've ever seen."

Langhorne didn't reply. Now was no time for talking, but Hurley didn't seem to know that.

"For a man on a confidential mission, you seem to keep anything but a low profile."

Langhorne glared at him. "What do you expect me to do, sit and watch?"

"Take it easy," Hurley said. "I'm just surprised at, uh, the destruction."

Langhorne let out a weary sigh. "So am I. I'll tell you, Hurley, I've had to kill before—but never with my bare hands." He turned his palms up and glanced at them for a moment. "There's a difference—between shooting a man, even up close, and . . ."

"I'm sure there must be."

"Hope I never have to do it again."

"You may be in the wrong line of work."

"May be." There'd be some prayer ahead, that was for sure. Now peace—that might be another story.

Hurley was silent for maybe fifteen seconds; then he spoke again. "I'm just glad there were some reliable witnesses who saw the whole thing. After your scrape with the police, they might've tried to prosecute you otherwise."

"Well, I'm leaving tomorrow, so that ought to put an end to it."

"Probably a good thing. Was it a robbery? Or do you even know?"

"I'm pretty sure it wasn't. From what one of them said, they must've been after Sandoval."

The consulate was just ahead, and Hurley increased the pace. "A newspaper editor can make a lot of enemies, especially when he doesn't pull any punches. You heard what he said—he knew more about the corruption down here than most anybody else."

"What a waste."

They reached the consulate and turned in. Hurley's clerk handed him a note.

"This came for you a few minutes ago."

Hurley led Langhorne into the office and shut the door. The consul looked over the paper quickly and raised his eyebrows.

"I have to go. And you'd better get back to your hotel room right away and lock the door. I'd say your leaving town tomorrow will be none too soon."

"How come?"

"Does the name Joaquin Escarra mean anything to you?"

Langhorne shook his head.

Hurley looked grim. "He's the man you killed. And he has relatives in high places."

CHAPTER 11

"For I am come to set a man at variance against his
father, and the daughter against her mother, and the
daughter in law against her mother in law."
Matthew 10:35

"Who is she?"

Fabiana's tone was mildly curious and just as mildly
impatient as she looked across the dining table at her stepmother
the next morning just after nine.

Jester sat two places down the table from Fabiana and
watched the two.

Guadalupe Medina spread marmalade on a piece of toasted
bread as she replied. "Her name is Luna Garcia, and she has
come to work for us."

Jester took a bite of fried egg. A new servant—that shouldn't
interfere with the walk he and Fabiana had planned in the
vineyard on the long slope just outside the walls of the hacienda.

Now he focused on his steak and eggs while mother and
daughter talked. It wasn't easy. Food still didn't sit well except
in small quantities, although things seemed to be getting better.
Fabiana's conversations with Guadalupe sure didn't help matters
either. They couldn't seem to talk without arguing, and Fabiana
was usually the one to instigate the quarrel. Who could
blame them, though, considering what they'd gone through?

"I think we have enough servants without hiring another one," the girl said. "After all, Papa didn't think we needed any more."

Guadalupe frowned momentarily. Then she smiled and said, "It's not just that we need another person to work in the house. I've done it for her good, as well. The poor girl would have ended up in the Valle Nacional or in Yucatan if she hadn't found a safe place."

Fabiana huffed. "We can't save every poor little Mestiza in the country."

"But we can save this one," Guadalupe said evenly. Her eyes darted toward the hall door, and she lowered her voice. "Be civil to her. She has been through a great deal."

"So have I, unless you've forgotten."

Jester kept his eyes on his plate.

A moment later a brown-skinned young woman came cautiously through the door bearing a plate of hot tortillas. She cast her eyes down as she approached the table and set the plate beside Guadalupe. The aroma filled the room, and Jester's mouth watered despite his restless stomach.

"Thank you, Luna," Guadalupe said, smiling warmly at her. "We are so happy that you have been able to come to work for us."

The girl still didn't look up. Nervousness was plain on her face.

"I am very happy to be here, Señora."

Still smiling, Guadalupe turned to Jester. "Señor Langhorne helped Luna and arranged for her to come here to us." She looked back at the girl. "Isn't that right, Luna?"

"Yes, Señora."

Guadalupe indicated Fabiana. "This is my daughter, Señorita Medina." Then she looked toward Jester again. "And this is Señor Jester, the friend of Señor Langhorne."

Luna nodded timidly at both of them.

Jester gave her the broadest smile he had. The poor girl needed to relax. "So you know Señor Langhorne, then, Luna. Tell me, what do you think of him?"

She looked very serious. "He is a great man. He saved me."

She meant it. She actually meant it. What could he say to that? Finally, he grinned.

"Yes, I fancy he does view himself as a kind of Christ figure, if I can use the literary term for it." He glanced at Fabiana. She seemed to be suppressing a smile—that was gratifying. Then he continued with Luna.

"Tell me, did Señor Langhorne mention me?"

For a moment, Luna seemed reluctant to answer. "You are Señor Jester?" She hesitated with the name, pronouncing it more like *Chester.*

"Jester. Yes, indeed, my dear."

She inched backward a bit. "Yes, Señor. He told me about you."

"Oh? What did he say?"

Luna backed away and gave a quick bow. "Excuse me, Señor. I must go back to the kitchen now." With that, she hurried out the door.

Jester smiled—always handy to cover embarrassment. "Well, I hope it wasn't too derogatory."

Guadalupe smiled at him. "She is just nervous. Now, tell me how you are feeling."

"Getting better every day." No need to mention the weakness, the draining fatigue after just a stroll through the patio. He *was* getting better day by day—that was definite—but it was so damnably slow. Still, if a fellow had to go through a period of recuperation, there were worse places—and much less pleasant company—for it.

"Are you walking with Señor Jester today?" Guadalupe asked

her stepdaughter.

"Yes. We're going out to the vineyard."

"There will not be anyone working out there," Guadalupe said.

"I know." The girl smiled. "The patios and the orchard seem so busy lately. Always someone standing around, or walking by." She stared boldly at her stepmother. "Or tending the plants."

Jester focused on Guadalupe. A chaperone would certainly dampen the enjoyment of the walk.

"Be careful," Guadalupe said.

"Oh, I will," Fabiana replied. "But I don't think poor Calvin is recovered enough yet to pose any great danger."

Guadalupe gave a quick little gasp, and the color rose in her face. "Of course, I was talking about wild animals."

"Wolves?" the girl asked.

"Anything that can do harm." She gave Jester a pleasant smile. "Are your injuries healing?"

"Yes. They're coming along quite well, Señora." Guadalupe was a gracious lady and didn't deserve to be baited by Fabiana. A little extra courtesy might provide her some compensation. "I much appreciate your hospitality and kindness."

"I suppose Sofia is still dressing your wounds."

"Every morning and every night." The old woman really had little inborn talent as a nurse. She cleaned his wounds and changed the bandages with about as much tenderness as she displayed when patting a tortilla out of a ball of dough, and she sponged off his body with less finesse than he used when rubbing down his mount at Fort Myer after a morning ride along the Potomac.

"She is a good old soul," Guadalupe said. "She has been here since before Augustin and I were married."

"Since long before," Fabiana said crossly.

Guadalupe paid her no mind. "Sofia is always ready to help."

Jester smiled. "I hope not to be needing much help from now on, Señora." Carlito stopped beside him and poured more coffee. When Jester reached for the sugar, pain stabbed his cracked ribs, and he grimaced through his smile.

Guadalupe touched his forearm for an instant, then just as quickly withdrew her hand. She shook her head sympathetically.

"You have not yet recovered so much, I think." She passed the sugar bowl over to him. "You will need Sofia for a while longer yet."

Fabiana said, "I think he needs the care of someone other than an old woman to make him mend."

"But one who nurses the infirm must be willing to get her hands dirty," Guadalupe said.

"Perhaps, then, Sofia would make a good walking companion, as well, for you," Fabiana said to Jester.

Jester took a drink of his coffee and cocked his head. "No one, Miss Medina, would make such a fine companion as yourself."

The words seemed to please her, and she stood up. "Then, sir, let us get started before you fatigue yourself further with all this conversation."

He smiled at Guadalupe and shrugged. "If you'll excuse us, Señora."

They walked to the French doors and out onto the gallery, then across the main patio to the *zaguan*.

It was before sunrise when Langhorne roused himself from the comfort of his bed. No telling when the first train south toward Mazatlan was, but it would be wise to be on it. He shaved, washed up, and was just getting into a suit and tie when there was a knock on his door.

Langhorne held his revolver behind his back and unlocked the door.

It was Hurley. "Thought I'd wish you a *bon voyage.*"

"Who was this Joaquin Escarra, anyway?"

"Have you ever heard of the *Acordada?*"

Langhorne shook his head.

"It's an organization throughout Mexico, part of the Diaz government," Hurley said. "You know, Sandoval and I told you about the police being involved with the labor agencies and the other corruption. Well, the *Acordada* is part of that. I suppose you could call it a network—a network of assassins."

Langhorne frowned. Things were getting worse with every answer. "Who do they assassinate?"

"Criminals they have no evidence against. Anybody who's inconvenient to the government. Anyone who gets in their way."

"This Escarra was a member?"

Hurley shrugged. "That doesn't make much difference. The important thing is, his brother Rodolfo is the *Jefe de Acordada* for all of Sinaloa and Sonora."

"The head man, huh? I picked a dangerous man to kill."

Hurley nodded. "That's about the size of it."

"But it's part of the Diaz government, and the Diaz government is gone."

"On the national level, yes. But remember what we said about the situation in Culiacan. Diaz people are still in place. The Maderistas haven't made their appearance here yet to take over. But even if they had, the *Acordada* wouldn't just disintegrate. It's a secret network, a powerful organization. Men like that won't give up their power easily."

"Glad I'm leaving town, then."

Hurley nodded. "But watch out. The *Acordada* has long arms."

While Hurley went down to settle the hotel bill, Langhorne pulled his shirts and trousers out of the wardrobe. He hurriedly tossed two pairs of trousers into his trunk but then stopped, pulled the pants back out, and carefully folded them. The bunch that murdered Sandoval weren't going to spook him.

He hired a carriage on the front step of the hotel to take him to the train station. There was no trouble along the way, and he made it aboard the first train toward Mazatlan and points south. He chose a seat in the back corner of the coach, with a clear view of all the other passengers.

The trip south was like the one from Nogales to Hermosillo, stop after stop at tiny stations or crossings, the cars steadily filling up and the temperature, outside and in, rising all along the way. They crossed several rivers as they paralleled the coast, and the humidity clung to his skin like a damp blanket, especially as they neared the Tropic of Cancer.

To pass the time, Langhorne bought a newspaper at one of the stops. The second page had an article about the local government in Mazatlan. Madero's people had taken over in the city and had a garrison of several hundred to keep things under control. A grainy photograph lent credence to the contention, showing one unfortunate Porfirista official against the wall with a half dozen Maderista riflemen poised to end his government career permanently a few seconds after the shutter clicked.

Apparently, that was the way in Mexico these days. The execution at Noria the first day and now Sandoval's assassination both added flesh and blood to the newspaper photograph. It was unclear which faction had done the shooting in Noria— presumably the Maderistas. But did it really matter? Whichever party held the advantage in a town would probably do the same to its opponents. He shook his head. For Mexico the prospects weren't good.

About half an hour of sun remained when the train finally began to slow as it approached the station at Mazatlan. During the last few minutes, Langhorne kept his eyes to the right for glimpses of the Pacific, deep blue to the far horizon and with a highway of brilliant gold running through the middle right toward him from the setting sun.

The same ocean had looked that way, hadn't it, blue and peaceful, eleven years ago, on an ancient transport on his way to the Philippines. It was empty, that vast expanse of water, sunrise after sunrise for weeks. The emptiness in his soul was much greater, though. It was still too soon after Catherine and Amy had passed, the void inside him robbing him of the will to live. Even the will to die. A sleepwalker—that's what he'd been like through those weeks and the months that followed. No interest, no hope in the world. Even his faith had lost its hold during the struggle. He'd never smile again.

And then one day he'd come back. Things just seemed to click into place again. He wasn't the same as before Catherine and Amy died, of course. He never would be. But it started with just tolerating living again. Then enjoying things, little things at first like the taste and smell of hot, black coffee. Who knows how it happened? The important thing was *that* it happened. Thanking God became possible again. Even smiling sometimes.

The locomotive's steam whistle sounded, and the train rolled into the station. It settled to a stop, and Langhorne looked up and down the platform at the rich and poor of Mexico.

He dropped his folded newspaper into the waist pocket of his coat and stepped down off the train. It was too late to go to the consulate. A hotel was what he needed, a good one, and little more than half an hour of fading light remained before night closed in completely. The station was crowded with travelers and vendors, the latter crying out their wares and buttonholing the easiest marks. Langhorne smiled—people from six to sixty hustling to make a living. That living was meager enough—no reason to object to their attempts.

He bought a piece of candied pumpkin from a ragged kid and munched on it while he arranged for a *cargador* to haul his trunk. There were plenty of people—any man among them could be part of that *Acordada*. Too bad they didn't wear nametags. The station had several wide doorways allowing a clear view from inside to the street. Most of the people seemed to be tending to their business, walking, talking. A handful stood here and there, looking out over the crowds like he was. Those were the ones to watch.

A man and woman were speaking English a few yards away, and Langhorne asked them to recommend a good hotel. Then he hailed a carriage and climbed up onto the seat behind the driver. Another man, a younger one, sat next to the driver. Apparently, he was an apprentice learning the trade.

"Hotel Sebastiano," Langhorne said. The driver touched his horse with a long prod, and the animal started into labored movement, its head down. Langhorne glanced back at the station as the carriage rolled away. Nothing seemed out of the ordinary. A tall fellow with curly black hair and a hat pushed back on his head was looking in his direction, but the man turned away quickly. A handful of men, skinny and unkempt in big sombreros, with ammunition bandoleers across their chests and holding a mix of Mausers and Winchesters, lounged by a wagon, making occasional comments when a pretty woman passed by. Probably members of the Maderista garrison mentioned in the newspaper. Had any of them been part of the firing squad in the photograph?

The carriage rolled through streets crowded with people as the workday drew to a close. There was little breeze, and it was still very warm, but Langhorne kept his coat on—his Colt revolver was there in the right waist pocket, next to the newspaper. The weapon wouldn't be going back in the trunk for a while.

The Hotel Sebastiano was situated on a slope that gave more of a glimpse than an actual view of the ocean. That was okay. This wasn't a sightseeing trip. Now there were orders to carry out, and then a return north to the hacienda as soon as possible.

Once he was settled in his room, which was on the front of the hotel, he got out his map of Mexico and spread it on the small table. To the south of Mazatlan, possibly seventy or eighty miles along the rail line, was the border of the Territory of Tepic. Another hundred miles along the route was the city of Tepic, where the railroad ended. East of Mazatlan, maybe a hundred miles and up in the mountains was the city of Durango. A rail line had been started to link the two, but it would probably be years before it was completed.

Langhorne sent down for room service and ordered a beef steak with beans and fried potatoes, plus a pot of coffee. A visit to Tepic might or might not be beneficial. The consul could probably advise him on that tomorrow. Durango was out of the question with no rail connection. Besides, Maddox and Alderman would almost certainly cover that city on their trek through the central part of the country. So what more was there for him to do than retrace his steps back up through Culiacan and into Sonora to the Medina ranch? Not very satisfactory from a reconnaissance perspective—there was so much more of Mexico and its rail system to reconnoiter—but the impenetrable line of the Sierra Madre made that all but impossible from this western coast.

His dinner arrived shortly. The steak really hit the spot. It was the first real meal he'd had the entire day. He read a couple of chapters in the Book of Judges in his Bible while he finished the pot of coffee. One statement repeated several times in the book seemed to stand out—"In those days there was no king in Israel: every man did that which was right in his own eyes." A lot like Mexico now, with neither Diaz nor Madero in real control.

He stretched and yawned. He'd find the consul first thing in the morning. Just before he turned off the lamp to climb into bed, he walked over to the window and pulled the curtain aside. The street was barely visible through the glare on the window, with a flickering gaslight directly across from the hotel. Someone was leaning against the lamppost. Langhorne reached over and turned out his lamp, then looked outside again.

It was a man, a tall one, under the streetlamp. He had dark, curly hair and a hat pushed back on his head.

CHAPTER 12

"And the damsel was very fair, and cherished the king,
and ministered to him: but the king knew her not."

I Kings 1:4

Jester was already awake when the rap on his door came. He'd come to recognize Sofia's knock, and this was it.

"Come in," he called, loudly enough for the old woman to hear it from the other side of the door. The routine had become predictable. There would be the sponge bath, which bordered on embarrassment, then the cleaning of his wounds with the hacienda's wine—one of the poorer vintages—and finally fixing new bandages in place. Some of the wounds probably wouldn't need bandages for more than another day or two; they were healing well, and the redness around the stitches was fading every day.

The door slowly opened about halfway, and the old woman peeked around it with her distinctive smile that showed a gap where one tooth had been lost. She might not have the gentlest way with her nursing, but the old girl certainly had a good heart. He gave her a sleepy grin and motioned her in with a *Buenos días.*

Sofia came around the door toward his bed, but she wasn't alone. Guadalupe followed after and stopped by the foot of the bed. She looked a little embarrassed—like him. At least the bedcovers were still up to his neck. On the other hand, though, he ought to stand up in the lady's presence. No, he'd stay covered.

"Good morning, Señor," Guadalupe said diffidently. "Please excuse this intrusion, but I wanted to speak with you for a moment."

What could it be about? Perhaps she was growing impatient with his presence at the hacienda. Or maybe it was Fabiana. If Guadalupe tried to keep them apart, the girl was likely to throw a fit. He might, too, for that matter.

Her smile put him a little more at ease. "Señor Jester," she said, "I know that Sofia is not skilled at tending the sick and that she sometimes could be more gentle."

Jester glanced at Sofia. She probably didn't understand enough English to be offended by the words. Guadalupe had certainly read his thoughts about the old woman's lack of finesse.

"I thought," Guadalupe continued, "that it would be best to let someone else care for your wounds."

Was she going to take over the bathing and dressing of his wounds herself? That would be exceedingly awkward. But there was another possibility, wasn't there? The most—and least—desirable of all. Fabiana!

It was certain to be a disaster, though, as delightful as it sounded in some ways. There had to be a gracious way to decline without hurting mother's and daughter's feelings.

Just then, Guadalupe motioned to someone behind the half-closed door.

Luna Garcia stepped into view a moment later, her hands clasped at her waist and her eyes looking shyly at the floor.

Jester just stared.

Guadalupe said, "Luna tells me that she cared for her employer's wife for several months when the woman was very ill. She will attend to you until you are recovered." After a few moments she cocked her head and looked quizzically at Jester. "That is, unless you disapprove of my choice."

Jester smiled quickly. "Oh, not at all, not at all, Señora." Of course Guadalupe wouldn't assign her daughter to nurse him, not when they could hardly sit outside at noon without a regiment of chaperones. Apparently, though, custom didn't apply with servant girls; nurses back home certainly didn't operate under such constraints. It just might work out okay.

"Now, I will leave you to them," Guadalupe said, edging toward the door. She spoke rapidly to the girl in Spanish, and Luna nodded gravely in return.

Jester was accustomed enough to the language after the past days that the message was clear—always leave the door ajar when she was caring for him. Then Guadalupe was gone. Looking up at Sofia and Luna as they came to the edge of the bed, Jester felt a bit like a swaddled infant.

Sofia reached out and turned down the bedclothes, then started to unbutton his nightshirt. He pushed her hand away and did it himself. Why hadn't he felt so prudish when Sofia had been there alone?

The women removed his bandages and sponged his upper body, then pulled the sheet and blanket down and washed his feet carefully. After drying him gently—Luna did that part— they started on the wounds with a cloth soaked in wine. Finally, the girl applied new dressings, and with a surer hand than old Sofia. A few quick questions passed between them in Spanish, and then Luna gave a brief, serious nod. Sofia patted her shoulder and hurried out of the room. The entire conversation was almost identical to one lieutenant relieving another as Officer of the Day. The only thing missing was the exchange of salutes.

The girl turned her back while he changed into his trousers, then helped him on with a corduroy shirt. The mornings had turned a bit cooler the past two days, and the heavy fabric ought to feel good in the crisp air. The day before, he and Fabiana had planned another stroll, this time out toward Viejo's shack for this morning after their *desayuno.*

He let Luna button his shirt for him; his fingers on the left hand were still stiff from the struggle with the bear, and she fastened the buttons expertly. He looked at her as she worked— her thick dark hair and large, liquid brown eyes. She wasn't a beauty, at least not in the classical sense like Fabiana. And she seemed so grave all the time—similar to Langhorne in that. He chuckled at the idea.

She looked up at him with that serious expression. Was it disapproval or fear? Her eyes cut for an instant to the open door. It was fear.

"I'm sorry," he said quickly. "You're doing fine."

"Thank you, Señor." She bowed her head for a moment and backed away to arm's length.

"I can manage from here, I think."

"Yes, Señor." She gathered the old bandages and hurried out of the room, shutting the door behind her.

Jester washed his face and combed his hair before walking down the hall to the dining room. Fabiana came in after a few minutes, and over coffee they made small talk, and she told him she'd take him on a picnic the next day.

"It's along a stream where my mother used to take me when I was a little girl," she said.

"It'll be my pleasure to see it."

"We'd eat and then I'd lie down on the grass with my head in my mother's lap and watch the sky." She gave a wistful smile. "I'd always end up falling asleep."

"Now that's something I seem to be doing a lot of lately. Like last night, for instance—I was dead to the world for nine or ten

185

hours. I trust you rested as well as I."

"I had a most unusual dream," she said finally, between bites of a ripe melon.

He waited for several seconds, but she continued eating, so finally he spoke.

"Well?"

She finished her melon and licked each of her fingers in turn, slowly, while she watched him from under her eyelashes. Finally she wiped her hand and mouth on a linen napkin.

"Come, let's walk," she said. "You're not eating anyway."

He followed her out the French doors and limped along beside her across the main patio. One of the hired men at the *zaguan* nodded and called out a greeting as they passed, and Jester wished him a good day in Spanish, for practice—not that his progress so far was impressive.

Fabiana tugged lightly at his sleeve as they went through the gateway, drawing his eyes back to her. They struck out across the rolling meadow in the general direction of Viejo's cabin.

"Don't you want to know my dream?" she asked a little impatiently. "You can talk to the ranch hands anytime." A mischievous glint came into her eyes. "Perhaps you'd feel more comfortable if I told you about it in Spanish. You're becoming so fluent."

He smiled and shrugged, his palms up. "I'm merely trying to accustom myself to your fascinating civilization, my dear. But I fear your story would be lost on me in my present state of ignorance."

"Ha! I think you understand perfectly—whatever I try to tell you. And about my civilization, as you put it—remember, I'm half American."

"Half Mexican, half American. The best of both worlds."

She caught his eye. "Or the worst."

They continued across the grassland in silence. The cool air felt good, and he quickened his pace. Fabiana pointed off obliquely to their left at the thick pines beyond Viejo's shack, and they altered course in that direction.

"Now will you finally hear my dream?" she asked.

"I didn't realize I was the source of the delay." He gave the slightest grin.

"All right, I'll tell you then, if you'll listen."

"Proceed then, Madame."

They entered the trees by the cabin, and she found a thick pine trunk, newly fallen, and sat down, indicating a spot on it for him a few feet away.

She cocked her head to one side, a slight frown on her face as if she didn't know exactly where to begin.

"Well in my dream, I was on the gallery outside the dining room when a bear came walking through the *zaguan,* growling and turning from side to side. He was black and not terribly large but fierce enough looking."

At the mention of the animal, Jester's face and limbs went cold. It was over in a moment or two, but how could the fear still grab hold of him like that?

"Go on, go on," he said quickly. Maybe she hadn't noticed.

"Of all people, Esteban was beside me on the gallery. I don't know why, but we didn't move. We just stood there watching. I didn't really feel any fear at the time. Then I noticed Sofia scrubbing some clothes in a big washtub by the stables. She had her back to the bear and didn't seem to hear him."

Jester focused on her now, and he nodded his head for her to continue.

"For some reason I didn't warn her," she said. "The bear got close to her, and she heard him and turned around. I especially remember the look of terror on her face. It was more vivid than anything else in the dream. She stood up to run but only got a few steps before he was on her, dragging her down. He clawed her with his paws and took her by the neck and shook her like a dog shakes a rat. He opened his mouth and let her fall to the ground, but she was still alive and started to crawl away. He kept following along, pawing her and biting her. I looked over where Esteban had been, but he was gone. My stepmother was nowhere to be seen, either."

The girl stopped there. Jester waited. Was that it? What a disappointment—and gruesome to boot. Of course, he wasn't going to tell Fabiana that.

"Quite a strange dream," he said.

"I haven't told you the strangest part."

She looked into his eyes and held them for several seconds. Those eyes of hers were beautiful, mesmerizing. Who needed any more of the dream? Finally, she blinked though, and that seemed to break the spell.

"The bear turned away from Sofia—I suppose she was dead by then—and started coming toward me, just walking. I remember not being afraid but just standing there, watching while he came on. He walked right up and stopped in front of me, not two feet away. And then he did the oddest thing. He leaned forward and licked my hand, just like one of our hounds." She shrugged. "And that was all. I woke up."

Jester gave a cagey grin. "Tell me, what did you have to eat last night?"

She frowned. "Don't make fun of it. What do you think it means?"

"Why should it mean anything? You're just remembering . . ." What would be the most innocuous words for the attack on him and Fabiana's father? ". . . what happened."

"All dreams mean something," she insisted. "I may not be very religious, but I do believe in dreams."

"Well, then." He hesitated. Was there anything about the dream that might make sense? "Perhaps something's gonna happen to Sofia." Of course that was foolishness, but maybe it would satisfy Fabiana.

She shrugged again, a puzzled look on her face. "I don't know. Dreams usually don't mean what they look like on the surface."

Jester edged closer to her on the log and gave her another grin. "You seem to be quite the interpreter of dreams. We'll start calling you Joseph."

That made her smile. "Besides, if something happened to Sofia, who'd be there to nurse you?"

"Oh, that's already taken care of," he said lightly. "Or didn't you know?"

She frowned. "Know what?"

"Why, the girl that Langhorne sent here. Your mother has assigned her as my new nurse—not that I really need anyone to take care of me now." He grinned again. She'd join in, certainly.

Instead, her frown deepened. "She *would* do something like that. I shouldn't be surprised."

"What's all the fuss? Your mother just—"

"She's my *step*mother!"

"Your stepmother just thought Sofia was clumsy as a nurse, so she assigned the girl to it. What's wrong with that?"

Fabiana stared hard at him. "You don't know?"

"The girl has a way with nursing. She's had experience."

"I'm certain she has!" Fabiana hopped up from the log and started off toward the hacienda without waiting for Jester. He stood up stiffly and followed after her as fast as he could. He had to push to keep up, and his leg hurt from the effort, but he managed to stay abreast of her.

They walked a good distance before Fabiana spoke again.

"You just said you didn't need anyone to take care of you any longer." It was like an accusation. "So why did you agree to it?"

What had gotten into her? And what could he say to mollify her?

Finally, he said, "I was fearful she might try to have you do the nursing."

"Me?" She gave a bitter little laugh. "I'm no servant. Or hadn't you noticed?"

The *zaguan* was close ahead now. That was good. The frantic pace was exhausting, and his leg was starting to really throb. Oh, to sit down and rest, with a hot cup of Carlito's coffee— that and silence.

"I've noticed it, all right," he said hotly. The words were out, too late to take back. What kind of Pandora's box had he opened now? He reached out to touch her arm. Would she forgive him if he asked, or just chew him up one side and down the other?

Instead, her beautiful face contorted, on the verge of tears. He shook his head. What a swine he was to do that to her. She was just a girl, after all, despite what she tried to pretend.

"I'm very, very sorry," he said, reaching out to get her to stop and to look at him. She shook off his hand and kept walking, through the gate and straight for the front door of the house, obviously fighting the tears down as she went.

Someone was standing on the gallery, watching their approach—Esteban Velasquez. That was just great. He stepped off the tiles and strode toward them, his eyes like fire. He stopped and held his arms open to Fabiana, but she brushed past without a word and hurried into the house.

Esteban caught Jester's arm and brought him to an abrupt stop, but Jester shook off the cur's grip and continued on into the house.

Fabiana was gone, probably to her room, and there was certainly no following her there. He walked on to his own bedroom, but all he could do was stand there. His leg ached. Sleep would at least give his mind and body some relief, but who was he kidding? Sleep wouldn't come now, not for a long time. He glanced around the room. This was no time to be cooped up within four walls.

Fabiana had brought him a stack of books yesterday, ones that had belonged to her real mother. Now he grabbed one from the stack without looking and hurried out, bound for the back door. He dropped into a chair on the gallery facing the private patio. How had he managed to ruin things so badly?

Ten or fifteen minutes of desultory reading didn't help much. The book was *Great Expectations*. He'd read it several times before, but now it took ten minutes to get past the first page. Dickens wasn't exactly the thing to bring a person out of the doldrums. Finally he set the volume down on a table. The soft scrape of a footstep sounded on the tile behind him.

"I hope I am not disturbing you, Señor Jester," Guadalupe said. She had a smile like a doctor checking on his patient.

"Not at all, Ma'am." He started to push himself to his feet.

"Please." She motioned for him to sit back down.

That was kind of her. If she didn't already know of his trouble with Fabiana, she would soon. That would burden her further. Her husband was only days in the grave, but good old Calvin Jester was there flirting with her stepdaughter and causing friction at a time when the two women needed each other more than ever. For some reason Langhorne came to mind again. The man would never have caused his hostess pain. Oh, to hell with Langhorne! Why did he always have to be there, even in his absence, setting impossible standards like some saint of old?

"Señor Jester. Señor."

Her words brought him back with a start.

"Sorry, Ma'am."

"Your walk fatigued you then?" Her expression said she knew there'd been trouble.

"Everything seems to fatigue me these days. I apologize for

imposing on your hospitality for so long, Señora. I expect to be on about my business in a short while." That might be too optimistic a forecast, as slow as his strength was returning, but being an invalid was no fun. Leaving wouldn't be either, though—not now, anyway. The hacienda was an oasis—or maybe a Garden of Eden. Complete with a young Eve.

"You are welcome to stay with us as long as you like, even after you are recovered," Guadalupe said, and her sincerity was obvious. She sat down on a bench facing him. "I believe your being here may be the only thing keeping my daughter from breaking down under grief."

Jester smiled. Her words put things in a better light.

"I must confess," she said, "that at first I worried about her spending so much time with you. In this country it is not customary for a young lady to keep company with a gentleman when there is no one to watch over them."

"I've become aware of your custom, and I promise you I'll not go with Fabiana again without a proper chaperone." Not so enjoyable, but Guadalupe deserved the consideration.

There was movement to his left, and he and she turned to look. Esteban had stopped on the gallery, staring at them. He turned without a word and disappeared back around the house.

Guadalupe shook her head. "No, there is no need for chaperones. Sometimes I think we are captive to our customs. *You* are an honorable man, Señor." She glanced back at the corner where her brother had been.

Jester nodded once to her. "I thank you for your confidence in me. I won't betray your trust."

"I'm certain you will not." Her face looked troubled again. Finally she said, "As for any more permanent understanding between you and my daughter—that would pose substantial difficulties, as I'm sure you comprehend."

A permanent understanding? With Fabiana, who could think

beyond the pleasures of the moment? But now the idea was out in the open. Marriage—it had always kept its distance, something that might happen "one of these days." But now— what a spooky thought.

"I suppose it'd have its difficulties," he said. What would it be like being married to Fabiana? Not the romantic physical part—a delightful prospect—but the practical aspects. His family, for instance. They were still back in the world before the war. Mother embracing a half-Mexican daughter-in-law? That'd be the day. And bachelorhood did have its advantages. But still . . .

CHAPTER 13

"Let us meet together in the house of God, within the
temple, and let us shut the doors of the temple: for they
will come to slay thee; yea, in the night will they come to
slay thee." Nehemiah 6:10

Last night's danger didn't seem nearly as great in the first rays
of morning sunlight. Langhorne spent a restless night, lying
awake for long stretches listening, but now in bright daylight
the fatigue and stress evaporated. Immediately upon getting out
of bed, he checked the street out front from his window. People
were moving to and fro on the sidewalks, but no likely sentinels
leaned against lampposts, or anywhere else, for that matter.
Still, the man out there had been flesh and blood, and the odds
were far better than even that he'd been sent by the *Acordada*.

After shaving and dressing, he buckled the revolver around
his waist. It had a reassuring feel to it. He looked in the mirror.
The weapon wasn't readily noticeable under his coat. Then he
removed the chair he'd wedged under the door knob last night
and went down to breakfast.

There was a guest telephone at the front desk of the Hotel
Sebastiano, and after his eggs and toast, Langhorne went to
give the consulate a ring. Hurley up in Culiacan had said he'd
contact the U.S. consul in Mazatlan, a man named Bryce Perriman, to tell him of Langhorne's mission and apprise him of the

trouble with the *Acordada*.

When the call went through and the clerk handed the telephone to him, Langhorne found himself talking to a male secretary at the consulate. Perriman, it seemed, was out of Mazatlan for the morning but would try to meet with Langhorne that evening, if all went well. In the meantime, the secretary said, he might try to contact Horace Walters, owner of a local shipping business and, at times when Consul Perriman was unavailable, a U.S. consular agent. That sounded good since Walters would be exactly the kind of man who could give him the information Colonel Powell was looking for. It took the hotel clerk ten minutes before he got a connection with Walters at his office near the waterfront, but once made, the consular agent's voice came through the receiver clearly, almost as if he were in the same room.

"This is Walters. What can I do for you?" He sounded impatient, a busy man.

Langhorne introduced himself. How could he convince this busy man to take time to meet him without letting the hotel clerk and everyone else loitering around the front desk learn more than they should about his confidential business? Lunch would be the simple solution, where they could "discuss a business matter." After all, everybody had to eat.

Walters was surprisingly amenable to the invitation. He suggested they meet at the American-European Lodge, an establishment whose members were foreign businessmen in Mazatlan and usually referred to the place simply as the "Gringo Club."

Langhorne found the Gringo Club situated on the Loma Linda heights. The elevation gave the club a remarkable view of virtually the entire city, including the harbor and dockyards on the bay east of the peninsula, plus the open blue Pacific just to the west.

Langhorne waited in the club's drawing room until Walters

arrived a few minutes later. The businessman gave the impression of being in a perpetual hurry, something a little out of place in a town like Mazatlan, known for a slow pace and relaxed atmosphere. He was a tall, overweight fellow with a florid complexion. He was sweating under his coat and tie, and the hand he held out to Langhorne was damp, but he had a good solid grip.

They found a table near the huge picture window in the dining room, and Walters settled his considerable bulk into a chair that barely contained him. A short Mexican waiter in white shirt and bow tie brought the day's menu cards and glasses of water and stood by discreetly to take their orders.

"Seafood's the thing here in Mazatlan," Walters said as Langhorne looked over the limited offerings on the menu. Walters nodded toward an adjacent table where a lone man was spearing boiled shrimp with a small fork and dipping them in red sauce en route to his mouth. "Best shrimp I've had anywhere," Walters said. He pointed to the east where the sheltered waters of the Bahia Darsena sparkled beyond the city. "The fishing boats are out now, most of them, but they'll be back in by late afternoon, and they tie up on that side of town. Nothing like fish right off the boat. The cooks here get it every day, and they really know how to fix it."

He recommended a dish of snapper baked in orange juice plus another called *camarones escorpionados,* named thus because the cooked shrimp resembled scorpions with tails curved to strike. That was what the man at the neighboring table had been enjoying.

A couple of meat dishes were on the menu, but Walters looked like he knew good food, so Langhorne followed his recommendations.

"Pretty sight, isn't it?" Walters said, looking east at the bay again. "Kind of empty at the moment, though."

Langhorne gazed out over the water. The only vessel of any size was a battered steamer maybe 200 feet long that looked like it had seen better days. A score of smaller craft were tied up or swung to their anchors.

"That's the *Miraflores,* the steamer there at anchor," Walters said.

Langhorne smiled. "I don't think I'd trust that one to cross the Pacific." Or even the bay.

"Oh, she just runs up and down the coast between here and Guaymas," Walters explained. "Carries whatever cargo her skipper can scare up, anything that turns a profit. Scheduled to weigh anchor and head back north late tonight, if I'm not mistaken."

"Sounds like you know what's going on in the harbor," Langhorne said.

"It's my bread and butter. We have bigger ships come in fairly often, though, but not on a regular schedule. Freighters mostly. You see those warehouses there in the dockyards?" He pointed in the direction of a cluster of commercial buildings near the water.

"Yeah."

"I own 'em." He said it with unmistakable satisfaction. "They bring in quite a handy profit, too. If somebody wants to store a big cargo in the port of Mazatlan, they usually have to come to me."

"Not a bad position to be in."

"You're damn right," Walters agreed. He pulled out a cigarette case and offered it to Langhorne, who declined. Walters struck a match and lit his cigarette. "We had three U.S. Navy destroyers in port this past week. Left yesterday. Those boys really painted the town." He laughed. "Probably helped the *menudo* vendors do a brisk business."

Langhorne chuckled. So it was the same here. A lot of

Mexicans on the border swore the spicy tripe stew was a sure cure for a hangover.

Their food arrived at that point, and as they ate, Langhorne steered the conversation into the subject of possible U.S. intervention. That exchange took the better part of an hour, during which Walters kept shoveling in the food—shrimp, snapper, potatoes, bread, salad, fruit, and caramel custard. Langhorne suppressed a smile. Not many men could've held their own with the fat fellow in an eating contest, nor were there many who seemed to find as much enjoyment in listening to themselves hold forth on U.S.–Mexican relations. But the man wasn't bad company despite all that. He certainly knew good food. And there was no doubt he thought American intervention would be inevitable.

They went out to a sunny terrace ringed by potted palms, where Walters lit a cigar and pointed out what looked like some kind of factory.

"That is perhaps the most important business in Mazatlan." Then he grinned. "The Pacifico brewery. I've managed to cultivate a *beneficial friendship,* shall we say, with the owners. Nothing like a cool bottle on a hot afternoon."

Langhorne drew him out about the Mexican rail system in the region. Walters proved to be the perfect man to question on that subject, being as experienced with rail transportation as he was with ocean shipping. Moving freight by rail was fairly efficient in the region, Walters told him, with a good network of tracks and sidings. The passenger system was better than in most parts of Mexico, too, and there was even a nightly sleeper train to Tepic, a rarity in the country. "Things don't always make sense down here," Walters explained.

Langhorne kept his notes brief and cryptic, as he'd done in earlier cities. Should he let Walters in on his real assignment? That would be a gamble, but the fellow finally asked him point blank if he was on business for Uncle Sam. Why hide the fact any longer?

"I figured you for a government man all along." Walters blew out a huge cloud of cigar smoke. It drifted over the terrace and on toward the open Pacific on a faint breeze.

"I'm sure I can trust you to keep it under your hat," Langhorne said.

Walters smiled broadly. "I may not control my appetite, and I may talk about myself too much, but I know how to keep my mouth shut when it matters, my friend."

"Good enough for me." Now there was one more subject to mention. Langhorne glanced right and left—no one else on the terrace was within earshot. "What can you tell me about the *Acordada*?"

"Huh?" Walters looked genuinely puzzled.

"The secret police."

"Oh, yeah. I've heard of them." He shrugged. "Never have bothered me. What about them, anyway?"

"I had a run-in with 'em back in Culiacan." Langhorne spent the next ten minutes describing the rescue of Luna Garcia and the fight with the three assassins.

Walters seemed to be amused by the whole story. He chuckled. "Cracked his head like Humpty Dumpty, eh? Served him right. So who was he?"

"I hear he was the brother of the *Jefe de Acordada* for Sonora and Sinaloa. A man named Escarra."

Walters nodded a few times. "I've heard the name. A man in my business here has to shell out a few pesos to the 'protectors of society' every now and again. Never had any dealings directly with him, but his errand boys have picked up some cash from me a few times. It's just the way business gets done down here."

For an instant the image of Sandoval lying in his own blood flashed across Langhorne's mind. "Yeah. I've seen the way business gets done here."

Walters stopped smiling. "That was Culiacan. You don't think they've followed you here, do you?"

"Followed, or wired to their boys here. I think a fellow trailed me from the station to the hotel last night, then stayed around to watch my room."

"Which hotel?"

"Sebastiano."

Walters brightened. "Oh, you travel in style."

"Less likely to get your throat cut in a nice place."

"I doubt if you've got much to worry about as long as you're there. The place is crawling with Maderistas, and they don't have much in common with old Diaz secret police."

There had been a number of soldiers at the hotel, now that Walters mentioned it. "What are the Maderistas doing there?"

Walters chuckled. "There was a hot little fight out at the *cuartel* when Madero's folks took over in town. Only lasted about fifteen minutes, but they shot up the barracks pretty good. While it's being repaired, most of the Maderista officers are living at your hotel."

"Sounds like they travel in style, too."

"Ha. When your side has all the guns, it's amazing how cheap you can get a hotel suite."

Langhorne smiled. "I suppose so. They can have my room in another day or so."

"Pulling out, huh? Your business will be done that quick?"

"Doesn't take long to get a little information. And I don't seem to be very welcome, at least with one element of the local population."

"You're really worried about that *Acordada,* or whatever you called it."

"Remember, they beat a good man to death right beside me."

"Yeah, you've got a point there, I suppose. Just stick to the hotel and the main streets, wherever you see the soldiers, and you ought to be all right. That's my advice."

It sounded like good counsel. Keep the eyes open and the revolver ready and stay out of dark alleys.

Walters leaned back in his chair and stretched, yawning. "After a lunch like that, I could take a good nap."

Langhorne looked around the terrace and out over the city and the blue water beyond. It was beautiful, no doubt about it, and the sun was warm on his back.

"Looks like a nice place for a person to retire."

Walters laughed softly. "No man ever said truer words. Mexico is a narcotic, my friend."

Langhorne purposely followed the busiest streets on his way back across town toward the hotel. On one stretch of several blocks, though, a pair of men seemed to follow wherever he went—crossing a street at the same spot that he had, stopping whenever he did, pretending to peer into shop windows if he glanced back in their direction. Wasn't one of them the man with the dark curly hair from last night? Hard to tell. Finally, Langhorne turned quickly and caught them both staring at him. They averted their eyes immediately, but that clinched it.

But what about their intentions—were they looking for a place to waylay him or merely keeping him under observation for future action? He'd done plenty of hunting through the years, but being the quarry was no fun. On the other hand, the roles of hunter and hunted could change in an instant.

Things were already uncomfortable in Mazatlan, despite the apparent safety of the hotel. If he stayed much longer, either his pursuers would grow bolder and come after him, or he'd make a mistake and play into their hands. Leaving town soon was essential, but which way? Returning to Culiacan would put him smack in the center of the *Acordada* in the region, and the local authorities were still Diaz men. Heading south to Tepic might make sense, although it, too, had drawbacks. Maybe there was a better way.

The consul might be able to help, and it was worth the risk of detouring a couple of blocks. He found the consulate easily enough. Mazatlan was not a difficult place to navigate. The male secretary greeted him at the door.

"Yes, sir, I remember talking with you," the man said. "I'm afraid Consul Perriman isn't here now. He came by for half an hour after he got back in town, but then he had to go on to his home. However, he said he'll meet you at your hotel at five."

"That'll be okay. Will he be back here before then?"

"He said he would."

"Good." It might not be prudent to wait. He looked at the man's desk. "I need to leave the consul a note." The secretary handed him a pad and pencil, and Langhorne began to write. When he finished, he folded the note in half. "Please make sure he gets it as soon as possible."

"As soon as he gets back, sir."

"Thanks." From the street door, Langhorne checked in both directions and started off. The office was on a corner of two busy streets, so the two men who'd followed him couldn't trap him between them. Sure enough, there they were again, together behind him, walking fast, and he hurried on to keep his lead.

By the time he got within a couple of blocks of the hotel, a number of Maderista soldiers were on the streets, and he relaxed a little. The two men were within half a block, but then they hung back and let him widen his lead. He reached the front door of the hotel and glanced back, but they were nowhere to be seen.

At ten minutes to five, Langhorne left his room and went downstairs to meet Perriman. A number of Maderista officers were in the lobby or going in to eat. The dining room was half full, and he got an out-of-the-way table near the back. A dark-haired man with the look of an American walked into the dining room a few minutes later and looked around until Langhorne caught his eye.

"Consul Perriman?" Langhorne asked when the man stopped in front of the table.

"And you must be Langhorne," Perriman said, extending his hand.

Langhorne wasn't very hungry—the big lunch at the Gringo Club and the prospect of trying to leave Mazatlan that night had his stomach tied up—but he ordered a good meal anyway, and Perriman did the same.

After the waiter brought their drinks and a salad, Langhorne said, "I'm glad you got my note early in the afternoon. I was worried you might not get back to the consulate today."

"That was quite an unusual list," Perriman said, with a wry expression. "I won't ask what all of it was for. I just hope everything was satisfactory."

Langhorne nodded. "Completely."

Perriman passed an envelope to Langhorne under the overhanging linen tablecloth. "Your money and the map," he whispered.

Langhorne nodded again and slipped it into a pocket of his trousers. "I was running a little short."

"So I gathered. Hurley up in Culiacan wired me yesterday about your situation—some Diaz big shot you got on the wrong side of—and told me to be ready to help."

Langhorne frowned. "Think there's much chance my friends got a look at that wire?" Hurley had been right about the long arms of the *Acordada*—the man with the curly hair had proven that.

"No chance at all. It was enciphered."

"You need to see my bona fides? The letter's in my belt, and I'd rather not have to dig it out here."

Perriman waved away the suggestion. "No need."

Langhorne checked his wristwatch. "You have the time?"

The consul grinned as he swallowed a mouthful of salad. "You don't trust that thing, huh?" Then he pulled out a gold pocket watch and popped open the cover. "Five twenty-three."

Langhorne smiled. "Just checking. This one keeps good time."

Their entrees arrived shortly, and they spent the next quarter hour eating and talking. Langhorne got all the information he could from Perriman about the situation in Mazatlan and the likelihood of U.S. intervention.

"Wish I could've talked to a few more Americans here," he said.

"But that's not as important as saving your skin."

Langhorne grinned. "You've got a point there." He folded his napkin and stood up. "And now, if you'll excuse me, I have a train to catch."

The consul stood up, too, and shook hands with Langhorne. "Good luck."

Langhorne nodded and walked off through the maze of tables.

A man eating with a companion at a table near the door followed Langhorne with his eyes as the latter left the dining room. So that was the one.

The man's companion, a bit shorter but solid, and with a pockmarked face, spoke softly in Spanish.

"Shall we follow now?"

The tall man kept his eyes on the doorway. "Of course. Get us a carriage, Pablo."

"Yes, Señor Escarra."

★ ★ ★ ★ ★

Langhorne had already sent his trunk downstairs before dinner, and now he checked out of his room and flagged down a carriage outside the hotel. Once the trunk was hefted aboard, he climbed up and told the driver to take him to the train station. The carriage moved off slowly, but he asked the driver to hurry, and that resulted in a somewhat brisker walk.

The sun was fast sinking to the western horizon, and Langhorne tipped his grey Stetson down almost to his eyes—the glare was bad. They rolled past people strolling lazily on both sides of the street and skirted the occasional parked oxcart or wagon. He should've left the hotel ten minutes sooner. The train south to Tepic would pull out around sunset, at least according to Walters.

Langhorne kept his eyes moving. Plenty of people were on the streets, many of them probably trying to get home before night fell. His carriage didn't pass a single automobile. That was fine—the contraptions weren't good for much except making him nervous. Thank goodness trains didn't have the same effect.

By the time the station finally came into view, the look of the people on the streets had changed. Men in coats and ties were almost completely absent now, replaced by those in the loose white cotton shirts and pants of the poor. The grimy *pulquerias* and cantinas were busy, though. Langhorne chanced a quick glance over his shoulder. Sure enough, among the pedestrians half a block back was the man with the curly black hair, his hat still pushed back on his head. Not very secretive, but maybe he figured he didn't need to hide.

The last rays of the sun were fading from a two-story building nearby when the carriage pulled up in front of the train station and the driver wrestled Langhorne's trunk to the pavement. Langhorne got a *cargador* to bring the trunk into the

205

station and wait while he got his ticket for Tepic—one of the sleeper compartments. The clerk told him to hurry because the train was getting ready to depart.

He found a compartment in one of the forward cars and settled in, having the *cargador* stow the trunk beside one of the seats. He tried to lock the door to the hallway, but the lock was broken, so he wedged the trunk under the door handle.

He sat on the threadbare forward seat, facing aft with a good view of the people boarding some of the cars. Quite a few were getting on, some rough looking characters among them. Which ones might mean him harm? That was anybody's guess, but some of them sure did. Maderista soldiers would've been a welcome sight, but there didn't seem to be any on this particular train.

Langhorne checked his wristwatch. It was six fifteen and darkness had already fallen outside even though the sun couldn't have been down more than a few minutes. Just like the Philippines—anywhere in the tropics, it seemed.

The train jerked and then started slowly forward. A series of lurches jarred his back as the slack between cars was taken up. He switched to the forward-facing seat and looked up the track. Only a few very faint lights were visible ahead beyond the locomotive, and they were far out to the side of the tracks. It looked like they were heading into a void.

The train crept along, starting and stopping, for ten or fifteen minutes before it had covered even two kilometers. By that time a nearly full moon had edged up over the distant mountains to the east. In a few more miles, the train would turn south onto the main line paralleling the coast.

Rodolfo Escarra leaned against the rail on the dark rear platform of the last car with his subordinate Pablo Sotero and carefully cut the tip from a slim Cuban *figurado*. He drew the cigar along his upper lip, inhaling the aroma, and the tracks behind slowly receded. The train finally began to accelerate.

Escarra reached into his pocket and pulled out a matchbox. Only one match remained, and he tossed the empty box away. He drew the match across the sole of his boot, but the stick broke, so he flicked it off the platform onto the track bed below.

"Here, Señor," Sotero said as he hurriedly pulled out a box of his own. He struck a match, and it flared into life, bathing their faces momentarily in yellow light. Escarra took the match carefully in his left hand and let it burn off the brimstone for a second or two. Then he held it close to the end of the cigar, slowly rotating the latter in his right hand above the tiny flame until the end was charred evenly. Finally, Escarra put the cigar in his mouth and carefully drew the flame in until the tobacco was fully alight. He held the first mouthful of smoke for several seconds, then blew it out with a sigh. That was the way to enjoy a fine cigar.

Sotero cleared his throat. Escarra just leaned on the rail. He drew in another satisfying mouthful of smoke. Before the night was out, there would be other satisfactions. Sotero finally spoke, slowly and with obvious deference.

"Should we take him now, *Jefe*? Aguirre and Lopez are watching his door."

Escarra still didn't look at the man. "All in good time, Pablo, all in good time."

He had worked out the plan quickly, once it was clear the Gringo—his name was Langhorne, Vega said—was taking the Tepic train. The man's light-colored hat had made it easier to keep him in sight even on the long, crowded station platform until he climbed aboard one of the forward sleeping cars. Escarra had simply decided to board the same train, along with Sotero and his other two who'd been following the man on foot, and deal with him when conditions were favorable. It had been very lucky that none of the Maderista troops were on the train. That would've made things more difficult. As it was, he'd delay any action until the train was about to pull into Rosario, sixty kilometers away and the only stop on the route. By that point they'd be far beyond any interference from the Maderistas in Mazatlan. Rosario was too small to warrant a garrison, and it would be late enough when they pulled in that few people would be at the station anyway. He and his three would force their way into the man's compartment and hustle him off the train with as little noise as possible. Once the train pulled out again, they'd find a quiet place and take care of business. Simple. And final.

The train's speed had leveled off at only about twenty-five kilometers per hour. No wonder it took the whole damned night to reach Tepic. That would mean maybe two and a half hours to Rosario. No matter—he had several cigars.

For the next few minutes he leaned on the rail, watching the tracks recede behind the train. The cigar was relaxing—they always were. Finally, he looked over at Sotero. The man couldn't carry on a very intelligent conversation, but at least he'd usually shut up and listen.

"Joaquin was my brother, you know. My little brother." Instantly he had Sotero's attention. Escarra took a long puff on the cigar then blew the smoke out slowly, looking off into the night. "I remember the times we played together as children. We were poor growing up."

Sotero seemed about to reply, but Escarra gave him no chance.

"We'd pick up grains of corn off the ground, sometimes dig it out of cow dung, believe it or not, to take home to our mother, just so we would have a tortilla at night. One tortilla! You don't forget those things." He smiled at the long lost memory. "We used to sling each other around by one arm. We'd get dizzy and stumble and fall." As he said those words, he stopped smiling and stared hard at the blackness. "And that damned Gringo—Langhorne—he slung Joaquin into a wall and broke his skull open!"

The power behind those last few words seemed to shake Sotero, hard man though he was, for his eyes opened a little wider and stared. After several seconds, he stammered out some nonsense about the killing of Sandoval.

Escarra turned on him. "I don't care about that! The circumstances don't matter!" He made himself take a deep breath. He said the next words very slowly, barely above a whisper. "I want him."

Sotero stood by the rail, gripping it so hard his knuckles showed white in the moonlight.

Escarra took another deep breath. He put the cigar to his lips again and drew deeply on it. That was better.

They spent the next minutes in silence, still leaning against that back rail while the night rolled past to either side of the train. The moonlight lay across the roadbed like a cool blanket, making it almost as clear as if it had been day. Escarra finished the cigar and tossed it away.

Sotero pulled a revolver from his coat pocket and checked the cylinder. Apprehension was plain on his face.

"Don't worry, Pablo," Escarra said, with heavy irony. "The Gringo won't bite." He spat over the side. "And yes, I have a pistol, too. But I don't want to use it. I want to use this." He dug into his coat pocket and produced a cord garrote, always his favorite for the special jobs. There was something about the feel of it, wound tight around a man's throat, biting into flesh and arteries and windpipe, as if he were reaching into his victim and ripping the life out of him.

He looked back out, idly watching the ground alongside the tracks. Then he saw it, a dark shape moving slowly in the moonlight. The contour of a man, and not just any man—a tall man with a light-colored hat on his head. Langhorne—it had to be!

Escarra grabbed Sotero's wrist and held a finger to his own lips. He waited until the man beside the tracks was twenty meters away before whispering in Sotero's ear.

"He's off the train, there, behind us. You see his hat?"

Sotero stared into the night and finally, softly said, "Yes! I will go get Aguirre and Lopez."

"No," Escarra whispered. "There's no time. He'll be gone in the night."

"Then let's get him." Sotero started to put a leg over the rail.

"Wait! I don't think he's seen us. If he does, he'll run into the darkness, and we may never find him. Let us get a hundred meters away and then follow." It was a gamble. Wait too long and they might completely lose contact with the man, but spooking him now would be as bad or worse. He mustn't learn that they were following. "Wait . . . wait." Finally the right moment came. Escarra slipped over the rail and dropped to the track bed, followed by Sotero. For a few seconds Escarra just crouched there. Fortune was smiling.

Far ahead was a spot of dull white, blurred by the night—the light-colored hat. And it was moving. The man was walking, back down the track toward the station. And he didn't know. Slowly Escarra followed, leading Sotero off several meters to the side of the track, so the Gringo would be less likely to spot them against the reflection of moonlight on the rails if he looked back.

"We're losing him!" Sotero whispered as a long curve in the track hid the man from view.

"Hunting men is my living, Pablo. Have patience." The poor fellow was capable enough in his own way and tough, but he had no idea of how to trail the prey. Escarra smiled. Patience, always patience—that's what had rewarded him. Even the Old

Man himself had called him the best manhunter he'd ever known. Escarra's eyes shone. The Old Man had actually called him that.

"Escarra," he'd said, "I am the master at forcing men to my will, but you—you are the master at hunting them." It was the time when he'd captured the traitor Aguinaldo after a pursuit of five days, first across the mountains and then the last day through the streets and alleys of Hermosillo—winding, backtracking, hurrying, creeping in turn, until at last the man had made his mistake. When it happened, Escarra closed the trap. Aguinaldo, the proud general, reduced to a whimpering, pleading woman of a man, as Escarra transported him back to face Porfirio Diaz. The traitor was shot on the spot. Escarra would've used the garrote.

Now he maintained the distance for ten minutes at least. Fortunately Langhorne hadn't left the tracks and struck out across country. They were getting back to the edge of town, with houses and other buildings more numerous and the smells and sounds of cooking, singing, laughing, and crying. Another ten long minutes and they were close to the station again. The American was going to march right back there, it seemed. Didn't the fool realize there were *Acordada* men waiting there?

After five more minutes, they were in the city proper again. The dim yellowish glow of the station lights was there, perhaps four hundred meters ahead.

Escarra's heart jumped—the familiar white blur was suddenly gone! Langhorne must've left the track bed and turned in among the houses. Escarra gritted his teeth. That would teach him to watch the ground instead of the man! And Sotero was no help—he hadn't been watching at all.

Escarra focused on the spot where he thought he'd last seen the man, and he hurried toward it. Had the Gringo seen them and bolted, or just randomly changed his course? Probably just changed direction. Escarra led on to the spot of his last sight-ing, stopped there, and leaned close to Sotero's ear.

"No more talking until I tell you."

It was a brushy alleyway between two houses, and he moved down it slowly. No sense in blundering into an ambush. Lang-horne was a dangerous man. And he'd avoided returning to the station. He might be lying in wait for them now, ready to spring on them quickly and silently—probably not, but maybe. Escarra kept one hand on the pistol in his pocket, just in case.

Joaquin had been a good brother—mean as hell sometimes and not always loyal, but blood meant a lot. The memory sent a surge of heat through his body, and he clenched his teeth and went on. Balance care with speed—the man could lose them quickly among the buildings of Mazatlan. Speed was more important now. They had to spot him again soon—yes, better split up.

At the first street, there was no sign of the man. Escarra sent Sotero forward along a side street while he drifted right, to meet two or three blocks ahead. The center of the city lay in that direction. The Gringo had to be moving that way, but he wouldn't know the city well.

Escarra knew the main landmarks, though. He and Pablo could move faster. And the lights from homes and cantinas here made for better visibility now, those and the blessed full moon. They'd catch sight of the man again soon. They had to.

When they converged again, Sotero waved desperately and pointed left at an angle. Escarra hurried to join his subordinate as quietly as possible. The sound of running footsteps could carry far in the night air. He was breathing hard when he reached Sotero, but that was all right. His luck had held. There was the light-colored hat, a bit clearer than before and bobbing slightly as the man walked, just seventy or eighty meters ahead.

But where was he going? There had to be a key to his destination. Figure that out, and they could race ahead on flanking streets and be there waiting when the man arrived. He smiled.

Langhorne stopped in front of a small restaurant, the sounds of dishes and conversation drifting out through open windows. He checked his map in the light that spilled from one of the windows. The big Mercado Romero Rubio, also marked with its local nickname, the Iron Palace, should be two blocks ahead, with the city's cathedral a little beyond that—if he was reading it right. Good thing Perriman had been able to draw up the map—one of the items Langhorne had requested in his note. The consul had marked the locations of several of the town's most prominent landmarks—the market and cathedral, the Gringo Club, the big Cerro del Vigia rising over the city near the southern tip of the peninsula, and the Cerveceria del Pacifico, the brewery that Walters liked so much. Those points would be enough to guide him through the dark streets.

He glanced behind him and around in all directions. There were people but no one who seemed to be paying him particular attention. Someone might be following, but if they were, they'd not made it obvious. No, there shouldn't be anybody on his trail now.

The escape from the train had gone fairly well although there were some problems. Shortly after they pulled out of the station, footsteps had come to a stop outside his door. A low exchange of male voices followed, but the words were muffled. The tone was clear enough, though—excited, stealthy, dangerous. Curly head and a friend, probably. Langhorne slipped the revolver out and held his breath, but they didn't even try the door. Maybe five silent minutes followed—the men had to be gone. That was good. A shootout among innocent bystanders wouldn't help.

After the train had traveled a mile or more in its frustrating stop-and-go fashion, the time seemed right to get off. He slid open his compartment window and climbed out, his boots finding a narrow strip of angle iron to stand on while he held to the window frame. That's when things started going wrong. He tried to drop to the ground beside the slowly accelerating train, but his coat caught on something, swinging him into the side of the car and knocking the revolver from its holster. It took him half a minute to free the coat and drop off the train.

He crouched down beside the tracks until the end of the train passed, and then he started back toward the station. He had no luck finding the pistol in the darkness. On the other hand, no one seemed to have seen him get off—no hue and cry, only the diminishing clack, clack, clack of the train as it puffed on toward Tepic. He smiled as he walked along. Whoever had followed him onto that train was still aboard. They were out of the race.

Now, in front of the restaurant, he started again toward the market. After half a block, there it was ahead, and he crossed to the other side of the street to stay out of its lights. Customers and vendors were still doing business under the massive metal roof. The sounds of conversations and haggling grew louder as he approached. Then, when he was abreast of it, he chanced a sudden glance back.

It was only a flash of movement a block back, a person by an alley then gone in the shadows in an instant. Langhorne increased his pace and didn't look back again. Maybe it was nothing—but it had a feel to it, almost like locking eyes with someone across a room.

In another block he reached a cross street, and a man fifty yards to the right ducked quickly into a doorway. Langhorne crossed the street as if he'd noticed nothing, but he cut his eyes right every few moments to see if the fellow reappeared. Sure enough, the man eased out of the doorway but hugged the darkness along a line of closed shops as he moved in Langhorne's direction.

One behind and one to the right—that was the score so far. His heart was beating faster now. Were any more out there on the other flank or up ahead? They might be funneling him into a trap. Time for a change in plan. He cut sharply left before he reached the cathedral, its domes and towers clear against the night sky ahead. The streets were darker in this direction, with far fewer people.

He set a brisk pace but not so fast as to let them know he was aware they were following. They'd realize it anyway if they were any good at this business—and they seemed to be.

He hurried east, block by block. The brewery loomed in the distance, its lights standing out in the darkness, many blocks away, near the bay. It looked different tonight than it had from the terrace of the Gringo Club.

Langhorne had picked up tricks from men and from animals over years of hunting and stalking, and he used most all of them now, but still the two pursuers wouldn't be shaken from the trail. He managed to stay ahead of whichever one happened to be behind him, but the other would invariably appear on the flank, the process steadily eating away at his lead. Twice he had to break from cover and move quickly to avoid being sandwiched between them. Why had he been so careless in losing the pistol? Without it, fighting could only be a last resort.

Finally, he reached a spot in front of a darkened store and stopped for a few moments to catch his breath beside the display window.

Escarra smiled as he hurried along the sidewalk. Things were looking up. Far fewer people were on these streets since the chase had turned east. It was easier to keep Langhorne in view and to distinguish him from the occasional other pedestrians.

Escarra stopped dead. There was the man now! His light-colored hat was like a beacon as he stood in the moonlight in front of a store window. So close—a quick dash ahead would cover the distance in what, twenty or thirty seconds? But that might send the man fleeing, and who knows what would happen then? No—patience.

Sotero was doing well, paralleling the man's route a block away to the left. A commendation might be in order after the hunt was over, maybe a bonus. Escarra scowled—he'd take it out of the salaries of those other two fools of his still on the train. They were probably halfway to Rosario by now and still unaware that the bird had flown.

The Pacifico brewery was only a few blocks away now. Up ahead, Langhorne rounded a corner to the left and was lost from sight. No matter. Escarra would reach the corner in less than two minutes, and Sotero would be coming from the right. They were closing the distance again.

The brewery—that was it! No hotels stood in this part of town, only tumbledown little houses and businesses closed for the night, if you didn't count the few cantinas with their low-class clientele, none of them the kinds of places a Gringo would be bound for. But the brewery—it was well lighted; it had plenty of workers still. A man fleeing for his life naturally gravitated to people and light. Or maybe he'd been going there all along. No matter. Now to trap the man between him and Sotero. It wouldn't take much longer.

He rounded the corner where he'd last seen Langhorne, and he almost laughed out loud. Luck was still with him. The hat was a little farther ahead than before but moving down a long straight stretch pointed right at the brewery three blocks away. Just then Sotero came into view on a side street a block over, and Escarra waved him on violently. If he could get there ahead of Langhorne . . .

Sotero seemed to get the idea and broke into a trot in that direction while Escarra quickened his own pace a bit.

His blood was pumping now, the sure sign that the chase was coming to a climax. A smile came onto his face involuntarily and stayed there, frozen in place. They might not be able to draw out the suffering, given the location, but it would be intense. The man was going to know who was strangling the life from his body, and why.

Escarra bolted to his left and rushed down an alley to get ahead of Langhorne before he reached the brewery. When Escarra came out on the next cross street, he stopped, breathing hard, and looked right. Seconds later, Sotero appeared two blocks over. Langhorne had to be on the street in the middle, coming into view between them shortly. Escarra would be there to greet him on one side, Sotero on the other, pistols drawn, covering him before he could make a move to defend himself. What a look that would bring to the Gringo's face. Escarra would shoot him immediately, a gut shot that would take all the fight out of him but still leave him alive enough to experience the terror and agony Escarra had in mind.

He hurried down the street, pistol in hand, as Sotero approached to meet him. Langhorne should be showing his face any moment now . . . any moment. Escarra slowed as he neared the middle street, and he motioned for Sotero to slow down, too. They both crept forward the last few meters, crouched and ready to spring. When Escarra reached his corner, he slowly peered around it, hardly breathing. Sotero matched his movements on the opposite corner.

A man was approaching, walking at a steady pace, but there was no hat. Was it Langhorne? The man was close enough now for Escarra to make out his size and build. Escarra scowled and rushed out, Sotero hurrying up in support.

It wasn't Langhorne. The man, obviously a local, jumped

when the two rushed out at him, but Escarra made no move to hurt him. After a few seconds' hesitation, the man hurried on in the direction of the brewery, casting furtive glances over his shoulder at Escarra and Sotero.

Escarra saw it now—the dull white spot halfway down the block, in a dark alcove. So the Gringo was there waiting. He probably didn't even know he could be seen. With a growl, Escarra rushed forward, waving Sotero on with him. It didn't even matter if the man emptied a gun at them. Langhorne would die with the name *Joaquin* in his ears!

The hat remained still as they ran forward, and long before Escarra reached the spot, he saw that it sat atop a low stone wall and not a man's head.

Langhorne took a deep breath and leaned against the steel bulkhead in his tiny stateroom. He'd made some big mistakes tonight. He was fortunate to be alive. But things had somehow worked out much the way he'd planned. Thank God, Perriman had gotten the items on the list—money, a map of Mazatlan, a new trunk, two big bundles of rags, and a message for Walters. The consul hadn't even asked him for an explanation.

The stateroom had very little floor space, especially with the new trunk taking up several square feet of it. Where was his old one now? Probably still in his sleeper on the train, filled with the rags to make it feel like clothing—an empty trunk might've made the porters remark on it. He'd packed his clothes in the new one at the hotel and then sent it out the back door by a *cargador* to Walters across town. The fat man, acting on Langhorne's message, had put the trunk aboard the *Miraflores* and booked Langhorne passage to Guaymas. Leave it to a businessman to get it right.

The bulkhead was cold against Langhorne's shoulder through his sweat-soaked shirt. He dug a fresh one out of the trunk and changed. The clean shirt felt good. All in all he'd come out okay—nothing lost in the evening's work but his revolver and the hat.

Where had his pursuers spotted him, though? Right off the train or somewhere along the tracks? He'd been a fool about the hat. Over the past days, it had become almost a part of his body. That store window was a godsend—the hat reflecting the moonlight. He chuckled for a moment. He passed off the hat to one of the rare pedestrians along a stretch out of sight of his pursuers. The fellow must've thought he was loco—ten pesos to take a nice hat two blocks closer to the brewery then leave it in the moonlight where it could be seen. No telling whether the man really left it or simply took it along as an extra dividend, but there was nothing he could do about that.

After that, he'd reversed course and stuck to the shadows and alleys, putting as much distance between himself and the hat as possible, as quickly as possible, while heading toward the docks where Walters had said the local fishermen moored their boats. One of them rowed him out to the steamer's anchorage, promising to continue on to a different spot for the night, so he wouldn't be around for questions if anyone else happened to appear at the docks.

The heavy vibration of the *Miraflores*'s engines shook the steel deck under his feet. The vessel steamed slowly through the Bahia Darsena and around Cerro del Creston to starboard. When he finally showed himself on deck half an hour after she'd weighed anchor, the city stood on the starboard beam, its dim lights twinkling a mile or two away.

The sea air was cool, and the stars and moon shone vivid in the clear sky.

Thank God he was leaving Mazatlan behind.

★ ★ ★ ★ ★

A few minutes after midnight, Escarra roused the Mazatlan harbormaster out of a deep tequila-based slumber and asked him a question.

Only one vessel, the coastal steamer *Miraflores,* had departed the city that evening. It was bound for Guaymas.

CHAPTER 14

"And he that sat upon the throne said, Behold, I make all things new." Revelation 21:5

Jester came awake the next morning with more energy than any time since the bear attack. Fabiana's promise of a picnic must've had something to do with it.

The girl, Luna, came in first thing to cleanse his wounds and help him dress. Her ministrations were more pleasant than Sofia's had been, but the picnic—that was going to be wonderful. Good thing, too, after the night he'd spent waking up, regretting his harsh words to Fabiana, then falling asleep again, only to repeat the cycle several times before dawn. He rehearsed the things he'd say to soothe her hurt feelings and then finally went to the breakfast table.

He went through four cups of coffee and ate more than he should've over the next hour and more. Twice, footsteps in the hallway made him turn quickly to the door, but by nine o'clock he stopped even listening. Fabiana wasn't coming—that was plain enough. Poor Guadalupe tried to engage him in conversation for a while, and he replied pleasantly enough, but that was all. Eventually, she excused herself, leaving him in the uncomfortable company of Esteban, who was gorging himself on meat and eggs seasoned with disdainful glances. At length, the man stood up and stalked out. Breakfast was definitely over.

Jester stood up and started for his room. The picnic would still happen. It would be fun. Who was he kidding? She might be finished with him for good. But why in the hell did it bother him so much? It never had before. Life here at the hacienda—that had to be it. So idyllic. And Fabiana's delightful company. It shouldn't ever have to end.

Luna was leaving his room when he came back, and she slipped out quietly, her eyes respectfully down. The bed was made, and the table and dresser straightened up neatly. She'd arranged the books standing up in a straight row, with a heavy inkwell at one end and an ancient jewelry box at the other, serving as bookends. The curtains were drawn back, and bright midmorning sunlight flooded the room. That was better.

He sat down at the table with the fountain pen and a sheet of stationery and quickly penned a message to Fabiana: *I regret not seeing you at breakfast. I look forward to our picnic this noontime. C. J.* He folded the paper and slipped it into an envelope, writing *Señorita Medina* across the front.

Jester smiled. Writing the note was almost as good as seeing her and patching things up. He hurried out of the room, whistling the Garry Owen under his breath. Sofia came out of another room down the corridor, and he walked up to her. She gave him her gap-toothed smile and took the note to deliver, looking as if she shared some great romantic secret with him.

Reading might make the time go by faster, so he took several volumes with him out to the gallery in back and sat in the same chair he'd used the day before when Guadalupe had talked with him. He opened *Great Expectations* again and settled back to wait for Fabiana's reply, however long that took.

This time the story got hold of him. He didn't even hear Sofia an hour and a half later until she stopped right beside him. He turned with a start, and she handed him an envelope. He smiled

222

and opened it quickly, then shook his head slowly as he read the girl's words: *Señor, I regret that I cannot join you this afternoon for the picnic as we had planned. I am ill with a headache.*

Well, that was that. She deserved the benefit of the doubt. Perhaps she really did have a headache. But then he saw her closing: *Your obedient servant, Fabiana Medina.* She'd underlined the word *servant* with such force that the paper had almost ripped.

At least he had his answer. There'd been quarrels and hurt feelings with young women before, even though he tried to always keep his ladies happy. Things had usually blown over quickly. So why was it so disturbing this time? Hurting the girl had been a knavish thing to do. Being a guest under her roof only compounded the guilt. An apology was the only honorable course of action, and he limped inside for paper and pen.

Please allow me to beg your forgiveness for my unkind words yesterday. I deeply regret having caused you distress. Yours, Calvin Jester. He dashed off the words quickly, but he meant them. Sofia again served as courier, and Jester returned to his seat outside to await his fate.

An hour passed. Then another. *Great Expectations* couldn't keep his interest although the title did seem rather ironic, under the current circumstances. For the next hour he alternated between the book and a mental picture of Fabiana's lovely face. Finally, he stood up and gathered the books in his arms. There'd obviously be nothing more between him and the girl. That was okay. There was more than one fish in the sea—he let out a deep breath—but then, the others weren't as pretty as Fabiana.

Sofia came out of the house then. She had a sober expression and handed him another message: *I accept your apology, Señor.* That was it, no signature, no hint of possible warmth.

He leaned back in his chair. A lot had happened in the past twenty-four hours. A lot had been lost. The veiled conversation with Guadalupe about the difficulties of "any more permanent understanding" between him and Fabiana was certainly superfluous now, a worry that would never come. How ironic, getting into trouble because of something he said to a woman. Always in the past, his way with words had facilitated romance, not extinguished it.

He pictured her face—beautiful. But would this kind of anger be the rule with her? If this was a sample of what a future with Fabiana Medina might bring . . .

He opened the note and read it again. Things were definitely over.

Jester managed a smile. Maybe it was all for the best.

In Culiacan again, Rodolfo Escarra's eyes lit on an old, beautifully framed map of Mexico on the wall of his study. The Old Man had given it to him on the occasion of Escarra's ten-year anniversary as *Jefe de Acordada* for Sonora back in 1906. He smiled bitterly. Things had been good then. And they got better, at least for a while. Two years later, Diaz increased Escarra's territory to include Sinaloa as well, the only *Jefe* with authority over two states. A raise in salary had come with the extended territory—the Old Man could be quite generous to the loyal and competent among his retainers.

He stood up and walked over to the map. Langhorne could be going almost anywhere on the west coast of Mexico. Those were the possibilities. But the probabilities—that was a different story. The American only had two modes of transportation available to him if he was planning to cover a lot of ground and not just pick a local spot and hide out there—the railroad and ships.

With his finger, Escarra traced the main north-south train line. It ran north through Mazatlan, Culiacan, the small junctions of San Blas, Navajoa, and Corral, and on to Guaymas and finally Hermosillo. From that point there were no more cities until the border at Nogales. Of course, the line also ran south from Mazatlan to Tepic, but Langhorne wouldn't go that way. Fugitives ran toward safety, not away from it.

If he went by sea, that narrowed the possibilities even further. A vessel from Mazatlan might go to La Paz over on the peninsula, but there was no railroad from there to the United States. Guaymas was the only significant port on the Gulf, besides being on the rail line north. Escarra tapped it with his finger.

"Pablo!" Escarra called out loudly enough to be heard through the closed door.

Hurried footsteps sounded in the hallway, and then the door opened slowly, and the man looked in.

"Yes, *Jefe*?"

Escarra went back to his desk and searched through one drawer. He found the paper he was looking for and pulled it out, studying it as he spoke.

"Wire our men in Hermosillo, Guaymas, San Blas, Navajoa, and Corral to watch the trains for the man, Langhorne. Send along a description. Have a drawing made and send it by train to the men as soon as it's printed. Oh, and those fools Aguirre and Lopez—they can watch the Mazatlan station and the port."

"Yes, *Jefe*."

"And our man in Guaymas—have him assign someone to watch the port there as well. What was that ship that left Mazatlan last night?"

Sotero frowned and stared off into the distance. "The *Monte-*something."

"*Miraflores*. Have him watch for it. He's to go on board when it arrives, search it, and check the passenger manifest. I have a feeling about that one."

"Yes, *Jefe*."

Escarra thought for a moment. "Is Zuniga still at Nogales?"

The Maderistas were in full control up there, but the agent might still be able to operate, if he was discreet.

Sotero scratched his head. "I don't know, *Jefe*. There's a rumor they stood him up against the wall."

Escarra cursed. "Don't risk sending him a telegram then."

"No, *Jefe*." Sotero kept looking at him.

"What is it, Pablo? Speak up!"

"What are your orders for our men? Do they . . . ?"

"Capture the man if they find him, of course. Keep him locked up somewhere under guard. Not the jail, though, some place hidden. We don't want the Yanqui consul finding him." Escarra smiled again. "Then I'll be along to deal with him."

Sotero smirked.

Escarra flourished the paper he'd pulled from his desk. "It seems he sent a wire to someone named Medina at Agua Blanca in Sonora. Find out if our man at Corral thinks the local gendarme at Agua Blanca can be trusted. If so, send him the description, too."

"So many books, Señor."

Luna, a broom in her hands, looked down like a child at the window of a toy shop as Jester sat with the five volumes he'd brought out from his room. The girl was sweeping the floor tiles on the gallery and probably wouldn't have spoken at all if he hadn't greeted her first.

Five books—that wasn't many, not in comparison with the hundreds in the library at the townhouse in Charleston. But to Luna it must've seemed quite a multitude. He'd always liked the sight of those rows and rows of volumes on their mahogany shelves, but now—maybe he ought to give some of them away when he got back.

Could it be Luna herself that was prompting his uneasiness? Timid, unsure of herself, seeking to please—she seemed to be everything that Fabiana was not. Jester smiled up at the girl.

"Do you like to read, Luna?" Funny, it was the first time he'd called her by name.

She looked down at the floor. "I do not know how to read the English good."

"There's nothing particularly hard about it when you already know how to read in Spanish."

She shook her head a few times and started sweeping with vigor. "No, I could not."

"Yes. Yes, you can," he said gently. "You're an intelligent young woman." He held open the book toward her. "This is a story by a man named Dickens."

Luna seemed to try to ignore the book, but she kept glancing over at it as she swept.

"It's about a young man who's infatuated with a rich girl," he said. "He's a poor young fellow."

She frowned. "What is infat . . . ?"

"Infatuated. He thinks he loves her."

"Oh." She looked a little frightened.

Jester pointed to a spot on the page. "Here, Luna. You can read that. I know you can."

Slowly, reluctantly it seemed, she propped her broom against a bench and took one side of the book in her hand while he held the other side. Her eyes studied the type for a long moment.

"Go ahead, try to read it." He kept his voice gentle. "This line right here."

" '*As she* gave' "—Luna pronounced it like *gavay*—" '*it me playfully—for her darker mood had been but momentary . . .*' "

"That word is *gave*," Jester said, smiling to reassure her. "But you're doing quite well. Go on, go on."

" '*I held it and put it to my lips.*' " She turned to him. "What does she give him?"

"Her hand, her hand, my dear."

Luna relinquished the book to him and took up the broom again. "I must do my work."

"Well part of that work is helping me, isn't it?" he asked. She didn't answer, and he continued. "Talking with you makes me feel better." He'd said similar things to girls before in various flirtations, but now he really meant it. She didn't look convinced, though. "Don't you believe me?"

"Señor Langhorne, he tell me you are a good man . . ."

"But what?" Langhorne again, always surfacing at the oddest moments.

"He say that I am not to believe everything you tell me."

Damn that Langhorne. But then he couldn't help chuckling. "He gave you good advice."

She looked at him for a long moment, as though she were trying to determine whether she should trust him or not. Finally she started sweeping again, but slowly, as if her heart were elsewhere.

Jester shut the book and took up another, a collection of poetry. He leafed through it until he found what he wanted, then looked up at Luna again.

"Let me read this part to you." he said. "A man named Robert Browning wrote it. It reminds me a little of you." She pretended to keep her attention on her sweeping, but it was obvious she was listening.

> "While brown Dolores
> squats outside the Convent bank,
> with Sanchicha, telling stories,
> steeping tresses in the tank,
> blue-black, lustrous, thick like horsehairs."

"And so forth," he said.

She looked totally puzzled. "What are they doing?"

"Why, the two girls are washing their hair in a pond."

"Oh. My mother's name was Dolores."

"And you see, they had thick, shiny dark hair like yours."

"I thought it said a horse's hair."

There was a touch of hurt in her eyes. She probably figured he was making sport of her.

"It's a compliment," he said quickly. "Their hair is thick and beautiful like a horse's mane." He nodded his head several times. "Really, he's saying a nice thing about 'em."

She didn't look convinced. Maybe a new poem would be best.

"This one's called 'Porphyria's Lover.' "

Her frown deepened, and she shook her head. "Porfirio Diaz, he was an evil man, an evil man. He hurt the people."

He started to explain, but then . . . Better try another. Turning back to the Wordsworth section, he located the one he wanted.

"This is called 'The Solitary Reaper,' " he said. "It's about a girl working in the fields, harvesting wheat."

> "Behold her, single in the field,
> Yon solitary Highland lass!
> Reaping and singing by herself;
> Stop here, or gently pass!
> Alone she cuts and binds the grain,
> And sings a melancholy strain;
> O listen! For the vale profound
> Is overflowing with the sound."

He continued on to the conclusion. Some of the words were beyond her understanding, but it would've broken the flow of the verse to stop and explain them. When he finished, he studied her face for a few moments. She looked a little confused.

"Do you ever sing when you work, like this girl did, Luna?" he asked.

She seemed embarrassed, glancing from him to the ground and back. Finally, she said, "Sometimes I sing—when no one else is near me."

"I'll wager you have a lovely voice, just like the girl in this poem."

That seemed to encourage her. "The man I worked for in Culiacan, Señor Dawes, he say I sing very pretty."

Jester smiled. "I believe it. I truly do."

Then Luna did something she hadn't done before in his presence—she smiled. It was fresh and innocent, and like someone had turned on a great golden light. Since crossing the line at Nogales, there'd been plenty of señoritas, dark-skinned, dark-eyed girls with a common but unremarkable beauty about them. Luna had been one of that number.

The smile changed things. It drove away, at least for now, the lingering picture of Fabiana. It made all things new.

Money could work wonders. Langhorne had seen it plenty of times in the past. Now it played out again as the tiny motor launch of the *Miraflores* puttered east in the darkness toward a scattering of lights on the mainland two miles ahead. He sat near the stern of the little boat, and a land breeze blew gently in his face.

It was a full day since the *Miraflores* had slipped out of the harbor at Mazatlan, en route to Guaymas, and now the steamer was making an unscheduled stop halfway along her track, to put Langhorne ashore. A hundred pesos was what it cost. He'd offered it to the vessel's skipper to let him off here, just in case the *Acordada* men had someone waiting for him on the docks in Guaymas.

The shore lights were the little fishing port of Topolobampo, where a spur line ran fifty miles to the main north-south railroad between Sonora and Sinaloa. Langhorne glanced behind him at the dark shape of the *Miraflores* riding to her anchor in the approaches to the tiny harbor. As the launch pulled farther and farther away, the night seemed to close around them.

The launch left him at a little pier where a couple of fishing boats were tied up. He waited until morning, catching a few hours of sporadic sleep, then hired a local man with a donkey cart to take him and his trunk to the railroad yard. It wasn't a station exactly, but he was able to catch an early freight for the junction at San Blas, where he switched to the main line. He rode a slow, crowded passenger train north to Navajoa on the Rio Mayo.

He debarked at that point. It was safer to leave the railroad there than risk being spotted by *Acordada* men who might be watching the bigger stations on ahead. A sign on a warehouse near the station proclaimed the building to be the terminal point of an American-owned mining supply company. That might be what he needed.

Inside, in a little office on one side of the cavernous warehouse, Langhorne found the local manager, an American with the unusual name of Demetrius Zeno. After showing the man his confidential letter, Langhorne spread out his map of Mexico on a cluttered work table and located Navajoa and the general vicinity of the Medina hacienda, where he penciled a small cross.

"I want to get from here to there, overland," he told Zeno.

"Looks to be eighty or ninety miles, as the crow flies," the manager said. "I'd go up the Mayo to Macoyagui, where the river splits. Take the west fork. You can follow it most of the way to where you're going. There's a few villages, Indians mostly in 'em. But you'll need horses, and I wouldn't go up there 'less I was well armed."

Langhorne gave him money to buy the animals and supplies, while he himself stayed back at the warehouse. There was no sense showing his face around the town unnecessarily. When Zeno returned a couple of hours later, he had two strong, shaggy horses and a small mule, plus the necessary gear. He also had a Mexican.

"You'll need a *mozo,*" Zeno explained, "and Paco's a good one. Trustworthy, and he knows the country." Zeno gave Langhorne a rifle he had in a storage cabinet, one of the ever-present .30-.30s.

Half an hour after sundown, Langhorne and Paco started out of town and up the west bank of the Rio Mayo.

CHAPTER 15

"Till I come, give attendance to reading."
1 Timothy 4:13

Jester was awake half an hour before sunup. His dream had been quite pleasant. Unfortunately, it had slipped away, just out of reach, almost like being unable to recall a person's name. Somewhere on the edge of his memory was the image of a girl or woman, elusive like a vapor. He lay there under the covers with his eyes closed. Maybe he'd drift back into the dream and discover exactly what had been so pleasant.

Dawn came on steadily. Clearly, he wouldn't be going back to sleep. He ought to check his wounds and then dress—but not just yet. Maybe it was the weather, overcast from the look of the light filtering through the curtains. Finally he swung his legs out of the bed and poured some water into the washbowl on the table. It felt good to wash his face. After that, he slipped back under the bedcovers and propped up his back with pillows.

A few minutes later a soft knock sounded on his door, and Luna peeked cautiously inside. Jester grinned and greeted her, and something of the pleasantness of the dream returned. She came into the room quietly, murmuring a brief good morning without smiling or looking at him. With anyone else, it might have indicated something was wrong, but it was how she always seemed to act—except for their brief, enjoyable conversation yesterday. The girl needed to show that pretty smile more often.

She helped him take off his nightshirt, then removed his bandages. She washed the wounds tenderly. "You are almost well."

He frowned for an instant. Why did the words almost seem like bad news? He looked down at his body to see if her estimate was sound. It was. The deep lacerations, which had once made him look like he'd gone through a meat grinder, were closed up, and the redness around them was fading.

He forced another grin. "It's because you're such an excellent nurse, Luna."

That made her blush and look down. She redressed the wounds. The touch of her hands on his chest was very pleasant indeed. If she felt any similar sensation, she did a good job of masking it. There was one brief moment when he glanced up and caught her looking into his eyes, but she lowered her eyes quickly and finished securing the bandages.

She took a shirt out of the bureau and laid it on the table. He asked her for the trousers that he'd draped across the back of the chair, and he put them on after she turned to face the other way. There was really nothing more for her to do there now. Even so, did she have to go?

"Do you want me to button your shirt?" she asked.

"Yes. Please."

He slipped it on and let her do the buttoning. There was something so domestic about the process—it was almost as if he were home.

"I'm going to teach you to read English, Luna." It was an impulse as the books on the dresser caught his eye. She shook her head, but he held up his hands and smiled. "Yes, yes. Do you have some time during the day when I could teach you?"

"Señora Medina, she lets me have time to eat after *almuerzo* and then again after *comida.*"

234

Jester shook his head. "I don't want to interfere with your meals. I'll speak with the señora and ask her if you can take half an hour in the afternoon."

"I have much work."

"I'll speak with her."

Luna stepped over to the half-open door but then lingered there instead of leaving. Things were a little awkward, but it was worth it to have her here a few more seconds. He put on his shoes and socks and looked in the mirror on its stand on the table while he used the comb. He threw a sidelong glance at her while he tried to get his thick blond hair to lie down properly— she was following his progress with that same serious expression of hers.

"You want me comb it for you?" she asked finally.

He shrugged helplessly. "I can't get it to stay down." He gave her the comb. She was too short to reach the top of his head easily while he stood, so she motioned him into the chair. He kept his eyes on the mirror as she stood behind him.

Luna went back over his entire head quickly, with a light touch. He had a cowlick near the back of his head, and she pulled the comb through it several times, but it wouldn't stay down. Finally, she dipped her fingers briefly into the wash bowl and rubbed them across the unruly patch. Then she ran the comb through the spot again a few times and hit it with a little more water.

"You like it?" she asked.

Jester turned his head one way and then another, staring into the mirror the whole time. He got the comb from her and tried adjusting his part a little, but that made the cowlick pop up again like a jack-in-the-box.

"Darn it!" He caught a glimpse of her face in the mirror, and she broke into a grin. She hid it quickly, or tried to, but he turned and looked up at her with his eyebrows raised. She seemed to teeter between embarrassment and amusement for a few moments, and then a smile spread across her face, and her eyes seemed to dance.

She took the comb back from him and ran it through the cowlick again, smoothing down the hair with her other hand. He ran his own hand over the spot, and a few hairs inexplicably shot up straight.

This time she laughed out loud, and he joined her. Her laugh was like music. Now she parted his hair down the middle instead of on the side, chuckling all the while. He looked ridiculous in the mirror, the hair on one side of the part lying down normally while the other side stood up like a bristle brush. Her hand rested lightly on his shoulder as they laughed.

At that moment, the door opened, and he turned quickly, his mouth open. Fabiana stood there, mild astonishment on her face. Luna seemed to take it all in stride, though. She quickly combed his hair back into its normal arrangement, laughing lightly, then gathered up her extra bandages and looked back at him one more time.

"He has such pretty yellow hair," she said pleasantly to Fabiana, and then she slipped out of the room.

"Such pretty yellow hair," Fabiana said, looking squarely at him.

There was an awkward silence for a few seconds. It was impossible to read her face or her tone of voice. Finally, she spoke again.

"I came to see if you'd like to have breakfast with me on the patio."

Jester gave her his best smile. "I'd be delighted, Miss Medina."

They walked out and sat at a table near the fountain on the east wall. Carlito brought them rolls and a silver pot of coffee along with a bowl of grapes and ripe plums.

"You know, my father and I often ate here in the mornings," Fabiana said. She looked around as if she were trying to find something she'd lost. Finally, her eyes settled back on him. "Do you think she's pretty?"

He needed a moment to collect his thoughts for a reply. "Do you mean the girl? Luna?"

She frowned. "Of course I mean the girl. Who else would I be talking about?"

"Well, I suppose she's pretty."

Fabiana leaned toward him. "No, I asked if *you* think she's pretty, not if she's pretty in some general way. Do *you* think she's pretty?"

Her eyes held his like a magnet now, and it was an effort to keep from matching her frown. "Yes, I do." He took a drink of hot coffee and forced himself to butter a roll—anything to occupy his hands. It was like being in the witness box.

A tiny muscle was working in her jaw. None of this was her fault, all her spoiled and apparently jealous nature aside. She was just a girl, after all, younger in her heart than in her body, and a very sheltered girl at that, her attempts to be sophisticated notwithstanding.

"I suppose the Mestiza type appeals to you," she said, with an edge in her voice.

He smiled as warmly as he could. "I'm a man, Miss Medina."

"My name is Fabiana."

"Fabiana. We find lots of girls pretty, almost all of 'em, whatever type they happen to be."

"And me? What about me? What *type* am I?" The words sounded like a challenge.

Jester looked straight into her eyes. "You, Fabiana, have a fine and exquisite beauty." She really did. But something was different than the day before, weaker, like morning fog burning off under a bright sun. In a contest of pure beauty, she'd outshine Luna hands down, but there was something about "the Mestiza girl," as Fabiana called her. Something.

His compliment, though, had an effect on Fabiana—that was obvious. Her eyes shone for a moment, and she almost smiled.

"Then perhaps," she said, "you'll not be so distracted by that girl."

"Oh, I'm not at all distracted by her." The words didn't sound very convincing, though.

"Huh. That was quite a heartwarming scene I walked in on. It makes me wonder what had been going on before I came." She raised her eyebrows.

"I assure you, nothing untoward happened before you came in. She changed my bandages and helped me button my shirt. Then when you arrived, the girl was merely helping me comb my hair."

"And you seemed to be enjoying every second of it."

To deny it would be an outright lie. He gave her a forlorn smile and just shrugged.

She didn't return the smile. "How can I compete with a maid? She has no requirement for a chaperone."

"You don't have to compete, I assure you." He said it with more conviction than he felt. He glanced right and left very obviously. "And I see no chaperone here."

"There can be eyes behind curtains. And it's clear you no longer have need of a nurse."

He smiled despite the unwelcome reminder. "No, I expect I've recovered my good health." He stretched then. A sharp pain knifed through his shoulder, and his ribcage felt the strain as well, but he didn't let on.

She lifted her coffee cup. "To your good health, then."

He clinked his cup against hers. What was Luna doing now?

He and Fabiana ate for several minutes in silence. Maybe

now it would be safe to venture back into conversation.

"I fear I've ignored your poor mother—uh, stepmother—this past day or more. Except for seeing her at mealtime yesterday, I haven't spoken to her."

"Well, you won't be able to see her today, at least not until late this afternoon." Fabiana picked a plum out of the bowl. "She's gone into Agua Blanca for the day."

"Enjoying herself, is she? That ought to do her good." He smiled again. "You should try it, too."

"It's difficult to enjoy yourself alone. And my partner has been otherwise engaged."

He ignored the remark. "You say the señora will be back later today?"

"Yes." A worried expression came onto her face. "She's gone to talk with an attorney."

"But isn't your uncle an attorney?"

Fabiana leaned closer and lowered her voice. "Yes, but she's consulting the attorney *about* my uncle. It seems he's tried something."

Jester frowned. There wasn't much incentive to like the man, and Fabiana's declaration only reinforced the feeling. "What has he done—if you don't mind my asking?"

"Not at all," she replied. "It seems he's trying to get some sort of court order about me and the hacienda."

"That's ridiculous." The man was a damned scoundrel, but Jester held his tongue. "What's he trying to do?"

"You'd better speak to my stepmother about that. I don't know the details of it."

"If he tries something—if you need my help, I'm at your service."

She smiled. "The gallant gentleman. But are you sure you won't be too busy?" Still smiling, she excused herself and went inside.

The verbal sparring with Fabiana was more exhausting than it seemed it should be. For ten or fifteen minutes after she'd gone, he just sat there sipping coffee and trying to sort things out. Fabiana wasn't easy to read. And there was Luna to think about. Could a fellow have too many women in his life? He'd never have figured it before. But now . . . And who would've thought they could make him take things so seriously? He slowly shook his head. Life as a bachelor officer at the War Department had been so much simpler, even with Washington debutantes to contend with.

Guadalupe Medina seemed far too feminine for the dark paneling and heavy furniture of the hacienda office, but during the past days she'd proven herself quite a capable woman. She motioned Jester to a comfortable armchair across from the big desk, and he settled into it. Her smile was weary but pleasant.

He asked, "Are you fatigued after your ride from town, Señora?"

"A little."

This lady who'd been so kind to him deserved his help. Whether she'd want it or even need it would be up to her. "I've learned that you may be having a, shall we say, misunderstanding with Señor Velasquez."

The color rose in her face. "I am embarrassed that you have to be burdened by our difficulty, Señor Jester. I assume you learned of it from my daughter."

"Yes. And I want to assure you that I'm not trying to interfere in your affairs. But sometimes a lady has need of a man's assistance when another gentleman is involved. I wanted to offer my services to you if I can be of help in any way."

"That is very kind of you." She tilted her head and looked him in the eye for several seconds as if she were deciding how much she could trust him. Finally, toying with a pencil, she continued. "My brother can be a clever man. As an *abocado*—"

"An attorney?"

"Yes. As an attorney, he has a great advantage over me in knowing the law. What I was doing in Agua Blanca was talking with another attorney about certain actions Esteban has taken concerning my daughter and this hacienda."

"Fabiana didn't say more than that."

Guadalupe glanced behind her at the partially open door to the corridor, then stood up and pushed it shut. Sitting down again, she leaned forward across the desk.

"My brother has applied to a judge for guardianship over Fabiana and for a court order putting this hacienda and all its lands under his control." The words seemed to frighten her.

"I know little of legal matters, Señora Medina, but I wouldn't think he could actually accomplish his designs here. After all, the land is yours by all rights."

"There seems to be an old Spanish legal provision requiring hereditary property such as this to be held by a man. I believe the English term is *entailment*. And with Fabiana, since I am not her real mother, she must come under the guardianship of a man for legal matters."

Jester frowned. "The attorney told you all this?"

"Yes. He said these attempts of Esteban probably will not be approved by the courts, but he cannot guarantee it." She kept rolling the pencil in her hand. "And for now, Esteban is acting as if he already has the court's approval for his actions. He is giving orders to the vaqueros and the other workers, and he demands that I allow him to inspect the account books for the hacienda."

"I think I should have a talk with Esteban."

"Señor Langhorne already spoke to him several days ago. But since your friend has been gone, my brother has grown bolder. And if he gets the court order he desires, I do not know if he can be stopped." She looked at him as if for reassurance; then finally she turned away and shook her head slowly. "I never realized how much I depended upon Augustin until now that he is gone."

"Have you thought about simply ordering Esteban off your property? Surely your workers will obey you rather than him."

"That would make him angry, and I want to avoid that. I still hope that he will come to his senses and stop his attempts to take our land and my daughter."

"Do you know how Fabiana feels about all this? Are you and she of one mind about it?"

Guadalupe looked uncomfortable. "My daughter and I seem to disagree now on many things. It was not that way so much before my husband's death." She shut her eyes tightly for several seconds then looked back at him. "You have seen how she defies me. I cannot blame her for it. She is sorrowful and afraid, even if she does not seem to be. And her . . . *other* feelings—perhaps she is only searching for another man to fill the spot her father held in her heart."

Jester nodded. Fabiana's sudden shifts in mood and her bursts of anger were certainly hard to read. Did she even know what she wanted—or whom?

"I confess, Señora, that I've been very flattered by the attentions of such a lovely girl as your daughter, and perhaps I haven't responded with as much caution as I should have."

Guadalupe smiled sadly. "I know you would not take advantage of her, Señor Jester. I am more thankful than you realize that you have been here during this time of our distress." She paused for a few moments. "I do ask that you give her no false hope. You are a man of the world, experienced in its ways and several years her senior."

"I'm twenty-seven, ma'am."

"Very much as I thought," she said, nodding her head. "And

Fabiana is not yet twenty. Please—be careful with her."

"Of course."

Guadalupe sighed and smiled. "I feel much better now. You must forgive me for burdening you with our difficulties. And I have not even asked about your health! Are you still recovering well?"

"Quite well, Señora. Almost back to my old self."

"And Luna? Is she giving you adequate care?"

Jester smiled at the thought. "She's a marvelous nurse. I'm completely satisfied."

"Oh?" Her eyes lit up, and she looked at him with greater interest. Maybe he'd responded a little too eagerly.

"Yes. In fact, I'm so far recuperated that I probably won't need her to help me for more than another day or two."

"I see."

"And that brings me to something I wanted to ask. Luna has taken an interest in learning to read English, and I wondered if you'd allow her to have some time off from her duties when I could teach her—say an hour or so in the afternoons."

"I think it is a wonderful idea," Guadalupe said. "And you would be such a good teacher for her. Yes, I think an hour shortly after midday would be perfect. You know that many of us at the hacienda often take the siesta at that time anyway."

"I appreciate your kindness, Señora Medina."

"Since it is already later than that today, you may give her the lesson now, if you wish. As you may have realized, it is my fondest desire that young women everywhere in our nation have opportunity to better themselves and live without being at the mercy of the unscrupulous."

Jester smiled again. "I shall find her and start immediately then." He stood up.

"Good. Luna is such a kind and pretty young woman, don't you think?"

"Very much so, on both counts."

She studied him for a long moment then smiled. "You know, Señor Jester, I think that Luna should continue to serve as your nurse for another week . . . or two . . . at least. We must guard against a relapse in your condition."

It was about an hour before sundown when Jester got several books together and took them out to a corner of the private patio where the sunlight still reached. Then, making use of his growing inventory of Spanish words plus simple sign language, he sent Sofia to find the girl. The old lady returned shortly with her, walking across the patio from their quarters, a small building on the east wall behind the main house.

Luna looked worried as she approached him. It was likely Sofia hadn't told the girl the reason she was being summoned. In fact, the old lady probably hadn't understood it herself when he'd sent her on the errand. Now he thanked Sofia, then offered Luna a seat on the bench beside him.

"There's nothing wrong, Luna," he said, smiling to put her at her ease. "Your *patrona* wants me to teach you to read English." She still looked unsure, so he went on to explain the arrangement Guadalupe had approved.

He picked Langhorne's book, *An Apache Campaign in the Sierra Madre,* from the stack he'd brought out.

"This is about the United States Army fighting the Apache Indians in this very region," he said, opening the volume and letting her hold the front cover while he held the back. "You've heard of the Apaches, haven't you, Luna?"

Her eyes widened a little. "The Apaches, they are very bad."

"They're all tame now. I hear we even use some of 'em for scouts nowadays."

She stared at him. "But they cut the people's hair off."

"Not anymore, my dear." He flipped through the pages to a

chapter where he wanted to start, and he held it open for her. From that point, he had her start reading aloud for a paragraph. Then he read the next paragraph. In that way they alternated for the next twenty minutes, covering a few pages. Her progress was slow at first, but she seemed to pick up a feel for the language as she went along. He had to help her with the pronunciation, especially those words with silent *e*'s and other tricky elements, but she seemed to remember those words that she'd had trouble with, so he seldom had to help her more than once or twice on any term.

"Well, how did you like it, Luna?" he asked, marking the page with a slip of paper and putting the book aside.

"It was hard. I don't think I read good."

"Nonsense." He smiled to reassure her. "You did quite well, quite well indeed. And you learned some history, too, I think. You know, I was only a little boy, a *muchacho,* when all that was happening."

She grinned. "You learn to talk Spanish?"

He chuckled. "Oh, just a few words like that. I'm trying to pick up as much as I can. It might do me good to know it later on."

"You will stay in Mexico?"

Jester took a pitcher of a fruit drink Sofia had made up earlier for him and poured a glass for Luna, then one for himself.

"I don't think so." A hint of disappointment touched her eyes—maybe it was just his imagination. Quickly he said, "But you never know." He held out his glass and tapped it lightly against hers. "Cheers."

"Cheers?"

He smiled at her. "That's what we say when we toast each other."

She smiled back. "I see that when I work for Señor Dawes. He and other men that come to eat the dinner, they touch glasses and say 'Cheers'—or some other words sometimes. They do that when they drink the wine."

Jester drank several swallows. "Now tell me what history you learned from reading with me." It might help her with the reading if she had to recount what they'd read.

Luna frowned, obviously concentrating. "The soldiers, they get Apaches to go with them to find other Apaches. And they go through trees and over mountains and rivers."

Jester nodded. "That's very good, Luna." Then what Fabiana had told him, back before the bear attack, about the hacienda's history came to mind. It might amuse Luna. "Say, did you know that this hacienda is named after you?"

Luna looked perplexed. When she didn't say anything after several moments, he continued.

"One of the names of this ranch is—let me see if I can remember it right—*Hacienda de la Luna de los Apaches.*"

She seemed to ponder the words a few seconds. Then a smile slowly spread across her face.

"Oh. That does not mean me. My name, it means the *moon.* The hacienda is *Moon of the Apaches.*"

Jester laughed and she joined in. For a few moments she looked into his eyes. Finally, embarrassed, he turned toward the other books on the table. Edgar Allan Poe might give her some interesting practice, and he opened the front cover, searching for the table of contents. He stopped for a moment—a dedication was scrawled across a blank page: *Con amor, Augustin.*

He quickly flipped away from the page—it was as if he'd intruded on a precious, intimate moment. Finally, he found the table of contents.

"I think we'll try 'The Purloined Letter.'" He turned to the proper page and held the book so she could see it. "Now don't worry about that line just under the title. It's in Latin. Start right here."

She looked at the first line and read aloud slowly. " '*At Paris, just after dark one gusty evening in the autumn of 18__.*' What does it mean, that line after the number?"

"The author, Mr. Poe, just doesn't want to give the exact year when this was happening."

She frowned and cocked her head. "But why not?"

"Never mind, Luna. It's just something authors do. It makes the story seem real."

"This is not true?" She looked disappointed, almost as if he'd actually told her a lie.

"No, it's not true, my dear." She stared at him. He shouldn't have used that last term. Luna might think . . . any number of things. He smiled to reassure her and called her attention back to the book. "Keep reading, please."

She went on, keeping up a fairly good pace for a new reader. Occasionally she'd stop to ask what *meerschaum* or some other unfamiliar word meant. Poe's style was more complex than Bourke's straightforward prose, and they didn't make as good time during this second half of the allotted hour, being only four or five pages into the tale when Jester had to call a halt.

"I want to know what happens," she said, smiling at him like a little girl wanting a present.

Before he could decide whether to tell her more, Guadalupe came out of the house and walked toward them. He and Luna stood up.

"Has the lesson been a success?" Guadalupe asked.

"Luna is a remarkable pupil—uh, a remarkable reader." Luna probably didn't understand the word *pupil*.

Guadalupe looked genuinely delighted. "Then we will continue the lessons every day if you wish." This brought a shy smile from Luna.

"I'd be very happy to do so," Jester said. He looked at Luna. "So you want to know what happens in the story?" He explained

Dupin's discovery of the letter in plain sight and what became of the characters involved.

As Luna bowed to him and Guadalupe and started toward the house to resume her work, Jester called after her. "So you see, Luna, the story shows that something of great value may be right in front of your eyes, unnoticed."

CHAPTER 16

"Mercy and truth are met together; righteousness and
peace have kissed each other." Psalm 85:10

Fabiana heard the plan quite by accident. Someone down the
hallway ahead of her stood in the doorway of the office, looking
in. It was Jester and he was talking to somebody inside the
room. She ducked into the cross hallway several yards away to
listen. The voice inside was her stepmother's, but her words
were masked. Jester's, however, were clear enough.

"You're certain you don't mind? I'll make sure I bring it back
in good condition."

Fabiana strained to hear her stepmother's words, but she still
couldn't make them out. Perhaps if she moved closer—but there
was no place to conceal herself if she did, and Jester might look
out at any moment.

Again her stepmother's voice drifted down the corridor. She
sounded as if she was enjoying the conversation, laughing like a
girl. Surely Jester couldn't be interested in Guadalupe—not in
that way, at least. At thirty-six, the woman was too old for him
to even consider. And only a few days had passed since her
father's death. Fabiana shuddered for a moment—the idea was
grotesque. The little Mestiza tart and now her stepmother—
who would've thought there'd be this much competition over
the man?

"Thank you, Señora," Jester said. "I'll be going when we're finished with the *comida*."

He backed into the hall, pulling the office door almost closed, and Fabiana started toward him, as if she were just now coming down the corridor. He smiled when he spotted her.

"Miss Fabiana. I was just going to the dining room. Would you care to join me?"

She smiled, too. "Certainly." It was hard to resist saying something about her stepmother. But she held her tongue—almost any remark would give away her eavesdropping.

Guadalupe and Esteban joined them for the meal a few minutes later. It was a long, uncomfortable affair, despite the excellent grilled steak, beans, a dry soup of rice, avocados, a stack of Sofia's hot tortillas, and fresh fruit. Esteban drank too much, as usual, and did his best to insult, insinuate, and make threats beyond his capacity to carry out. Her stepmother responded with as much steel as she could muster. Fabiana forced herself to stay at the table, but the continual combat of these past days was exhausting.

And then there was Jester. It was too bad in a way that he had to endure this feud, through no fault of his own. If only her father were still alive. He would've sent Esteban packing, and she and Jester could've enjoyed each other's company without distraction—from servants and family alike. But now, that seemed less and less likely.

The meal ended at last, no one except Esteban staying to linger over the last of the wine. Jester should've mentioned his plans and offered her a chance to join him, but he'd said nothing. If that was the way he wanted it—two could play at hide and seek.

She didn't have to wait long. As soon as he'd picked up a coat and hat from his room and a rifle from the office, he walked out to the stables and saddled a horse, the palomino gelding

he'd ridden before. She watched from just inside the front
doorway. He worked expertly, as if he handled horses all the
time—that was a surprise.

Jester mounted a bit stiffly—obviously he wasn't completely
healed yet. He turned the horse's head and urged him into a
trot toward the *zaguan*. Fabiana hurried along the gallery and
across the courtyard to the stables and had Elonzo saddle her
thoroughbred gelding.

By the time she rode through the *zaguan*, Jester was out of
sight. She spurred out quickly to a slight rise and looked in
every direction. There he was, off to the south, trotting along
toward the far edge of the vineyard. Her thoroughbred could
overtake him easily—but that would take the fun out of the
hunt. Instead, she skirted the vineyard on the east, keeping him
under observation. She'd done it before to her father and others, following them just for the thrill of the chase and the fact
that they didn't know they were being stalked.

As she cleared the far end of the vineyard, she pulled up to
stay well back of Jester. He hadn't looked around. Obviously, he
didn't know she was shadowing him.

He put his horse into a lope across a huge rolling meadow.
Fabiana had no cover now. Would he turn and spot her? A shiver
went up her spine, and a smile froze on her face. He didn't look
back, though. She kept pace with him, but back on his left
quarter at two hundred meters.

There were no shacks or outbuildings this far south of the
hacienda, and the country looked as wild as it must've back
when her ancestor the Marques was in his prime fighting the
Apaches. Riding the hills and meadows alone was always
wonderful—how much better having Calvin Jester not far ahead.
When would be the best time and manner to reveal herself to
him? Some dramatic way, something that would surprise and
impress him.

Jester disappeared over a gentle hill. Beyond lay a thick forest of pines. Fabiana skirted the hill to the left. Hopefully, he'd come in sight again but not be looking back when she reached the other side. She held her gelding to a walk—no sense blundering into Jester's view.

She finally completed her circuit of the hill and—no Jester! The pines began a short distance ahead, and she scanned them from left to right. Was the brown of his coat or the tan of his felt hat out there? Nothing.

She pulled up and sat her horse, checking now far to the left and right. He might've turned sharply after crossing the hill. What was he thinking? Where was he going? Papa had taught her that tactic for hunting. It should work as well on a man. Jester had been talking to Guadalupe—maybe she'd suggested a spot to visit. There was a beautiful stream, clear and icy cold, rushing between scattered boulders two or three hundred meters into the pines. It was a favorite place of hers, and her stepmother knew the spot, too. It was worth a try.

She spurred her horse into the trees, then slowed to a walk again to move more silently. Her eyes moved from side to side as she rode along. This was starting to get irritating. She stopped to listen.

The forest had a sound of its own—soft wind, the creak of a branch, birds, a rustling through the pine needles by a small animal. All of those were present now, but nothing else, no jingle of a bridle, no whinny from Jester's palomino, nor signs of nervousness from her own horse, nothing to give direction.

She inhaled deeply and let it out in a long, impatient sigh. This wasn't fun any longer. He could be a mile away by now, in any direction. She frowned and started her gelding forward again at a walk. The stream wasn't far ahead. Why not go see it since it was so close—a poor consolation prize, though, compared to catching Jester unawares.

Fabiana rode on to a spot where the edge of the stream brushed against a gravel bank. She slid to the ground, dropping her reins so the gelding could drink. It was cool in the shade of the pines, and the boulders reinforced the chill. She rubbed her arms.

The water was so clear that it served like a magnifying glass, lending a vivid sharpness to the stones beneath it. Fabiana stared hard into the water, focusing on one pool that looked no more than a foot deep but must actually be close to a meter. A dark green object seemed to hover just off the bottom, swaying almost imperceptibly with the current. She watched it for a long time. Finally, when her horse raised his head and began looking calmly from side to side, she picked up a stone and threw it into the pool, and the trout darted out of sight among the rocks.

"You shouldn't scare the poor fish like that, Señorita."

Fabiana jumped, as frightened as the trout. Before she'd turned all the way around, she knew who it was. He would pay.

Jester grinned sheepishly and held his arms out to his sides, palms up.

"I couldn't resist."

"How long have you been back there?" she demanded.

He seemed to think about it for a moment. "Oh, ever since you rode into the woods."

She frowned. "You mean you've been behind me for the past ten minutes? Where did you . . . ?"

"I fell in behind you right after you came around that little hill. I'd spotted you a lot earlier, though, almost as soon as you left the hacienda. I noticed you tended to bear left every time. So, as soon as I came off that hill, I turned right and hightailed it back around the hill and came up a hundred yards behind you. I guess you never thought to look behind you." He laughed softly—that made it worse. She tapped the riding crop nervously into the palm of her left hand.

"I suppose your, uh, experience has taught you to spot people who are following you." She'd almost said "military training," but caught herself—that would've given things away.

"I just like to know what's going on behind my back." His expression was a little more contrite now, and that helped dampen her irritation.

"Some things are better left unknown," she said.

"I think the expression is 'better left unsaid.'"

"Do you think you always know best?" she demanded. It would've been worth a thousand pesos to be able to tell him that she knew who he really was and why he was in Mexico. But if she did, he'd probably leave within the hour, and then she'd never see him again. That would never do. Calvin Jester belonged to her, in a way by right of conquest—government orders, little Mestiza maids, and stepmothers notwithstanding.

"By no means, Miss Fabiana." He still had that infuriating smile on his face.

But it was such a handsome face. She did the only thing she could think of at that moment—she stepped up to him, put her hands on his shoulders, and kissed him hard.

The kiss hit him like being in a column of troops ambushed out of nowhere. He kissed back, at first by reflex but then by desire, his body responding of its own volition. After a few exquisite moments, though, he reluctantly stepped back out of range.

"Fabiana, I think we'd better leave this place." His body didn't agree with that idea at all, but Guadalupe's words and Luna's smile teamed together to stiffen his resolve. "I gave your stepmother my word that I'd be a gentleman around you."

She had a sensuous smile on her face as she stepped closer again, and as clear as any words, the smile said *I own you.*

"But my stepmother's not here, is she?"

She leaned in, putting her arms around him and searching

for his mouth with hers, but there was awkwardness in her attempt. She'd probably not done this before. That helped him muster the willpower to push her gently away.

"I must admit, you tempt me sorely, Fabiana. But my word means something to me." That sounded a hell of a lot more like a statement that would come from Langhorne's mouth rather than his own. The man was everywhere.

Anger flashed in her eyes for an instant, but then that possessive smile returned. Inexperienced she might be, but it was plain she knew what she could do to a man. A tactical withdrawal in the face of superior forces seemed to be in order.

"Will you ride with me back to the hacienda?" he asked. He gathered his reins and climbed onto the palomino.

Still smiling, she said, "I'll find my own way home, thank you."

The sound of distant gunfire drifted across the grassland even before Jester was out of the pines. It was a steady series of individual shots, with an interval of three or four seconds between them. They had the distinctive *pop* of a pistol, no doubt about that, and they seemed to be coming from the direction of the hacienda.

Jester kept his horse at a walk. No point in coming on too quickly before identifying the source of the gunfire. When the hacienda finally came into view, he pulled up and stared hard until he was certain who was shooting.

Esteban Velasquez stood alone, just out from the *zaguan,* and fired at a plank stuck upright in the ground. Anyone trying to enter the hacienda's courtyard would have to pass between him and the target.

Who could tell what the man had in mind—probably intimidation. Jester glanced down at the rifle he'd taken along in case of another bear, but he didn't pull it from its scabbard.

He stopped a few yards short of Velasquez's line of fire.

"Hold your fire while I pass through," Jester said.

Velasquez squeezed off another shot, then another, as if he'd not even heard. Finally, with exaggerated nonchalance, the man turned in Jester's direction.

"Do you shoot?" Velasquez asked.

"Occasionally." When there was a good target.

Velasquez was bleary eyed, and his hand holding the pistol down by his side was a little unsteady. "Join me."

Jester considered the offer. Snubbing him now might make him less tractable toward Guadalupe. He climbed down and let the reins fall. A boy had been lounging near the *zaguan,* watching Velasquez shoot, and Jester motioned him over to take the horse back to the stables.

A small table had a couple of boxes of ammunition. Velasquez's revolver was a Smith & Wesson New Model 3 in .44-caliber, an excellent weapon that Jester had fired a few times in the past. Velasquez broke open the revolver and reloaded. Sure enough, his hand had a slight tremor as he pushed the fresh rounds into the cylinder.

The plank was close to fifty feet away and eight or ten inches wide, not a particularly difficult shot. Velasquez stood sideways to the target, and extended his pistol in the offhand position. He shut one eye, and Jester waited for the first shot—and he waited. For an instant the memory of Miss Higginbotham and of Langhorne's final shot in the rifle competition came to mind. Jester couldn't squelch a momentary grin.

The pistol wavered until Velasquez finally pulled the trigger. The weapon bucked in his hand and seemed to surprise him.

A miss.

Velasquez thumbed the hammer back and aimed his second shot. He rocked back a little as the pistol went off, and again nothing hit the target. The third shot came a few seconds later with similar results. Velasquez scowled and fired more quickly the next time, and the bullet struck the edge of the board. That brought a brief smile to the man's lips. His remaining rounds missed the target.

Velasquez practically tossed the revolver to Jester.

"My arm is getting tired after all this shooting," he said.

Jester broke the weapon open and reloaded quickly. Should he try to hit—or make sure he missed? Humiliation might push Velasquez's vanity to extremes, and Jester's back was a lot bigger target than the plank. So was Guadalupe's hacienda. But letting the lout win after his schemes about the estate, and Fabiana—to hell with it.

"I've seen you with that new girl," Velasquez said. "What's her name, Maria or uh . . ."

Jester stiffened. Something unpleasant was coming.

"Luna."

Velasquez grinned. "You are giving her lessons, reading lessons, eh?"

Jester looked at him. "That's right. She's a bright young lady."

"Bright possibly. A lady, no. You know, I think I'll give her some lessons myself."

Jester lowered his voice and stared hard at the man. "You keep your distance from her. She's an innocent girl."

The grin was still on Velasquez's face, lewd and mocking. "Servants are there to serve."

Jester pointed and cocked the pistol, sighted down the barrel, and squeezed off his first shot. It hit dead center in the board at eye level. He cocked and fired again, and again, and again, until he had put five of six bullets into the board at various points. Not an expert's pattern, by any means, but they both knew which man was the better marksman. He turned toward Velasquez and smirked.

"I'd say you're the one that needs lessons, Esteban, old boy."

He set the revolver on the table and walked away toward the gate, not giving Velasquez another look. A bullet in the back? The fellow didn't have the guts.

CHAPTER 17

"Two women shall be grinding together; the one shall be taken, and the other left." Luke 17:35

Luna removed the stitches from Jester's wounds first thing the next morning. She seemed to take extreme care not to hurt him. At one point she had to work the point of the scissors into the skin to cut a stitch, and he jerked in pain. She touched his cheek with her hand and looked almost as if she'd cry. After the procedure was complete, he tried to joke with her, but she had to go on to her other duties and just smiled at his words and hurried from the room. That smile of hers—it warmed him like sunlight.

He skipped the *desayuno* that morning. The heartier *almuerzo* would come soon enough, about nine o'clock. By eight, however, coffee sounded mighty good, and he followed its delicious aroma toward the kitchen.

Sofia and Luna were hard at work preparing the meal. Sofia was cutting vegetables and tending the pots on the big, black wood-burning range, but she took time to pour him a steaming cup of coffee. Luna knelt on the floor beside a huge pottery bowl, with the big stone trough and the rectangular stone bar, rather like a rolling pin, that he'd seen Sofia using several days before when he and Langhorne had looked in. The trough and bar were used in making the tortillas he enjoyed so much, but

259

the exact procedure was a mystery.

Luna looked up and gave him a shy smile as she washed the trough and bar. Jester grinned back and leaned against the doorpost to watch.

"Are you gonna make some tortillas?"

She nodded her head rapidly. "Yes, I make the tortillas."

She went about her work vigorously, smiling all the while. Having an audience must've pleased her. She scooped a double handful of swollen corn kernels out of the bowl and placed them on the trough.

"Luna, since I teach you how to read English," Jester said, "I'd like you to teach me what you're doing."

She looked a bit embarrassed but said, "Yes. This is the *nixtamal*."

"The corn?"

"Yes—after you boil it and rub off the outside."

"And what are the two stone pieces?" he asked.

She picked up the bar. "This is the *mano*." Then she pointed to the trough. "And this is the *metate*. You do like this." She drew the *mano* toward her, catching some of the corn under it, then pushed the *mano* back toward the lower end of the *metate*, crushing the corn as it went and pushing it off into a pan under that end.

Luna rocked back and forth slowly and rhythmically as she continued the process with more and more of the corn from the bowl. She stopped at last and gathered the ground mixture from the pan and piled it onto the *metate* again.

"Now it is called *masa*." She went through the grinding process again and yet a third time, until the *masa* was a fine, smooth dough. Finally, she formed it into little balls about the size of an egg and laid them in the pan.

She reached behind the big bowl of corn and pulled out a smaller one, also with the prepared kernels. Jester looked closely.

This corn seemed whiter than that in the large bowl.

"What's the difference?" he asked.

"I take the dark part out of these," Luna replied. She picked up one of the kernels from the large bowl and held it up for Jester to see. Then she held a kernel from the smaller bowl up beside the first. Sure enough, the black base was missing in the second kernel, leaving a grain almost pure white.

"Must be a lot more work," he said, "taking them out one by one like that."

"A little."

"But why do you go to the trouble?"

"It make a tortilla that is very white."

"I know that, Luna. But why would you want to do that?"

She placed a mound of the special corn on the *metate* and started grinding. She kept her eyes on her work, apparently reluctant to answer his question. Finally, he asked her again.

"Why?"

She squirmed a little. "I make these special—for you. No one else."

What a surprise—but at the same time, something made it seem like the most natural thing in the world. He cocked his head and looked at her for several seconds. "Why, Luna, that's about the nicest thing anyone's ever done for me. Thank you."

Luna kept her eyes down, but a pleased smile spread across her face, and she attacked her grinding with vigor. He watched her work. She could feel his eyes on her—that was obvious. It was also plain that she was enjoying his attention as much as he enjoyed giving it.

She finished grinding the pure white corn quickly—too soon—and then formed the masa into balls like before. She laid an iron sheet across the top of the range.

"This is the *comal*," she said. While it heated up, she patted one of the masa balls between her hands into a tortilla. When she finished, it was a perfect circle—impressive. She rubbed a rag across the *comal* and laid the tortilla on the hot surface.

He watched, still at the doorway, inhaling the tantalizing aroma from the baking tortilla and sipping his coffee. Luna patted out more tortillas and baked them, using her thumb and forefinger to turn them or snatch them off the *comal* when they were done. Such dexterity—and she never seemed to burn her fingers. As tortillas finished cooking, she piled them on a plate and kept the growing stack covered with a cloth.

"You know, Luna," he said after a while, "back in South Carolina, we made what they call corn dodgers."

She laughed. "That is a funny name."

He grinned. "Yes, I suppose it is. They're thicker than tortillas, and we fry 'em in bacon grease in a skillet."

She wrinkled her nose. "You should eat tortillas instead."

"I like tortillas very much."

She glanced over at Sofia, who was peeling potatoes, and then Luna handed him one of the pure white tortillas she'd just pulled off the *comal*.

"Thank you, my dear," he said. He held her gaze for a few moments, until she turned back to her work. He rolled the tortilla, shifting it from hand to hand for a while to keep from burning his fingers. Finally, he bit into it. Good heavens!

Luna kept glancing shyly at him as she worked, and he smiled at her.

"That is, without a doubt, the best thing I've ever put in my mouth," he said, and that brought a huge smile to her lips.

"My mother teach me how to make the tortillas when I was very young, just a little girl."

"She taught you well."

"She die last year," Luna said slowly.

Jester hesitated for a few moments. "I'm sorry, Luna. That must've been hard for you."When she didn't reply, he continued.

"Is your father still living?"

"He die, too. When I was twelve." She picked two tortillas off the *comal* and placed them on the stack, then began patting out another one.

"Any brothers and sisters?"

"No."

"Don't you have any relatives at all?"

"No."

Too bad he couldn't kick himself. He'd managed to ask every question that would impress upon the poor girl how utterly alone she was in the world and how pitiful her prospects were. He leaned against the door frame in silence for a while then and watched her work. She was a stoic one—admirably so. More than he'd be, in her circumstances, no doubt. After a minute or two, she stole a glance at him, though, and just the hint of a smile came into her eyes.

Maybe he could lead the conversation in a more positive direction this time.

"It's a beautiful place here, this hacienda, don't you think, Luna?"

She smiled. "Oh, yes, very beautiful."

"You like the mountains?"

"They are pretty—yes, the green trees, the blue sky. I like them all very much."

Shyly, she held out another tortilla, pure white and right off the *comal.* He grinned and took it. She hurried over to refill his coffee cup and then returned to her place by the range.

"Thanks, Luna. Do you like working here?" The question might not be fair; she wouldn't be likely to admit it if she didn't like it. She was too polite for that. But when she smiled, he knew she was going to tell the truth.

"Oh, yes. I like it very much here." Her eyes lingered on him for longer than usual, and he hurried on to another question.

"You have a nice place to stay then?"

"I have my own room, with a bed and a chest. And the señora, she give me some nice clothes to wear and says I can keep them, they are mine."

"That was kind of her. I think the señora likes you, Luna. You've brightened up this hacienda with your smile."

She seemed to blush a little, although with her dark skin it was hard to tell for sure. The girl deserved some praise—a lot of it.

From down the hallway a female voice startled him. "That coffee smells heavenly." Fabiana.

She walked toward him, a saucy smile on her face. Her long-sleeved white blouse and black skirt set off her figure to great advantage. She stopped beside him in the doorway and told Sofia, in Spanish, to get her some coffee. The old woman poured her a cup, and Fabiana took a long swallow, then turned to Jester.

"I see you had the same idea," she said, glancing at the cup in his hand.

"I suppose I did." He smiled politely. "And a good morning to you, Miss Fabiana."

"I trust you found your way back to the hacienda yesterday on your own," she said with an arch stare. "I didn't have the opportunity to ask you."

"It wasn't difficult. But then, I wasn't trying to follow anyone else. I did run into your dear uncle, out by the gate." Esteban's remarks about Luna came to mind, and Jester's smile disappeared. "We shot for a while."

Fabiana smirked. "At each other?"

Jester had to grin. "Yes. But he missed."

She looked him up and down. "I'm very glad to see it." Jester took a bite of his tortilla, and Fabiana raised her eyebrows. She looked over at Luna as if she'd just noticed the girl's presence.

"Give me one."

Luna smiled and handed her one of those with black flecks in them. Jester watched Fabiana—she hadn't noticed the difference. No sense in calling her attention to it. She took a bite and cocked her head while she chewed it.

"I think I like Sofia's better," she said at last. "Especially her flour ones. Why don't you make flour ones, girl?" Luna hesitated to answer for a moment or two, and Fabiana repeated the question in Spanish.

"Luna speaks good English," Jester said.

"Yes, I speak English good," Luna said pleasantly.

"*Well,*" Fabiana told her. "A person doesn't speak *good,* he speaks *well.*"

Luna was starting to look confused. Maybe it was time to divert Fabiana's attention from her.

"I've been teaching her to read, you know," Jester said.

"Yes, I know. It's been hard to miss you two out there in the patio in the afternoon. I wonder that she's able to get her work done."

"Your stepmother gave her permission, or I wouldn't have done it."

"Strange. We're running a kind of school for the servants, it seems."

Jester frowned. Too bad Fabiana had ever come down the hall. Things were much more pleasant with just Luna to talk to.

"Why don't we take our coffee out to the gallery," he suggested. At least that would get Fabiana away from the girl. He started into the hallway, but Fabiana made no move to follow.

"No. I'm curious what you find so fascinating about tortillas." She looked at Luna with obvious distaste. "I mean, you don't like a beautiful spot beside a mountain stream and want to get back to the hacienda as fast as you can, but then you spend an hour in a hot kitchen with smelly servants."

Jester glanced at Luna. She wasn't smiling any longer but went about her patting and baking with a blank expression.

"It hasn't been more than a few minutes," he said, "but I have to say those minutes have been very pleasant." That was for Luna's benefit, and she smiled a little.

Luna looked up at Fabiana. "I teach him how we make the tortillas, *Patrona,* like he teach me to read the English."

Fabiana turned to Jester and smirked. "I'm sure that knowledge will come in very handy for you."

Jester smiled as blandly as he could manage. "It's been quite enlightening, and I'm delighted to have had the experience."

"You seem to be delighted by the strangest things," Fabiana said, "and repulsed by others, most unaccountably."

"I'd hardly say repulsed, Miss Fabiana. Just wary of what I can't control."

"How can a guest have control over anything?"

Jester glanced over at Luna. The girl seemed puzzled by the veiled exchange, but she kept at her work. Timidly, she turned toward Fabiana again.

"I show him how to make the tortillas because it is what women do for the men. All women in Mexico. You and me and all of them." She held out a ball of masa, some of the pure white kind, toward Fabiana. "You make the tortilla for him. He will like it."

Jester stiffened up. Luna meant well, trying to offer Fabiana a kind of honor, an opportunity to make food for him. Making tortillas came naturally to Luna through long experience, as naturally as breathing. But it probably wasn't such a natural act for Fabiana.

Fabiana ignored Luna for a few moments, but the servant girl pressed the offer, holding the masa out almost in front of Fabiana's face.

"Luna," Jester cautioned, "I think your *patrona* would rather not make me a tortilla just now."

Luna grinned. "Oh, no, Señor. She like to make the tortilla for you. Every woman make tortillas for her man."

Suddenly, Fabiana slapped Luna's hand away, knocking the ball of masa across the kitchen.

"I don't know how to make your stupid tortillas!" Fabiana glared at the girl, then at Jester. "And he's not *my* man!"

Jester's heart pounded and Luna looked horrified. Fabiana seemed to teeter between fury and tears, and he stared at her. A moment later, she rushed from the room, sobbing angrily.

He glanced over at Sofia, who was staring open-mouthed at him and Luna. The old woman found her tongue, and a torrent of Spanish poured out, aimed in Luna's direction. It was too quick for Jester to understand, but from the tone, it had to be lecture, warning, or maybe a combination of both.

Luna looked completely bewildered. Jester stepped over beside her and put a hand on her shoulder. Hopefully, she wouldn't start crying, but no one could blame her.

She looked up at him. "I just want to let her make the tortilla for you. I just want . . ."

"I know, I know, Luna." He smiled to reassure her. "It'll be all right. I'll talk to Señora Medina and make sure she knows this wasn't your fault."

She touched his hand on her shoulder. "Will you, Señor? Oh, thank you, thank you."

Her hand felt rough, not at all soft like Fabiana's, but that made no difference at all.

Jester braced for a stormy day, but the remaining daylight hours were relatively calm. Fabiana didn't appear for *almuerzo*—no surprise—but she was there for *comida* about two in the afternoon and actually seemed in good spirits, although she talked mostly to her stepmother. Esteban had left the hacienda early in the morning, *en route* to Agua Blanca. Guadalupe simply said he'd decided to return to his house in town but gave no reason; thank goodness, regardless of the cause. The women ought to be more at ease with Esteban gone.

Late in the afternoon, Jester gave Luna her daily reading lesson. This time, however, he had to make do only with Langhorne's Apache volume because the books Fabiana had provided him were gone when he went to his room to get them. Carlito said that she'd made him retrieve them earlier in the day.

Sometime after seven that evening the calm ended.

Jester was sitting on a bench on the back gallery, right outside his own window, when some kind of ruckus began inside—female voices raised in either fear or anger. It sounded more like an argument than actual danger, and intruding again in a family squabble seemed ill-advised. After two or three minutes, though, the apprehension and curiosity were too much.

The commotion sounded like it was coming from near the kitchen, so he went in the back door and walked to the junction of the two hallways. He peeked as discreetly as possible around the corner into the lateral corridor. Fabiana was standing near the door to the kitchen, screaming in Spanish at a cowering Luna and grasping the neck of Luna's blouse.

Jester froze. Did he need to intervene? A moment later, Fabiana drew her other hand back and slapped Luna hard across the face, and Luna began to wail. Jester rushed into the corridor to go to Luna's aid and almost ran into Guadalupe, who was hurrying down it toward the altercation. She shot him a horrified glance as she slipped past, and he followed right behind.

Fabiana had her hand raised to strike a second time, but Guadalupe forced herself between the two, facing her stepdaughter and shielding Luna.

"What are you doing?" Guadalupe demanded.

Fabiana made as if she'd reach around her stepmother to hit Luna, but Guadalupe remained in the way, and the girl seemed to relent.

"I want her out of this house!" Fabiana screamed. "Out!"

Jester stepped forward. Maybe his presence would dampen the girl's fury. But she continued screaming at poor Luna like he wasn't even there, so he just stood close in case he had to intervene.

The rage continued for perhaps half a minute, and then Fabiana seemed spent. She stood there, her chest heaving as if she'd run a mile, and stared at Luna with dazed eyes. Guadalupe, for her part, put an arm around Luna's shoulders and tried to comfort her on the one hand while attempting to calm her stepdaughter on the other.

Jester fidgeted, useless and out of place. It was tempting to just go to his room and shut the door. But how could he, with his responsibility in the matter? Fabiana was angry because of him, because of his attentions to Luna, no matter how much he'd like to deny it.

He stood there for several minutes, until he was certain he wouldn't be needed. By that time, Guadalupe had calmed her stepdaughter sufficiently. Then he took Luna by the arm and guided her a few yards away from the two. She was sobbing a little, but she shrunk away from him when he tried to put an arm around her shoulders.

Guadalupe looked back at her. "Luna, dear, you may go back to your room for the rest of the evening."

Luna nodded her head nervously and slipped away down the hall.

Jester hesitated another moment, and then went to his own room as quietly as possible. When he shut the door behind him, he stretched out on the bed. What had he done?

When would Langhorne get back, so they could be gone from this place? But then, what might happen to Luna here? Was there a simple answer to all of it? One thing was certain, though. Just as Fabiana had said, he wasn't her man.

CHAPTER 18

"Thou shalt not be afraid for the terror by night."
Psalm 91:5

Jester woke up later than usual the next morning. The day looked drizzly from what he could tell through his curtained window—probably why he'd slept late.

A picture of Luna's smile came into his mind as he lay on his back, his hands locked behind his neck. She'd be coming in soon to help him, even though the time for really needing assistance was past. Still, Guadalupe had said the girl would continue for several more days—he certainly wouldn't argue.

It would be nice to be back in the United States, though. Now why would he think of that? Probably a connection with Fabiana's volatile temper over the past few days. When he and Langhorne had first come to the hacienda, he couldn't spend enough time with her. Maybe he'd even been falling in love with the girl—if he was capable of it. But now, everyone needed to take cover whenever she came on the scene. More and more often, there was some kind of outburst.

He waited for what must've been half an hour and was about to dress and go to the dining room, when the knock came on his door. Luna would come in now, as she usually did, peeking in first to make sure he was ready for her. But the door remained closed. After a few seconds the knock came again, and this time he answered.

"Come in, Luna." He smiled. It would be nice to see her face, just the thing to brighten the dreary day. She was such an honest, uncomplicated girl. And there was her beauty—simple but with a stirring quality hard to define.

The door opened but it was Guadalupe who peered around it for just a moment before withdrawing out of view again.

"I am sorry, Señor Jester. I didn't know you were not dressed."

The blood warmed his face. "My apologies, Señora. Please give me just a minute."

"I will come back when you are ready to get up," she said, but he hopped out of the bed, assuring her that he'd be present-able momentarily. When he'd donned his shirt and trousers, he called to her to come in.

He was pulling his suspenders over his shoulders when she entered. She looked decidedly ill at ease.

"I know you must've been expecting Luna," she said. "I have decided that it would be best if I assigned her to other duties." Her eyes seemed to hold an apology, and he hurried to reassure her.

"That's perfectly all right with me, Señora Medina." He forced a smile. Things couldn't have lasted, though. It had been easy getting attached to the girl and her solicitous ways. Better to call a halt now than risk doing something they'd both regret. At least that sounded good, but darn it—damn it!—why couldn't she be here now instead of Guadalupe?

"As you may have guessed," Guadalupe said, "my daughter's wishes were largely responsible for my decision. I thought it would help keep peace in our home. But I apologize to you for the change. I know that you have come to look upon Luna with favor."

"She's a very pleasant, helpful girl. I wonder, does this change mean that I won't be able to continue her English lessons?"

Guadalupe smiled. "No, not at all. I hope you will take every opportunity to teach her. And she will, of course, have the same time off from her duties every afternoon for those lessons."

"That's very kind of you, Señora."

"I beg you not to think too ill of Fabiana. She is sad and confused, and those feelings have led her to act in a way far different from her usual temperament."

"I quite understand. She's been through a lot. I only hope my own conduct hasn't added to her difficulties."

"Of course it hasn't." She put her hand on the door knob. "I will leave you then. Perhaps I will see you in the dining room later if you're coming for *almuerzo.*"

He held up a hand. "If you'd stay for a moment. I wondered if there's been any word from my compatriot, Señor Langhorne."

She shook her head. "I am sorry. We have heard nothing." She smiled and continued. "Tell me, are you getting anxious to be on your way?"

He returned the smile. "Is it obvious?"

"I just sense your energy returning. I think it will not be a welcome prospect to one young lady I know—or possibly two."

"No, Ma'am. I confess I have mixed feelings about the possibility of leaving."

Ah, those girls. Had there ever been a more pleasurable—or nerve wracking—time in his life? He chuckled. Being a self-confessed ladies' man wasn't always what it was cracked up to be.

Then her eyes brightened as if she'd remembered something. "I have received some good news of another kind, however."

"Oh?"

"Yes. My attorney has sent word that it appears my brother's attempt to gain control of the hacienda—and guardianship over my daughter—will not be considered by the court. He said that

273

Esteban's claim had not impressed the judge. You can appreciate my relief after hearing that."

"Indeed, I can, Ma'am, and I'm delighted things have turned out this way. You've had enough troubles these past days without adding that to them."

She sighed. "Thank you, Señor."

With that, she slipped out the door and closed it softly.

The remainder of the day was unusually serene, the English lesson with Luna was especially enjoyable, and he retired about ten. A long night's slumber sounded wonderful.

Jester came out of a deep sleep around midnight. Someone was screaming.

But where was it coming from? He listened for maybe fifteen seconds. It had to be from somewhere behind the house. He sat up in bed and kept listening until his mind cleared completely. It was a woman! He bounded out of the bed and pulled on his trousers, then his boots.

Other people were awake now in the main house. Worried voices moved down the hallway, and Jester hurried to join the others and find out what was happening. His hand touched the doorknob and stopped. The revolver. He turned back to slip it into his pocket.

Guadalupe was bustling through the corridor in a robe, her hair down and disheveled and her face marked by apprehension, but looking extraordinarily beautiful nonetheless. Carlito followed her with a coal oil lamp. She was speaking to him in Spanish.

Jester caught her eye and joined the procession. "What's happening?" he asked.

Without turning around, she said, "It came from the patio, or possibly the servants' quarters. I do not know what it is."

They hurried out the back door and into the darkness. The

clouds had departed at dusk, and a million stars twinkled overhead in the chill of the night. Carlito stepped in front of his *patrona* to lead the way with the lantern, and Jester fell into step beside her as they followed the yellow circle of lamplight across the ground.

The scream came once again, most definitely from the servants' quarters this time, and they turned in that direction. Then came the sound of frantic weeping. A faint light came on somewhere in the quarters, and an agitated female voice started speaking in tandem with the weeping, but the words were indistinct.

They pushed through the outside door and into a short hallway with two doors on either side. The first door on the left was ajar, and Carlito stood aside to let Guadalupe and Jester enter. The only light in the room came from a lone candle flickering on top of a small chest of drawers. Luna stood on her bed in a white nightdress, weeping and gasping, while Sofia held her hand and spoke softly to her.

In rapid Spanish, Guadalupe asked the women what had happened. Sofia was the one to reply at first, Luna still too distraught to give a coherent answer. Jester strained to catch the gist of what the old woman said, but it was all so rapid that he only picked up a few words—one in particular was puzzling. He turned to Guadalupe.

"What is that *alacran* she keeps saying?"

After a moment she looked at him, deep concern on her features. "A scorpion, she thinks. Luna did not see it, but she was stung, there on her shoulder—as she slept."

Jester stepped close to the poor girl, who was trembling now as she stood barefoot on her bed. He reached up toward her with both hands, and she held her arms out to him and melted into his embrace. For what must have been half a minute, she sobbed and shook, her face buried against his chest. He tried to

275

comfort her with soothing words, and eventually she did seem to calm down.

He looked at Guadalupe. "What's to be done?" he demanded. Oh, why had he made that sound so abrupt? But Luna needed help without further delay. Time might be of the essence.

Guadalupe translated into Spanish for Sofia, and Jester nodded his head nervously as the old woman slowly answered.

"We must open the spot with a knife and squeeze out the poison before it gets well into her system," Guadalupe told him at last, her face a pale mask.

Jester tried to push Luna a few inches away, so she'd look at him, but the girl kept her face buried against his shoulder like her life depended on it. He stroked her back with one hand.

"Luna, we've got to get you to lie down here."

"No!" She jerked upright.

"I will check under the bedcovers, Luna," Guadalupe said, pulling them back to the foot of the bed, but there was nothing under them. She patted the sheets by Luna's feet and said, "Why don't you lie down here, dear." Luna did, after a few moments, but her eyes were still wild with fear. Jester kept a hand on her shoulder the entire time.

Sofia looked around at the rest of them and said something. Immediately, Carlito stepped forward and opened a thin-bladed pocket knife. He held it out to the old woman, who took it hesitantly.

Jester looked into Luna's eyes.

"Now, dear, where did it sting you?"

Slowly she pulled the night dress off her shoulder to reveal a spot about the size of a half dollar, red and angry even in the dim candlelight. A point in the center was of a darker red.

Jester tried to keep his voice as calm as possible. "Now, Luna, Sofia's going to have to cut you a little, so we can get the poison out." It was unclear whether she'd comprehended, but after a few moments, she gave a tentative nod.

"We will have to hold her," Guadalupe said. She took the girl's hands in hers. Jester put both of his hands on Luna's head but stroked her cheek with a finger to soften the effect.

Sofia was beginning to look as frightened as Luna. The old woman leaned over the girl and slowly brought the knife over the sting. She touched Luna's shoulder with the blade, but her hand began shaking, and she drew it away. The shaking did not subside.

Jester looked around at the others and swallowed—all their eyes were focused back on him. The only time he ever cut a living creature was when he cleaned fish or dressed game, but now it was plain that this job had fallen to him. If he could only keep his hand from trembling as much as Sofia's and not hurt Luna too badly.

He swallowed again and wiped his palm against his trousers. He tested the point of the little blade against the tip of his finger. It was sharp indeed, almost like a needle. He leaned forward to get a better view. He took her upper arm in his left hand and moved the tip of the blade into contact with the dark red spot. She winced momentarily but then seemed to relax. He could delay no longer—he pushed the point of the knife into the spot and then drew it down a bit, making a cut a quarter of an inch long. Thank goodness it was sharp. He didn't spare Luna a look—he might not be able to continue with the process if he did.

Jester squeezed the spot between his thumb and forefinger, but his efforts didn't force more than a drop of blood from the cut. What should he do next? He looked at each of the others in turn, but their expressions were blank. Perhaps a sting was treated like a snakebite.

He put his mouth to the wound and sucked hard. Luna winced, and Jester backed off for a moment, spitting onto the floor. But he had to continue if it was to do any good. He bent down again and sucked more from the spot. He repeated the process three more times. Was he accomplishing anything? The liquid did taste of more than simple blood.

Jester wiped his mouth on his sleeve and peered down at the spot. The skin around the sting looked white and puckered. Now he could look at her face. The pain was gone from it, but she was pale, and her eyes had a hollow cast to them. Had he put her through this for no good?

Guadalupe released her hold, and Luna struggled to sit up, keeping her feet off the floor, tucking them under her. Jester sat down beside her and put his arm back around her shoulder. Her body was slightly feverish, snuggled limp against him. She rested her head on his chest, and he stroked her hair lightly with his free hand.

He chanced to glance up at the door, and raised his eyebrows. Fabiana stood just outside it, her features half in shadow in the eerie glow of the lantern and candle. Her face held no expression at all—no anger, pity, or even curiosity—and she seemed to avoid his eyes. He glanced away for a moment, but she was gone when he looked back.

Guadalupe, Carlito, and Sofia stayed along with him for quite some time, and the old woman cleaned the little cut on Luna's shoulder with some of the hacienda's wine. Finally, the girl's breathing became deeper and more regular. Jester didn't move for several more minutes—anything to keep from disturbing the poor girl's slumber. At length, he slowly disengaged himself from her, and with the help of Sofia and Guadalupe, he lowered her head, very gently, onto the pillow and pulled the covers up over her shoulders.

One of the ranch hands was sent to Viejo's shack, and the vaquero returned shortly after, with a handful of leaves for a poultice to be placed on the sting.

Guadalupe insisted on staying up with Luna and insisted equally that Jester and Sofia go back to bed.

"I will watch her carefully," she said.

Jester stepped quietly over to the door and took one last look back at the girl, sleeping peacefully now. He might even be able to sleep himself now.

He closed the door softly behind him and walked to the outside door, where he paused for a moment. The stars seemed even more brilliant, and a frosty chill hung on the night air. When he stepped out onto the ground and started toward the back door of the house, his foot kicked something hollow. He bent down to pick it up and then carried it with him into the house and to his room. The light of the lamp there revealed it clearly—a small wooden box, dark red and open.

CHAPTER 19

"Bring forth the men that are come to thee, which are
entered into thine house: for they be come to search out
all the country." Joshua 2:3

The next day was a time of waiting. Guadalupe had dispatched
one of her vaqueros to Agua Blanca before daybreak to fetch
the doctor, and they'd returned to the hacienda by ten. The
doctor could do little to treat the sting, but he thought Luna
was doing well. He ordered that she be kept calm and be allowed to sleep as much as possible. He wasn't certain whether
Jester's efforts to suck the poison from the sting had been effec-
tive, whether the scorpion had been one of the less dangerous
types, or whether it simply hadn't injected a full load of venom,
but in any case, Luna had fared better than many another victim
in the region. He predicted she'd be up and around like normal
in a day or two.

Jester watched the doctor gathering his implements in
preparation to leave. Would it be worthwhile to tell him that it
had been one of the small red scorpions? It probably wouldn't
benefit Luna, and it might do more harm than good. After all,
what could he prove? What was important was that Luna was
recovering.

Guadalupe had Sofia and a couple of other workers clean the
servants' quarters completely, remove and shake out all clothing

and bed linens, sweep every corner and dark place, and generally expose any areas that might furnish cover for scorpions. A couple of the creatures were found and killed in a storeroom down the hall from Luna's bedroom, but they were big, straw-colored ones that everybody agreed had painful but not dangerous stings.

It was mid-afternoon before Jester saw Guadalupe again, when she came to the dining room to eat *comida*. She sat across the big table from him, her dark eyes hollow. The few hours she'd had in bed after the doctor left probably hadn't made up for the time watching over Luna. He glanced at the door frequently—Fabiana might appear any time. The food had little appeal today.

"Is your daughter going to join us?" he asked finally, after they'd been eating alone for fifteen or twenty minutes.

"No. You did not know? She accompanied the doctor back to Agua Blanca."

"Whatever for?"

Guadalupe looked at him through tired, half-closed eyes. "She has gone to visit a friend in the town. I confess that I hope it will calm her. She needs to relax. Possibly a change of scene will help her get back to normal."

"I sincerely hope it will." The poor lady apparently had no inkling of Fabiana's part in the matter. And would anything bring her back to normal again? It would be best for Guadalupe, for Luna, and for everyone at the hacienda if Fabiana left and never came back—maybe even for the girl herself. In any event, Luna would be safe, at least for that day.

Who could ever like Agua Blanca? The smell—Fabiana wrinkled her nose as she rode the last thousand meters to the little town. Its muddy streets were more like wide alleys. No picturesque quaintness here, despite its mountainous surroundings. Instead it was nothing but a mining town, with just enough of the machine age to give it a rusty veneer.

After parting company with the doctor, she walked her horse past the fragile wrought iron fence that surrounded the town's tiny, weedy plaza, and fifty meters down a cross street to one of the few decent houses. Unlike most others, its walls were plastered and painted, in a sky blue, though a few raw adobe bricks stood exposed where the coating had eroded away.

Her stepmother thought she was coming to visit her friend Manuela, so of course she had to make an appearance at the girl's home—Guadalupe might check later. The woman was like that. Manuela and her sister and mother seemed happy to see Fabiana, and the mother especially seemed quite sincere in her condolences over the death of Augustin Medina. Fabiana kept her expression sweet—they couldn't imagine the wreck of her whole world. She endured the *comida* but departed shortly afterwards in a shower of distasteful embraces and well-wishing, claiming she had to run an important errand for her stepmother before the long ride back to the hacienda.

Now she started on the real errand. She rode by a surreptitious route through the town's irregular web of streets to the back of another decent house, this one a bit larger than Manuela's and painted a soft yellow—nothing, however, remotely approaching the size and fineness of the Medina hacienda. Fabiana tied her horse to a small flowering tree and slipped around to the front of the house, taking care not to be seen by the few people on the streets nearby.

A dark, sullen servant in white peon garb opened the iron gate and led her through a cool corridor to an open courtyard where bushes and flowering vines grew around a tiny tiled fountain that held a few inches of muddy water. The man indicated a wrought iron chair, then disappeared through a doorway across the courtyard.

Fabiana looked around her, drumming her fingers on her knee. The sooner this was over, the better. But it would probably be worth the distaste. In a brief few moments, footsteps sounded past the far doorway, and her uncle Esteban Velasquez strode out into the daylight.

He was smiling. "Ah, my dear niece Fabiana. What a surprise to see you here in my humble home. I am at your feet."

At your feet. Calvin Jester had said those very words. From him they'd been tantalizing.

He bowed extravagantly and tried to kiss her hand, but she slipped it out of his grasp. He dropped into a seat across a small table from her and leaned forward. "To what do I owe this pleasure?"

She almost shivered but then went on. It would be worth the unpleasantness.

"Esteban, I, uh, hope you are well."

"How could I not be so when such a beautiful creature as yourself is before me."

Fabiana took a deep breath. Perhaps the little red box should've been placed in *his* bedroom.

He looked intently into her eyes. "I've missed you since I departed the hacienda. Yes, I've missed you quite sorely."

It would've been nice to dispense with the ritual of compliments, but the game had to be played. Gratify him, make him more amenable—but her plans themselves would probably be agreeable to him no matter how she acted.

"You are kind, Uncle," she said. "Now I'd like to speak frankly. We're both adults." For a moment his eyes went over her body as he might've done in appraising a fine horse. It made her skin crawl but might be advantageous.

"Yes, niece, so we are. Tell me what's on your mind."

"You've made no secret of your wish to have the hacienda." She lowered her eyes demurely and then looked back up into his in a bold stare—hopefully the way an experienced woman would entice his desire. Yes, it would probably work. "And, I understand, you've expressed an interest in . . . me, as well. In one way, it seems that you want to extend your protection to me by becoming my legal guardian. In another, it would appear that marriage is what you have in mind."

The words seemed to take him by surprise. "You're very direct, Fabiana. I, of course, have only your welfare at heart when considering these possibilities." He called for his servant, and when the man appeared, Esteban ordered cool drinks brought to them. Was he just doing it to collect his wits again?

He turned back to her. "My poor sister has experienced a great shock and loss, as you have, my dear, and I cannot in good conscience stand by while she struggles with the responsibility of running the hacienda. It's a task beyond the delicate abilities of a woman. You, being a minor before the law, are in need of a man as protector and guardian." He smiled benignly. "As for any thought of a marriage being made between us, I suspect that to be the work of people with overly fertile, or even sordid, imaginations."

The servant brought out a pitcher of fruit juice with chunks of ripe melon floating in it. He poured two glasses and set them on the table then quickly disappeared again.

Fabiana took a sip from her glass and gave him her most convincing look of disappointment. "You mean you have no interest in ever considering the possibility of making me an offer of marriage?"

Again he appeared to be caught off guard. "Well, of course any man would consider himself fortunate indeed to unite in matrimony with such a young woman as yourself." The desire took hold in his eyes again. "Some would bring up the argument that we're kin and unable to entertain the possibility." He smiled. "But I assure you that there'd be no legal obstacle at all.

As an attorney I can say without equivocation that our kinship, being by my sister's marriage to your father and not by blood, would in no way prevent or even discourage you and me—if you'd ever consider it—from entering into a marriage."

Fabiana put a fist to her mouth. It was hard to keep from laughing at the whole idea, but also at his language—as convoluted and complex as one of the legal documents she'd sometimes glanced over in her father's office, certainly not the ardent declaration of passion he seemed to think it was. She kept a straight face, and tried to look both innocent and alluring at the same time, no easy combination. But what did her poor acting matter now? Esteban apparently had reached the point where he was thinking with his glands rather than his brain. She couldn't help a slight smile at the expression—old Sofia had used it once when telling another servant about an amorous experience from her youth.

He apparently misinterpreted her smile as avid interest. "I haven't broached the topic of marriage seriously before, Fabiana, because I thought you too young and inexperienced to have that choice thrust upon you. But now I see that you have a maturity of mind well beyond your years." He took a long drink from his own glass and then called out to his servant to bring a bottle of white wine. "You know, my dear, that a man of my experience and position could offer you many advantages as a husband. I, as an eminent attorney, a professional man, widely respected in this town and the entire region, can commend myself to you as a worthy match."

Fabiana held her palms toward him. "Please, Uncle. You proceed too fast. While I don't find your attentions unwelcome, I'm not ready at this time to rush into such an undertaking. I'm still in mourning over my father." That was the truth. "And I wish to become much better acquainted with you"—that certainly was not—"before seriously considering the possibility."

"Oh, of course, of course, my dear."

"I've heard, Uncle, that your hopes to, uh, *help* my stepmother manage the hacienda have been dashed. At least, that's what her attorney has indicated."

Esteban's face showed his embarrassment. "Well, these things can be extremely complex. I wouldn't at all say that the issue is decided." A lie.

"From what I've heard," she said, "your suit has no chance for success." Was that revealing too much cynicism? No—the time for feigned innocence was over. Boldness was needed now. "Of course, if you could find some way of gaining the favor of the court, of the judge in this case, I suspect your position would suddenly become much more favorable."

The wheels were turning in his mind. It was so obvious. It was easy to guess his next words.

"You know of such a way?"

Fabiana smiled. "Perhaps."

"Will you tell me?"

The servant came into the courtyard again, carrying a bottle and two wineglasses. Esteban frowned while the man uncorked the bottle and poured. He filled the glasses too full—not surprising that her uncle couldn't get a well-trained servant in a backwater like Agua Blanca and for the little that he'd pay.

Esteban shooed the man away impatiently and drank down half the glass, and it seemed to steady him.

"Are you going to tell me, Fabiana?"

"I'm going to show you." She reached into a pocket and withdrew a folded envelope. "You would consider yourself a patriot, would you not, Uncle?"

"Certainly, certainly." His eyes shifted between her face and the envelope.

"And someone who might do harm to our nation—you would be glad to expose such a person, would you not?"

"Yes, yes. Of course I would. I am first, last, and always, a Mexican."

"I was sure you were." She slowly removed a sheet of paper from the envelope and held it out to Esteban.

He snatched it and began to read. After a few moments he frowned. "This is nothing but a copy. Did you write this yourself?"

"From the original."

"The American is here on behalf of the United States government?"

"Obviously."

"But what is he doing? Is he a spy?"

"He must be. Why else would the letter be marked 'Confidential'?"

He frowned in thought for several seconds, then looked back at her. "Perhaps he's been carrying confidential information to the representatives of his government here. That wouldn't be espionage."

She frowned at him. "If you wish to believe that. But it seems to me that the simplest explanation is likely to be the true one—he's working against our government and our nation."

"Where is the original?"

"Back at the hacienda."

"In your room?"

"Back at the hacienda," she said, a little more slowly this time. It was back in the hidden pouch in Jester's belt—he would've been alarmed if he'd found it missing. But it would probably be easy enough to get the original again if she needed it.

Esteban frowned but didn't press her further about the location. "Why is it, my dear niece, that you're telling me this? What is it you want?"

Fabiana flashed an innocent look. "I, too, am a patriot, Uncle, and I wish to stop him from harming Mexico." Esteban's frown deepened, and he cocked his head. She had to smile. "And I wish to see him punished."

"Ah, you don't like the American's interest in that servant girl. Well you won't win him back this way, if that's what you had in mind."

"I don't want him back." She held his eyes for a long moment in a provocative look—her best effort at it, anyway. "My affections have changed. But I want him to suffer for what he's done—to our nation, of course."

"This letter could damn him."

"I hope it does."

"And Guadalupe?"

She paused for a moment and sighed. "I bear her no hatred. But neither do I have any great love for her. If she suffers, she suffers."

Esteban gave a cynical smile. "The obedient daughter."

"She's not my mother! My mother was a wonderful woman, and she made my father happy. Guadalupe tried to take her place, but she never could."

"Of course not."

"The letter should help you get in the court's good graces."

He folded the paper and tucked it safely into a pocket. "Tell me, my niece, don't you have the slightest apprehension about helping me? After all, it gives me a very good chance to convince the court to transfer the hacienda to me—and possibly to put you under my guardianship, as well."

She smiled serenely. "Without the original letter, you have no proof that it's genuine. You might've written it yourself. So you see, you must rely on me to prove your accusation." Really, did it matter if Esteban came to own it? She'd still be the one to control it, one way or another. But punishing Calvin Jester—now that was what mattered. And Esteban would most certainly be the instrument of that punishment, armed with her copy of the confidential letter.

He smiled at her. "You're really quite naïve despite that devious mind of yours, Fabiana. I have no doubt you could be persuaded to give up the original if I have need of it—and to agree to anything else I might desire."

The smile left her face suddenly. Could he be right? Had she overplayed her hand?

Esteban cocked his head. "But for now, there's no need of such persuasion—as long as we work on the same side. Remember, I'm a very generous man to those I'm fond of."

She forced a proud smile. "We'll work on the same side, Uncle. Never fear." If Esteban tried in the future to go too far—in any direction—she'd find a way to deal with him.

Fabiana bade her uncle farewell and slipped out of his house, again taking care not to be seen. A cluster of trees stood a hundred meters away, and she led her horse there, tying it out of sight and kneeling behind the foliage where she could watch Esteban's front door. Now to see if he'd do anything immediately. Probably not. He was far too lazy to act with any real energy, as his present difficulties, financial and otherwise, indicated.

Kneeling among the trees was uncomfortable, and when fifteen minutes had passed without his leaving the house, she rode off past the railroad station in the direction of the hacienda. The local gendarme, a heavy man with a big black moustache and a perpetual scowl, eyed her from the platform as she went by. She never remembered seeing him in a uniform in all her years, although everyone in the area knew he was a policeman. He wasn't likely to cause her any problems.

Fabiana turned a corner and the station disappeared from

her view, and she stopped her horse. Would Esteban alert the gendarme to the letter? Would he try some other way to capture Jester? It would be because of her actions if he did, her fault—and Jester had such beautiful blond hair. She sighed and shook her head. If it happened, it happened. He shouldn't have treated her the way he did. He'd had his chance.

About half past five that evening, Jester took Luna to her room to rest and started off across the courtyard and past the main house, toward the *zaguan*. He'd been with her most of the day, first sitting on the gallery and later out in the sunshine of the private patio. She said she wanted to soak in the warmth of the sun, and it did seem to do her good. Her face was losing some of its pallor, and she'd eaten a modest *comida* of salad and peaches.

Now, exercise sounded like just the thing, a brisk walk out toward the vineyard. He turned south past the *zaguan* and covered the ground with long strides. It was great to be out beyond the walls in the mountain air.

The pines and the meadows all around and the mountains that rose to the east in razor-sharp focus made an impressive panorama—beautiful. He breathed in deeply. It was good to feel almost normal again. Damn that bear.

He was almost to the vineyard when mounted men came in sight to the south. They came in at a trot over a grassy rise, a quarter mile out. Two horsemen, there were, and a third animal behind, horse or mule—still too far to tell.

An uneasiness hit his stomach, nothing definite. Any strangers warranted a good lookover these days. He slowed his pace and glanced around. There ought to be a place to hide somewhere close, if it proved necessary.

He squinted. What was it about the one on the left? The man's erect posture—he'd seen it somewhere before. By the time they'd closed another fifty yards, he had his answer.

They'd spotted him too, by now, and headed straight for him. A broad smile came onto his face, and he stood there, arms crossed. Too bad they'd caught him in the open. It might've been amusing to give them a surprise. At twenty yards, the one rider broke into a grin.

"Lose your horse, sonny?" Langhorne reined up and slipped down from the saddle. He gripped Jester's hand. "Good to see you back in the land of the living."

"Likewise, sir. Welcome back to paradise."

Jester spent half an hour drumming his fingers on a chair arm on the back gallery while Langhorne bathed and dressed. The man's return would bring changes in the routine, but welcome ones in some ways.

The evening meal was delayed for Fabiana, who rode in when it was almost totally dark. Jester raised his eyebrows when she hopped off her horse at the front door. Her eyes danced with life, despite the long ride from Agua Blanca, and she'd never looked more beautiful—but there was no warmth, no softness, more like a graceful mountain cat. He shook his head slowly after she passed him on the way to the dining room—what had become of the girl?

Dinner—not the usual light *cena,* but a very substantial meal of beef steak, vegetables, salad, and plenty of warm tortillas with butter—was a lively affair. Fabiana talked more than ever, but with none of the anger that had been so common to her these past few days. She was pleasant and almost respectful to her stepmother, and she seemed to hang on his and Langhorne's words. What was going on?

Guadalupe didn't seem to know what to make of the girl's pleasant demeanor after the conflict of the preceding week, but after a while she began to look relaxed and comfortable.

Langhorne said little specific about what he'd done since departing the hacienda, but he indicated they'd be leaving soon. He asked Guadalupe about the land to the east where the Sierra Madre formed a rugged barrier between Chihuahua and Sonora. She told him what she knew of the route used by the few travelers who chose to make that difficult crossing rather than taking the long but easy detours by rail to the north or south around the range.

"Sometimes," he said, "the best route's not the flattest one."

When they finished the caramel custard *flan*, Jester and the others rose from the table. It would be good now to relax on the back gallery with Langhorne and listen to his travels in detail. So far, he'd mentioned little to Jester of any trouble, but something must've caused him to avoid the railroad and return to the hacienda overland.

Langhorne lingered in the dining room to speak with Guadalupe. Jester snatched another tortilla from the stack to take with him to the patio. It had black flecks in it. He dropped it on the table and poured a cup of hot coffee instead.

When he got out in the chilly night air, Fabiana was standing there. She had to be waiting for him. Why couldn't she leave it alone?

"You may sit with me if you'd like," she said, dropping into a chair and crossing her legs. She indicated another chair. Might as well oblige her. She had another bottle of wine and, with a rather unsteady hand, poured herself a glass. Was that her third?

He opened his mouth, but there was really nothing to say. Instead, his eyes went across to the servants' quarters where Luna was resting in her room. It was unnecessary, but he turned his chair to be able to watch that door while he kept his eyes on Fabiana.

"You haven't asked me about my trip to town to visit my

friend," she said innocently. Her words had just the slightest slur.

He did not reply for perhaps fifteen seconds. "No. I hope you had a good time."

"Oh, I did. Thank you. My friend Manuela and I are very close. Very close. We tell each other everything." She giggled for a moment just like any young girl might, but the sound held no magic now. "She and I talk about who we like—sometimes about the young men we think are handsome. Of course there aren't many handsome young men that come to Agua Blanca or the hacienda. Those that do come, we especially like."

"That's nice." Langhorne ought to hurry up.

"Yes it is. You know how girls are. I'm sure you've had a great deal of experience with girls. You know how to please them." She looked closely at him. "And how to hurt them."

Would it be good to tell her he knew what she'd done to Luna? No, it probably wouldn't. He looked away from her, keeping his eyes on the door to the servants' quarters.

Fabiana glanced in that direction, too, then back at him. "Is there something interesting out there? I can't imagine what, but you seem to keep looking." Finally, she shrugged. "No matter. You know, Manuela can have an unforgiving nature. There was a young man that she was fond of, but he treated her horribly. He took an interest in another girl, one of no family or education, and flaunted it in front of Manuela. It broke her heart, poor thing. Well, do you know what she did?"

He looked back at her. It would be quite satisfying to slap the hell out of her. Of course, he couldn't—he wouldn't—ever. "No, I can't say that I do."

"This young man wasn't what he seemed on the surface. Manuela learned of his secrets and exposed him for the scoundrel he was. He's in prison today, I believe in Hermosillo."

"And the other girl?"

Fabiana shrugged and drained her glass. "She died, I think. She wasn't important anyway." She smiled sweetly at him. "Now isn't that a sad story?"

Jester turned away again, his eyes back on the servants' quarters.

After another half minute of silence, Fabiana abruptly stood, bottle and glass in hand.

"Good night, dear Calvin." She started for the back door.

"Good night, Miss Medina."

In a moment she disappeared into the house.

Langhorne stepped out onto the gallery only seconds later.

"Did you two have words?" He sat down where Fabiana had been. "The girl brushed by me without a glance, lookin' like she was about to cry."

Jester frowned and looked over. "It's not her words that bother me."

"It's plain *something's* bothering you." He had a cup of coffee, too—as always—and he took a long sip of it. "Mm. Paco didn't make it like that on the trail."

"I assume, sir, that you've done more than drink coffee and give advice these past two weeks you've been gone."

Langhorne looked surprised at him for a few seconds, then began to chuckle. "Relax, will you, Jester. I'm not the enemy."

Jester sighed and smiled himself. "My apologies. I'm anxious to hear how you've been entertaining yourself while I've been holding down the fort. I doubt you returned here cross country by choice when there's a perfectly comfortable railroad."

Langhorne settled more deeply into his chair and nodded. "I guess you could say I killed the wrong man's brother." For the next minutes he recounted his run-in with Sandoval's murderers and his flight from the *Acordada* by ship, train, and horseback.

Jester kept a slight smile on his face the entire time.

Recounted by anyone else, it might've sounded too dramatic to be swallowed whole, but Langhorne didn't have the air of an exaggerator. Instead, the entire account came across in the same understated tone as an after-action report in a regiment's monthly returns. Of course, Lieutenant Colonel Powell had mentioned Langhorne's experience. Jester looked at him.

"You've killed men before?"

Langhorne looked uncomfortable. "Yeah. But it never gets to be commonplace."

Jester cocked his head. "Think you'd do it again if you had it to do over—this last one, I mean?"

"I don't know if I'd kill *any* of 'em again." There was a long pause. "But I probably would. It's part of what I do—what I was put here to do, if you understand what I mean."

"You're not the easiest fellow to understand."

Langhorne sighed. "No, I suppose not. But what I'm trying to say is just that, since there are some pretty bad people in this world, there have to be some soldiers. I think God's suited me to be one of them. Sometimes killing goes along with the job. I wish it didn't."

Jester leaned back in his seat. "I guess I never gave it all quite so much thought. Maybe you don't have to if there's not a war on."

Langhorne smiled. "You don't seem to be quite the joker you were when we first got here. Did the bear take that much out o' you?"

The question was a surprise, and one that took a little reflection. "I've had to look at things a little more seriously than I ever did in the past, especially in regard to young ladies."

Langhorne just nodded once, slowly, and took another drink of his coffee.

After a few seconds of silence, Jester spoke again. "I was curious about what you were discussing with the señora after supper. Anything to do with me?"

Langhorne smiled. "No. I just asked her to point out the route east across the Sierra—the one she'd mentioned—on a map she had in the office."

"You know, I'm thinking I might just need to stay here a little longer." It had been nagging at him all evening—not so much that he didn't want to leave, but there was Luna's safety to consider. Of course, there was no denying she'd worked her way into his heart.

"A fellow down in Mazatlan told me something that bears repeating for the unwary. He said, 'Mexico's a narcotic.' "

Now what did that mean? Was it true? And how did it apply now?

"You think I'm in love with Luna?"

"Her or maybe Miss Medina. Them and this place." He glanced around at the dark patio, the house, and the servants' quarters, all under the brilliant night sky. "Like you said, it's a paradise here."

Jester took a sip of his own coffee, but it was cold, and he slung the rest onto the ground. "I'll have to admit, I may be a little sweet on Luna. But that's not it. Not all of it anyway."

"What is it then?"

Jester related his dealings with Fabiana and how things between them had "gone to hell in a handbasket," especially since Luna's arrival.

"Sounds like a young girl's way," Langhorne said. "Can you fault her too much for being a little jealous? After all, you're quite a catch." He didn't laugh, but there was a definite twinkle in his eye.

"You won't think the rest is funny. A couple of nights ago, she tried to beat Luna. Guadalupe and I stopped it, of course. But then last night, Luna got stung by a scorpion."

The humor had left Langhorne's eyes now. "Yeah, trying to

hit the poor girl is way outta line. But a scorpion sting—those things happen in this part of the country."

"You remember the day when Señor Medina and Fabiana showed us around the ranch? You and he were looking at cattle or something, and Fabiana took me to see this old man she called Viejo. He had a collection of herbs and potions, and a few varmints, too. There was one little red scorpion he kept in a red wooden box. Very dangerous, he said. Well, last night when I left Luna's room and started out across the patio toward the house, I found that little red box on the ground, open and empty."

Langhorne didn't reply for several seconds. "I see what you mean. Some people would call that attempted murder. From what you've told me, Miss Medina sounds as unpredictable as a mad dog."

The chill in the night air seemed suddenly more intense. "Why don't we take our conversation inside where it's warmer?"

Langhorne offered no protest, and they went in to Jester's room. He got on his bed and leaned back against the headboard while Langhorne took the chair.

"I'm sorry, but you'd better get your things in order," Langhorne said, "because we'll have to be leaving in the next couple o' days."

Jester sighed. "I guess that's that, then." He slipped his suspenders off his shoulders and locked his hands behind his neck. It felt good to relax, even now. "There's not much to get in order. I can pack the night before we go."

"Just make sure you have your letters of introduction—both of 'em. Who knows if we'll have to use them again on the way home."

Jester slowly got to his feet and went over to the bureau. He found the regular letter of introduction, then opened a drawer and pulled out the belt that had the hidden zippered compartment. "The 'confidential' one's in here," he said, working the stiff zipper open slowly. He pulled the paper out carefully. Something did not seem right.

"What's the matter?" Langhorne asked.

Jester unfolded the letter and looked at it carefully. "Someone else has had this." He looked at Langhorne, who was frowning. "I'm quite fastidious when it comes to my papers. I only fold them one certain way. I suppose it has to do with my literary nature."

"You mean it's not folded to suit you?"

"I never fold a paper this way. I tell you, someone else has seen this letter." There was Fabiana and the story about her friend. "And I think I know who."

"Miss Medina?"

"It's something she said. She was a little tipsy when she said it."

"Go on."

"She told me this tale about a girl who found out a man's secrets and exposed him, sent him to prison, she said. It was just a cock and bull story, but I think she was trying to let me know she'd found this letter and told somebody about it— somebody who could make real trouble for us."

"Velasquez maybe?" Langhorne said. "Or maybe she went straight to the law. She was in town today. Either way, we'll need to move our departure up to tomorrow—first thing."

"I don't know."

"Tomorrow morning."

The urgency was understandable, but there was still Luna to consider.

Langhorne seemed to read his thoughts. "She'll be okay. Believe me."

"I think I've got to watch over her a little longer."

"Better get packed, Lieutenant."

That last word—Langhorne had to pull rank again. But what

could he do? Maybe one last try, but halfway in jest. "As I've been trying to tell you, my bar is just as silver as yours."

"First thing tomorrow. And she'll be okay."

CHAPTER 20

"Get you to the mountain, lest the pursuers meet you;
and hide yourselves there three days, until the pursuers be
returned." Joshua 2:16

Fabiana came awake in stages over what must have been twenty
or thirty minutes. Her head was pounding and her mouth dry.
When she finally opened her eyes just a little, she quickly
squeezed them shut again. There was activity outside—talking,
horses, and movement.

Oh, to stay in bed. Not luxury but necessity. The wine had
been mercy last night, but now it was judgment. The commotion outside wouldn't go away. A few minutes more, and she
dragged herself out of the warm bed and pulled on a robe over
her night dress. Where were her slippers? Outside—yes, it had
to be. The law or Esteban must've arrived. She found the slippers under the bed and hurried on for the entertainment.

She stepped outside and looked toward the stables, but where
were Esteban and the officers of the law? Instead, Calvin Jester
and Mr. Langhorne were both swinging into their saddles, and
the little man who'd arrived with him yesterday was already
mounted, all of them surrounded by vaqueros and others of the
hacienda's workers. Old Sofia was there, tears rolling down her
leather cheeks.

Fabiana scowled. That damned lazy Esteban was probably

still in Agua Blanca, lingering over a lavish breakfast or lying in bed with his young housemaid, while that damned Calvin was slipping from the trap. She hurried out through the crowd to join her stepmother, who was standing beside the men's horses, exchanging farewells.

Jester leaned down toward Guadalupe. "Watch over Luna, won't you." He looked worried. Fabiana smiled for a moment. She'd give him something to worry about. When he glanced over at her, his frown deepened. He said nothing but their eyes met and held for several seconds. Then he looked back at Guadalupe, tipped his hat, and the three men turned their horses toward the *zaguan*.

Guadalupe put an arm around her shoulders, but she shook it off. Who needed the woman's pity? Fabiana hurried along behind the riders, following them outside the gate and right, along the wall. When they reached the corner, they turned east toward the Sierra and put their horses into a lope.

She stood there at the corner, looking after them for a long time, until they disappeared into a stand of big pines four hundred meters away. They reappeared beyond it two or three minutes later, so far away now that all she could make out was the color of their horses.

Fabiana fought back tears. Damn it all! For a moment she looked around for a rifle. She'd ride after them and serve justice on Calvin Jester herself. But no—she kicked the ground and stalked back through the gate and on to the house.

Esteban showed up sooner than expected—after his initial failure, she hadn't really thought she'd see him until the afternoon or later, but he rode into the courtyard and pulled up in front of the main house no more than forty-five minutes after the Americans had left.

Two *rurales* were with him.

Fabiana hurried out to meet her uncle and the lawmen and

told them of the escape of the two Americans and their *mozo*. The officers remounted their horses immediately and followed her out through the *zaguan*, where she stopped by the northwest corner and pointed out the fugitives' route. Esteban hurried out to join them again and rode out with them on the trail, the trio breaking into a gallop toward the crests of the Sierra far to the east.

Fabiana watched them go. There was a certain satisfaction to it, after all. Despite their beautiful grey clothing and sombreros, those *rurales* were tough and dangerous men. Her father had told her of their skill in running criminals to ground. And there was what others had whispered more than once in her hearing—*rurales* operated under the simple maxim of finding lawbreakers and killing them on the spot, without the inconvenience of a trial.

A thought struck her and she smiled—how convenient it would be if Esteban happened to catch a bullet as well.

Langhorne and Jester followed the vaquero called Rubio south, out of the pines and through a little valley, sheltered from view by the higher ground between them and the hacienda. The two vaqueros who'd been waiting in the pines with Rubio had ridden on east with Paco, being careful not to come out in sight of the hacienda again until they were too far away to be recognized. According to Langhorne's plan with Guadalupe Medina, Paco and the two would draw any pursuers toward the Sierra, keeping well out ahead, for the rest of that day, then filter back toward the hacienda during the night. Paco would break off to the south and return overland to his home in Navajoa, a hundred-peso bonus from Langhorne in his pocket.

With Rubio leading, Langhorne and Jester swung in a wide arc south and west, skirting the hacienda at half a mile and always out of sight from it. Langhorne held Rubio to a gentle pace to give plenty of time for the *rurales* to ride far to the east before he and Jester started along the trail back to Agua Blanca.

"I don't quite understand how you knew when we needed to ride out this morning," Jester said as they neared a crude corral and barn. They were well to the west of the hacienda by this time.

"Something I worked out with the señora last night after supper. I asked her to post a man with a fast horse four or five miles from the hacienda just off the trail to Agua Blanca. If he saw anyone coming out from town toward the ranch, he'd hightail it there and give us warning without letting 'em know they'd been spotted. Sure enough, this morning he caught sight of Velasquez and the *rurales*. Glad they didn't see him."

"And then Rubio here and the other two rode out to the pines to wait for us," Jester said, nodding his head slightly as if the plan was becoming clear to him now.

Langhorne grinned. "You're catchin' on." His expression became serious again. "But you know, if you hadn't noticed that letter of yours had been tampered with, we wouldn't have taken the precautions. They might've caught us flatfooted."

"I feel better already."

"Of course, you shouldn't have left the letter unguarded in the first place."

Jester raised his eyebrows. "I do apologize for being mauled by that bear, sir, and having to take to my bed to recover. It was quite thoughtless of me."

"Apology noted."

Rubio led them straight on to the barn, and they pulled up there. A saddled bay mare was in the corral, tied to a fence post. Langhorne stepped down from his horse and Jester did the same.

"Rest stop?" Jester asked.

"Just got to pick up a passenger." Langhorne couldn't keep

from grinning. Poor Jester looked puzzled.

Luna emerged from the barn carrying a brown leather grip. It probably held most all her worldly possessions. When she saw them, a shy smile came on her face, and she walked over.

Jester laughed, and he took her by both shoulders and looked into her eyes. Then he glanced over, and Langhorne said, "You didn't think I was really gonna leave her here, did you?"

"I had no idea. I was worried sick about her staying on with you-know-who still around."

"That was another thing Señora Medina and I talked about," Langhorne said. "But Luna couldn't very well leave with us. The señora had one of her men smuggle Luna out covered in a shawl and then bring a horse for her."

"Sounds like you and Guadalupe thought of everything."

"That lady is the real hero of this whole affair," Langhorne said. "I don't think we could have done it without her help— and her vaqueros."

"What do you think'll happen to her?" Jester stepped into the corral and untied the mare but kept his eyes on Langhorne all the while.

"I think she'll be okay. I wouldn't have left her if I thought otherwise." He waited while Jester led the mare out and helped Luna climb into the saddle. "We're the ones they're after, not the señora. Besides, she's got a ranch full o' vaqueros who aren't likely to let anybody bother her, even the *rurales.*"

Langhorne mounted, and Jester followed a moment later, they swung their horses to the west, Langhorne shouted an *adios* to Rubio, and they were off at a trot toward Agua Blanca and the railroad home.

Jester and the others reached the first outlying shacks near Agua Blanca. It seemed more like six months since they'd first come through the town rather than just a couple of weeks. The town was no more attractive this time than before. The sooner he boarded the train and left the place behind, the better.

They watched the station silently from across the street for a couple of minutes, and finally Langhorne spoke.

"I'd better lie low as much as possible in case any *Acordada* men are watching. Luna shouldn't attract any attention buying the tickets, though."

"I could go," Jester said. Involving Luna might put her in danger.

"But your Spanish isn't that good." Langhorne grinned. "We might end up with passage to Panama if you bought 'em. And that blond hair of yours is like a flag."

So Luna went into the station for the tickets, and they unloaded their baggage under a tree and rode to a livery stable a short distance away where Guadalupe had asked them to leave the animals. Langhorne left the Winchester there, too, in the scabbard on his saddle.

"Can't very well take a rifle on the train."

"I've got my revolver anyway," Jester said.

"I have a telegram that I have to shoot off to a friend of Señora Medina's," Langhorne said as they started up a dusty street back toward the station.

Jester didn't say anything for a few moments, but finally he had to ask.

"Something to do with Luna?"

"Yeah. You knew something had to be done. She couldn't very well come back to the States with us."

Jester let out a long, troubled sigh. "I suppose not."

"Being a ladies' man catches up with a fellow sometimes, I guess."

"That sounds like something I thought recently myself, believe it or not." Parting from the girl, probably for good—he shook his head. There'd been plenty to distract him up to now, but suddenly it was there staring him in the face.

Langhorne glanced over. His smile was sympathetic at least. "That little girl really got hold of you, didn't she?"

Jester nodded. There'd been plenty of lady friends—society girls, great beauties, young women with charm and manners. It hadn't been a problem keeping them at a distance, figuratively speaking, even while he'd enjoyed those charms and that beauty. Now to be smitten with a young woman like Luna, a servant girl—that hit from out of the blue. Surely they might find a way.

He turned to Langhorne. "I was thinking . . ." Before he could say anything further, Langhorne spoke.

"The wheels are turning in your mind. You want to figure a way that she can be with you. She's about as innocent as they come. And I think you'd agree that you're not. She'll go with you if you ask her to—I saw it in her eyes there at the barn. You can take her along, and she'll be happy and so will you, for now, and things'll end up with you breaking her heart. Or you can make her stay down here, make her a little sad for now— but give her a chance for a decent life, where she won't be cast off like an old shirt."

An old shirt! Jester looked hard at him.

"I assure you, sir, that my intentions are honorable."

"With Luna, I believe you."

That was a surprise. "Well . . . I thank you for that."

"But you know what they say about good intentions."

Did Langhorne think he was the Pope or something? But there was a more practical objection. "Things may go bad down here. There's no telling if the whole country'll fall apart. She could be killed if she stays in Mexico."

"That's a possibility. But what I'm telling you is a sure thing." Langhorne stopped in front of a building, and Jester did, too. "I won't stop you if you try to take her along. That's not my place. But I'm asking you to consider the girl."

Jester stared at him. There had to be a reply. But no words would come.

Langhorne nodded toward the building. "Here's where we're going."

The word *Telegrafo* was stenciled in faded letters on the wall next to the door, and Langhorne led the way inside. A man sat behind a counter at a telegraph key, and Langhorne handed him a paper and said something to him in Spanish. After passing the man some coins, he waited with Jester while the fellow tapped out the message and got an acknowledgment from the other end.

"That friend of the señora," Langhorne said, as they started out the door, "is part of some network of folks around the country working to stop the slave traffic and help the peons— folks like Diego Sandoval was. I told you about him. Señora Medina is part of it, too, of course. Anyway, the friend is up in Hermosillo."

"Which is on our way home." Convenient.

"That's right. We probably won't be able to make it there today, knowing the Mexican railroads. I doubt if we can get farther than Guaymas tonight."

The railroad station was only a block from the telegraph office. Luna was sitting on a bench under an awning, glancing nervously from one side to the other. Jester started to cross the street to her, but Langhorne caught his sleeve.

"If anybody's watching that station for you or me, it'd be best for us to show ourselves there as little as possible." He led Jester back to the spot where they'd left their baggage beside a tree. When a boy walked past them a few moments later, Langhorne stopped him and pointed over at Luna, said something in Spanish, and handed the kid a coin. The boy grinned and ran across the dusty street to the girl. She looked over and then hurried across, smiling.

"I thought you were gone," she said. "I was very worried."

"No need to worry, my dear," Jester told her, casting a quick frown at Langhorne. "You can trust us."

She glanced down shyly and then looked back up at Jester. "I know I can trust you."

Langhorne held out his hand. "May I see the tickets, Luna?" She handed them to him, and he looked at them. "On to Corral and then to Guaymas. Did they say if we'd have to wait in Corral? Never mind—I'm sure they didn't." He turned to Jester. "Mexican railroads seem to run on the philosophy of 'we'll get there when we get there.' "

Jester grinned. "I recall it well from the trip down here."

They waited there for half an hour until a train pulled in from the north.

"That's got to be ours," Langhorne said. He took Luna by the elbow and started across the street. They walked with her between them, their hats pulled low over their eyes and looking no one in the face. There were no compartments on this branch line train, so they found three seats in a second-class coach and sat down, bags at their feet. Their trunks and some of their clothes were still at the hacienda, sacrificed for the sake of speed and stealth in their hasty exit. Jester didn't mind—clothes could be replaced.

The coach was half full, and a few people were still boarding as the train pulled out. An old woman with a scarf around her head sat down across the aisle from them, and a heavyset man in a cheap suit dropped into a seat near the other end of the coach, looking none too pleased behind his bushy moustache.

Jester settled back. It would be good to have a pleasant journey.

CHAPTER 21

"But then shall I know even as also I am known."
1 Corinthians 13:12

The Hotel San Lorenzo where they spent that night in Guaymas suited Jester just fine. They had three separate rooms, with Luna's between his and Langhorne's. Jester slept well the first part of the night but woke up about three and only dozed after that.

Langhorne knocked at seven, and Jester answered the door, shaved and fully dressed.

"You look a little the worse for wear," Langhorne said, with a wry grin.

"I feel, sir, a little the worse for wear."

"Coffee ought to fix you up. Let's get Miss Garcia and head down to the dining room." Jester was stiff and bleary-eyed, but Langhorne led him next door to Luna's room, and the sight of the girl was like pulling back the curtains on a sunny morning. The improvement would only be temporary, of course, because they'd be on the next train to Hermosillo soon and the meeting with Guadalupe Medina's friend. As they walked along the corridors and down the broad stairway, Luna remained tucked between them almost like a child. Jester edged a little closer to her and put a hand under her elbow.

As Langhorne had promised, coffee did the trick for Jester.

The fatigue lifted off of him as if it had been a physical weight. His mental state was something else. He looked across the table at Langhorne and frowned. How could the fellow be so cavalier, smiling and digging into a plate of ham and eggs, toast and orange marmalade? Luna smiled back at both of them in her shy, diffident way. She only ate a little of her pastry, though. Did she realize they were going to leave her soon?

Langhorne was the one to broach the subject. "Do you know where we're going this morning, Luna?"

"The señora, she tell me we go to see her friend in Hermosillo. He is a good man, she say, and he will take me in."

Jester raised his eyebrows. At least she realized what was happening. His mind went over the route home, back up to Nogales—but how much nicer it would be if Luna could ride it with them. She probably wouldn't have any trouble at the border, not with him right there. And Langhorne had said he wouldn't interfere—that was something. The journey on from there was something of a blank, though, no matter how hard he tried to imagine it. El Paso, Washington, amber waves of grain beside the tracks stretching between the two cities—those visions were plain enough, all right, but Luna was nowhere in them.

If she had no place in his army world, then he could always resign his commission. They could stay on the border. He could find—what?

He looked at the coffee in his cup. Too bad it wasn't straight bourbon.

The railroad station was bustling with Mexicans of every class and age when they arrived there at half past nine. The ticket clerk told Langhorne the train north should be very crowded and advised them to wait for the next one, which would be along in an hour or two. It wouldn't be wise to delay, though, and Langhorne bought their tickets. They found a place to sit in the third coach back from the coal car, but it was only two seats for the three of them. They piled their luggage in the aisle beside their seats and waited for the train to start moving, the air close and warm already, heavy with the smell of unwashed bodies.

The trip was sluggish, with scarcely time for the train to build up speed after leaving a station before it began slowing again into the next town. Luna and Jester talked nervously, half-heartedly to each other. It was plain they both dreaded the parting that was ahead. Langhorne didn't spend all his time watching them—there was the return to Fort Bliss to think about. Would Lieutenant Colonel Powell be there to receive their report, or would they have to travel all the way to Washington before seeing him? And what of Stemmons? The threat of a court of inquiry was still there, nagging. From most men it would've been a hollow threat, but Stemmons was just vindictive and unreasonable enough to actually carry through with it. The train's slow speed didn't help matters. Langhorne sat there, cramped beside Luna and sweating in his shirt and coat. Would he even have a career after the next few days? Starting over would be hard. And what else did he know how to do but soldier? God would provide. It would be nice if He provided a horse right now, though, and some wide-open spaces.

It took three or four hours to make Hermosillo, and it was like he was a prisoner given a precious reprieve when they finally began the last slow deceleration. People were already stepping off onto the platform before the train came to a full, steamy stop. The platform was just as crowded and noisy as it had been when he and Jester had come through on their way down.

Langhorne hoisted Luna's bag and his own and followed her and Jester out the back door of the coach and down the steps onto the platform. They pushed their way through the crowd and found a rough wooden bench in a less hectic part of the station and sat down. Langhorne spotted a boy who looked like he wanted to make some money and scribbled a quick message to Guadalupe Medina's friend, asking him to meet them to escort Luna to safety. He gave the boy the friend's address and sent him on his way with a promise of another peso if he'd hurry.

The wait was uncomfortable for all of them, with the crowds and the heat. Langhorne made small talk with Luna to keep her mind off Jester, and glanced occasionally at him. Was he actually going to let the girl go? He could've ordered Jester to do it, just to be on the safe side—but that was a decision no man ought to make for another. Besides, he'd given Jester his promise.

Langhorne looked over at Luna. The important thing was that she got a chance for a decent life. He got up and walked over to a vendor and bought a fruit drink for each of them. Luna accepted hers gratefully. Jester nodded his thanks but didn't take more than a sip. His mind was obviously working. Too bad he'd fallen so hard.

"Señor!" It was the errand boy's voice above the din of the crowd. He came toward them, accompanied by two men, one young and the other middle aged and heavy. The younger was Jorge, Diego Sandoval's assistant. Jorge's eyes brightened as he looked at Luna there on the bench.

After giving the errand boy the promised extra peso, Langhorne nodded to Jorge. "I didn't expect to see you here, friend."

The young man grinned. "I have been staying with Señor Torreon." The grin disappeared. "I had not left Agua Blanca when I got word about Señor Sandoval. The lady, Señora Medina, sent me on to Señor Torreon here in Hermosillo. We did not think it would be safe for me to return to Culiacan."

Langhorne nodded. "That was wise." He made the introductions.

"A pleasure," Torreon replied, nodding his head grimly as he gave Langhorne and Jester a quick handshake. His tight collar seemed to strain under big, gleaming jowls, and his eyes went from Langhorne to Jester, then finally settled on the girl. "Is this the young woman that Guadalupe told me about?"

Jorge spoke up eagerly. "Yes, she's the one. This is Señorita Garcia."

Luna looked like she didn't know quite what to make of it, suddenly being the center of attention of four men.

"The girl's been through quite a lot," Langhorne said. "You'll have a safe place for her?"

Torreon smiled for the first time. "Yes, we will take care of her. She will be quite safe."

The man looked like he meant it, and Langhorne let out a deep breath. Maybe he could let her out of his sight now without so much apprehension. He glanced at her. She and Jester had their eyes locked on each other, as if they were the only people in the entire station.

He gave them a few more seconds then finally spoke. "Well, Calvin?"

Neither Jester nor Luna stirred for a few more moments, and at last Torreon said, "Come. We must hurry."

Jorge edged closer to Luna and looked like he was about to speak, but Jester put a hand out and lightly stroked the girl's shoulder.

"Well, Luna, I guess it's time to say goodbye."

Langhorne could hear the Carolina drawl break a little as he said it, and tears were forming in Luna's big eyes.

"In the United States," she said, "you will have a blond woman to make your tortillas."

"I don't think so, Luna," Jester said.

"Yes." She smiled through the tears. "But she won't make them pure white for you."

"No one would ever do that but you, dear lady."

Torreon's voice was insistent. "We must go now."

Jester took his eyes from Luna and glanced over at Langhorne. "May I give Miss Garcia one of your books? I have it in my bag."

Langhorne smiled at him. "Sure thing."

Jester bent down quickly and rummaged in the bag, finally pulling a volume out and holding it out to Luna.

"It's the book about the Apaches."

She smiled and took it from his hand.

Langhorne studied her face for a few moments. She looked like she was on the verge of a real crying spell.

"You're quite a romantic, Calvin, giving her *that* book."

Jester looked over and managed a grin. "We read through some of it together."

Langhorne took one of the girl's hands in his. "You'll be all right, Luna."

She looked up at him. "Thank you, Señor Langhorne. Thank you for saving me."

He couldn't reply at first. It'd be a fine thing if *his* voice cracked now. Finally, he said, "I think all four of us here had a part in it—us and the señora."

"Guadalupe is a wonderful woman," Torreon said. "The equal, in courage, of any man I know."

"Amen to that," Langhorne said. He shook hands with Torreon and then Jorge. "Take care of her, Jorge."

They turned and walked away through the crowded station, and a long, ragged sigh came from Jester.

Jester stopped at the ticket window. Things were a little better now that Luna was out of his sight. It was going to be a long time, though, before she'd be out of his mind as well. He and Langhorne bought their tickets for the train north to Nogales, which was scheduled to leave very soon, and they carried their bags to an out-of-the-way spot near the platform, beside a deserted vendor stand. Langhorne scanned a local newspaper while they waited. Jester shifted his bag from one hand to the other, then back again half a minute later. It would be good to talk, but Langhorne seemed intent on his paper.

Something hard nudged Jester's ribs. Langhorne looked up suddenly, and Jester chanced a cautious glance over his shoulder. The man standing there seemed vaguely familiar— yes, he was one of the people who'd boarded the train with them back in Agua Blanca, a heavyset, unpleasant looking fellow with a thick moustache.

"You will stay where you are for now," the man said, revealing a revolver held down by Jester's back where none of the people around them were likely to see it. "Do not think of trying to get away or doing anything else. I *will* use this if you give me any trouble."

Langhorne's voice was steady. "What do you want from us?"

The man ignored the question and checked his pocket watch, then dropped it back into his vest pocket.

"I asked you what you wanted with us," Langhorne said.

Jester swallowed. Langhorne shouldn't press things. Then the stranger answered Langhorne's question.

"You will wait here with me until the *Jefe* arrives. Then I will give you over into his custody."

Jester glanced at Langhorne. "Is he talking about the man you told me about?"

"That's right." He turned to the man. "I'll make it worth your while if you'll leave us and walk away. He won't ever know."

"He knows everything." The man shrugged. "Anyway, I'll have your money when he gets here. He doesn't care about that, just you."

Jester glanced at the man again. "Sounds like we don't have

much to lose then by making a break for it, Señor."

The man pressed the revolver painfully against Jester's back. "If you do not consider your lives to be of any value then go ahead—because I will shoot you dead. My name is Juan Narvaez, and I am a professional officer of the law, not an ignorant peon."

Jester looked at Langhorne, who shook his head ever so slightly.

The tempo of business in the station hadn't slackened. People shuffled by, talking loudly and jostling those that got in their way, and there was the low, constant rumble of creeping locomotives. If they were going to end up getting shot, at least Luna had gone before the danger threatened her.

And then, there she was, damn it, coming back!

She was short but she craned her neck to see past the crowd, and when she spotted him, her face lit up just like it had back at the hacienda. Jorge was right beside her, steadying her by the elbow, and Señor Torreon followed close behind, reluctantly, judging from the expression on his face.

How could he warn them away? But no—he'd just end up with a bullet in his back. Langhorne made no move to give the alarm either although he was probably waiting for his moment. The pistol barrel pressed harder into Jester's ribs.

He spoke more loudly than normal when Luna and the others were still ten or twelve feet away.

"Why did you come back?"

He was frowning. His words and expression might strike the girl as unkind—what an odd thought, though, when there was so much more to worry about.

She stopped a little short of him, with a puzzled look, and then held out the book toward him. She glanced down then back up at him.

"I, I want you to write your name in my book."

Jorge said, "She insisted on coming back for this. Please."

Narvaez moved quickly, shoving Jester away and leveling the revolver at all of them, sweeping it quickly back and forth from one to another.

"Stay back!"

Somewhere in the distance the "All aboard" was announced for Nogales.

The next moments seemed to play out in slow motion. Langhorne flipped the newspaper toward Narvaez's face, Jester tried to strike at the man's gun hand, and Jorge threw himself in front of Luna. The pistol discharged, and the report reverberated off the ceiling of the station, and the bustle of movement all around them suddenly froze.

Langhorne was on Narvaez in that instant, landing a solid blow with his fist to the side of the man's head, which sent him senseless to the floor, the revolver clattering away.

Luna was frozen in place for several seconds. Jester stepped over to her, checking her for injuries—she couldn't be shot, not now! In a moment he noticed Jorge's forearm, blood slowly running down his sleeve. Nothing was certain, but the young man had very likely saved Luna from being hit. Jester stared for a moment—too bad he couldn't have been the one to save her.

Quickly, he and Langhorne pulled Jorge's coat off and rolled up the sleeve of his white shirt, now stained bright red. Apparently, what the young man had done dawned on Luna then, and she stepped in and tried to stop the bleeding. It looked like a flesh wound, thank goodness, albeit a severe one.

A moment later, Langhorne said, "I don't think it hit bone or artery."

Luna was making over Jorge, dabbing his wound with her handkerchief and speaking *Pobrecitos* to him as if he were a child, and Jorge seemed to bask in the girl's attention despite his obvious pain.

"We'd better get him a doctor," Jester said.

"She seems to have things under control," Langhorne said. He turned to Torreon. "I suggest you get Jorge and Miss Garcia out of here, Señor, before you have to answer a bunch of questions." Quickly he caught Luna's eye and nodded at young Jorge. "Take care of him, Luna."

"Yes, Señor." Luna spared Jester one long, meaningful glance, full of concern, then turned that concern back to Jorge and, with Torreon's aid, helped him away until they were lost from sight in the crowd.

Jester stood there looking after her. Finally, Langhorne's voice brought him back.

"We've got a train to catch, Calvin." He nodded toward Narvaez, who was still out cold on the floor. "Nothing to worry about from him. But this"—he bent down and retrieved the book, which had apparently fallen from Luna's hand during the fracas. "Maybe you can mail it to her once we get back to the States."

Jester shook his head slowly.

Langhorne shrugged and dropped the volume into the waist pocket of his coat. "No, I suppose not. I expect Jorge will have her attention for the foreseeable future—most likely for good, from the way he's been looking at her."

"Let's get on that train." Jester gritted his teeth and started grimly down the platform, and for once Langhorne followed *him*.

Rodolfo Escarra was already on the Nogales train when the Americans came aboard. He chose an aisle seat in the second car from the rear, the coach closest to where he'd seen them standing near the platform. When his own train from the south had pulled in a few minutes before, he'd debarked hoping to find Narvaez, whom he knew vaguely, holding Langhorne in his custody. Narvaez did indeed have a man who had to be Langhorne, along with another gringo, in an out-of-the-way spot. Escarra had started toward them just at the moment when things fell apart and the shot was fired.

His plans changed immediately. He had no jurisdiction here, no official authority whatsoever anymore, even though an unofficial and illegal network of men like Narvaez still functioned, held together by nothing except Escarra's own fearsome reputation. With Narvaez out of action and the attention of everyone in the station focused on the Americans, the chance to take them quietly was gone. Even if he could capture or kill them here, his own chances to escape were greatly diminished. Police or troops—*Maderista* police or troops—might appear at any moment, and that fearsome reputation of his might well earn him a spot against an adobe wall. No, the train north offered much more promising possibilities.

Langhorne and his blond-haired companion entered Escarra's coach when they came aboard, and he allowed himself just the hint of a smile—his luck hadn't deserted him. It never would.

They passed right by him down the aisle, Langhorne even brushing against his shoulder as he went by. How tempting it was to grab the man right then and there, and choke the life out of him. He clenched his teeth, and his enemy passed. He'd make his own opportunity to repay the man for killing his little brother—repay him with interest. It wasn't going to be an easy death.

The two Americans found seats near the forward door of the coach, and again Escarra smiled. It would be easier to keep an eye on them that way and watch for the best opportunity to present itself. Maybe it would've been wiser to bring Sotero along, but there'd been no time. Having the two gringos together might present difficulties although he had, on occasions in the past, taken two or even three men together. It all depended on waiting for the right circumstances, the moment of vulnerability and inattention—then strike and strike mercilessly! This time would be no different—except more satisfying than ever.

He patted the pocket of his coat—the pistol was there, his little Smith & Wesson .32-caliber hammerless revolver. He'd chosen it rather than the bigger, more powerful Webley .455 in his suitcase. The smaller pistol was easier to conceal and not as loud, and a wound from it could make a suspect talk without killing him. Besides, it was only a secondary weapon for what he had in mind this day. The cord garrote was in his trouser pocket, where he always kept it.

Escarra bided his time while the train cleared the station and began the series of runs from village to village, advancing steadily but slowly northward toward the border. Perhaps a fairly deserted stop would be best, although all of them might be crowded. He settled back against the greasy upholstery of his seat and waited.

It was hot. Not as hot, or as crowded, as the original ride south had been two weeks before, but hot nevertheless. They went through the first two stops, and by that time the sun was really beating down on the metal roof of the car. Jester looked back over his shoulder. The coach was full—poor men in peon white, businessmen in dark suits, one vaquero holding his *tapaderos* on his lap, and a scattering of grandmothers in *rebozos*, pretty young mothers, and children. Many were eating and drinking—something cool to drink would taste mighty good now.

He nudged Langhorne, who was handing a five centavo coin to a little boy of six or seven who'd stopped to stare at them. "You think they sell refreshments on this train?"

Langhorne laughed. "This isn't the Washington to Baltimore, first class. Who knows, maybe you can find somebody aboard

who's willing to sell you a cup o' lemonade."

Jester got up and eased past Langhorne into

get one for you, too, if I find anything." He sta

where the majority of the cars were.

"Don't be long," Langhorne called after him.

Jester glanced back at him for a moment. La

looking back and from side to side, seeming to tak

of everybody in their coach.

The other cars were full, too, and the p

uncomfortable as those in his coach. Finally, on

Jester found an old woman who was willing to sel

of cups of a sweet orange drink, *naranjada,* she ca

He worked his way back toward their coach t

narrow aisles, past the only lavatory he'd seen

next car back. What a hell of a stench, even thro

door! He'd sweat out the orange drink if he was

have to visit the lavatory himself later.

Langhorne was engrossed in a newspaper he

somewhere. The man took the cup of orangeade

a "thank you" and drained half of it in one draug

"That was a pretty good idea of yours." Lan

the remaining liquid around in the cup.

Jester gave him a lazy grin, swigged the remair

drink, and tipped his hat over his eyes.

Escarra watched the Americans.

He'd made it a practice over the years, whe

Man had assigned him a particular offender, to st

habits, his preferences, the patterns in whicl

moved. Those revealed his victim's vulnerabilit

Power—the power of knowing without being kn

Now he went over what he knew of Langhor

man had acted and reacted in every incident.

considerable information on Langhorne and what he'd
e in regard to the Mestiza girl. And then there was the situ-
1 with Joaquin. Escarra stopped for a moment and tried to
e the pictures from his mind—pictures of his brother as a
: boy, as an awkward young man of fourteen, and finally as
strong man he'd become, a constant and faithful companion
1 if he was hotheaded and bent toward cruelty. Joaquin,
quin—little brother. Escarra swallowed hard. Did anything
matter?

he pictures faded of their own accord, slowly. Then he
:ed back over the things he knew about Langhorne. After a
e, a thought began to form. He latched on and laid it out
rly in his mind before it could slip away. And then, finally,
e it was—something he could work with.

ghorne stretched and checked his wristwatch. They'd been
eling for almost four hours from Hermosillo, certainly
vay or a little closer to the border. Jester stirred beside him,
ed his hat away from his face, and looked over.

\s much as I hate to subject myself to the indignity, I fear I
t make use of the lavatory."

anghorne chuckled. "That bad, huh? You can't wait another
hours till we get to Nogales?"

'm afraid that would be out of the question."

'ith an uncomfortable expression, Jester stood and edged
into the aisle, then started toward the front door of the
h and disappeared through it a moment later.

anghorne glanced back over his newspaper. He'd exhausted
y item of interest two hours ago, so he dropped it under his
There was a tug on his sleeve.

señor." Langhorne smiled—it was the little boy to whom
given the five-centavo piece earlier. The child looked seri-

ous and explained that his mother needed help in the car behind theirs.

What kind of help could she need? Langhorne got up anyway and followed after the boy, who ran ahead to the back door of the coach and on outside. Langhorne stepped through the door onto the platform between cars, but the boy must've already gone into the next coach.

But there was someone off to the side. Yes, it was a man whom he'd noticed earlier in the coach, a man in a business suit and pointing a revolver.

Escarra shot Langhorne.

The air burst out of the gringo's lungs in a hoarse grunt, and he dropped. One shot, low along the waist—with luck, it hadn't killed him. The shot had worked well in the past when he'd had no accomplice and so wanted to incapacitate, to take all the fight out of a man before dealing with him further. Now he was free to strangle the man slowly—Joaquin deserved no less satisfying justice to avenge his murder.

Escarra put away the revolver and drew the garrote from his pocket. It was a simple tool, a thick cord with a small wood grip on either end, but there was nostalgia about it like a fine hunting rifle that had brought down many trophies. He stretched the cord and worked it free of kinks. There was time to enjoy this— the man groaning on the platform wasn't going anywhere.

Escarra glanced at the doors to both coaches. No one had looked out from either one—not interested or, more likely, too scared to show their faces. The other gringo, the blond one, was still around—but the pistol would take care of him if he happened upon them.

Langhorne was stirring now and gasping, trying to suck in air as he lay on his back, dazed grey eyes looking up in Escarra's direction. It would be easier if the man was on his stomach,

323

easier to use the garrote from behind. On the other hand, straddling his chest and facing him, watching his eyes while the life was slowly choked from his body—now that would be satisfaction.

Escarra knelt down with his knees on both sides of Langhorne's body and his hands grasping the wooden handles of the garrote. He raised it to loop it over Langhorne's head.

A light seemed to come on in the man's eyes, and they regained their focus. What was happening? It was just a moment's hesitation, and then Escarra started to whip the cord around the man's neck.

Langhorne's left hand grabbed the cord between the handles and jerked it sharply toward him, drawing Escarra along, too, and he swung his right elbow in an arc. Stunning pain reverberated through Escarra's jaw, and he blinked quickly.

Langhorne pushed him off and got to his feet. Escarra shook his head to clear it—he had to stand up, but . . . A fist hammered his left eye. Then his nose cracked under another blow, and he reeled back into the door of the rear coach.

The revolver was still in his coat pocket, and he pulled it, but Langhorne was already on him, shoving him hard against the coach. The pistol—damn it, it slipped from his hand! He swung and caught Langhorne in the mouth, driving him back.

Where in the hell was the pistol? There, down on the coupling between the cars. Escarra dropped to his knees. He could get it—if he only could reach far enough. He stretched, and then stretched farther, more than he'd ever done before, down toward the pistol. His fingertips brushed it. Then his hand closed on it! He smiled through the blood. Now!

Something—what was it, the sole of a boot?—planted itself on the seat of his pants and shoved like a mule's kick. He was toppling now, grappling for a hold on the platform and then on the coupling itself, his fingers missing both, and he was tumbling toward the cinders and ties rolling smoothly past below him like in a dream.

Jester threw open the rear door of their coach, revolver in hand. Langhorne stood bent over on the platform, breathing hard and bleeding from a split lip.

A long, tortured groan like a soul in hell came from somewhere below, and the train lurched slightly, just for a moment. Jester's skin turned cold in the hot afternoon, and he hurried into the last car and down the aisle to the back, then out onto the rear platform. He looked back down the track. A man's red body lay between the rails—at least, half of a man's body.

By the time Jester got back to the platform between the cars, Langhorne seemed to have caught his breath. Jester stared at Langhorne's coat and frowned.

"Are you shot?"

"I sure thought I was." Langhorne pulled a mangled book from the waist pocket of his coat. "I'm kinda glad Luna didn't keep this." He held it up, and Jester saw the bullet lodged in the thick leather cover. It had gone almost all the way through, and the lead tip was visible just peeking through the leather. Langhorne rubbed his waist and winced. "Just nicked my skin, but brother did it pack a wallop—like getting kicked by a mule. Couldn't breathe for a minute or two there."

Jester took the book from him and held it up in the sunlight, his eyes twinkling mischievously. "I am surprised—and delighted, of course—to see that you're not dead, sir."

"A thirty-two, I think. A larger caliber probably *would've* killed me. Or if he'd shot me in the chest. Who knows why he didn't."

Jester kept the straight face. "You must live right."

"Mercy of God, more likely."

"Was that the fellow whose brother you killed?"

"I suppose so. Escarra was his name, I think."

Jester looked off at the dry, rolling hills going by beside the tracks. " 'Nothing in his life became him like the leaving it.' "

Langhorne could not help a smile. "I think you're on the mend, friend—back to quoting poetry. *Hamlet*?"

"*Macbeth*."

CHAPTER 22

"They departed into their own country another way."
Matthew 2:12

El Paso looked better to Jester the next morning as they pulled in than Washington or New York ever had. The night train from Nogales had been loud and slow for the first hours, with several groups of enlisted men playing cards and joking crudely in the coach, and then quiet and fast for the rest of the trip after the troopers had de-trained at Douglas. Jester had slept little—who could after what had happened on the ride north to the border?

Once off the train, he and Langhorne found a streetcar that took them to the post, and from there they walked on to the bachelor officers' quarters. A few minutes lying down in his room would be just what the doctor ordered—that and a slow, hot bath. Langhorne had telegraphed Lieutenant Colonel Powell from Nogales right after they'd crossed the line last evening, and Powell had instructed him to report to the commanding officer of the Fourth Cavalry at noon. He added, ominously, that Colonel Vandreelan hadn't yet returned to command of the regiment from his duty at the War College. Jester was to join Powell at the train station at four in the afternoon.

Jester soaked in the tub and scrubbed the accumulated grime of the preceding twenty-four hours off his body. It was no use, though, trying to focus on Washington and how comfortable things would be again very soon now. For every minute thinking about the parties, the fine dining, and the society girls, there were three on the hacienda there in Sonora. All of it was there, as vivid and fresh as when it had happened—the grizzly, the legend of the Apache moon, the walks and rides with Fabiana Medina . . . and more than anything else the moments with the Mestiza servant girl who'd worked magic on his heart.

Damn it but there'd been a lifetime in those weeks, and this present existence was something new and alien. It would take some getting used to again, this gringo life.

He settled back against the tub and let his mind dwell on Luna Garcia one last time.

Powell had said noon, and Langhorne appeared at the regimental offices five minutes early. He was going to be cool and calm when he faced Stemmons—but his palms were damp by the time the clock struck the hour. He stepped up to the commanding officer's door and knocked briskly three times. A voice inside told him to come in, and when he opened the door, there was Stemmons—no, actually nobody was behind the big desk, and Langhorne let out a deep breath. Powell was seated against the wall.

He got up and returned Langhorne's salute, shook hands, then indicated a chair.

"I'm sorry to say Colonel Vandreelan won't be back for another week. I hoped he'd be in command here again by the time you two got back, but you returned earlier than I'd expected."

"Yes, sir. Circumstances forced us to head back ahead of schedule." Langhorne glanced uneasily toward the door, and Powell spoke again.

"He'll be back in, in a couple of minutes."

Langhorne shifted his weight. The reunion with Stemmons

wouldn't be joyful. Any hopes that the man would forget about the court of inquiry simply wouldn't hold water, not with Stemmons's personality. The man never seemed to forgive a mistake, real or imagined, and there'd been plenty of the latter. Two months back he'd relieved the captain of C Troop for being a few days late with his officer evaluations, and that while the troop had been on arduous patrol duty at the scouting camps along the river.

"While we're waiting," Powell said, "why don't you fill me in on how my aide performed on this mission."

"Lieutenant Jester performed very commendably, sir." He handed Powell a manila envelope. "It's in here, sir—my report on the mission." He'd skipped getting any sleep himself that morning in order to pound out the report in time for the meeting.

Powell pulled out the typed sheets and started looking over them. He grinned. "A bear, huh? That took a hell of a lot of nerve."

"Yes, sir. He kept fighting the animal even though he was badly injured."

"I wasn't talking about Jester." Powell turned another page. "This information on the Mexican rail system is excellent—just what I wanted." Footsteps approached in the hall outside, and Powell slipped the report back into its envelope.

Langhorne stood up and faced the door as the knob turned, his heart beating like a drum on the parade ground.

Powell chuckled as the door opened. "Well, Langhorne, here's Major Sommerset, the Fourth's acting commander."

Langhorne could've melted onto the floor. A moment later he was able to smile. After the exchange of salutes, Sommerset smiled and motioned for Langhorne to resume his seat. The major went around the big desk and sat down.

"Glad to see you back, Langhorne." Sommerset, English by

birth, was a fine officer and a fair one.

"Thank you, sir."

"I forgot to tell you, Langhorne," Powell said with a wry grin. "I suppose you were expecting Lieutenant Colonel Stemmons to still be in command."

Langhorne wanted to frown at Powell, but he couldn't do it.

Powell looked at Sommerset. "I didn't remember to tell the lieutenant here about Colonel Stemmons's transfer." He turned to Langhorne. "He got some fitting orders—assignment as co-ordinator of our team for the 1912 Olympics." He laughed. "It's amazing what working on the General Staff allows me to accomplish."

Langhorne didn't join in the laughter, but he did smile. "No mention of a court of inquiry, sir?"

"He didn't have time to even think of it. I got the orders approved a couple of days after you left, and he was packed up and gone the very next day. I tell you, Langhorne, because of you a lot of men are going to be unhappy."

Sommerset said, "Confidentially, sir, I don't think Lieutenant Colonel Stemmons was that popular here."

Powell grinned again. "I was talking about those poor athletes."

"You don't really have to see me off, old boy," Jester said as he and Langhorne crossed the street and entered Union Station in downtown El Paso. It was ten minutes to four in the afternoon, and the Texas and Pacific train to Washington was scheduled to depart just after the hour. The prospect of the capital was beginning to look just a little brighter.

While Langhorne went off to locate Powell, Jester put down his bags and sat on a bench on the platform next to the train. A blond young woman sat on the opposite end of the bench. She was pretty—what else could he do but talk to her? At first she

seemed reluctant to give more than polite answers of the brief-
est sort, but she opened up after a while—courtesy and a soft
Carolina accent were usually handy for wearing down female
reserve. By the time Langhorne reappeared, things were
definitely looking up. Jester turned toward him and smiled.

"Why, Lieutenant Langhorne, I just found out the most
interesting thing. It seems that Miss Williamson, here, is also
going to Washington. What a pleasant journey that'll make it."

Langhorne nodded back over his shoulder. "Lieutenant
Colonel Powell is here."

So he was. Jester stood up and saluted as Powell approached.
"Colonel, I'm so glad to see you again, sir. Can you tell me
which compartment we'll be riding in?"

Powell looked down at a ticket. "I'll be in this car, compartment C, Lieutenant." He looked Jester up and down for a few
moments. "Well, it seems that bear didn't damage you too
severely. I trust you're feeling fit again and ready to ride."

Jester beamed. "Fit as a fiddle, sir. What was my compartment again, sir?"

Powell grinned. "Ride as in horses, not trains."

Jester couldn't find his voice. What in the devil?

Powell handed him a set of papers. "You're being assigned to
the Fourth Cavalry, son, and with my recommendation that you
serve in the same company as Langhorne, B Troop."

Jester had a half smile on his face, and he struggled for the
words. "Why, sir, I had expected to, uh, resume duty as your
aide."

"You don't have to thank me, Lieutenant," Powell said.
"Langhorne's glowing report on your work convinced me that
the Fourth couldn't do without you."

Jester glanced from one to the other. Which scoundrel was to
blame?

Powell extended his hand, and Jester automatically shook it.

"Don't worry, Calvin. It'll be a lot easier than fighting bears."
He grinned at Langhorne and shook his hand. They exchanged
salutes, and the colonel was up the steps and onto the train.

Jester looked at Langhorne, shrugged, and grinned. He picked
up his bags and turned back toward the lovely Miss Williamson
for a moment.

"I don't suppose you know how to make solid white tortillas,
do you, Miss?" The girl looked a bit puzzled and shook her
head slowly. "I wish you a very pleasant journey home then," he
said, nodding to her. She smiled and boarded the train as the
conductor began to shout his "All aboard." Jester stood watching the train as it prepared to get underway. Without looking at
Langhorne, he said, "She must not be the one, then."

Langhorne patted him on the back.

Still watching the train, Jester said, "You know, now that
we're back from Mexico, we can be true equals. As I've said
many a time before, my bar is just as silver as yours."

Langhorne pulled a paper out of his pocket. "Yeah, your bar
may be the same color." He held the paper out to Jester, who
took it carefully. "But now I've got two of 'em."

Jester looked at the paper and whistled softly. "So your
promotion finally came through. Well, if I may quote Walt
Whitman, 'O Captain! My Captain! Our fearful trip is done.' "

"You can say that again, Calvin."

Langhorne looked far down the platform. It would be nice
not to see another train for a while—a real long while.

EPILOGUE

"And when they had opened their treasures, they
presented unto him gifts." Matthew 2:11

Captain C. W. Langhorne studied the envelope in his hand for a
moment and tapped it on the desk a couple of times, then
glanced up.

"It's got a Sonora postmark," he said. Calvin Jester, standing
on the other side of the desk in the tiny B Troop office at Fort
Bliss, had a grin on his face.

"You may borrow my saber to open it if that's what's holding
things up, sir."

"Looks like a woman's handwriting."

Jester reached out and took hold of a corner of the envelope.
"May I, sir?"

Langhorne relinquished it. "Don't rip it apart now, Calvin.
Remember, it's addressed to me." Making Jester wait was fun,
but that had lasted long enough. It was time to find out what
was inside and who it was from.

Jester inspected the envelope from one direction and then
another. Finally, he held it to his nose and sniffed.

"Definitely a lady." He smiled and handed it back to Langhorne. "I'd say between thirty-five and forty, dark haired, good
figure, beautiful. Oh, and she speaks with a slight foreign accent."

"Amazing, Mr. Holmes."

Jester's eyebrows went up. "Oh, you're familiar with Doyle's work then? I *am* impressed, sir."

"I like a good yarn. I listen to you enough, don't I?"

Jester seemed about to reply but stopped when Langhorne slipped his thumb under the seal and opened the envelope. He pulled a sheet of folded stationery out and spread it on the desk top while Jester stood there fidgeting and craning his neck.

Langhorne grinned up at him. "It's from her, all right. *'My dear Señor Langhorne. It pleased me greatly to receive your letter of the 20th of February. I had wished to be able to correspond with you and to be assured that you had been able to return safely to the United States. Of course, my friend Benjamin Torreon informed me in September of your departure from Hermosillo, but beyond that, I knew nothing.'* "

"So you wrote to the señora last month," Jester said.

"Yeah. I wanted to see how she was—and the others, too. I gave her General Delivery, El Paso as my address. Didn't want to tell her Fort Bliss. That would've pretty much given the whole thing away. I figured the less she still knows about what we were doing down there, the better."

Langhorne looked back down at the letter. "Anyway, she goes on. *'We went through a tragic time when you were here, but you and Señor Jester were like anchors for me. I can never thank you enough for the help and support you gave me.*

'Another tragedy has touched our lives more recently, just days ago, in fact. My brother Esteban has lost his life in the revolution that continues in our country.' "

Jester grunted. "I'm surprised he lasted this long, knowing his glowing personality."

Langhorne gave him a cross glance and continued. " *'I am certain that you are aware of the recent rebellion by Señor Pascual Orozco in Chihuahua. Esteban had made some unfortunate state-*

ments in support of Señor Orozco weeks before the rebellion began, and those caused his arrest by the federal military commandant in this district. It seemed that he was about to be released, and my daughter Fabiana even spoke with the commandant personally on Esteban's behalf, but the following day he was executed by firing squad. I can hardly think of it without weeping.' "

"Neither can I," Jester said drily.

"He was the lady's brother," Langhorne said. "Have a little respect."

"I wonder what sweet Fabiana had to say in *behalf* of her uncle. Perhaps she crossed the commandant's palm with silver, as they say. Convenient way of getting rid of the dear man."

Langhorne raised his eyebrows. Jester had probably hit the nail on the head. Langhorne looked back at the letter. " *'Fabiana herself is gone from me now, and will be for the coming twelve months or more. As you surely remember, she was unhappy and has continued to be ever since her father's death. I finally decided, and she readily agreed, that she should travel to Spain, where a portion of my family still resides. She will remain with them until the spring of next year. It is my fervent hope that the change of scenery and company will restore her spirits and her peace of mind. I solicit your prayers for her mind and her troubled soul.' "*

Langhorne let out a deep breath. "She's a troubled girl, all right. I just hope she never becomes a danger to Guadalupe."

"I have the feeling that she may be a danger to anyone she's around."

Langhorne glanced through the rest of the letter. It might be better if he could just fold it up now and put it away. But Jester would never allow it.

"There's a little news of Miss Garcia," Langhorne said, looking at Jester. There was eagerness on the lieutenant's face, but some apprehension as well.

"Go ahead."

" *'Luna is doing very well, from the reports that my friend Señor Torreon has sent me. He keeps me informed of her situation at least once every month. She is teaching young children to read. Please tell Señor Jester she will always be thankful for the time he spent teaching her.'* "

Langhorne studied Jester's face for a moment. Jester was listening, but his eyes were fixed on the opposite wall. Langhorne continued.

" *'She and Jorge Rodriguez were married six weeks ago, and they are very happy. I hope that they will be able to live in peace and happiness in these unsettled times.'* "

Jester let out a sigh. His face was sober. "Well, I hope so, too. Luna deserves a good life. And a good man—one who won't be looking at every pretty face that comes walking by."

Langhorne hurried on into the final paragraph. " *'For now, life goes on here at the Hacienda El Valle de Ajalón much as it always has, as it did when you and Señor Jester were here. I have no plans for leaving but pray the dangers that plague so many parts of our nation now will bypass our pleasant valley.*

" *'May you both enjoy good health and good life. My home will always be yours.*

" *'Your obedient servant.'* "

Jester chuckled at that.

" *'Guadalupe Maria Velasquez de Medina.'* "

Langhorne looked up at him. "Like you said once, Calvin, her name's almost like a song." He glanced down at the letter again. "There's a postscript here. It says she's sent a package along that'll have some significance for me. For us both, I expect." He called through the door to his orderly in the hallway outside. "Tate, do you have the package out there?"

The private looked inside. "I'll have it for you right away, sir."

Jester frowned at Langhorne. "What is it?"

"Well, I'm not sure, but do you remember that beautiful rifle that Don Augustin had, the seven-millimeter Mauser?"

"Quite a fitting gift for a marksman such as yourself, sir," Jester said.

The sound of considerable grunting came from out in the hallway, and a moment later the orderly and another soldier manhandled a long wooden crate into the office and began prying off the lid.

Jester gave an uncertain grin. "I may be wrong, sir, but I don't remember that rifle being quite so large."

Langhorne just waited, frowning, while the two troopers set the lid aside and wrestled the contents out of the crate and onto the floor. Then he smiled. Well, well.

"I'd say that might have considerable significance—to both of us."

Spread out before them on the polished wooden floor was a rug made from the hide of a huge brown bear.

HISTORICAL NOTE

The United States government was understandably alarmed by the upheaval in Mexico that unseated the relatively stable dictatorship of Porfirio Diaz. The War Department did indeed dispatch two army officers in 1911 to make a clandestine reconnaissance of the heart of Mexico and to seek information from Americans living there about the likelihood of U.S. military intervention becoming necessary. Those officers, Captain Charles D. Rhodes and Captain Paul B. Malone, traveled through the central plateau of Mexico during September and October of that year, going as far south as Mexico City, and returned to the United States without incident to make their report to the War Department.

Like Langhorne and Jester in the novel, Rhodes and Malone were furnished false names and phony identification and used employment with the *Washington Times* as the cover for their intelligence gathering activities.

Eventually, of course, the United States did intervene in revolutionary Mexico, most notably during the occupation of Vera Cruz in 1914 and the Punitive Expedition in 1916.

ABOUT THE AUTHOR

Loyd Uglow is a history and writing professor at a university in North Texas. His special areas of interest include the American West, the Mexican Revolution, and military history from all eras. He is a retired naval surface warfare officer.

Fiction is his primary love in writing, although his earlier books were all non-fiction. Those include *Standing in the Gap,* a history of army scouting camps used in Texas Indian campaigns, and two biographies for children, on Benjamin Franklin and Abraham Lincoln. His first novel, *Marksman's Trinity,* dealt with military action along the Rio Grande in 1916. He has honed his writing skills by working as a professional editor for several years.

He lives with his wife and two sons.

The employees of Five Star Publishing hope you have enjoyed this book.

Our Five Star novels explore little-known chapters from America's history, stories told from unique perspectives that will entertain a broad range of readers.

Other Five Star books are available at your local library, bookstore, all major book distributors, and directly from Five Star/Gale.

Connect with Five Star Publishing

Visit us on Facebook:
  https://www.facebook.com/FiveStarCengage

Email:
  FiveStar@cengage.com

For information about titles and placing orders:
  (800) 223-1244
  gale.orders@cengage.com

To share your comments, write to us:
  Five Star Publishing
  Attn: Publisher
  10 Water St., Suite 310
  Waterville, ME 04901